VENGEWAR

BY KEVIN J. ANDERSON
FROM TOM DOHERTY ASSOCIATES

The Dark Between the Stars
Blood of the Cosmos
Eternity's Mind
The Nebula Awards Showcase 2011

WITH A. E. VAN VOGT
Slan Hunter

WITH DOUG BEASON
Kill Zone
Ignition
Ill Wind

WITH BRIAN HERBERT
The Road to Dune
Dune: The Butlerian Jihad
Dune: The Machine Crusade
Dune: The Battle of Corrin
Hunters of Dune
Sandworms of Dune
Paul of Dune
The Winds of Dune
Sisterhood of Dune
Mentats of Dune
Navigators of Dune
Dune: The Duke of Caladan
Hellhole
Hellhole Awakening
Hellhole Inferno

VENGEWAR

WAKE THE DRAGON, BOOK 2

KEVIN J. ANDERSON

A Tom Doherty Associates Book · New York

VENGEWAR

Copyright © 2020 by WordFire, Inc.

All rights reserved.

Maps by Bryan G. McWhirter

A Tor Book
Published by Tom Doherty Associates
120 Broadway
New York, NY 10271

www.tor-forge.com

Tor® is a registered trademark of Macmillan Publishing Group, LLC.

The Library of Congress Cataloging-in-Publication Data is available upon request.

ISBN 978-1-250-30213-7 (hardcover)
ISBN 978-1-250-30214-4 (ebook)

Our books may be purchased in bulk for promotional, educational, or business use.
Please contact your local bookseller or the Macmillan Corporate and Premium
Sales Department at 1-800-221-7945, extension 5442, or by email at
MacmillanSpecialMarkets@macmillan.com.

First Edition: January 2021

Printed in the United States of America

0 9 8 7 6 5 4 3 2 1

As a writer, I have the lives of my characters in my hands, but in the real world lives don't follow any plan. I dedicate this book to those so recently lost, but not forgotten: Jonathan, Andy, and Neil.

BlueWater River

Crickyth River

Konac's Castle

Convera

BGM

Fulcor

BGM

VENGEWAR

1

THERE are things you must know as konag," Utho told the young ruler. "The future of the Commonwealth depends on your leadership." His voice had the force of a battering ram, implacable, because Mandan needed to face his new reality after the murder of his father. As harsh as The Brava might sound, he would not coddle the former prince. Some actions were simply necessary.

Looking younger than his twenty-five years, the new konag appeared doubtful and overwhelmed. His large hazel eyes, red-rimmed with tears in his narrow face, avoided Utho's gaze. Ever since that terrible night on Fulcor Island, nightmares had harried Mandan like crows.

Utho spoke firmly to his ward. "I trained you all your life, and that training must continue. But it is no longer a mere exercise. From now on, everything you do becomes history. You rule the Commonwealth, like Conndur the Brave before you."

Long life and a great legacy.

Under Utho's stern regard, Mandan seemed to dredge a core of steel from the rubble of his personality. Good. The young man would need to get through his dead father's remembrance ceremony. Going through the motions, the konag donned his regal clothing, topped by a crimson cape trimmed with snowfox fur.

Though he had known he would someday rule the three kingdoms, Mandan was clearly still frightened inside. The grisly sight of Konag Conndur's butchered body had devastated him, but the bonded Brava was his strength, his mentor. Utho would guide him into the obligatory war against Ishara, a true vengewar.

At last!

Clad in his usual black Brava tunic, leggings, and finemail-lined cape, Utho pulled on his black leather gloves. "Come, Mandan. Your people need to see their true konag."

As the young man followed, he said in a small voice, "How can I be what they need when I am so alone?"

"Not alone, my konag—never alone while you have me." They left the royal chambers.

Convera Castle stood at the point of a high bluff that overlooked the confluence of two great rivers. In the main city below stood the remembrance shrine, an imposing stone building that preserved the names and lives of countless generations.

Humans built such shrines in every village and town to memorialize those who had lived before and the descendants they left behind. Families took great care to commemorate their loved ones, paying for written records, stone engravings, or painted tiles to be kept in the shrine through the ages. Once a person's life and works were forgotten, it was as if they had never existed.

Convera's shrine was the largest in the Commonwealth, seven stories tall, with records dating back almost two thousand years, to the end of the last wreth wars. Two stone lions guarded the entrance, each one nearly as large as a dragon. The shrine held many storage chambers and reading rooms with shelves crammed full of ledger books. The most prominent names were chiseled into the smooth marble walls and floors. A basement vault held scrolls for poorer people, who paid scribes a few coppers to record the names of their loved ones.

Crowds had gathered in front of the great shrine, where the remembrance ceremony would take place. Stonemasons had already prepared a slab of white marble, which looked as slick and pure as boiled bone on the raised entry platform between the two stone lions. A skilled mason had already engraved the name of Conndur, and covered his work with a canvas, leaving only a few strokes to be completed for the ceremony. The man stood ready, with his eyes down and his hair mussed. He held his mallet and chisel, looking nervous as thousands of people stared at him.

As Mandan and Utho approached the remembrance shrine, the crowd responded with a swelling murmur of appreciation, respect, and sorrow. Utho doubted the young konag would ever earn their cheers or adoration—it wasn't in his character—but the people would follow his commands. Hatred for the murderous Isharans would bond them.

Chief Legacier Vicolia emerged from the open doors of the towering building and took her place next to the covered marble slab. She was a tall, thin woman with pinched lips and an expression as serious as her duties; she wore a brown legacier's robe trimmed with gold at the sleeves and hem. Resplendent in his cape and crown, Mandan joined her, while Utho waited respectfully off to the side by one of the stone lions, a dark figure with steel-gray hair.

"The Commonwealth remembers Konag Conndur the Brave," announced the chief legacier. Her voice was deep and rough, as if she had breathed too much dust from her books. "He leaves a great legacy for us to remember."

"My father's life was too short," Mandan blurted out, and then he stepped forward, facing the gathered crowd. The people fell silent, sensing this would not be a traditional ceremony. "Conndur fought in the Isharan war thirty years ago, but in recent days, he mistakenly decided to trust those animals. He believed the Isharans might actually want peace."

His eyes sparkled with spiteful tears, his skin paled further, and his voice was wrong. "My father met them on Fulcor Island to negotiate the end of hostilities." Mandan visibly shuddered. Utho was proud of him. He did not mention the wreths or the dragon Ossus, the real—if ill-advised—reason Conndur had been so desperate to speak with the Isharan empra. "And they chopped him to pieces! They hacked off his hands, gouged out his eyes! They . . . they cut out his heart!" His voice broke, and he degenerated into shivers and sobs. "I saw it!"

The crowd remained as silent as death itself, and the chief legacier fidgeted. Utho let Mandan weep publicly for a few moments before he came forward and stood as a bastion of strength by the new konag. He gestured to the stonemason. "You know your work! Let the marble preserve Conndur's legacy forever."

The mason pulled aside the canvas covering to reveal the marble and the bold, impressive letters. With a bright percussion of steel and stone, the mason used his chisel to follow the charcoal lines and finish carving the last letter in CONNDUR THE BRAVE. Vicolia watched like a schoolmistress, nodding in cautious approval.

When the mason finished, Mandan stared at the name as realization struck him anew, and dropped to his knees in front of the marble, weeping.

Placing a black-gloved hand on the young man's trembling shoulder, Utho said in a low voice, "You can grieve only so much, my konag. You have a kingdom to rule." He increased the pressure, squeezing until Mandan managed to compose himself. "And we must prepare our war of vengeance against the Isharans."

⌘

Even before the Commonwealth ships departed from Fulcor on the night of the murder, Utho had set his plans in motion. The Brava was saving the three kingdoms by preventing Conndur's awful, naïve proposal to seek peace with the Isharans. Such a choice could cripple humanity's future. He had done what was necessary, as appalling as it was.

Conndur had been his friend, and secretly murdering him was the most difficult thing Utho had ever done. But that act, and placing the blame on the Isharans, had provided the necessary trigger to unite Mandan and the whole Commonwealth in destroying their enemy. Everyone believed Empra Iluris had ordered the despicable crime.

Still reeling from the horror he had witnessed, Mandan deferred the planning to his bonded Brava, who was happy to take the reins. In the name of the konag, Utho ordered numerous Commonwealth ministers and advisors to catalog the resources the three kingdoms could bring to bear for a full-scale war. The main army needed to be armed and supplied, and the vaults of stored armor, swords, arrows, and spears beneath the castle had been emptied and inventoried. Soldiers would be recruited from across Osterra, Norterra, and Suderra. Since the enemy was across the ocean, he required ships—hundreds, if not thousands of ships—to strike the other continent like an executioner's ax.

The Brava race had wanted this vengewar for centuries. *A vengewar is not a quick thing,* he thought, *but it is necessary.*

When a courier brought a letter from the king of Norterra, Mandan sat on his throne and stared at the message as if he didn't know what to do. It was addressed to Konag Conndur and sealed with wax impressed with the mark of King Kollanan. Obviously, the message had been dispatched weeks ago.

The sweaty, exhausted courier swiped a hand across his forehead. "I regret that it took me so long, Sire. I had to ride far to the north to find a passable road over the Dragonspine Mountains." He heaved a deep breath. "Kollanan the Hammer said this was most urgent information for Konag Conndur."

"My father is dead," Mandan said.

Utho stood beside the tall throne. "If this message is the business of the Commonwealth, then it is your business. *You* are the konag now." Still, the Brava felt uneasy, though he didn't know why. Not wanting an audience, he dismissed the courier from the throne room so they could read and discuss the message.

Hesitant, Mandan broke the wax seal and unfolded the letter. Without showing Utho, he read with widening eyes and his skin turned as pale as milk. When Utho tried to read the letter for himself, Mandan snatched it away, accusing. "Is this true? What did you do, Utho?"

Though he dreaded the news, the Brava spoke in a calm voice. "If I am to advise you, my konag, I must know what it says." He forcibly took the letter and scanned the words, and struggled to control his shock at what Kollanan had revealed. Impossible! He had never expected to deal with this.

His mind raced to choose the best course of action. Finally, trusting his relationship with the young man, he admitted, "Part of it is true, Mandan."

Mandan said, "That Brava woman Elliel accuses you of betraying her! Did you really wipe her memory and tell her she committed awful, false crimes?" He stared at his mentor, aghast. "Why, Utho?"

He stood implacable. "For the good of the Commonwealth—as always—and to save us all. In her mind, I'm sure Elliel considers it a betrayal, but she sees only a small part of the picture." Utho's thoughts spun, but he continued to speak, slow and reassuring. No excuses. He was loyal to the konag.

"But it's so . . . dishonorable!"

"I would never lie to you, you know that, but King Kollanan does not have the full explanation. Lord Cade runs a vital operation in his holdings. Even your father was not aware of the hundreds of Isharan prisoners who work to repay the innocent blood they have shed over the centuries. Elliel was Lord Cade's bonded Brava and she oversaw the saltpearl harvesting. Even Konag Conndur didn't know about it."

And a good thing, because Conndur would have wanted to free them as a foolish gesture of goodwill.

Mandan snatched the letter back, crumpling a corner of the paper. But he listened.

Utho continued the story. "Elliel became Cade's lover, and that is when it all fell apart. She was not rational."

"This . . . this says he raped her."

He could see the young man was wavering. Mandan would believe what he wanted to believe, if given the proper nudge. "I'm sure that is how she remembers it now, but Elliel's memory is damaged—as she admits in the letter. When Cade's wife learned of the affair, she threatened to expose the Isharan prisoners to the whole Commonwealth, just to punish Elliel. Lady Almeda was a spiteful, scorned woman. The scandal and uproar would have sent shock waves throughout the three kingdoms, and the Isharans would have launched an all-out war against us. We needed to prevent that, at all costs."

With great effort, he kept his voice neutral, and Mandan listened with rapt attention. "Elliel had to pay the price. It was the only way to solve the problem. So we erased her memory. I myself tattooed the rune of forgetting on her face, and created a false narrative that should have been too horrible for her to investigate. Elliel should have made a new life and a new legacy for herself. It was a small enough price to save the Commonwealth, wasn't it?"

Though he maintained his outward calm, Utho couldn't comprehend how Elliel had broken the spell. The rune of forgetting was ancient magic that Bravas knew but didn't completely understand. Now she remembered everything, and had revealed the whole story to King Kollanan.

But Utho had much bigger things to worry about, with the start of the vengewar. He needed to steer Mandan back onto the correct path.

Fortunately the young man's own hatred did it for him. "Are these Isharan prisoners still working under Lord Cade? To atone?"

"Yes, my konag. They give their sweat, their blood, their lives if necessary. They harvest saltpearls at great risk, and those riches are used to fund our great army. For the good of the Commonwealth."

Mandan turned toward his mentor and made no further mention of Elliel. He dropped the letter to the side of the throne. "Take me to Cade's holding so I can see it with my own eyes."

2

⪦⪧

KOLLANAN was still reeling over the crippling news from Convera. His heart and mind could not believe it.

As the lords gathered in the main hall at his urgent summons, Tafira, his beloved wife of three decades, sat beside him. Her long hair had once been raven black but now was frosted with silver that, if anything, made her look more distinguished. Although her dusky skin, generous lips, and pointed chin indicated Isharan heritage, Tafira was his queen here in Norterra, far from the land where she had been born.

She looked at him with concern. "I know you too well, beloved. I can see the news is bad."

Koll nodded only slightly as he stared beyond the raised dais into the large chamber.

Lords Bahlen, Ogno, and Cerus muttered to one another, probably about their temporary victory at Lake Bakal. Bahlen's bonded Brava Urok stood like a statue just behind his lord. Other vassal lords appeared uneasy, waiting for the king to address them.

At the edge of the room, a restless group of escort soldiers from Convera still wore their Commonwealth uniforms. Perhaps they would be the most shocked. Conndur had dispatched Captain Rondo and twenty men to escort Kollanan home just before the eruption of Mount Vada. These soldiers were impatient to ride back to the konag, but scouts and traders reported travel difficulties over the mountains, so the escort remained as Kollanan's guests in the barracks.

After today's news, though, they would be even more insistent on riding back to the capital.

Koll could not wait any longer. He rose from his throne and spoke out in a voice that silenced the entire room. "Konag Conndur is dead." He paused for a thunderous intake of breath. "My brother was murdered on Fulcor Island by the Isharans. His body was . . ." Grief filled his throat like hot wax. "Prince

Mandan found him in pieces. There was a great battle, and Empra Iluris was gravely injured, perhaps mortally, but the Isharans escaped."

Captain Rondo let out a loud cry. "What of Prince Mandan? Is he safe?"

Koll's vision blurred, but he forced himself to go on, one word after another like plodding footsteps. "He is safe. Apparently, Utho protected him." Koll locked eyes with his own bonded Brava, Elliel. She looked nauseated to hear the name of the man who had done her so much harm. A hot flush came to her cheeks. Next to her, the dark wreth stranger Thon stared at her, then at Kollanan, then at the others in attendance, trying to understand what he was hearing.

"Mandan is now the konag. I am . . . in mourning for my dear . . ." Koll couldn't go on. The words simply hung in the air. *My brother.* His shoulders shook under the crushing weight of memories.

The escort soldiers uttered low angry sounds, and restless hands strayed toward their swords. One of the men glared daggers at Queen Tafira. "Isharan animals," he muttered, as if he blamed her.

"Norterra must decide what to do," Kollanan said. His normally rough voice came out sounding like a lost waif's. But he was the *king.* "And so must I."

"Decide what to do?" Captain Rondo looked at his companions in disbelief. "We must ride back to Convera and offer our swords to Konag Mandan against Ishara!"

"Maybe so, but I will require you to stay here for a little longer. I must compile a report to . . . to the new konag about what is happening in Norterra. We must prepare for what the frostwreths will do to us here."

❧

Once the news had time to sink in, the king called his vassal lords for a private war council. After Koll's recent strike on the ice fortress at Lake Bakal, they all knew the very real possibility that bloodthirsty wreths might sweep across Norterra and attack human settlements.

Kollanan squeezed his large hand into a fist. "King Adan and I traveled together to Convera. We warned Conndur about the wreths, but my brother was more worried about Isharan raids on the coast. Prince Mandan even scoffed at the idea of wreths. He is under Utho's thumb." Koll sighed. "After Mount Vada, though, I think Conn was convinced, and he went to Fulcor Island to enlist Empra Iluris as an ally. But if the Isharans did assassinate him, Mandan will not concern himself with our problems here." His eyes stung with thoughts of his poor brother, but more painful still was the clear memory of his daughter and her husband, his grandson, and all the others blithely killed by the frostwreths at Lake Bakal. "We need to save ourselves from whatever comes down from the north."

"And it will come," said Elliel, imposing in her black Brava outfit. Her grim expression was marred by the rune of forgetting tattooed on her face.

"We will be strong—I certainly am! Ha!" said Ogno, the biggest and most intimidating of his lords. "We will be ready, Kollanan the Hammer."

Koll rested his bearded chin in his hand. "Adan knows the wreth threat, too, down in Suderra." His voice caught again. "He will also have received word of his father's death. I need to go to him, so we can discuss how our two kingdoms can defend themselves. If the sandwreths and the frostwreths are intent on destroying each other, we will be caught in the middle."

Tafira's dark eyes sparkled. "Maybe you could convince the sandwreths to fight on our behalf, against a mutual enemy."

Koll's eyebrows drew together. "I would ask Adan's counsel on that first."

Elliel sat up straight. "I will accompany you on the ride to Suderra." She shot a questioning glance at mysterious Thon, who nodded that he would join her.

"And I as well," Lasis said. The Brava had served Kollanan much longer than Elliel, and had been captured and left for dead by the frostwreths.

Kollanan shook his head. "No, Lasis. While I am gone, I need you here to protect my queen."

Tafira smiled. "*And* your kingdom."

The other Brava bowed. "Yes, Sire. Perhaps we should ask Captain Rondo and his Commonwealth soldiers to remain as added defenders, while you are gone?"

"Yes, that is reasonable," Koll said.

"We need regular scout riders, Sire." Lord Teo ran a finger down the left side of his long mustache. "They can give us warning if the wreths move."

"What good is a warning, if they can wipe us out with a blast of cold magic?" Lord Bahlen asked.

"It would give us a chance to evacuate the villages," said Vitor. "Scatter our people into the wilderness. Some of them might be saved."

Alcock said, "My county has open grassland and hills. We're farmers with spread-out villages, and there is no safe place for them to go. We do not have fortress walls like Fellstaff."

Teo said, "Norterra hasn't been at war for centuries, barely even a squabble among holdings. We are vulnerable."

"That is the weakness that peace brings," Ogno grumbled.

"I fear the time of peace has ended," Kollanan said.

Urok, Bahlen's normally silent Brava, said, "We can shore up our defenses. We must."

"Even if I wanted to, what sort of walls could I build against the wreths?" asked gaunt Cerus. "What material can stand against a frostwreth attack?"

Thon spoke up in a distant, musing tone. "Were the wreths not at war with one another for centuries? Their own defenses stood against the most destructive attacks, and those walls still endure." He glanced at Elliel with strange eyes that sparkled like crushed sapphires. He looked almost human, but not quite. "Elliel and the scholar girl showed me one of the old wreth cities."

"Ah, the ruins! Shadri is still determined to explore them more," Elliel said. "Many abandoned wreth cities are still intact and could be turned into fortresses if we repaired them."

Kollanan sat in his heavy chair. "Fellstaff has the greatest defenses, the thickest walls. We were always strong for the sake of the Commonwealth." Another wave of sadness unexpectedly came upon him at the thought of Konag Conndur, his brother, his companion, his friend. The three kingdoms had to stand together, but faced with his own crisis, Koll felt distant from any Isharan threat across the sea. He had loved his wife for far too long to think of all Tafira's people as inhuman animals, even if it was true that they had butchered Conndur.

"I have a large wreth city in my county," Bahlen said, sounding pleased with the idea. "We could make it into a stronghold."

Alcock lowered his head, scratched his dark goatee. "We've always avoided wreth ruins as bad places, maybe even haunted."

"Now they might save us," said Lord Iber.

That night in his chambers, Koll sat by the fire, holding a small carving of a cow, which he had whittled from a scrap of wood. Not his best work, but it kept his hands busy. Tafira had made honeysuckle tea, and she sat near the fire, reading a chronicle from Fellstaff's remembrance shrine that told the life story of their daughter Jhaqi, as written by the scholar girl Shadri. Koll loved watching his wife read the story and comfort herself by keeping their memories alive.

Koll kept their memories alive as well, but at the moment he was preoccupied with thoughts of his brother. During the Isharan war, he and Conndur commanded divisions of the Commonwealth army that roamed the new world. They had gone to punish the Isharans for some imagined slight that Koll couldn't even remember.

Conndur the Brave and Kollanan the Hammer, war heroes.

Koll and Conn.

The legaciers exaggerated the legends of the two brothers, but Koll remembered how dark those times were, on both sides. His own men had lost control, intending to raze a village, and the Isharan villagers, just as ruthless, decided to sacrifice an orphaned girl, Tafira, to their godling. Koll had rescued her as his prize and his bride-to-be. When that war ended unresolved, Koll had thought he would never worry about Isharans again.

Now, as he whittled a few more details into the wooden cow, he remembered his raid at the frostwreth ice fortress. Koll had hoped to rescue his captive grandson, but Birch wasn't there. Instead, the boy was being held a prisoner up at Queen Onn's palace, and Koll had no idea how to get him back.

With the tip of his dagger he scratched detail lines, then set the carving aside and picked up a new piece of wood. He had made many toy animals for his two grandsons. Someday he hoped to give this one to Birch.

3

~∞~

T HE walls exuded cold, turning the boy's every breath into fog. The ice blocks distorted the weak sunlight that flowed into Queen Onn's throne room. Outside, frigid winds whistled around the ornamental spikes of the palace in unsettling mournful music.

Numb with cold, Birch huddled under his tattered blanket, but he was alert, watching every detail.

Onn sat on her throne, languid and relaxed in her frozen surroundings. Her long hair was the color of ice and bone chips, and her large eyes had an undertone of steel.

Behind her hung an ancient wreth spear wrought with magic and metal, powerful enough to slay monsters. In a boastful voice, Onn had told the boy how one of her ancestors had stabbed the great dragon Ossus, breaking the shaft. Now Onn displayed the artifact as a trophy, as her predecessors had.

Birch crouched on the floor at the side of the throne, quiet and ignored. The queen treated him like a pet, a curiosity, although she didn't seem to know what to do with him. Her interest had waned, and he instinctively knew to stay as quiet as possible; remaining unnoticed was his greatest protection. Birch was hungry and cold, but he was alive, and he meant to stay that way. Birch needed to be *resilient*. His grandfather had taught him that word.

With a frenetic bustle, five drones entered through the arched doorway, bearing small plates with morsels of food. Queen Onn thrived on the attention more than the food itself.

In ancient times when the land thrummed with untapped magic, wreths had fashioned the human race. But after the world was battered and drained by the wreth wars, the frostwreths were unable to create anything better than these drones as new servants. Small in stature and genderless, the drones had grayish skin and poorly formed features.

From what Birch had seen, frostwreths considered the drones expendable.

The obsequious drones offered the queen spiced lichen, tundra ferns, and small silver fish that swam in cracks within the glacier. Bowls of frost-sprinkled blue berries made Birch's mouth water. He couldn't remember the last time he'd been fed; likely, Queen Onn couldn't remember either.

She accepted a bowl from a drone, plucked out a berry, and popped it in her mouth, savoring it. The drones made small noises that weren't quite words. Birch knew the creatures were intelligent, though he wasn't sure the frostwreths realized it.

After munching on a still-wriggling silver fish, the queen smacked her lips. Birch looked at her with shadowed eyes, his hunger apparent, and when Onn noticed him, she responded with a disapproving frown. "How pathetic you are." She tossed him one of the berries, which he gobbled. When his performance amused her, she handed him the whole platter of twitching fish, and Birch wolfed several down.

"Perhaps that is all you are good for—to eat my leftover food," Onn said with a snort. In front of her, the drones held up more plates, beseeching her to take them. "When Rokk brought you to me, I thought he was a fool to have captured you in the first place." She smiled. "But he does like to give me things. Rokk is a magnificent lover, boy."

Boy? Birch stopped eating and crouched, forcing himself to remain silent, though he wanted to scream, *Birch! My name is Birch!* Memories swirled in his head. *And my brother was Tomko. You killed him. And you killed my parents.*

"You are fortunate my Rokk saved you and brought you to live among the frostwreths," Onn said with a smirk. "Appreciate that."

Birch pressed his lips together and thought back to that terrifying day at Lake Bakal, the fishing boats on the water, the surrounding hills thick with silver pines, the steep mountains that framed the lake. It was a happy place, peaceful. His father was the town leader, and his mother was the daughter of Norterra's king and queen.

On that last afternoon, he and Tomko had been with their friend Piro in front of their house. Birch and his brother played with carved animals that their grandfather had given them.

His mother came out to call the boys inside, concerned by a line of ominous weather rolling in from the north. They all watched white clouds pour over the mountains like a frigid flood. It did not look like anything Birch had ever seen.

A party of fierce, pale frostwreth warriors appeared before the frigid wave, riding white-furred steeds that looked like wolves. The oncoming cold had shattered trees and turned the deep lake into solid ice. His mother had shouted for the children to get inside the house. But a wreth warrior had seen Birch first, seized him, and protected him—for no reason other than curiosity.

Then the cold caught the rest of the village, froze the people solid and left them like fish buried in a snowbank. Tomko died next to their friend Piro, who clutched one of the wooden pigs his grandfather had carved. His mother and father had collapsed in the cold, covered with ice, buried in snow that fell all too gently upon a dead town. . . .

"Eat your fish," Onn snapped at him. "If you do not appreciate the food, I will stop feeding you."

Birch ate the last two on the plate, licked his numb fingers. He withdrew, shivering, and pulled the blanket closer. In front of the throne, the many drones shifted position, but stayed close at hand, hoping for the queen's attention.

A female wreth warrior strode into the throne chamber with a swift deliberate pace, her boots clicking on the metallic ice floor. She approached without any bow or gesture of respect. "Queen Onn, our fortress at Lake Bakal was attacked."

Birch's ears pricked up. He had been held for a time at the fortress under the lackluster care of Rokk until he had been brought back to Onn at the northern palace.

The warrior was gruff, unemotional as she delivered her announcement. "The attacking army used some strange magic to thaw the lake. The ice and water swallowed our warriors like the jaws of a trap. Many wreths at the fortress were killed, including your lover."

"Rokk!" Onn groaned, more with surprise than grief.

Choosing the wrong moment, a drone scuttled forward to offer the queen more food. Enraged by the interruption, she extended a hand, and waves of cold shot out like a volley of arrows. The drone froze solid, then shattered into fragments of flesh-colored ice. The other drones dropped their dishes and fled the chamber. Birch wished he could go with them.

Onn lunged down from her frozen throne, confronting the warrior. "Who struck our fortress? Did the sandwreths attack?" She glanced behind her at the jagged spear.

"Not sandwreths, my queen. It was a *human* army, led by King Kollanan."

"King Kollanan." Onn rolled the name around in her mouth and spat it out. "I do not understand this. Humans cannot cause such damage to wreths!"

"And yet, they did," the warrior said.

Huddled beside the throne, Birch heard the name of his grandfather and smiled.

As he and his wife approached the council chamber, King Adan already heard shouting.

Penda leaned on his arm as if she needed his help in her advanced pregnancy, but Adan leaned on her just as much. She gave him strength to face the crises blowing in like sandstorms from the Furnace.

Despite the uproar coming from the room ahead, Penda forced a sense of calm on him. Her long dark hair flowed back, enhancing her deep brown eyes. "Breathe, my Starfall."

"How can you be so calm?" he asked.

"There's an Utauk saying: 'In the pause between a flash of lightning and the sound of thunder, a person can find a stillness to weather the worst storm.' That is what you need now." With her free hand she traced a circle around her heart and whispered the mantra of her people, "The beginning is the end is the beginning."

Riding on her shoulder, the green reptile bird flapped his wings and burbled as if in agreement. Xar, her pet ska, was fierce and devoted, bound to Penda by a heart link. With his talons, he gripped a padded leather patch on her shoulder to keep his balance. The hawk-sized creature always vied with Adan for Penda's attention.

Adan allowed himself a moment to consider his love for her, to let it drive away the turmoil and shadows for a brief instant, like the pause between lightning and thunder. "Thank you."

Arm in arm, showing a grace that belied his distress about the world falling apart, the king and queen entered the chamber where the vassal lords, advisors, and military commanders had gathered. They had already begun their debate, expressing dread over the turmoil in the three kingdoms.

When Adan stepped into the room, one lord rose to his feet. "Sire!" The others rapidly stood, showing their respect and relief.

Adan said in a wry attempt at humor, "I see you have solved all the problems without waiting for us."

Penda's father, Hale Orr, grinned, flashing his gold tooth. "There you are, dear heart." He wore the maroon and black silks of his tribe and a distinctive shadowglass pendant in one ear.

Adan said, "We have much to discuss, much to fear, and much to decide. Events happen swiftly, and news travels at a much slower pace." He led Penda to the head of the table, where they each took a seat. Behind the queen's chair was a wooden T-shaped ska stand, where another young ska perched. Ari fluttered her blue plumage in greeting as Penda placed Xar on the stand beside her.

One lord, who often did not think before he spoke, called out, "Tell us of the dragon hunt in the Furnace. And the sandwreths!"

Beside him, another advisor glanced at the restless blue ska on the crossbar stand. "Sandwreths . . ."

"And with Konag Conndur murdered, what will happen to the Commonwealth?"

Adan paused as another unexpected wave of grief rolled over him. "My brother is konag now," he said, hoping that might reassure them, even though he could not believe it himself. Mandan, as konag? He turned his thoughts to Suderra. "Let us talk about the sandwreths first, and dragons."

Taking turns, he and Penda described how the sandwreth queen and her hunting party took them into the barren wastelands and summoned a dragon for sport. "The monster caused great havoc before the wreths finally killed it. They called it a *small* dragon," Adan said.

"The slain dragon rotted away within seconds, as if its evil were dissipating into the world." Penda reached into the foldpocket of her maroon-and-black skirt and removed a tooth as large as a hatchet blade. "This is one of the few fragments that remained. Voo herself gave it to me."

"But why would wreths hunt a dragon in the first place?" asked his war minister, running his fingers through stringy hair. "Why provoke it?"

Adan was surprised they didn't all know the ancient mythology. "The wreths were charged by their god to slay the great dragon Ossus, so the world can be remade into a perfect form. This one was practice."

Penda added with a frown, "The sandwreths seem most interested in destroying their rivals. They do not want the frostwreths saved when the world is changed."

Adan's chief armorer leaned forward on the table. "If Ossus is so horrific, shouldn't they work together to kill their common enemy?"

"*Cra*, one would think," Hale muttered.

"The human race is doomed, no matter what," grumbled another vassal lord.

"Vengeance drives otherwise sensible people to do irrational things." Adan clenched his fist as a flood of emotions filled his mind, anger and grief blotting out his thoughts. Mandan's message had said their father was betrayed and murdered by Isharans, his body mutilated . . .

Adan remembered how he and Conndur had watched the stars from the observation deck of Convera Castle, wondering what the patterns might mean. His own name, Adan Starfall, came from a night when they had seen a meteor shower against a clear black sky.

"Queen Voo asks for an alliance with us," Penda said. "She wants the armies of Suderra to help her fight the frostwreths. She says she wants to protect us." She pressed her full lips together. Both skas twitched and clicked, sensing her emotional outpouring. "We now know she is lying."

She took the blue ska from her perch and touched the mothertear diamond in the collar. In a blur above the table, disturbing projected images showed a prison camp with hundreds of human slaves working in the desert heat, their clothes tattered, their bodies gaunt.

"During the dragon hunt, my adopted sister Glik came looking for us out in the desert. She stumbled upon this camp and was captured. Her ska recorded these images as she flew away."

The glowing picture showed the skinny girl trying to flee down rock-walled canyons. Copper-skinned wreth warriors rode her down on two-legged lizard mounts. Glik was dragged away to the camp while her ska escaped.

"*Cra*," Hale muttered, though he had seen the images before.

"We can't ally ourselves with those monsters!" said one of the Suderran generals.

"We do not have the strength to defy them either," Adan said. "Queen Voo could send her warriors against Bannriya and enslave us by force." He had seen what the wreths could do, the capricious disregard for life or pain. They had weapons, magic, strength. They thought humans were beneath their notice, which could work to Adan's advantage. "We need to be careful, and smart."

Penda drew another circle around her heart, and her expression became sly. "Voo is not aware that we know." She stroked Ari's blue plumage. "We don't trust her, but we can play along until the time is right—to stab her in the back."

5

GLIK usually considered herself fortunate. She hadn't chosen to be an orphan, but what she did with her circumstances was up to her. She had the freedom to travel the land by herself, relishing the independence. She did not feel alone. Whenever she wanted to, she returned to Utauk camps for companionship and supplies before heading out again. It was a rugged life, and she had endured hunger and storms, frigid temperatures and baking heat, and countless other hardships, but that sort of life was her choice. Because of her wits and the lessons she learned daily in her explorations, her survival skills were unmatched.

And those skills would help her escape from the sandwreth labor camp. She was determined to find a way out.

The high canyon walls served as prison barricades, so Glik studied every cleft, every pebble. She would need the information to escape from this grim, harsh camp in the desert. She was used to being free to travel at will. She felt suffocated. Glik had always gone where she wanted instead of where she should.

Looming nearby, the wreth guards wore breastplates and shoulder spikes enhanced with bone and burnished metal. They carried ivory spears and hooked chains they could hurl out like a scorpion's sting. Occasionally, the wreths made an example of a prisoner to keep the weak and terrified captives in line, and that made Glik cautious. The guards didn't hate them, simply saw the humans as a resource, bodies to fight and bodies to work as part of their larger plan. Glik drew no attention to herself.

Learn, plan, stay alert, she told herself. *There will be a way out.*

One guard snapped at a sluggish worker pushing a cart of ore over the uneven ground. The metal-tipped whip whistled out and struck sparks from the stone wall only a hand's breadth from the slave's head. The man leaped to work.

The bleak camp's dwellings were made of sand, hardened mud, and rock shaped by wreth magic. Mages deflected the wind that whipped through the canyons. For shade, fabrics and skins were stretched over frameworks made of gnarled hardwood.

Glik sat under the meager shade of her tattered awning. Bright sunlight poked through the holes, warming her arm as she used a rough rasp on long sticks to fashion arrow shafts. The slaves were making thousands of arrows for some upcoming titanic battle. Glik tossed her finished arrow with a clatter onto the pile of similar shafts. Others would sharpen the wooden tips and cover them with a resin that hardened like glass. She had no idea where fletchers would get arrow feathers out here in the desert, but that wasn't her task. *The beginning is the end is the beginning.* She was trapped somewhere in the middle. For now.

As heat waves rippled from the desert canyons, she saw dust and smoke rise into the sky from mining operations in the striated mesas where workers extracted ore for smelting. Dour mages watched over the work crews, adding spells and drawing upon what magic remained deep within the landscape.

Among the captives Glik met survivors of entire villages overrun by wreths, whole populations bound and whisked away, leaving behind only whispers and ghosts. These people had no one to write down their lives, and many died here without anyone even recording their names. That made Glik sad, because a person's legacy, their *name,* was all they contributed to the universe. She drew a quick circle around her heart.

Seeing her, others made the gesture, muttering the same phrase. Individual Utauk traders and even large caravans had fallen afoul of wreth raiders. She was not alone here, but in a sense their isolation—where they were watched over at every moment—had rendered all of them alone. She vowed she would get to know them, build a sort of alliance.

As her hands worked on the next arrow shaft, she fell into a fugue. Although her fingers were sore, bleeding in some places and callused in others, and the work was so routine, she forgot what she was doing.

At least Ari had escaped. The beautiful reptile bird was another reason Glik rarely felt alone. Their companionship was so close they could feel each other's emotions even when they were apart. When Glik was captured, the ska sensed her terror through their heart link, but Glik had pushed her away to keep her safe. The reptile bird had pumped her wings, darting among the thermals to fly far from the slave camp. Because she could still sense her ska, a part of herself remained free.

Now from her canyon prison, Glik looked up into the blue depths of the sky and focused her inner sight, going higher, rising beyond any clouds. She felt dizzy, falling up into nowhere, yet she pushed farther into her vision. Intending to search for her ska, Glik was startled to sense another great reptile with large scales, an ominous presence out there. She had seen something like this once before, glaring at her from behind a resinous shell in a mountain eyrie, just after she had found Ari's egg. As Glik drifted in her strange waking dream, she also envisioned skas, thousands of skas coalescing and then breaking apart . . . wings, countless small wings. And then gigantic wings.

A dragon's roar shattered her trance, and Glik blinked back to awareness to see a wreth mage standing nearby, inspecting the workers. He was broad shouldered and bald, his face deeply chiseled, his eyes gold and intense. He wore a heavy robe of oxblood-dyed leather imprinted with arcane runes. The garment looked like a book of dangerous spells.

Mage Ivun led this labor camp and sometimes even deigned to speak with the prisoners, as if he thought that explaining the wreth mission would make the slaves work with greater fervor. Glik stared at the ugly man, still trembling from the vibrant vision that had just consumed her.

Ivun addressed the workers in a booming voice. "You will help the sand-wreths triumph in the coming war. With your assistance, we shall exterminate the frostwreths, then we shall wake the dragon and destroy it, so that Kur rewards us. You will be part of our victory."

Ivun's intense eyes were like lodestones sending out shimmers of energy. Forced to listen, the wretched captives stopped their work, but their lack of response seemed to disappoint the wreth mage.

When Ivun lifted his left hand, the leather sleeve fell back to reveal a shriveled arm like the forelimb of a dead beetle. The mage straightened his arm to point a gnarled finger toward the captives. "In our great wars long ago, thousands of human soldiers wore sandwreth armor and carried our weapons. They fought the enemy for our glory. That battle is not over. Now we call upon you again. We created your race. You owe us your service." He grumbled in his throat and scanned the squalor of the camp. "There can be no greater meaning to your existence. This is why you were all made."

The captives muttered in low tones, a mere murmur that could not be identified. Disappointed by the reaction, Mage Ivun strode barefoot across the rocky ground toward his stone headquarters. The wreth guards pummeled the captives back to work.

In silence, Glik observed how cruelly the guards treated her fellow captives. How did the wreths believe they had the right to destroy so many lives? Lives of good people?

Humans had lived without wreths for thousands of years now, creating their own civilization, making their marks in the world, creating a legacy. They had earned the right to be their own masters, not just to be tools for wreths to use or throw away.

Glik could survive this place. But survival was only the first step. She had to help these people *escape*.

6

As the Isharan warship entered Serepol Harbor, black fabric dangled from the red-and-white-striped sails to signal that something terrible had happened on Fulcor Island.

Cemi stood at the bow, feeling very alone as they sailed back home with the wounded empra. Her view of the bustling harbor appeared to be blurred with an ocean fog, but when she felt the trickles running down her cheeks, she realized that tears had clouded her vision. Her mentor Iluris was alive, and dead at the same time—unresponsive, empty.

The young woman's body hitched as the horrible memories flashed through her. She had burst into the empra's guest chamber to find her on the floor, her head smashed against the stone ledge. An assassin who looked like the Brava Utho had attacked, holding magical fire in one hand and a knife in the other. Treachery from the Commonwealth, the same people who had lured the empra there under pretext of peace!

Cemi had felt in a daze since their frantic escape on that stormy night, rushing the wounded empra down to the ship. Now, days later, though her head was bandaged and the blood had stopped flowing, Iluris had not spoken, not opened her eyes, not moved at all. A faint whisper of breath came from her mouth, and she still had a heartbeat, though it was faint and erratic.

"Oh, Iluris . . ." Cemi whispered, and the sound was lost in the hissing curl of water at the warship's prow as they sailed into the harbor.

Loud war drums from the warship's deck called the crowds as they gathered on the waterfront to cheer the return of their beloved empra. But the black hangings gave them pause.

Captani Vos joined Cemi in the open air, his golden armor polished and gleaming, his scarlet cape ready for a formal ceremony. "Empra Iluris is safe with us. We hawk guards will not let our mother suffer any further harm."

Although he treated Cemi as a friend, Vos acknowledged that she was the empra's intended successor, though no formal process had been completed.

Cemi could not believe that a street girl from Prirari could be chosen to rule an entire continent, and she didn't want to do it without Iluris. "Should I go back to her cabin in case she needs me?"

His eyes were weary and sad. "She has not stirred."

"I'm sure she knows I am there."

For much of the return voyage, she had locked herself in the guarded cabin, sitting beside the empra's motionless form. Cemi had tenderly washed her skin, bound clean bandages around her head, but there was nothing else to do. The rocking of the ship through the rough storm waters had made Cemi sick, but Iluris had not responded at all.

Now as the ship glided to its place in the harbor, Key Priestlord Klovus strode up and down the deck, riling up the crew in preparation for docking. He bemoaned the fact that if only they had brought a godling along, they could have protected the dear empra. Several nondescript soldiers hovered close to the priestlord, guarding him from harm. A strange concern aboard an Isharan warship, Cemi thought, but her mind had been so fogged with fear and grief that she didn't pick up on the small details at first.

As the sailors threw down ropes and the ship tied up to the dock, Cemi stood pale and brave at the bow. Next to her, Captani Vos seemed to be sculpted entirely of duty. After losing his family, Vos had been adopted by the empra as a surrogate son, just as with the other handpicked hawk guards.

Klovus stood in the sun in his dark blue caftan, and his enthusiasm overshadowed any grief he might have displayed for the empra's grave condition. The priestlord shouted to the crowd even before the gangplanks had been lowered. "The Commonwealth set a trap against us, just as I warned. The empra is grievously injured! Only by focusing the power of prayer and sacrifice can we keep her alive. Hear us, save us!"

The chant roared back. "Hear us, save us!"

City guards lined up to push back the crowds and clear the way, and Klovus stepped to the front as if he were the ruler of Ishara. As the key priestlord, the highest priestlord in all of Ishara, he controlled the godlings that defended the land. With the empra incapacitated, it made sense that the religious leader would speak on behalf of the returning mission. Cemi herself had no standing to speak, but it still made her uneasy.

"We will bring the empra," Captani Vos announced. "No one may touch her but us."

Cemi followed the hawk guards to the empra's guarded cabin, where they looked at the motionless woman with respect and sadness. Vos issued orders, and two hawk guards together gently lifted Iluris onto a pallet, which they carried in a brisk procession out into the sunshine.

Vos said privately to the hawk guards, "She is not dead. This is not a bier being carried to a funeral pyre. We will bear our mother through the city to the safety of the palace. Iluris is still our empra."

Cemi took the lead, wearing a grave expression as they descended the gangplank behind Klovus. Resplendent in their gold and scarlet uniforms, the hawk guards followed the larger soldier escort along the docks.

Xion, the ur-priest from the harbor temple, waited for them along with many followers of his own godling. He had heavy brows and dark hair cropped very close to his skull. "Prayers and sacrifices will be made in the harbor temple as well, Key Priestlord. Hear us, save us! My godling can share its strength with the people of Ishara, for the empra."

"Your godling?" Klovus said, as if it were a criticism. "That temple and its godling used to be mine before I became key priestlord. The harbor godling traveled with me when we struck the town of Mirrabay in Osterra." He gave a condescending smile to the ur-priest and his earnest followers. "I can muster all the godlings for the defense of Ishara."

Unable to bear it any longer, Cemi spoke up sharply, her small voice breaking through the hubbub. "Iluris remains the ruler of Ishara, and she will awaken."

Hearing Cemi's confidence, the crowd responded with a cheer as well as a prayer. "She will awaken! Hear us, save us!"

Klovus frowned at the interruption, but rapidly shifted his expression. "Of course, dear girl, that is what I meant."

At a swift, unwavering march, the hawk guards rushed Iluris along the main thoroughfare that led to the palace. A tall man wearing dark robes and a thick chain of office intercepted the party. He had a lantern jaw, large eyes, and heavy brows. Chamberlain Nerev had accompanied Iluris throughout the districts of Ishara in the search for her successor. Seeing the older woman stretched out and pale on her pallet, the chamberlain stifled a gasp. The lines in his face looked as if they had been pounded in with a chisel. "What happened? She still lives?"

"She still lives," said Captani Vos.

Nerev turned to Cemi, showing deference and respect. "What are we to do?" Clearly, he expected the young woman to give him an appropriate answer.

Nearby, concerned with his own followers, Klovus raised his voice in a shout. "Only we can make our people strong. Hear us, save us!" While the hawk guards hurried the motionless woman to the palace, the key priestlord thrived on the attention as if he drew energy from the believers just as godlings did.

The key priestlord followed them to the fountain courtyard of the palace under the soaring stone arch, but he remained outside as the hawk guards took their burden inside. Cemi was concerned that he showed such little regard for the injured empra, but she was also glad he didn't accompany them.

Instead, Klovus climbed to a speaking dais and bellowed his story in a commanding voice. As they hurried the empra into the cool shadows of the palace, Vos said to Cemi, "Klovus has the crowd's attention, and he will speak at great length." He sounded relieved.

"He always speaks at great length," Chamberlain Nerev said with clear disapproval.

The hawk guards were swift and professional, their boots and jingling armor echoing in the vaulted portico. For Vos, it was a tactical matter. "That gives us time to take our mother to the tower quarters. We can secure her and set up a cordon of hawk guards."

Cemi trusted his instincts. "I approve. No one will approach unless we allow it." She was surprised at how readily the guards followed her lead. Nerev looked at her and nodded.

Outside, the crowd's murmur built to a roar as the key priestlord continued his speech. Using inflammatory language, Klovus explained how Konag Conndur had tricked Empra Iluris, offered Fulcor Island to atone for all the crimes the Commonwealth had committed. Cemi frowned as she paused to listen. That wasn't exactly what Conndur had said.

Waving his hands as if to shoo away gnats, the key priestlord painted a bloody and vindictive picture of how the treacherous konag had sent his own Brava to kill the empra. "We were vulnerable. The empra's greatest mistake was to trust the godless, and she nearly paid with her life. Brave Isharan soldiers carried her to safety—but this is not over." He raised his voice to a shout. "Oh no, it is not over! Hear us, save us! We must prepare our revenge." When the people shouted in anger and dismay, Klovus continued, "Go to your temples, make your sacrifices, give your blood to strengthen our godlings—to strengthen Ishara."

Inside the grand entryway, Cemi looked at Vos, whose brows were furrowed with concern. Chamberlain Nerev cleared his throat. "Cemi, why are you not addressing the crowds?"

"Me? But I—"

"We know Empra Iluris wanted you to replace her."

"No one is replacing the empra," scolded Captani Vos. "She still lives. She needs rest and medical attention."

Cemi still struggled with Nerev's comment. "You may know it, Chamberlain, but Iluris made no announcement to the people, did not anoint me. I can't just—"

They listened to the crowd grow angrier as Klovus continued. "We should have strengthened Ishara thirty years ago. Our Serepol godling must be stronger than any other force in the world." He paused, then turned his speech in an unexpected direction. "The Magnifica temple was always meant to be the cornerstone of our strength, not just for Serepol but for the whole land. As key priestlord, I hereby order construction efforts to resume. All resources, all workers shall be brought to the city center, and the temple will rise, the grandest ever constructed! We need it for the defense of Ishara. When our godling thrives, we will conquer the hated Commonwealth. We will wipe out the godless!"

Cemi was alarmed by how bold Klovus had already become. "Iluris has to get better."

As they crossed the main entry hall bearing the empra, an old woman rushed along the polished tile floors, clad in a drab but clean dress. "Excellency!" Analera had been a loyal and dedicated servant for all of Iluris's life, and now she pushed herself in among the hawk guards. "Oh, my lady! I will call the court physicians."

Recognizing her, Vos and the hawk guards relaxed. Cemi had also talked with the old woman many times during her days of tutoring sessions. She said, "Make sure the empra has whatever she needs in her quarters. We will all be with her." Her voice cracked. "We may be there for some time."

"It's a defensible position," said Vos. "Our best option to guard her."

Wearing a look of determination, Analera hurried off. "I will take care of everything."

7

ᘛᘚ

FULCOR Island was a fortress in the middle of the sea protected by an expanse of empty water. Only expert navigators could thread their way through the jagged reefs to the sheltered harbor cove, which was little more than a cleft in the cliffs. Stairs made of iron and wood bolted onto the sheer rock allowed people to climb single file up to the stronghold above.

Even with such defenses, Klea did not feel entirely safe. The battle-scarred Brava woman stood on the garrison walls and gazed across the threatening waters. Utho had stationed her on Fulcor as the new watchman, and she could not let down her guard. The Isharans were out there.

On that blood-filled stormy night, when the treacherous enemy had attacked during what was supposed to be a peace conference, Klea had killed many Isharans, but those casualties did not pay all the vengeance that was required. She remembered swinging her sword and striking down enemy after enemy . . . but it had not been enough to save Konag Conndur, and that weighed heavily on her heart. A failure.

Utho was the expedition's lead Brava, sworn protector of the konag, but Klea and another Brava, Gant, had also been assigned to protect the diplomatic mission. Somehow, a murderer had slipped into the konag's chambers. Utho had whisked Mandan away to safety, and the enemy had also escaped with the gravely injured Empra Iluris. Klea wished she'd been able to break the bitch's neck with her bare hands.

A hundred Isharan soldiers had been left behind that night, abandoned by their own ships. The desperate enemy had fought under the sheeting rain and flashes of lightning, but Klea had led the Commonwealth soldiers to victory. Now, six days later, her soldiers raked the gravel in the courtyard to remove the scars of combat. Others scoured blood from the walls and floors in the main keep.

Standing on the thick surrounding wall, Klea watched the grim work as cold sea breezes scrubbed her face. A seasoned Brava, she was in her middle forties, muscular but not stocky, dressed in traditional black boots, pants, jerkin. Her heavy cape hung from her shoulders, protection rather than a burden. She carried a long sword, which she used for everyday killing, and the burnished gold cuff of her ramer for when extraordinary violence was required.

Klea looked down at the courtyard barracks, watching her people repair damage to the building exteriors. After that night, the fallen Commonwealth soldiers had been respectfully laid out, relieved of their armor, weapons, personal possessions. A scribe documented the names, writing down any detail that observers could see or remember, in order to preserve their legacies. Since Fulcor had no spare wood for funeral pyres, the bodies of those heroes were consigned to the sea, taken one at a time to the cliffs above, their legacies read aloud, before they plunged into the foaming water to vanish into the purity of the sea.

While this slow, sad process continued for two days, the dead Isharan bodies were left where they were. Under the hot sun, the corpses became discolored and bloated. Gulls circled above the high walls, and Klea let the birds feast while her crew completed more important work.

In all, seventy Isharan soldiers had been captured alive and locked in a prison barracks where they were allowed no sunlight or food. After the rainstorm, the roof cisterns were full, so she did give the prisoners a little water to keep them alive.

Finally, when all the dead Commonwealth soldiers had been respectfully buried at sea, Klea released the enemy prisoners in small well-guarded teams, and ordered them to strip the armor and any valuable keepsakes from their dead comrades, who had already been relieved of all weapons.

One Isharan soldier retorted through a bruised mouth, "I will not defile the bodies of my brothers. They should be taken to the sea as they are, out of respect."

Klea drew her sword and struck off his head, then told the other prisoners they now had one more body to deal with.

Sullen and resistant, they peeled breastplates, boots, and greaves from the stinking bodies. While stripping one of the empra's bodyguards, a captive found a knife hidden under the chest armor. He seized it and launched himself at Klea with a roar. She raised her gauntleted hand to block the blade, which could not penetrate the finemail in her glove. She grabbed his wrist, squeezed until the bones cracked, and the knife fell.

Refusing to acknowledge the pain, the Isharan glowered at her with black soulless eyes. Klea saw no humanity there, even though these people were descended from the same humans created by wreths long ago. As Klea held the man's gaze, she stomped her bootheel on his bare foot, shattering his ankle. He collapsed with a gasp, after which she calmly crushed his other foot, crippling him. She would not need the captives much longer anyway.

When the remaining prisoners finished stripping the enemy cadavers, her soldiers sorted the valuable armor and weapons from the filthy garments. They piled the useless debris in the courtyard and set it on fire. The blaze sent a column of smoke into the clear sky, a beacon of victory and defiance that Klea hoped could be seen all the way to their capital city of Serepol.

As she stared at the smoke, one of her soldiers came up to her, dissatisfied and impatient. The wind whistled around them accompanied by the scolding seabirds. The man still had a bandage on his left arm, crusted with blood from an injury on that terrible night. "Do we know when reinforcements are coming from Convera, Watchman? When will they change the station guards and let us go home?"

"Fulcor Island is your home now," Klea said.

"I was not part of the garrison here," the soldier said. "I accompanied Konag Conndur on his diplomatic mission. I wasn't supposed to be left behind during the fighting."

Klea frowned, hearing the criticism in his voice. "I am certain there will be supply ships soon as well as other war vessels, but for now we must hold the island. You should be pleased to serve among the Fulcor defenders."

"But this place is just . . . a cold and windy rock," the soldier sneered. "No resources, only rainfall for water." He shook his head as he looked at the imposing garrison walls. "Why must we fight so hard to defend it?"

Klea scowled. "Because the Isharans want it, and they have always wanted it. They stole Fulcor from us many times, but we always captured it back."

"But why?" The soldier's words had a whining tone. "Why is it so important?"

"This is a strategic island, halfway between the old world and the new. When the first colonists sailed away in search of a new home, it was their stopover point. Olan led his group of Brava colonists here on his way to establish Valaera." Her lips twisted to remember that old tragedy, and the wind felt colder around her face. "All those hopeful colonists, following their dream, harming no one . . ."

"I was trained as an officer in Convera, and even there no one could explain why Fulcor Island is considered strategic. We've shed so much blood over this worthless rock . . ." He looked up to the gray skies.

"It is not worthless," Klea snapped, struggling with her own thoughts and angry that she had no ready logical answer for him. "This island belongs to the Commonwealth, and the Isharans are willing to sacrifice many lives to seize it back. Therefore, we need to hold it."

When he continued to argue, she silenced him and sent him off to his duties.

The next day, the stink of the piled corpses finally became too much inside the garrison walls. Klea commanded the Isharan captives to carry the bodies up to the wall and throw them without ceremony over the cliffs to where the sharks could devour them. This was not beautiful like the legacy ceremony she had given her fallen comrades. This was just disposing of garbage.

The crippled prisoner was carried up to the wall, still moaning in pain, sweating and feverish. He had endured the agony for more than a day. Klea nodded, and two of her soldiers tossed him over the wall. He did not start screaming until he was halfway down the cliff, as if he didn't realize what was happening.

As her black cape rippled behind her, Klea raised her voice. "In response to the crimes you committed, I sentence you all to death." The murder of Konag Conndur gave her more than enough reason, but Isharans also bore their ancestors' guilt for massacring the innocent Brava colony of Valaera. "Your bones will be scoured by the reefs. Your legacies will be forever forgotten."

The Isharan captives were angry, but their hands were bound, rendering them helpless. "Godless bastards!" one of the Isharans snarled. Some screamed and struggled, while others accepted their fates with straight backs. Klea had no more and no less respect for any of them, no matter what they did.

At swordpoint, they were driven over the cliff edge, one after another.

When every captive was gone and the foaming waves erased the blood, Klea turned to the remaining soldiers in the garrison. "Fulcor must never again feel the poison touch of an Isharan. This island is ours."

8

W HEN Suderran lookouts saw the sandwreth party riding their reptilian mounts toward the walled city of Bannriya, King Adan ordered
the entrance to be swung open. He remembered all too well when Queen
Voo's brother had battered his auga to death against the barricaded gate, just
because he was impatient.

Hale Orr joined the king and scowled as the gate opened. "Are you just
going to let them in, Starfall? You know we cannot trust them."

"No, but we don't want to declare war, at least not yet," Adan said in a low
voice as the sandwreth riders approached. "We are smarter than that. Let
them think we are all good friends."

Queen Voo rode to the gate, sitting high on the tooled leather saddle. Beside her rode her lanky, aloof brother Quo and the craggy wreth mage Axus.
Voo looked at him and said with a sniff, "King Adan Starfall, why do you
even bother with these walls? You know I could turn them to dust if I truly
wished to see you."

Adan looked regal in his formal garments as he returned her gaze. "There
are other enemies and dangers in the world. These walls have stood for almost two thousand years. You told us we should learn how to fight and
defend ourselves."

She considered, then nodded. "Indeed, a weak army is of little use to me."
She gestured into the city. "We will go to your palace! It has been weeks since
our dragon hunt, and we must begin arming your people against the frostwreths. I intend to make this alliance strong. We are partners."

Though bile rose in his throat, Adan kept his expression calm. "Of course.
Follow me." He knew Penda was already at work, rushing the staff to create a
reception that would not insult the capricious queen.

Knowing Voo would never leave her entourage outside the walls, Adan
and Hale mounted their horses and rode off, accompanied by an escort of
Banner guards. They guided the party through the winding streets of the old

city. Curious observers peeped out of windows, watched from doorways, or stood under colorful awnings.

Outside Bannriya Castle, Queen Penda had erected an Utauk-style pavilion and a wooden table spread with a colorful variety of foods. Near at hand, the weathered statue of an ancient wreth man, long ago salvaged from the ruins, lay toppled on the ground.

As they arrived, Penda waited beside the old statue, smiling. She had chosen this location intentionally, to subtly remind Voo of her fallen race. She looked beautiful in a fine dress that mixed casual Utauk practicality with more formal Suderran attire, allowing for the swell of her belly. Hale Orr dismounted and stepped up protectively beside his daughter, who was perfectly capable of protecting herself.

Her two skas perched on a single crossbar in front of the yellow pavilion. Seeing the wreths, the skas clicked and hissed. Adan's squire Hom tried to calm the reptile birds, but jerked away in fear when they snapped at him.

As Voo came close to inspect the toppled wreth statue, her lips quirked in a smile. "We have historical records back in my desert palace, but this worthless man was nothing of note." She tossed her long hair, making the little metal ornaments jingle. "I am glad you found some use for him."

Ignoring the selection of drinks, candied fruits, and sliced meats on the table, Queen Voo approached Penda. "I can sense the life growing within you." Boldly, she reached out to touch the curve of her belly.

The Banner guards raised their spears or rested gauntleted hands on sword hilts. The wreth warriors accompanying Voo were alert but confident that no human could pose a threat. They seemed amused at the defensive posture of the guards.

When the sandwreth queen touched her, Penda's expression changed to one of pain or fear, as if a knife twisted in her gut. She jerked away and spoke in a cold, commanding voice. "Please don't touch me."

Adan stepped between them. "Some might consider that a threat to my wife." His voice held controlled fury and firm command. "Step away."

Voo shrugged. "I meant no insult. There is a beauty in such pregnancy, but I also see pain, because it makes us remember why we hate the frostwreths. When my ancestor Raan became pregnant with Kur's child, her own jealous sister poisoned her, nearly killing her. And she lost the baby." Voo raked her golden gaze across them. "That triggered our generations-long feud with the frostwreths, and the tragedy was why Kur left us. We must destroy Suth's descendants before the world can be pure again."

Ari bobbed on her perch, glaring at the strange guests. Beside his sister,

Quo sniffed the air as if he could find answers there. He leaned closer to Penda. "I know little about how humans give birth. When is your baby due?"

"It will be soon," Penda said, uneasiness clear in her voice.

Voo seemed fixated on the baby. "What do you intend to do with the child when it is born? Will it be useful?"

Indignant, Adan said, "It will be our son or daughter. We will raise it and love it and hope to make it the best person possible."

"Ah." Voo sounded disappointed. She gestured for her entourage to take seats at the table.

They all began to dine on the variety spread before them, but no one seemed interested in the meal. The servants were clearly uneasy, and the squire Hom was jumpy each time the sandwreths snatched samples from a plate. Hale Orr was as tense as a strung bow.

Penda sat across from the sandwreth queen. "Why did you come here?"

Voo mused, "Queen Onn created her own workers, which she calls drones. Inferior things, I have heard." She looked at Adan and Penda, ignoring everyone else. "I see much greater potential in humans. Your army will be a valuable asset in the coming war. There will be many obligations and requirements, possibly even some sacrifices in order for your race to survive."

Quo picked up a forkful of sausage, sniffed it, then set it aside. "So long as your people continue to breed. We expect significant losses in the coming war. We will need many children as replacements."

Adan felt boxed in and ready to explode. He wanted to demand that Queen Voo free all of the human captives he had seen in the mothertear images, but he forced his emotions beneath the surface. He took a breath, released it slowly.

Queen Voo said, "Adan Starfall, you rule only one kingdom in this land, but the konag rules all of you. Why has he not come to see me? Does he insult me?"

The mage Axus grumbled from his chair near Hale Orr. "If Adan Starfall is not the most powerful king, then why waste your time with this man?"

"Because he is still powerful, and he is nearby," Voo said with a sniff. "And I find him charming."

Adan, though, felt stung by the comment. "Konag Conndur was murdered by our enemies across the sea. He . . . my brother Mandan is konag now. We only just received word of what happened." He pushed back the grief that welled up. He also knew that his brother discounted the magnitude of the wreth danger. "I think you should speak with my brother, convince him how important your war is."

Voo blinked her topaz eyes and spoke in an imperious voice. "Tell your Konag Mandan to come to the desert, and my warriors will escort him to my palace." Her smile went only as deep as her teeth. "I am eager to see how he measures up to you."

Hale spoke up in disbelief. "*Cra,* you want the konag himself to ride into the desert and hope that someone notices him?"

Quo practiced stabbing the meat with his fork. "We are always watching. No one enters the Furnace without us noticing."

Glad that he had distracted the sandwreth queen from her fascination with Penda and her baby, Adan said, "I will send a message to my brother right away. I, too, want him to talk with you."

9

⚭

R IDING with Elliel and Thon on his mission to Suderra, King Kollanan felt safe in their company, but he knew that any feeling of security was a lie. Unexpected threats had risen out of history like steam from a volcanic vent. Meeting with Adan about the wreth threat was vital, but he was also uneasy about being gone for long from Fellstaff.

Until recently, even a king had been confident traveling alone. Sometimes he had taken Lasis along with him, but he liked to be by himself, at peace. He no longer found peace in simple everyday things, though, as he had before the frostwreths attacked Lake Bakal.

Elliel looked resplendent in her black Brava garb, confident now that she had reclaimed her memories. Her rich cinnamon hair was cropped short in a warrior's cut, and she seemed happy with the love she and Thon shared. Handsome and powerful, the dark wreth regarded the world around him with curiosity, surprised by the smallest things. Thon was eager to see the southern kingdom, to walk in the ancient streets of Bannriya, and to meet King Adan.

Kollanan's warhorse abruptly sidled back and forth, snorting, as if he sensed a predator. Elliel was on her guard, touching her sword.

Suddenly, Thon gasped in pain. Barely managing to halt his horse, he stumbled out of the saddle and took two staggering steps. Elliel jumped down and ran toward him. "What is it?"

The words were torn out of his mouth. "I feel it . . . breaking!"

The forest shook with silent thunder, as though from some great blast underground. The pines around them hissed and rushed together as if shaken by some giant hand. Thick boughs broke and crashed down from the tall silver pines.

The dirt road split, and loose brown earth tumbled into the widening fissure. Kollanan fought to control his horse Storm. Could the dragon be stirring?

Elliel held Thon's shoulders as he writhed in agony. His face was tight, his eyes squeezed shut.

The ground continued to rattle and shake. Gradually, the deep shocks stopped. The world became quiet again, though it still seemed to throb with exhaustion.

Dismounting, Koll hurried over to Elliel, who knelt beside Thon with great concern. The wreth man lay sprawled on his back, staring up in confusion. The inner pain had wrung him out. "I was being shaken and torn apart, just like the world was." He pushed himself up to a sitting position. "There is something deep inside the land and deep inside me . . . something dangerous."

Elliel helped Thon to his feet, brushing off his tunic and silver leggings. She looked intently at him. "Are you sure you're all right?"

"I am sure of nothing, and I have no answers." Thon fashioned an odd smile. "That is why every day is filled with discoveries. The scholar girl taught me that." He ran his hands through his long dark hair. "Let us hope future discoveries are less painful."

He was shaky as he climbed into his saddle, grasping the reins like a lifeline. He looked down at the ground. "This may be a sensitive place that feels the vibrations of Ossus. Perhaps I will be safer once we are far away."

The three of them pressed on well into twilight until they were finally forced to camp. They chose a spot by a narrow stream, and Elliel gathered enough deadwood for the fire to last the night. After she stacked the dry branches, Thon ignited the fire with a tentative touch of magic. Soon water boiled in a cookpot filled with beans and root vegetables. Elliel laid out a blanket to share with Thon, though they would take turns at watch. The king found a comfortable place across the fire from her. He sat against a rock, pulling his knees up. To an outsider, the scene might have looked idyllic, but they remained tense.

Thon hunkered down beside Kollanan, pressed his palm against the dirt. He closed his eyes, let out a long breath, and nodded. "Solid and stable. There is no cause for worry."

Koll raised an eyebrow. "A king who does not worry is not protecting his people."

"Perhaps protecting is my job too," Thon said. "Maybe I am here to hold the world together while everything else tears it apart."

Kollanan leaned against the boulder, feeling the rough stone against his shoulder. "I saw what you did at Lake Bakal. In the coming battles, I intend to rely on you, though I do not know what you are."

"I am a mystery to myself as well, King Kollanan," Thon said with a shrug. "When I find the answer, I hope we will all be satisfied."

"About his power," Elliel said. "There's also a gentleness in him to counteract it." She brought them each a bowl from the pot and sat down. "Thon reminds me of a fine blade. One should admire its beauty but beware of its edge."

"At least I know what a blade is," Koll said. "Do we even know whether you are a wreth, Thon? You look like one, but I am no expert." He had seen only the frostwreths at Lake Bakal.

"There are similarities," Thon admitted. He held out his hand, inspected it, tugged at his dark locks. "And if so, what sort of wreth am I? Obviously not a frostwreth, and I do not believe I am similar to sandwreths either. The two lines descended from Raan and Suth. I do not see how I belong to either of them."

"Another race perhaps?" Elliel said. "I know little about wreth history, but what if Kur created another line of people, people who look like you?"

Thon raised his eyebrows.

"You are an anomaly," Kollanan said. "A useful one."

"A powerful one," Elliel said.

"Then how and why was I sealed inside a mountain with my memories erased, like some unhatched creature in a cocoon? Who am I, and what Am I meant to do?" He frowned, deep in thought. "Did other wreths turn against me?" He touched the strange tattoo on his face. "And why strip me of all my memories? Were they that afraid of me?"

Kollanan said, "Your powers alone could give people reason to fear."

"They frighten me, too," Elliel said. "Even though I know you are no threat to us." She reached out to touch the markings on his face. "I didn't know my identity either until you brought my memories back." Finishing her meal, she set the bowl on the ground and removed the golden ramer band from its place at her hip. In wonder, she held it up to the firelight. "You made me a Brava again, helped me find the power in my own blood."

She squeezed the cuff around her right wrist until the metal fangs bit into her veins. Blood trickled down the pale skin of her arm, providing the catalyst to ignite her ramer. Bright flames encircled the cuff and covered her hand. When Elliel concentrated, she extended the fire and raised the slender bladelike torch high in the forest clearing. "I am a Brava again!" She lowered her voice, spoke to herself. "And I will never forget what Lord Cade and Utho did to me."

Intent on the ramer, Thon reached toward the blazing blade. He twitched his fingers, twirled them, and the fire changed color from orange to yellow to a pure white, which then dropped down to a deeper blue, then violet before cycling to a dark crimson. Elliel shuddered with pleasure as his wild magic surged through her.

When Thon released his invisible grip, Elliel's shoulders slumped, and she let the ramer flame sputter out. She removed the red-stained golden cuff, and the blood flow at her wrist stopped.

"Your ramer is interesting," Thon said to her. "I wonder if Kur envisioned such things when he created the wreths."

Kollanan said in a gruff voice, "Their god has nothing to do with us."

"If Kur created the world, you are still part of it," Thon said. "Although according to the story, Kur vanished long before wreths created humans. He has not seen anything of the world in a very long time. He is waiting for the wreths to complete the task he gave them."

For most of his life, Kollanan had dismissed the legends of Ossus sleeping beneath the Dragonspine Mountains. Up until a few months ago, he'd considered the wreths themselves little more than legend. . . .

"The world will be made perfect—if we can believe wreth history," Thon said. "I do not know if the world is imperfect. I have seen nothing of it . . . in a very long time."

"That's what you just said about Kur." Elliel turned, and her voice became tentative. "Could there be some connection?"

Thon was intrigued. "A connection between me and Kur?"

"Think about it. Kur created wreths in his own image, so therefore their god would look pretty much like a wreth. A perfect wreth. That's what *you* look like." Elliel's voice rose with excitement. "You must admit, you have incredible and unexplained powers."

Kollanan blinked when he realized what the Brava woman was suggesting.

Thon's brows were raised in a quizzical look not understanding, until Elliel said, "What if *you* are Kur?"

Thon gave a surprised laugh. Then a sober look came over him and he considered for a long moment. "My memories end at about the same time. It is not an . . . impossible idea."

"But if you were a god, why would wreths subdue you and seal you inside the mountains?" Koll asked. "Could they truly have been so afraid that they considered you a threat?"

"Whether you're Kur or not, *how* could they do it?" Elliel pressed.

Thon pursed his lips as he followed another thought. He ran his fingertips along the tattoo. "What if I allowed them to do it for some reason?" His brow furrowed. "Or what if I did it myself?"

10

∽

I WANT to depart as soon as possible, Utho," said Mandan, leaning forward on a cushioned chair in his royal suite. "It's time the people see me as their new konag."

The Brava watched him, sure that the young man's eagerness would wane during the hardships of travel. A private dinner had been set out for them, but Utho had no interest in the food. The large fire in the hearth made the room too hot for his taste.

Mandan's eyes took on an avid expression. "And when our procession reaches Lord Cade's holding, I wish to see the Isharan slaves and witness the defeat in their eyes."

As he ate sliced venison with blackberry sauce, the young man turned his attention to the maps that covered one entire wall of his chamber. He would spend hours pondering the boundaries of Osterra, Suderra, and Norterra. During his studies as prince, he had become interested in geography. He knew where every holding ended, could name all twenty-one counties that served Osterra, the fifteen counties in Suderra, and the eight large counties in Norterra. Mandan could even identify most of the vassal lords by name, though he had little personal relationship with any of them.

Most of his knowledge had come from books and tutors, since Mandan had not seen much of the Commonwealth. Utho was pleasantly surprised by the young man's idea. "I, too, should inspect Cade's prison camp, my konag. It will be a long ride, many days on the road. We will try to find inns or holding houses along the way, though we will be prepared to camp."

"I studied the route." Forgetting about his dinner, Mandan walked to the lavishly detailed maps on the wall. "There are places in Osterra I want to see, vassal lords to meet along the way." His gaze had turned steely, and his mind had gone from panic to an irrevocable focus on revenge. "I intend to take my father with me."

Utho was startled. "What do you mean?"

"Konag Conndur was cut into pieces, which have been preserved. The entire Commonwealth must understand the barbarity of our enemy. What better demonstration than to dispatch processions throughout the three kingdoms so the people can behold the proof of what the Isharans did to our beloved ruler."

Utho remembered exactly what had been done to Conndur's body. After all, he had staged the scene to generate maximum horror. He had cut off the konag's hands, gouged out his eyes, cut out the heart and placed it on the man's groin. He had splashed blood on the walls of the chamber to imply the greatest violence, though in his only spark of mercy, he had at least killed Conndur first.

Utho nodded slowly as he realized that such a procession would continue to enrage every person in the Commonwealth. "It is a good plan, Mandan."

The young konag beamed at the praise. "We will take my father's heart with us and send the other pieces elsewhere."

⁊⁊

The procession departed three days later with supply wagons, tents, comfortable camp beds. With the banner-bearers and escort in the lead, Utho rode alongside Mandan of the Colors. His black Brava garb was in sharp contrast to the young konag's multicolored cape, jerkin, and leggings. Behind them walked a pure white horse, perfectly groomed, bearing the colors of Conndur the Brave. Bound to the saddle was a gilded chest, evident and ominous for all to see.

The people came out to cheer the konag each time the procession arrived in a town, but as news spread of the grim trophy, the crowds grew more somber. Murmuring with respect, the people recounted tales of Conndur's exploits, when he and his brother had led Commonwealth armies in Ishara thirty years ago.

On the second day the procession arrived in the county of Lord Goran, who came out to greet them with a retinue of personal guards. Goran had prepared fine quarters for the konag in his holding house above the river, and Utho did not doubt that Goran, who was a petty man, would assume the meeting bestowed great importance on him.

Looking at the crowd, the Brava saw some people wearing drab clothes and haunted looks. Many refugees from the devastated mining town of Scrabbleton had resettled here after the eruption of Mount Vada, but had not yet rebuilt a normal life.

Lord Goran had a high forehead, a cleft chin, and dark lips that gave him a pouting look. Standing in front of the procession, Goran turned his attention to the gilded box on the white horse's saddle. He fought to maintain an expression of respect.

After dismounting, Mandan walked up to the small chest. "You want to see my father's heart." He stroked the horse's mane. "Let me show you what the Isharans did."

Goran bent closer as the young konag undid the metal hasp and raised the lid to reveal a wrapped lump in folds of blue velvet. Mandan spoke in a husky voice. "They cut it out of my father's chest. They pried apart the ribs and reached in with their bare hands to rip out his heart. Then they shoved it between his legs, still leaking blood."

Goran's face went as pale as fresh cheese. "I . . . I'm sorry, Sire."

Utho watched, pleased by Mandan's performance. He had coached the young man, showing him how to add passion to this speech. The konag's voice rose so he could address all of the people, not just the sallow-faced lord. As he described the events on Fulcor Island, he relived his nightmares and gave the listeners nightmares as well.

In the weeks since that night, Utho had seen a real change in the young man. As prince, Mandan had been shy and weak, bored and impatient with his duties, but now vengeance made him strong.

One man with thick arms and broad shoulders hung his head. "First Scrabbleton is destroyed, and now this terrible news! The world is full of evil and pain. What are we to do?"

Unpracticed, Mandan fumbled for words, and Utho interjected in a gruff voice. "You can help. You can be more than refugees. There is a war coming, and we are building our army." He looked at the man's obvious strength. "A person who spent his life breaking rock could be a great fighter. We'll train you to be a warrior." He raised his voice to the crowd. "Anyone who wishes to be part of the Commonwealth army is welcome."

Standing beside the open box, Mandan looked at Lord Goran's escort soldiers. "You already have some fighters that you will give to us."

The sallow lord balked. "So many sacrifices, so much pain and suffering! The Isharan animals must pay for their heinous crime, but we are also in danger here in Osterra." He flicked a glance at Utho. "My konag, you have this powerful man next to you, but I've lost my bonded Brava. Klea was my protector, but she selflessly joined the expedition to Fulcor Island, and she never returned to me."

"Klea has other duties now," Utho said, his voice hard. "She remains on Fulcor as the new watchman commanding the troops there. The Isharan animals are sure to come back. That is where she belongs."

"But she's bonded to me!" Goran said. "What am I to do without protection?" Beside him, his armed soldiers flinched, offended by the comment.

Utho had no sympathy for the man. Bravas could swear their loyalty to a nobleman or some other wealthy employer. "You will have to make do." Though Goran needed no such protection, he had always basked in the prestige of having a bonded Brava at his side.

"I am so sorry for your great sacrifice, Lord Goran," Mandan said with thick sarcasm. "I cannot imagine the pain you must be feeling. Does it compare to mine at losing a father, or that of the Commonwealth losing a beloved ruler?"

He shut the lid of the chest that held Conndur's heart and fixed the hasp with a sharp click, letting his palm linger on the gilded wood as if he could feel his father's heart still beating inside.

11

THE Fellstaff remembrance shrine felt like another home to Shadri. Proud of her new title as the queen's legacier, the young scholar had spent many days there with books spread out on the long table, reading by sunshine or candlelight. She asked persistent questions, because she wanted to learn *everything*. Today, rather than studying alone, she was glad Queen Tafira offered to accompany her.

Silent and serious as the queen's protector, with his black cape flowing behind him, the Brava Lasis led the two of them through the streets to the two-story remembrance shrine. Shadri continued talking, her conversation as erratic as a bumblebee in flight. "Maybe the legaciers will tell you more answers than I've been able to learn, my lady. Legacier Thooma seems impatient with me when I ask too many questions."

Tafira frowned. "They should be pleased that someone is so interested in our history."

Lasis broke his silence. "Perhaps they do not like it when they don't have the answers."

Shadri grinned at him. She was a sturdy and self-sufficient young woman who wore thick bundled skirts and layered upper garments, because they offered plenty of pockets to keep all the things she might need. When she had wandered the land alone, Shadri carried an enormous pack stuffed with supplies like food, notebooks, darning needles, sulfur matches, nubs of candles, a lead stylus, and little packets for specimens she found along the journey.

Ever since arriving in Norterra, Shadri had been eager to talk about everything she had learned in her travels. She pestered everyone from the firewood boy Pokle to Queen Tafira herself with anecdotes and with whatever questions popped into her mind.

Lasis opened the door of the remembrance shrine, and Shadri peered inside. This was one of her favorite places. She had read dozens of volumes and scrolls, studying names and the associated lives, talents, tales, treasures, and descendants. Her eyes were shining when she looked at Tafira. "So many people left so many different stories!"

"Pay attention to the living ones as well, dear girl," Tafira said as they entered the building. "A person's legacy should be experienced, not just remembered."

"I'll keep that in mind," she said. The books and scrolls around her had a wonderful smell.

Lasis pulled the door closed behind them, and Shadri caught a glimpse of the long scar across his neck. He had told her the story—only because she asked him repeatedly—of how the frostwreth queen had slashed his throat when she grew bored with him as a captive lover, but his Brava magic had kept him alive. Shadri wrote down that story and logged the document into the remembrance shrine.

The young scholar strutted forward, looking at the tables and shelves of books, wondering where she should start today. Once they entered the foyer, Legacier Thooma came to greet them. Upon seeing Shadri, the matronly legacier showed a wary, put-upon expression, as if she had suffered a multitude of the girl's questions, but she gave a warm and respectful welcome to the queen.

Tafira rested a hand on Shadri's shoulder. "My personal legacier has done great work chronicling the story of the recent attack on Lake Bakal. She has acknowledged the generous assistance your people gave her."

Legacier Thooma responded with a pinched smile. "Of course, my queen. I tasked two of my junior legaciers with fetching any documents she requests." She sighed. "It must be quite an exhaustive history she is writing."

"It's our legacy." Shadri felt defensive. "We need to share it, fill the archives with details and supporting documentation on all the vassal lords, the soldiers, and their families. Everyone in the Commonwealth has to remember the people who fought at Lake Bakal, and the people who died there."

Lasis stiffened. "They deserve to be remembered."

The queen's expression fell. "Often I come here by myself so I can reflect on my life and the legacy I leave. I consider the turmoil I've endured and the love I have experienced to counterbalance the pain."

Shadri's words came out in a rush. "Can I write more of your story, my lady? Everything you remember about your home village, the local godling, and what happened when the Commonwealth army came?" She imagined telling a romantic tale. "And how your beloved Kollanan swept you away?"

A fleeting smile touched the corners of Tafira's lips, before her expression shifted. "It was not an entirely joyous tale, dear girl. Perhaps not all of the details need to be remembered."

Sunlight streamed through the many-paned windows, illuminating the main reading room beyond the first line of shelves. Tables were covered with old volumes, some open for reading, others stacked. Shelves along the walls held books organized by family name and by year. Helpful legaciers moved about assisting patrons who came to remember lost loved ones, history students, solicitors researching property disputes, young couples studying their genealogy in preparation for marriage.

As they followed Thooma into the reading room, they saw the group of Commonwealth escort soldiers at one table, still wearing their capes and doublets with the open hand of the Commonwealth. Thick leather-bound books were spread out on the table, but Shadri doubted the men had been researching long-lost uncles.

When Captain Rondo looked up and saw the queen, his expression tightened. He offered a stiff nod, the briefest gesture of respect. "Queen Tafira."

"I did not know history was one of your interests, Captain."

"As the people say, each day brings a new surprise. My men had a surprise today, as well. King Kollanan asked us to remain in Norterra, even though the konag has been murdered and the three kingdoms must prepare for war."

"The king asked you to remain behind while he traveled south to Suderra to meet King Adan," Tafira said. "We are glad for your added strength to help protect Norterra, if anything should happen while my husband is gone."

The guard captain looked away, frowning.

Shadri spoke up. "Scouts say that many roads are impassable due to the eruption of Mount Vada."

"And yet, the courier made it through, with his news of Conndur's murder." Rondo reached across the table and pulled a large volume toward him, which displayed a map of the Commonwealth. "The high route should still be open, far north of Mount Vada, although the snows will close it soon." He closed the book. "But we will stay, as King Kollanan commanded. I hope he is not gone too long." Resentment roughened his voice. "While my men and I wait, we intend to gather information that may help the Commonwealth. We will add it to the report the king sends to Convera." Two of his soldiers perfunctorily looked down at the books in front of them.

Shadri took quick interest. "And what information is that? Can I help?"

Rondo looked at her and did not seem to know who she was. "We search for evidence of any other Isharans who might be in this land. They could be spies or saboteurs. The konag must know." He looked down at the book in front of him. "Norterra is safe and far from Ishara, and thus it would be a good place for the enemy to hide. There may be spies."

"Oh, I doubt you'd find Isharans here," Shadri said, matter-of-fact. "I haven't seen any."

Other soldiers distractedly traced the patterns on the pages, avoiding Tafira's gaze. The queen remained proud, her eyes bright. Her long dark hair was bound in distinctive, colorful scarves that made her stand out, made her look foreign.

Rondo said, "I can't even sleep at night, knowing what the Isharan animals did to our beloved Conndur. Cutting him to pieces!"

"His bonded Brava should have protected him," Lasis interjected, as if to shift the focus of their ire. "Utho failed in his most important duty."

Shadri knew the terrible things Utho had done to Elliel, as did Lasis. But the soldiers were not distracted by the Brava's comments. Shadri sensed anger and unease rippling from the Commonwealth soldiers like heated air from a stoked fireplace.

Rondo said, "Even a Brava can't defend against outright betrayal. Konag Conndur was wrong to trust any Isharan."

One of the other soldiers, Sergeant Headan, muttered, "Isharans aren't human like the rest of us. They don't understand the same pain or the same loyalty."

It was clear even to Shadri, who often didn't notice such things, that his sharp tone was directed toward Queen Tafira, whose exotic garb, dusky skin, and large brown eyes were distinctly Isharan.

Bristling at the comment, Lasis placed a hand on the pommel of his sword and tossed back his black cape to give him more freedom of movement. The Commonwealth soldiers shifted and several stood, ready to assume fighting positions.

But Tafira raised her hand. "What you say may be true about some Isharans, Captain." She looked at him until he turned away. "When I was just a girl, my stepmother hated me, because my father had gotten a farm girl pregnant. He accepted me and loved me as his daughter, but she cast me out of the house the day after he died.

"I survived by helping people, doing odd jobs. I thought they liked me, but when Commonwealth raiders came burning fields and razing villages, my people believed their only hope was to make a sacrifice to our local godling." Rondo's soldiers listened, though with clear reluctance. "Ours was a gentle godling, but the villagers were desperate because monstrous Commonwealth soldiers were raping and slaughtering and burning their way across our countryside. There was no way to stop them."

She leaned closer to the table, intruding on the space of the uneasy soldiers. It seemed that Captain Rondo and his fellows stopped breathing.

"My people needed blood for their sacrifice—and they considered me the most expendable person in the village, the least wanted. They were going to sacrifice me." She squeezed her ringed hand into a fist. "But Kollanan rode in and stopped them, and he prevented his *own* soldiers from committing atrocities. He saved me that day."

Rondo and his men were uneasy. "I didn't fight in that war," he said. "But I will fight in this one."

"As well you should, and I hope you and your men can keep yourselves from committing the atrocities of your predecessors," Tafira said. "Our features and our clothing did not make us enemies, Captain. Neither does the name of the land where we were born. What matters is what is in our hearts."

The queen turned to leave, and Lasis ushered her away with Shadri in tow. Though the scholar girl had been unable to study any new documents this day, she had learned a great deal.

12

∽

ICY winds scoured the towers, but the movement of chill air inside the frostwreth palace was as faint as the last breath of a dying man.

Queen Onn lectured Birch as she glided through the corridors on slender legs. "For many centuries we remained dormant in our glacier, restoring ourselves through periods of spellsleep." Her gown was silver and white, as if woven from strands of hoarfrost. "The sandwreths crawled under their dusty rocks to recover, while we preserved ourselves in the purity of the ice. Now we are strong again."

When the queen flashed a pale smile toward him, Birch flinched. She seemed disappointed that he wasn't awestruck. Onn led him deep into the ice, where passageways had been carved by magic, melting and refreezing the water until it was as smooth and hard as glass. Their footsteps barely whispered on the slick floor, and Birch hurried to keep pace with her.

"I want to show you our numbers, boy. Maybe I will even let you witness the coming battle when we slay the sandwreths. After that, we wake the dragon Ossus." When Birch didn't respond, she snapped, "Are you glad to be with us?"

"Yes," he said, adding nothing else. He had learned that the less he said, the less chance there was of accidentally making Onn angry.

As she strolled along, the queen muttered more to herself than to him, "The children of Raan must pay for how they corrupted the love that Kur shared with my ancestor Suth. They are an inferior race, just as humans are. And my drones are even more disappointing." She seemed frustrated with herself.

Onn strode into a complex of giant grottoes hollowed out of the glacier ice. Wreths of different castes moved about: armored warriors, aloof nobles, dour mages, and burly lower-caste workers performing necessary functions. Teams of drones also moved underfoot and beneath notice.

"Thousands of us were injured during the last wars," Onn continued, "and lay dormant as the centuries passed. The land was drained of magic, and we had hoped the world would regain its power after so much time. Thus far our mages have not recovered fully." She shook her head. "But I will never consider myself weak. No frostwreth is weak."

Tiers of frozen chambers, like sealed-over cells in an insect hive, studded the grotto walls. Thin, transparent ice covered the chambers like a window, and each cell held the motionless, blurred figure of a dormant wreth.

On walkways above, drones scampered about performing incomprehensible tasks with the spellsleep chambers. Warriors strolled along in full armor as if trying to impress one another. Mages pressed their palms against the ice windows, monitoring their frozen comrades inside.

"Thousands of frostwreths underwent cycles of spellsleep," Onn continued. "See how many still remain to be awakened! Using spellsleep, I sidestepped the centuries, awakening only a few days at a time so that my body did not age. See, I am still young and ready for war." She touched her face with sharp silver fingernails. "I lost neither my beauty nor my strength." She drew in a deep breath and exhaled a cloud of frost.

Drones shuffled about, getting in the way. A wreth warrior cuffed two, knocking them aside. The creatures scuttled away, avoiding further blows.

Onn sneered at them. "If my magic were at full strength, those drones could have been magnificent creations, like our humans, but they are lacking in so many ways." She gave a wistful smile. "Fortunately, we have superior warriors of our own."

The queen led Birch to a nearby cell, where a bald mage smoothed over the ice window. Thin tubes like vines ran through the ice and into the rectangular chamber, pumping a silvery fluid. The tubes emerged from the chamber covered with icicles connected to aquamarine jewels that powered them, pulsing with faint blue light.

The spellsleep enclosure contained a muscular male warrior clad in diamond and sapphire plate armor. His neck was thick, his jawline strong. He seemed to exude enough power to melt the ice even in his frozen state. Queen Onn pressed her face against the ice, breathing so that a sheen of melted water appeared like liquid diamond droplets. With one of her nails, she scratched a thin line on the surface.

"Irri—that was his name. I wonder why . . ." Her voice trailed off. "Now that Rokk has gotten himself killed, I think I shall wake this one. Irri can comfort my loneliness. He was quite good at it, I recall." She glanced at Birch, then issued orders to the mage tending the spellsleep chamber. "Make certain we balance our overall awakenings so that we have the proper proportion of warriors, nobles, mages, and support workers. Our numbers will increase dramatically." Her gaze bored into the mage's craggy features. "Do it properly."

The bald mage bowed. "Of course, my queen."

Onn strolled along, peering into the transparent ice at her preserved frostwreths, and on the second tier she paused before another chamber. The frozen cell held a tall, beautiful woman with pale, bone-cold hair. Unlike the other wreths, who wore armor or garments in their chill sleep, this woman was naked, her skin as pale as snow. Her features reminded Birch of Queen Onn's.

"My daughter. I will wake her along with the others, because I need all my frostwreths," Onn muttered, as if she had forgotten the boy standing next to her. "But Koru is often intractable." She looked down at him. "I also had two sons, but they were killed in the wars. Koru remains. By staggering our spellsleep cycles, she and I manage not to be awake at the same time. I did not see eye-to-eye with her."

Looking at the naked woman in the ice, Birch finally spoke. "That's your daughter?"

"See how beautiful she is."

The boy obliged with a nod.

"Koru was strong in battle, although she argued against me as much as she fought against the sandwreths."

"Will she fight Ossus?" Birch asked. "The dragon?"

Onn frowned. "Yes, she will fight Ossus. I will have to wake her." She seemed to be bracing herself. "We need all of my subjects."

"Maybe she can kill the dragon with the spear behind your throne," Birch said.

"Maybe," Onn said. "Or maybe *I* will."

13

∽

THE empra's tower rose above Serepol, stretching skyward as if the architect believed he had the strength of a godling. In the spacious upper chamber that was Iluris's private residence, Cemi gazed out the large windows, which were open in hopes that the fresh air might revive the unconscious woman on the bed. The empra did not stir, but the breeze ruffled Cemi's short brown hair.

Two hawk guards, resplendent in gold and scarlet armor, kept watch inside the main chamber; three more guarded the outer door, with additional ranks stationed in the corridor.

Cemi usually enjoyed the view from this dizzying height, but today she felt overwhelmed, as if she were falling free with no landing in sight. Inhaling the salty air that blew in from the nearby harbor, she surveyed the waterfront, where the streets were cluttered and crowded, filled with craft districts, smithies, tanneries, weaver shops, merchant offices, warehouses, fish markets, and the docks themselves. In the opposite direction, wide streets stretched toward the city center, where the long-dormant Magnifica temple would soon rise high.

Crowds filled the entire fountain square directly below, in front of the palace. People of all professions and classes, knowing that Empra Iluris was gravely injured, came to offer their support and energy. Even from so high up, Cemi could hear the murmur of their prayers, and she drew strength from it. The chants rose and fell, followed by a lull, then an even louder resurgence. The people were passionate, summoning their faith to strengthen their beloved empra. Those prayers were a safety net that kept Iluris safe and alive.

Leaving the open window, Cemi went to the woman who lay on her lavish bed with colorful silk sheets. The unconscious face of her dear mentor was etched with deep lines that might have been worry, might have been pain, or might have been nothing at all. "Please get better," she murmured.

Iluris's head was freshly bandaged with white gauze. Cemi and one of the trusted court doctors, whom the loyal servant Analera had chosen with the approval of Chamberlain Nerev, changed the dressing and inspected the wounds daily, but Iluris's condition remained the same. She appeared lifeless, but a mirror held up to her nose showed the faint exhalation of breath. Cemi sat next to her, talked with her, though it was a one-sided conversation and a confession.

Captani Vos carried a jeweled cup to the bed, and Cemi shook her head. "I just tried to give her some water."

"No, this is for you. You must also care for yourself. There may soon come a time—"

She cut him off. "I'm fine. I've gone days without food or water before."

"But you don't have to, not if I have anything to say about it. I insist that you eat meals as they are brought in. Stay strong for all of us, and for her."

Cemi felt a weight lift from her shoulders. "Thank you for taking care of me."

"Someone has to, apparently. And it will help you take care of the empra."

She took a sip of cool water, smiled at Vos. "When I first tried to sneak in and see the empra in Prirari, you did everything in your power to keep me away from her."

The captani's expression shifted to amusement. "It was my job. You climbed the walls and tried to break into her guest quarters. I had to consider you a threat." He flushed with embarrassment. "And I failed to protect the empra."

Cemi smiled at the memory. "I wanted to see if I could do it. I think our godling was watching over me that day."

"You were fast and bold, but you shouldn't have gotten through," Vos said. "Iluris should have called for my execution, or at least dismissed me from service."

"I'm glad she didn't, because we sorely need you now." Together, they looked down at Iluris. Outside, the prayers continued to swell, adding strength to the air. "I'm glad she didn't," she repeated in a whisper.

"I know I can trust you. Our mother placed so much faith in you." Vos reached out to stroke the older woman's smooth, dry cheek. "She wanted you to be a good empra, Cemi."

The young woman glanced at the books of mathematics, political science, diplomacy, and trade summaries that Chamberlain Nerev had brought at her request. Cemi had so much time sitting here in the empra's presence, she was determined to continue her instruction. That was what Iluris would want her to do.

A signal from the corridor alerted Captani Vos, as one of the guards issued a stern challenge to stop an approaching visitor. "Priestlord, what is your business here?"

"I am *Ur*-Priest Dono," said a man's nasal voice. "I have come to pray at the empra's side and give her the godling's blessing."

Vos went to the chamber door.

The hawk guards glanced at the captani, and Vos stepped forward to take charge. "Isn't the godling powerful enough to see her from the temple? Can it not extend its power and bless our mother from where it lives?"

"It would be more effective if I directed the godling's attentions," Dono said. "That is what priestlords do."

"But that is not what you will do today," Vos said. "The empra is in danger, and the hawk guards must protect her from any threats."

"Threats? I come to pray for her. How can that be a threat?"

"We cannot be too careful. If we had been more suspicious on Fulcor Island, then Empra Iluris would not now lie injured." Vos's voice became grating. "We do not know who might be a Commonwealth sympathizer, a spy come to finish the assassination. They have many tricks."

As Ur-Priest Dono expressed his outrage, the hawk guards closed in and prevented him from catching even a glimpse of the empra on her bed. After a tense moment, the priestlord turned about and retreated down the corridor.

❧

The construction site of the Magnifica temple left much to the imagination, and Key Priestlord Klovus had tremendous imagination. He had needed a catalyst for more than two decades, and he had wasted no time after returning from Fulcor Island. In light of the unconscious empra, when he issued his confident command for the temple work to proceed, no one pushed back.

For years Iluris had blocked him at every turn, and now she couldn't speak out against him. Her chamberlain, her advisors, and the young girl she had taken as her ward had not rallied to push back against him now in this time of crisis. To a frightened, angry people, the key priestlord's orders made perfect sense.

On Fulcor Island, Klovus had directed his Black Eel assassins to kill the empra and make it appear as if the konag's Brava had done the deed. Something had gone wrong, which still baffled Klovus—how could one woman, even an iron-willed empra, stand against a Black Eel? Zaha, the leader of his assassins, had told a wild story of a mysterious invisible force that had inter-vened to save Iluris, which made no sense.

Perhaps all was for the best, though. Even comatose, the empra served his purposes. With no other clear leader of the land, Klovus could command that his pronouncements be followed. The ambitious work on the Magnifica was a perfect example.

Priestlords from the city and the surrounding districts answered his call, and labor crews were starting work already. The site had been cleared decades ago, when Klovus's predecessor announced the original grandiose design of a construction so vast it would concentrate unimaginable power here in Serepol. Emprir Daka had agreed.

But the war against the godless Commonwealth had stalled construction, with all resources diverted to the defense of the land. After Daka's death, the new Empra Iluris called a halt to all construction, concerned that the Mag-nifica would vest too much power in a single godling. Her stubbornness had frustrated Key Priestlord Klovus for years. But now she could not stop him.

Standing at the edge of the huge open plaza, Klovus marveled at the ex-panse of the foundation alone. He folded his hands into the voluminous sleeves of his caftan and felt an air of importance rippling from him like a godling's strength. He inhaled deeply and exhaled pure satisfaction.

Because the Magnifica would be so enormous, the foundation went deep beneath the streets to a full labyrinth beneath the city. The priestlords had continued their construction out of sight over the quiet decades. But a god-ling deserved praise and needed extravagance to make it stronger. A godling's sheer power was dependent upon the faith of its people.

Soon—maybe in only a handful of years, if the workers devoted them-selves properly—this entire plaza would be dominated by a stepped pyramid that rose even higher than the palace. That was fitting, because the primary godling was more important than any human ruler.

Part of the temple's second level over the base foundation had been con-structed over the years, but much of the open expanse still held only tempo-rary structures, stands, altars, and blood-offering receptacles. Ornate statues had been placed at strategic points where titans would one day stand, anchor points for the beliefs of the faithful.

Klovus stood at the northeastern corner of the square, looking down at the detailed scale model of the temple on display. It was an embodiment of his dreams. The model stood five feet high and eight on a side, showing the stairsteps of the gigantic pyramid, each layer reserved for certain types of worshippers. The walls and steps would be emblazoned with carvings and mural paintings, gold sculptures embellished with jewels. The model alone was a work of art, and Klovus imagined that the completed Magnifica would be almost too grand for mere human eyes to behold.

At his command, valuable materials were confiscated from construction sites across Serepol: slabs of stone, structural timbers, bricks, mortar, iron, and steel—anything the city had on hand. As word spread, eager work crews raced to Serepol from the thirteen districts of Ishara. The quarries of Rassah and Ishiki sent wagonloads of granite and sandstone blocks. The hardwood forests of Janhari provided endless logs. Clay from the riverbanks in Mormosa and Salimbul would be used to make bricks.

Everyone would provide, because everyone believed. Isharans knew the potential of their godlings, even if their empra had grave reservations. Klovus himself fed upon the people and their faith, drank in their open worship, which was fuel to the fire of the godlings.

It annoyed him, though, that so many devotees now prayed so earnestly for Empra Iluris. She had been the single most frustrating impediment to Ishara's growth! At least now she could cause no further delays.

At several sacrifice stations around the construction site, priestlords rang bells and called for volunteers. "All your sacrifices!" a voice boomed out. "We take all your sacrifices. Feed the godling. Make us strong!"

The devout approached, some carrying jars or urns, others with sacks of gold, keepsakes, even food offerings, but the most powerful and simplest sacrifices occurred at the blood receptacles, where priests stood with sharpened knives to slash bared arms or open palms, spilling the life fluid down below to strengthen the godling.

"Hear us, save us!" they chanted.

"Hear us, save us," Klovus responded and smiled. He could picture the Magnifica, complete and breathtaking. Soon. "Hear us, save us."

14

❧

THE brown leather was soft but strong, and Glik knew it would be thick enough to blunt a sword blow. She sewed a second layer on the breastplate she was assembling. Her needle was dull, but she pushed hard, using a wooden thimble. The needle pierced the leather and slipped out the other side. She pulled the thick thread and tugged the stitch tight, then shoved the needle back through again. The stitches made the breastplate leather look like a patchwork scar sewn up by a battlefield surgeon.

Glik didn't know where the leather came from, nor did she dare ask. She quelled her thoughts, kept working. Whenever possible, she palmed small scraps of leather, hiding them among the folds of her clothes. The young girl never missed an opportunity to snatch resources that might be useful at some point. She never knew what small thing might be the key to escape and survival.

Glik paused to draw a circle around her heart with a quick subconscious gesture. She got through each day with the slow tedium of a quiet trance, but no new visions had come to her in two days. Even though Ari's unexpected images had terrified her dreams in the past, she missed them.

Mage Ivun prowled through the camp, without seeming to see anything. The steady rhythm of work being completed convinced him that all was well. Many of the prisoners felt weak, eaten up by their own terror, but Glik did not let herself feel the despair. She would find a way out of this.

Her fingers poked the sturdy needle through the leather, worked the thread down into a seam, pulled back up to complete another stitch. The leather breastplate was slowly coming together. Whoever wore it would likely die on some pointless battlefield.

A few of the stronger captives donned the armor, heavy gauntlets, and leggings so they could be trained in combat. The sandwreths wanted to fashion their captives into a viable army, though Glik didn't know who the enemy was or why slaves would throw down their lives for their captors. Forced to drill, the human fighters practiced without enthusiasm, battering one another with blunted swords.

Glik paid particular attention to a group of captive fighters, actual Bravas, half-breed descendants of wreths and humans. She wondered if they felt any different toward the sandwreths than she did. The eight Bravas were intrinsically stronger than the other captives, able to endure hardships better than most. One Brava woman with a long, oval face and short brown hair trained with unexpected dedication. Glik watched her swordplay against two Brava men who fought back with equal verve.

Though the Bravas seemed to have no interest in satisfying the wreths, they threw themselves into the training exercises and even seemed to enjoy the fighting.

After a while, the Bravas paired off, working themselves into a sweat in the hot desert air. They struck blade against blade, bashing shields to throw their opponents off balance, and then clashed again.

After observing the Bravas with a critical eye, the aloof sandwreth guards pulled their bone swords and long copper spears. The guards waded into the fray laughing, as if this were a mere frolic, and the Brava captives were just as happy to fight them.

"You gave us real blades to train with," said the lone Brava woman. "Now we can test you." She slammed her sword against a copper spear, forcing the wreth man to stagger back, startled, before he came at her with redoubled fury.

"We gave you real blades because you are no threat," he retorted.

All eight Bravas joined forces, and in a dramatic clash of blades and a crack of wood against bone, they retaliated against their enemy. "Give us our ramers back," challenged a Brava, "and we'll show you how we fight."

The wreth warriors snorted. "Mage Ivun keeps your strange weapons locked away. Once you prove yourselves with swords, perhaps we'll let you play with your fiery bands."

The Brava woman struck a guard in the face with the flat of her blade. The unexpected blow snapped his head to one side and left an angry red mark on his bronze skin. In fury, he turned his full attack against her and unleashed a burst of wreth magic that even the Brava couldn't withstand. The blow bowled the woman back into the dust.

The wreth leaped at her and raised his spear for a killing blow, but one of his companions knocked him aside with a grunt. The woman sprang back to her feet, shifted her grip on her sword, and faced them, ready to keep sparring.

The humiliated guard managed to control himself. He issued orders to the Brava captives. "Teach yourselves to fight better, and then teach the other humans to fight, too. Maybe you will earn our respect."

"I don't need your respect," the woman retorted. "I have my own."

The metallic sound of a copper gong resounded through the canyon. The prisoners gathered for their midday meal of dried strips of meat and a bowl that contained a paste of beans and grain. It was enough to keep them alive. Glik had survived on meager rations before. She had collected spare scraps whenever she saw the opportunity, squirreled the food away in case she needed it later. She always had to be ready.

She knew many of the prisoners by now, although each person was isolated and separate. Even before her capture, the orphan girl had spent much of her life wandering outside the circle. Few people were likely to notice she had gone missing. At least Ari had escaped. . . .

Taking her food, Glik impulsively squatted on a rock next to the Brava woman, who glanced at her, then went back to silent eating. The tall woman had not bothered to tend her bruises and cuts. Apparently Bravas healed swiftly.

"My name is Glik. From the Utauk tribes."

"I can see where you're from." After a long pause, she added, "I'm Cheth."

"Why train with the wreths? Because you're half-breeds?"

Cheth glowered. "My people have wreth blood in our veins because wreths raped my ancestors."

"Then why do you fight for them?"

"I don't fight *for* them, girl! I fight because that's what a Brava does. I fight because by doing so I maintain my skill, and someday I will turn that skill against them. They are fools to let us train right in front of them."

"Those three guards were beating all of you," Glik pointed out.

"We allowed them a false sense of confidence for next time."

"Hard to believe," Glik snickered. Cheth merely shrugged.

"If Bravas are great fighters, how did they capture all of you?"

Cheth was reserved, chewing on her gruel. "With great difficulty. We had twelve Bravas, and four of us died. So did two of their warriors."

"*Cra*, sounds like you need a lot more Bravas."

As if dismayed by the idea, Cheth placed a hand on her abdomen. "That is our problem. We breed and try to maintain our numbers, though we are not always successful." Her green eyes stared into the distance as if she could see right through the canyon walls.

"Will you train me how to fight? You're supposed to train humans, aren't you?"

The woman stared at her for a calculating moment. "You look scrappy enough."

"I am." Glik drew a circle over her heart. "Won't fight for the wreths, though."

"I certainly wouldn't want you to."

They finished their meal together as sandwreth patrols moved up and down the canyons, overseeing the scattered slave crews, rounding up workers. The wreths relished the afternoon heat, but the captives grew more sluggish, needing additional water.

Ivun strode to a crack in the red slickrock wall and used his bare hands to spread open the stone as if splitting the rind of a fruit. He stepped back and cool water bubbled out, summoned from a spring deep underground. The captives came forward to drink, then were sent back to work. The Bravas returned to fighting practice.

Glik went back to sewing leather armor, but she observed how the Bravas moved as they fought. She glanced up at the sky and felt sudden joy when she spotted black specks dancing in the air high above.

For a moment, she thought Ari had returned, but she felt no familiar tug on her heart link. Although these were just wild skas, the reptile birds gave Glik a sense of peace nonetheless, a glimmer of bright hope.

The wreths spotted the skas as well and jabbed their pointed spears upward in impotent threat. For a moment, Glik was surprised by the guards' frustration. Then she understood. While she had been staring at the sky longing to see skas, it seemed the wreths were watching out for dragons.

15

HALE Orr presented the Utauk man to Adan and Penda in their royal quarters. On the stand, the two skas flapped their wings hoping for attention. Penda rested in a leather chair with a cushion behind her back.

King Adan rose from the desk to greet the visitor. "Who is this, Father?" He faltered as soon as he spoke the offhand familiar term. Hale Orr always beamed when his son-in-law called him that, but now the word served as a painful reminder that Adan's real father was dead.

Hale nudged the guest deeper into the room. The long-haired Utauk was in his mid-forties, lean, with a scant, scruffy beard, wearing clan colors of green and tan. "This is Donnan Rah, the perfect courier to take Queen Voo's message to the konag. Rah has my highest recommendation. Let me tell—"

Penda interrupted him. "The man can speak for himself, Father."

"Indeed, I can." With one finger, Donnan Rah drew a circle on his chest. "I've crossed the three kingdoms several times, both in large caravans and small parties, but I prefer to ride alone. I travel light and unseen. I can leave right away, and I'll reach Osterra in less than a week."

"Even with the difficult roads over the mountains?" Penda asked.

"I know a way through the south." He smiled at her. "Do not worry."

Adan was glad Hale had found someone so quickly. "Voo is not a patient person, and Mandan needs to receive the message as soon as possible. It's imperative that my brother meets *her,* so he can see how powerful the wreths are. He is preoccupied with hatred for another enemy, for—" He felt the sudden, unexpected grief press on his heart again. He paused, drew a deep breath, let it out slowly. "I am outraged at what the Isharans did to my father. Mandan and I stand together in that, but personal vengeance cannot be more important than saving my kingdom."

"Or saving the world," Penda added. "The wreths want to wake the great dragon."

The courier gave a quick bow. "I have contacts at Convera Castle and will present your letter directly to the konag." His lips quirked in a sly grin. "I've done it before. I have ways."

Xar clicked on his crossbar stand, and Ari chittered at a higher pitch. Donnan stalked over to the reptile birds and scratched each under its beak. They trilled and fluffed their feathers, accepting the attention as their due.

"You've done this before?" Hale asked.

Donnan Rah smiled at him. "Konag Conndur used my services several times. He paid me to take secret messages and gather information. I can be swift and discreet, when I need to be."

Adan was surprised. "You were a spy?"

The man brushed the green fabric of his sleeve. "I prefer to call myself an observer who provides useful information."

Hale snorted. *"Cra,* you worked for Osterra and you told none of us!"

"I did not work for Osterra. I was paid by Osterra. I gave Conndur what he requested, while I also gathered information useful to the Utauk tribes. Shella din Orr has all my reports." The man's expression became grave. "Strange occurrences across the land, empty villages, caravans disappearing."

"Now we understand why," Penda said, looking at the blue ska who had delivered images of the slave camps.

Adan placed his hope in Donnan Rah. "Convince my brother. Once he stands face-to-face with Queen Voo and sees the sandwreth armies, he will realize this threat is unlike anything we have ever faced." It pained him to add, "The Isharans can wait."

Donnan sketched a circle over his heart. "I shall do my best."

வ

Penda kept track of the moon and studied how her body felt, while Adan monitored the calendar. The baby would arrive in less than a month.

They dined together at the long banquet table. Hale took his plate of food back to his own quarters, and Hom flitted about adding wood to the fireplace, refilling their goblets, and avoiding Xar, who harassed the squire every time he passed too close.

Adan smiled at Penda, whose large eyes were filled with longing and love. With a bittersweet pang, he recalled his father's delight upon learning Penda was pregnant. Conndur often complained that his older son had refused to accept any of the viable brides that had been offered to him, but Mandan was a difficult person to love. Adan was lucky to have someone he cherished.

Conndur the Brave would never see his first grandchild. Adan felt tears burn his eyes, and he bent his head down to concentrate on the rich barley and lamb soup. "Our child will have a long life and a great legacy."

"So will we," Penda said. "I can feel it." The Utauks had a faint connection with the remaining cobwebs of magic in the land.

Adan had seen Penda's intuitions proven correct many times. "I believe you."

One of the Banner guards hurried into the dining hall. "Sire, three riders arrived at dusk. It's late, but we let them through the gate. They asked to see you right away."

Penda whispered, "Such visits usually don't bode well."

"That's what I was thinking." Adan rose to his feet, bracing himself for another crisis. He put a hand on his wife's shoulder.

The guard broke into a grin. "It is King Kollanan from Norterra, Sire!"

Adan let out a relieved laugh. "I doubt he brings good news, but I'm always glad to see my uncle. Send him in."

Before the guard could leave the dining hall, Adan heard footsteps and loud voices coming down the corridor. The king of Norterra marched through the door, spreading his arms wide. Kollanan wore riding leathers and a long, warm cape, dusty from travel. He was a handsome man with a body strengthened from hard work and training. His well-trimmed beard gave him a paternal, commanding air. He tugged the gloves from his hands. "Adan Starfall!"

The younger man accepted his uncle's bear hug. Both men—both kings— pounded each other on the back.

Behind Kollanan came a cinnamon-haired Brava woman in her mid-twenties and a strange man with long black hair and deep blue eyes. His exotic garments, silver leggings, shoulder pads, and chest armor reminded Adan of Queen Voo and her retinue. The stranger and the Brava woman had nearly identical tattoos on their faces.

Penda made a strange sound. "Is that a wreth?"

Koll glanced over his shoulder. "This is Thon. As to what he is . . . that remains to be seen. Elliel is my new bonded Brava. She came to me at Fellstaff, and she has quite a story to tell. In fact, we all do. So much has happened since you and I left Convera."

"My father is dead. That changes everything." Adan and Kollanan heaved a heavy sigh together, thinking of Conndur.

"Ancestors' blood, it's much more than that," Koll said. "That's why I had to come in person."

The two skas took wing from their perches, circled Thon, and landed across from him on the dining table. They watched him, curiously bobbing their heads. The wreth man regarded them with sparkling eyes. "I see you have little dragons. Fragments."

"Dragons . . ." Adan gestured for Kollanan, Elliel, and Thon to take seats. "We've had our own experience with dragons. . . ."

Kollanan settled heavily onto a sturdy wooden chair. "And I have to tell you about our battle against the frostwreths at Lake Bakal, and how Thon helped us defeat them."

Adan sat back and called for more food. "It will be a long dinner."

16

SHADRI had previously explored the abandoned wreth city, but there were countless more things to discover there. When Queen Tafira suggested inspecting Lord Bahlen's new fortifications while Kollanan was gone, Shadri asked if she could go along. "Now that the wreths have reappeared, we should understand their history more than ever before. We might even help Thon unlock some of his memories."

The road from Fellstaff to Bahlen's holding was well traveled, but the wreth city was off the beaten path and had been shunned for generations. On horseback, Tafira mused, "I have lived in Norterra for decades, but spent little time exploring the land. These ruins never seemed relevant before."

Shadri squirmed in the saddle. Riding horses might be faster than walking, but it was certainly more uncomfortable. Road dust kept getting in her face. "I'm excited to show you some of the things I found in the ruins last time, my lady."

Lasis accompanied them, insisting that the queen not be left alone even for a short journey to the nearby county. He was an imposing escort in Brava black.

Shadri wiped grit from her cheeks, shaded her eyes, and looked toward the ancient city as they approached. She hardly recognized it with all the new construction work. "The place was so quiet before! Look at the restored wall!"

Lasis led them ahead to the bustling camp. Work crews moved throughout the ruins as if the city itself had come alive again. The main gates had fallen to ruin long ago, but Bahlen's workers had built a new wooden barricade and reassembled much of the stone wall, though gaps remained.

The nearest town was Yanton, a mile away, and Lord Bahlen drew on it for labor and supplies. Horse carts rolled in on fresh roads, beating down the grasses as they delivered wood and stone. Sturdy canvas tents were pitched in open plazas, and courtyards were filled with bedrolls, pillows, and extra clothes for the ever-expanding work teams who moved temporarily to the wreth city. Cauldrons over cookfires simmered soup for everyone.

Shadri looked around at the ancient buildings. "I wonder if Lord Bahlen found the fascinating magical relics and places I saw last time. Is he a man with much curiosity?"

"He is a man who wants to protect his people if the wreths come back," Tafira said. "He may explore more thoroughly once he feels safe."

The noise of hammers and picks grew louder as they arrived at the main entrance. Aside from the significant portion of the northeastern perimeter that had collapsed in some long-ago quake—Ossus stirring at the heart of the world?—the rest of the wall was remarkably intact.

Inside the city, crumbling buildings were being taken down, the walls disassembled piece by piece and the materials used to shore up the outer barrier. Burly stonemasons strained with ropes, pulleys, and counterweights until their biceps looked ready to pop. They shifted enormous blocks and lowered them onto reinforced wagon beds. Carts with the material from dismantled buildings rolled off to work sites. The activity reminded Shadri of a stirred-up anthill.

Lasis nudged his horse forward and raised a black-gloved hand. Seeing them arrive, workers set picks and shovels on the ground to watch.

Bahlen rode among the work teams, sitting tall on a dappled mare and wearing a cream-colored cape. He shaded his eyes and stared at them, then trotted his horse forward. "Apologies, my queen. I was expecting another work crew, but I am honored to have your company." He gestured around the broken city. "As you can see, we've been busy. This place is already far more defensible than Yanton or any of my other holdings."

He led his visitors through wide streets, showing off what he had done. "Many of the buildings are intact, and many are easily restorable. If wreth armies attack, my people can come inside the wall for shelter and barricade the entrances. Mayor Cleff and I have already discussed this." His thin face was etched with deep lines of worry. "I hope it will be sufficient."

"Far better than an undefended farming village," Lasis said.

Shadri pointed at a soaring structure marked with graceful curves. "I remember that spiral tower, but I never went inside. See how it tilts! I wonder if it's about to collapse. Or do you think the wreths built it at that angle on purpose? They might use mathematics or magic that humans can't understand."

The tower's outer wall was carved with a serpentine scaly back. The dragon tail wound up the spire, but the apex stones had broken away, as if the dragon had escaped.

Shadri remembered everything so clearly from her previous visit. "I want to show you something else, my lady. Over here."

She guided her companions between tall buildings and through over-grown promenades, until they reached the heart of the ruins, where a large sinkhole swallowed an entire plaza, leaving a sunken crater.

Bahlen hesitated, despite the scholar girl's eagerness. "We avoid this place. It seems unstable. There must be tunnels under the ground." He lowered his voice. "Sometimes, noisome mists rise from below."

Shadri went to the sloped edge of the sinkhole. "See the opening down there, at the center? Like a sunken well. We could go through there to get underground and explore." The crater radiated with questions, and her goal in life was to fill the emptiness with answers. "Lord Bahlen must have torches and rope."

"I wouldn't advise it," Lasis said.

"Not this time, dear girl," Tafira said. "We can explore after we know the people are safe."

"My crews have too much work to do," Bahlen said, impatient to get back to the construction. "Mayor Cleff is bringing a new crew and supplies. I have to be at the gate to greet them."

Shadri gave them one final, silent plea, but their stern expressions told her they would not change their minds. Maybe later she would come back on her own. This old city held so many questions.

That evening they ate bowls of sausage soup in the command tent, joined by Cleff, the harried but somehow cheerful mayor of the nearby village. Bahlen was proud of the detailed chart he had made of the abandoned city, showing the streets, the intact buildings, the sections of wall that still needed repair or reinforcement, the lookout towers he meant to erect. Shadri peppered him with hundreds of questions until the man grew exhausted. Queen Tafira just smiled and suggested it was time to go to bed, so they could ride back to Fellstaff early in the morning.

On the journey home with the rising sun behind them, Shadri kept up a patter of conversation. Lasis said nothing at all. Tafira made small comments, but primarily she listened. Since the queen did not seem bored, Shadri told more stories that she had read in the remembrance shrine.

Once back in Fellstaff, they saw lookouts watching over the city and the surrounding area. Scouts patrolled the surrounding lands, concentrating on the northern road, the direction from which a wreth army might approach. Everyone remained on high alert, ready for an attack.

When they reached the castle, Shadri and Tafira left their horses with La-sis in the stables and headed to the main courtyard. Near the guard barracks, some of Captain Rondo's escort soldiers sat sharpening their swords. Other escort soldiers had set up practice dummies, like scarecrows on crossbars. Queen Tafira paused, her gaze drawn toward the figures. The straw-stuffed targets were garbed in colorful fabrics draped in a loose exotic cut. Isharan clothes.

The soldiers lined up with bows, taking aim at the practice dummies. "Another round!" Rondo called. "Kill more of the enemy."

A volley of arrows sank into the straw-stuffed chests. Tafira's jaw set hard.

Laughing, the escort soldiers nocked more arrows. Rondo noticed Shadri and the queen standing in the courtyard. "Ah, Queen Tafira! As you can see, we're practicing to defend Norterra against invaders who come to kill our people, pillage the towns, rape the women."

"We must all be prepared to defend Norterra," she said coldly. In a flash Tafira drew the throwing daggers at her waist and flung both knives at the same time. The blades spun in the air, and each one plunged up to the hilt in the forehead of a practice dummy. A perfect strike.

"Impressive," Rondo admitted.

The queen retrieved her daggers. "Tell your men to keep practicing, Captain. Make sure they know how to recognize a real enemy when they see one."

17

❧

ONCE Irri was thawed from spellsleep, Queen Onn called the handsome frostwreth warrior to her chambers.

When he arrived, Irri paused in the curved doorway, clad in blue metal armor and crystalline scales. He preened in front of Onn, and his skin glistened as if beaded with oil.

She glided toward him. "You are beautiful. The spellsleep preserved you well." From then on he absorbed all her attention. They didn't even remember the captive boy was there.

Wrapped in his blanket, Birch sat on a small stool in the corner, knowing how to stay invisible in her presence. He held the carved wooden pig that his grandfather had given him—the only keepsake he still had from his old life. He was careful to hide how much he valued the object so the queen wouldn't take it from him.

Irri's long white hair hung in a thick braid on the left side. Sapphire and aquamarine crystals embellished his body. His expression had a haughty confidence. "I am glad you asked for me again." He reached out and stroked her cheek. Onn's eyes fell closed, and she exhaled a whispering sigh. "I knew Rokk would not satisfy you for long."

Her eyes snapped open, and she drew back. "Rokk was a fool, and he was weak. I commanded him to build a fortress for me at a defensible lake, but humans got in the way."

"Humans? Do they still exist? I am surprised they survived."

"They survived, and they think they are powerful." When the queen glanced at Birch, Irri noticed the boy for the first time. Onn continued, "Rokk underestimated them, and the humans killed him." She made a sound of disgust. "How did I ever let a weakling like Rokk touch me? It makes my skin crawl." She stroked the warrior's chest, trailed a finger down his arm, and led him toward the bed. "Come and love me. Afterward we will plan a real war. I am awakening all wreths from spellsleep. The time is now."

Irri took her head between his hands, slid his fingers into her hair, and drew her face toward him. "Yes, the time is definitely now." He kissed her savagely, and she moaned.

Suddenly she pulled away, hurling a glare at Birch. "Why are you still here spying, boy? Leave us—or should I just kill you now?"

Irri said, "I hear the blood of a child can be an aphrodisiac."

Queen Onn considered, then twined her fingers in Irri's hair. "I do not need an aphrodisiac."

Birch grasped his blanket and wooden pig and ran out the door. Gaining distance in the corridor outside the chamber, Birch fell in with four drones who were performing incomprehensible tasks. Onn frequently told the drones to care for him and then forgot about Birch entirely. He had a feeling this would be one of those times, and Onn might not think about him again for days, especially if the new warrior kept her entertained.

He was glad to be left alone. The drones folded around him and moved away from her chambers at a rapid pace. The diminutive creatures were his size. As far as Birch had been able to tell, they didn't have names and didn't see themselves as individuals, but still he felt a kinship with them.

Whenever a mage or noble strode past, the drones would huddle close to the wall, pretending to be invisible. Birch did the same. The wreths never looked at them, simply walked on. Rarely, one might cast a withering glare of disapproval before continuing his business.

The drones seemed to know more than their masters about the curved corridors and unmarked chambers of the palace. After they scuttled down frozen staircases, the drones entered a storage room that held a treasure trove of salvaged items: scraps of clothes, a dented cookpot, strips of leather, wood from broken furniture, skeins of yarn, furs, even a couple of woolen blankets. Birch's own blanket was tattered and dirty, and though he was wistful for the memories it carried, he traded it for a warmer one, as well as a fresh set of clothes. The patchwork garments fitted him poorly, but they were mended and clean, and he felt better. He wondered who had once worn the small shirt and trousers. The drones must have salvaged them from Lake Bakal or some other village the wreths had destroyed.

Birch followed the drones through kitchens, workrooms, armories. Along the way, they collected remnants discarded by the wreths: scraps of metal, fabric, broken tools, worn furniture, knobs of crystal, tubes, polished bits of stone. The drones spoke a strange chittering language among themselves that made no sense to him, but he listened closely.

In large, smelly laboratories inside the glacier, grim wreth mages performed horrific tests on animal victims and test subjects. Birch watched in nause-ated silence as they tortured huge white bears and reindeer captured outside. Bound to a rack of silver and crystal, one of the wreths' large wolf-steeds, which they called oonuks, had been flayed of its fur; the agonized beast snapped and twisted, its body a mass of glistening red meat upon which the mages burned runes.

Fascinated and sickened, Birch didn't dare make a sound. After they hur-ried beyond the hearing of the mages, the drones spoke more easily. They strove to teach him, and he tried to imitate their language. When they showed him the words for *wall* and *sword* and *queen,* he responded with human words, and the drones shared the new words among themselves.

The party grew larger as more drones joined them over the course of their activities. By the end of the day, when they emerged from the frozen palace into the biting wind and open sky, Birch knew more than a handful of their words. He began to make conversation, and the drones chittered back at him.

In the frigid air, the drones dumped their gathered bounty into a midden pile out of sight of the palace. More drones sorted through the day's prizes, and bits of shiny metal or fragments of crystal caught Birch's eye. He real-ized some of those scraps were substantial enough to be sharpened, turned into makeshift weapons.

Birch had had a knife once. It was larger than Tomko's. Their grandmother Tafira had given each boy a dagger and taught them how to throw them. She was quite proficient, entertaining the boys with her tricks.

He pocketed some metal and crystal fragments. Maybe he would use them to make a knife.

Birch followed the drones to their low huts and ducked to enter the stuffy interior. The air was thick with a rotting stench, but at least it was warm, and he enjoyed the company. Although he was different, the drones accepted him.

Sitting inside, they exchanged more words. Birch learned how to say *pot, water, fire, teeth,* and he taught them his language as well. Their gestures were complex, and he could tell they understood far more than Queen Onn imagined.

As the drones watched him, he withdrew the wooden pig from the pocket of his new trousers and set it on the frozen dirt floor. The drones gathered around, bending close to admire it. "Pig," Birch said. He picked up the toy and moved it across the floor, making snorting and oinking sounds, as if it were alive.

The drones repeated the word and the pig sounds, but they didn't have a corresponding word in their own language. Birch wondered if the drones had ever seen a live pig this far north. The Lake Bakal village had been frozen and dead before the frostwreths brought any drones to the fortress.

He thought again of his grandfather King Kollanan carving little animals as gifts for him and for Tomko. The frostwreths fashioned drones in the same way, like toys to be discarded.

The wind picked up outside, flapping the skin walls of the hut. He enjoyed the stumbling conversation with the friendly drones. He pointed to the cookpot that contained shreds of meat, grease, and simmering liquid over heating crystals. "Cook," he said, trying to demonstrate the concept. He took out the sharp fragment of metal, found the pointed edge, and sliced a gouge on the frozen ground. "Cut," he said.

The drones chittered and each took something sharp and cut a gouge in the floor. They shared their equivalent word.

Birch thought of the hated wreths, his dead family at Lake Bakal, and everything that he endured as a captive here. Someday, he hoped his grandfather would come and rescue him.

If he made his own knife, Birch could help in the fight. He and his drone friends could hurt the frostwreths.

As the drones served up a pasty mixture of salvaged food, Birch reviewed the words he had learned. He had actually enjoyed teaching the drones and learning their language.

He wasn't sure how he would convey the idea of *revenge*, though.

18

⟋⟍

IN Serepol Harbor, seven Isharan warships prepared to launch against Fulcor Island. The seagulls in the air above reminded Klovus of the screams of the dying.

Feeling good, he stood on the main docks wearing a dark caftan embroidered with the marks of his high office. His freshly shaved scalp and cheeks glowed with softening oils, and his belly was full from a fine breakfast. He had rested well despite being entertained by a skinny but winsome young lady no more than fifteen, whose parents had offered her as a sacrifice for a special blessing from the godling, and Klovus had been happy to oblige.

Crowds along the waterfront cheered the uniformed soldiers who marched forward in perfect ranks, wearing dispassionate expressions. They seemed completely confident that they would recapture the strategic island.

After tapping into the outrage of the people, he knew the best way to keep them firmly in line was to launch this attack as soon as possible. Very few in Ishara actually cared about Fulcor Island, a rock that happened to be a good anchoring point between the two continents, but after the atrocity committed against their beloved empra, the populace now considered Fulcor the most important piece of land in the whole world. Klovus wanted them to keep believing that.

His authority to order such a bold strike might be questionable, but with the empra incapacitated, Klovus had filled the void before anyone else dared, even that street girl who did not know her place. As key priestlord, he was a leader of Ishara, too. He merely helped facilitate what they all knew needed to be done. Who would dare contradict his orders to avenge their beloved Iluris? Anyone trying to stop him would have been torn limb from limb.

The cheering crowd gave the soldiers energy as they marched along the docks to the waiting warships. Commercial vessels had been anchored out in deep water so that the seven warships had the primary pier all to themselves. Preparing to set sail, the naval crews adjusted rigging, checked the anchor chains, and made way for the soldiers to board. Porters lifted crates of dried food, blankets, firewood, lamp oil, arrows, and other supplies to stock the garrison for months, once the Isharan army recaptured the island.

After the main ranks boarded, a last squad of Isharan soldiers moved along the dock in perfect formation. Their leader, a nondescript man with a plain face, paused before Klovus. He spoke in a low voice. "We are in place as you requested, Key Priestlord. We will ensure your victory on Fulcor." Startled, Klovus realized that the man was Zaha, leader of his Black Eels. The assassins could shift their appearance to mimic anyone they chose.

Klovus gave his blessing, and the soldiers—his handpicked assassins— marched aboard the lead ship. He already felt confident about this mission. Now they just had to wait for their secret weapon, the godling.

A gong rang from the harbor temple at the end of the docks, and the carved wooden doors swung open wide. In awe, the people murmured, "Hear us, save us!"

Ur-Priest Xion emerged from his temple, eyes intent on the harbor. His weathered face and rough skin signified his earlier life as a fisherman; the man had faced storms and even survived a shipwreck before he felt called to become a priest. With his devotion and coolheaded command, Xion had risen quickly in the priesthood, and now would serve an even greater calling as he commanded his godling to a victory for Ishara.

Aware of what was coming, the awed crowd backed away, clearing the street.

With a humming, swirling sound, like a thunderstorm comprised of bumblebees, a terrifying shape oozed out of the temple's open doorway. Summoned from its arcane realm, the godling extended tendrils of smoke, which retracted and swirled into a ball of snakes. Faces appeared on the indistinct body, a smoky mass of screaming human visages, frantic expressions of power and anger. Small bolts of lightning skittered through the amorphous form.

"Hear us, save us!" the people chanted, their voices growing to a roar. Klovus was glad to hear they had stopped whimpering their grief over the comatose empra.

Klovus felt a chill as he saw the monstrous harbor deity. Because he had served in Xion's position for years, tending the harbor temple early in his career, he felt a special bond with this godling. He had recently taken this entity on a warship to raid Mirrabay.

Xion led the entity toward the waiting warships with a proud and confident gait. The godling rumbled and seethed behind him, completely under his control. If unleashed, it could wreak incredible damage, a swift storm filled with monsters of superstition, terrors of the deep sea. Only a strong priestlord could guide such chaotic power, and this time Ur-Priest Xion would lead the attack.

The crowds parted to make way for the godling. Dock boards creaked and splintered, some parts smoking, other sections covered with a sheen of frost.

Klovus stood at the boarding ramp. "We have been attacked and betrayed. We have been *insulted* by vile people who do not deserve to live." He drew a long breath through his nostrils and gestured behind him to the seven warships. "Our powerful navy will break down their defenses, but you and your godling will be the key to conquering Fulcor Island."

Xion gave a minimal bow. The thundering entity roiled and shifted behind him, like a pack of wolves turned into mist and lightning. "Key Priestlord, we will protect our land." For the first time he showed a flicker of uncertainty and he lowered his voice. "Are you sure I should leave my followers without their godling?"

"You need not fear for the people here," Klovus said. "The Magnifica godling grows stronger every day, and we can easily protect Ishara. Our greatest threat is the Commonwealth, and yours will be our first blow against them."

Xion raised his hand, showing a long scab across the palm where he had gashed himself to sacrifice blood. "As I take my godling far from Ishara, its strength diminishes. Will we be strong enough for a battle so far away?"

Klovus scoffed. "The beliefs of our people anchor it and give it form. The godling was strong enough to devastate Mirrabay on the other side of the sea. It will be sufficient to take over Fulcor Island."

Xion bowed and moved up the boarding ramp. "Hear us, save us."

The godling boiled behind him, rushing, pushing, lashing out a tendril of smoke, then drawing it back. On the warship's deck, the soldiers withdrew in fear. Near the waterline, all hatches had been covered with wooden shutters. The cargo hold was ready.

As the ur-priest walked aboard, the godling rolled onto the ship, leaving burned spots and a smoking, misshapen footprint on the deck before it extended an appendage toward the open cargo hatch and poured itself down into the hold below.

By himself, Ur-Priest Xion swung the hatch shut and secured the bolt in place, sealing the godling inside the hold. He called out, "We are ready."

The seven warship captains shouted to one another across the harbor. The crews worked the ropes, climbed the masts, set the sails, pulled up the anchors. While the godling simmered in its confinement, the seven formidable vessels headed out of Serepol Harbor.

19

∽

THE upper tower of the empra's palace was well guarded. Neither Captani Vos nor Cemi left the chambers, and other hawk guards took their stations in regular shifts so that each man remained rested and alert.

The empra lay pale and still on her sumptuous bed, looking too much like a perfectly preserved corpse. It startled Cemi every time she looked at her. She touched the woman's cool hand, was relieved to feel a faint pulse on her wrist. She spooned tepid broth between the Ilursis's dry lips, enough to keep her alive.

Cemi spent all day, every day with a hard knot in her heart. The entire land teetered on a precipice and the slightest change could send them all tumbling into an abyss. Setting the soup aside, she gripped Iluris's hand, muttering, "We are here to help you, but you have to help us. Hold on!"

Chamberlain Nerev arrived at the end of the corridor. His expression sagged, and his eyes looked sad and weary as he requested entrance into the royal suite. Cemi looked at Captani Vos. Since taking refuge here, the two of them had had many quiet discussions, sharing their concerns. They both agreed the chamberlain was on their side. Vos gave a signal to the guards.

Nerev wore black and purple robes stitched with patterns, and a heavy amulet hung from a gold chain around his neck. Moving ponderously, he paused before the empra's bed and bowed deeply, his gold chain swaying, then he turned to Cemi and gave her the same gesture of respect, though he didn't seem to know which title to use for her.

"My lady, Key Priestlord Klovus just dispatched the Isharan navy to recapture Fulcor Island. He sent the harbor priestlord and his godling to aid in the attack. I thought you should know."

From the tower windows, they had already watched the red-and-white sails depart, sailing out onto the ocean. "I do not disagree with that. It is important for Ishara . . . after what happened there." Still, Cemi tried to think of reasons why the barren island had been worth fighting over for so many generations. Was it just for the symbol? When she and Iluris had first seen the bleak, craggy rock from the deck of their diplomatic ship, Cemi had not been impressed. "It is a necessary military mission."

Nerev rubbed his lantern jaw. "The point remains that Key Priestlord Klovus should not have given the order. None of the military advisors would speak out against him because they support the same course of action, and Klovus offered to send the harbor godling to guarantee victory. But it makes me uneasy. No priestlord commands the military of Ishara. That is the authority of the empra."

Captani Vos also seemed unsettled, but he lowered his gaze. "Klovus claims he is doing what the empra would command, and she isn't able to contradict him." All the guards muttered their agreement. Vos seemed to be convincing himself. "But how can we object? Striking Fulcor is the obvious course of action. After what happened to our mother there, we must purge the island of godless vermin. They deserve to die." He looked down at the gray form of Iluris, and Cemi noticed that his lips were trembling. "All of Ishara wants the same thing."

Cemi brushed a strand away from the empra's forehead. "It has to be done. Who else would give the order?"

The chamberlain looked pointedly at her. "Why not you? With each command Klovus issues, the next one becomes easier, and the people grow more accustomed to listening to him."

Cemi tried to think what Iluris would say or do. Cemi had grown up in the gentle Prirari District, a place of orchards and rivers. Parentless, she lived on the streets, scrounging for her existence, occasionally offering sacrifices to the benevolent Prirari godling. Here in Serepol, she had learned only the rudiments of statecraft, thus far. She studied hard, but there was so much she did not know yet. "I am not ready. You realize that, Chamberlain, as did Iluris."

Nerev focused his attention on Cemi, rather than on the silent woman on the bed. "I've served the empra throughout her reign. I know Iluris as well as anyone, better than any of her husbands. Her wishes were plain. She wanted you to be her successor." He looked around at the hawk guards standing at attention in the room. "The rest of you understood that as well."

All of the guards gave nods or murmurs of agreement.

Cemi just wanted her beloved mentor to wake up and for things to go back to the way they were. "I am still studying, but I am not wise enough to be empra!"

Nerev grew more serious. "Nevertheless, I know what my empra intended, and I know that your heart is not corrupt. Ishara needs a leader. Now."

"I'm not ready to rule," Cemi insisted, but her objection felt weaker. She understood in her heart that it was indeed what Iluris would have asked of her.

"No one is, but I suggest we begin to prepare." When Cemi nodded, he straightened his robes and turned to exit. He moved with his usual ponderous gait, but she could tell he left a heavy part of his burden behind.

❧

The loyal servant Analera delivered broth and juice for the empra, along with more substantial food for Cemi and the hawk guards. She had a bent back and fragile bones, so old that she seemed a marionette made of sticks and leather. Since the day they had returned home, the old woman had tended all of them, taking charge of the other servants, overseeing the empra's care, escorting physicians who ultimately could not do anything beyond healing her external wound. Other servants under Analera's guidance took shifts to bring what was needed, but she often did the work herself. She showed as much devotion as the hawk guards.

Entering the tower chamber at noon, the woman carried a tray that seemed to weigh more than she did. A tremor in her hands made the dishes rattle, but she did not waver as the guards let her pass. With a slow, careful process, Analera placed the tray on the side table. The open bowl of broth smelled of beef and mild spices. Cemi thanked her. "You take good care of us."

The old servant paused, fighting back tears. "Iluris has always been my purpose. I worked to keep her safe and alive most of her life. This isn't the first time someone has tried to kill her, you know." She ladled the soup into a bowl and placed it in Cemi's cupped palms. She offered to spoon broth into the empra's mouth, but Cemi insisted on doing it herself.

Analera continued, "I was a girl of sixteen when I entered palace service. I began under Emprir Daka . . . who was an awful man." She made a disrespectful noise, then muttered, "Hear us, save us," as if in apology.

She continued, "One should not speak ill of the emprir, but he . . . he had his way with me, back when I was young and pretty. Three times." Her wrinkled throat tightened. "That was before I learned to avoid him. Daka destroyed his wives, drove them to misery, broke their hearts, their health, and their spirits. He tried and tried to have sons, but produced only daughters."

Cemi dribbled the rich liquid between the empra's cold lips, then used a napkin to dab a drop at the side of her mouth. She raised her eyebrows. "But isn't Iluris his only daughter?"

Analera's face tightened, like a raisin drying in the heat. "Oh, he had others, and they all died. Convenient accidents. Daka didn't want them around."

Her expression darkened. "I failed to save the first two babies, but I vowed to keep Iluris alive. The household staff knew what sort of man he was, and we saw that the priestlords would support any terrible thing he chose to do. By the time little Iluris was born, another girl, another disappointment, we'd had enough. I talked with the other servants.

"The girl's mother was weak and broken, and we knew that it was up to us to keep the poor baby alive. We protected the child, made sure she was never alone with Daka. A wet nurse fed her, one of our chosen staff. We kept Iluris out of the emprir's sight. It is a miracle the child survived to adulthood."

She gave a harsh sigh. "Knowing what sort of man Daka was, it is also no surprise that he turned his lust toward Iluris. The poor girl was fifteen, I believe, when he first ravished her. By then, it was beyond our ability to help her. The harsh treatment certainly shaped her, changed her. I have been with Iluris for nigh on fifty years now."

Cemi finished feeding the empra as much of the broth as she could manage, then she herself ravenously ate the meats, cheeses, and fruits that Analera had brought for her, leaving half the plate for Vos. The captani accepted the food, but did not eat yet. He was still on guard, but he continued to listen to the old servant talk. The love in her eyes was unmistakable.

Analera continued, "Then, after the beginning of the last war with the Commonwealth, Emprir Daka stumbled out that window and fell to his death." She gestured toward the arched windows. "Iluris called it an accident, but the rest of us saw it as a miracle."

Leaving the tray behind, Analera gave a respectful bow and shuffled back toward the door. "I continue to serve Empra Iluris. You have only to tell me what you need, and I will make it happen."

"I value your service. Thank you." With a heavy heart, Cemi pondered the fact that she was now about the same age as Iluris had been when she became empra. Cemi would study while taking care of her mentor.

After the old woman departed, Captani Vos wolfed down his meal. He took up his position on the opposite side of the bed, hovering near the empra's pillows. Cemi could feel the emotion radiating from him.

He had joined the Isharan military because his family had too many mouths to feed, but after he left, his parents and siblings had all died of the coughing flu. Empra Iluris had adopted the orphaned young man as a surrogate son, just like all the hawk guards. And like Cemi.

Vos bent close and touched her cheek in a surprisingly intimate gesture, whispering into her ear. Only Cemi could hear him. "We will watch over you." Tears hovered in his eyes. "I cannot lose my mother again."

20

THE konag's procession passed through three other counties on the way to Lord Cade's holding. The somber spectacle served Utho's purpose of fanning the flames for the much-anticipated vengewar.

As they passed from village to village, Mandan always looked north with a hungry sparkle in his eyes. Utho sent heralds ahead to announce the coming of the konag. Though sad and sober, the young man drew strength each time he revealed his father's preserved heart to awestruck spectators. Utho was satisfied with his behavior.

Finally, the procession reached the main town in Cade's holding. The lord had already called out his people, so that peasants, craftsmen, and merchants, as well as Cade's private soldiers, lined the streets leading to the small remembrance shrine.

Coldly handsome, the nobleman himself waited at the main entrance dressed in a blue cape and a vest with gold buttons over a ruffled shirt. His chestnut hair hung long and smooth, and his beard was shaved thin with such precision that it looked like a prominent outline of his face.

For years, Konag Conndur had remained oblivious to how much power Lord Cade wielded or the extent of his large private army. Although the vassal lord paid extravagant taxes with saltpearls harvested from beneath the rugged cliffs, Conndur had never asked about their origin. Utho had gone to extreme lengths to keep the secret, using Elliel as a scapegoat. It disturbed him that she had regained her memories; worse, she had revealed the scheme to King Kollanan of Norterra. Fortunately, Mandan already understood hard realities that Conndur the Brave had been too soft to embrace.

Standing in front of the remembrance shrine, Lady Almeda made her husband look meek and humble by comparison. Her painted face and hair twisted into bejeweled braids made the arrogant lady look more like an ostentatious effigy than a real woman. He remembered his own wife Mareka, who had needed no such gaudiness to be beautiful and strong. The last image of her face was burned into his mind. . . .

Cade stood beside his replacement Brava, an ugly man named Gant, who had also been with them on that terrible night on Fulcor Island. He had bristly hair, heavy brows, and a misshapen nose that looked as if it had been bashed too many times. Pockmarks dotted his cheeks. Almeda had chosen Gant specifically because of his coarse features, since Cade had been too tempted by beautiful Elliel. Utho quietly despised Lady Almeda, because her shrewish jealousy had turned a mere problem into a crisis that *he* had been forced to solve.

Now, Lord Cade stepped forward and bowed to the young konag, ignoring Utho, the white horse, and the crowds. "Welcome to my county, Sire. You have our respect as your loyal subjects, and you also have our sympathy and anger for the appalling crime that was committed against your father."

Mandan began to speak, then faltered. A shadow fell over his face. His voice cracked, but he pressed on. "We remember the legacy of Conndur the Brave, and we must never forget what the Isharan animals did to him." Mandan dismounted, tossed his fur-lined cape over his shoulder, and walked to the white horse. He placed his hands on the jeweled box, looking toward the town's remembrance shrine. "This is the end of our procession."

He undid the leather straps that secured the chest to the saddle, then raised the lid. Lord Cade, his Brava, and his wife all came forward to look at the grisly object in the box. After they made the appropriate sounds of anger and grief, Mandan turned to show the preserved relic to the crowd. "I will leave the heart of my father here, and your legacier can display it for all to see. Remember what happened to him and tell everyone you know."

Cade's chest swelled. "We are honored to provide a permanent home for such a priceless gift."

Gant carried the chest through the open doorway of the shrine, leading Mandan and Lady Almeda inside. Utho hung back just enough to walk beside Cade as they entered the wooden-walled building. "Once this ceremony is over, the konag wants to see the camp and the captives."

അ

After they were settled in at the holding house, Mandan and Utho accompanied Lord Cade and his Brava that afternoon as they rode out on the dirt road to the northeast. After traveling several miles, Utho could smell the salty air and felt a chill from lingering fog as they neared the coast. The day was blustery but not unpleasant.

Riding beside him, Mandan looked ahead and shaded his eyes against the wind, eager to see the slave camp. His cheeks were flushed.

Before long, a large army settlement blocked further travel down the dead-end road to the headlands. Hundreds of foot soldiers, archers, and cavalrymen lived in canvas tents and permanent wooden barracks for Cade's private army.

The nobleman led them at a trot down the main thoroughfare. The soldiers paused and fell into respectful ranks as the party passed, then they returned to their combat exercises. The wealth from his saltpearl operations funded such a large standing army to protect Cade's holding from envious neighboring lords, though no one had challenged him in years. Utho was confident that the private army would be a vital part of the Commonwealth military against the Isharans.

The party rode through the army settlement and continued miles up the road to a primitive camp surrounded by fences, wooden barricades, and sharpened spikes that were not pointed outward to defend against invaders, but turned inward to stop the inhabitants from breaking out.

Gant hunched forward in the saddle of his gray horse, while Cade sat tall and confident. Mandan drank in details as they passed Cade's guards into the camp. He shrugged off his warm cloak to show off his konag's cape and tunic.

Inside the fence, people stood around like tattered dolls, dressed in rags, their hair unkempt, their bodies unwashed. All Isharans. Although Cade had the resources to feed and clothe them properly, the captives were purposely kept miserable, and Utho agreed that animals deserved to live in pens. Sixty men and women came out to stare with hollow eyes as the visitors halted in the packed clearing.

"The main crew is at the cliffs harvesting saltpearls to earn their keep," Cade explained. "Soon enough, these will take their place for another shift."

Mandan raked a pitiless gaze across the Isharans. From his garments, they could immediately see he was a young man of great importance. They beseeched him, eyes wide with hope, but he didn't respond. "Look at them, Utho. You can see how they are inferior, their hair, their expressions. I can tell they're thinking evil thoughts."

"Certainly they are, Sire," Utho said.

Gant grunted in what might have been agreement.

Another set of riders approached from the opposite side of the camp, leading an open wooden cart. Cade frowned and led his companions ahead to intercept the returning party. "It's too early for the workers to be back from the cliffs. The tide won't come in for hours yet."

A body lay sprawled in the bed of the cart, a half-naked Isharan, his skin bashed and bruised. A red welt encircled one ankle. The skull had been broken so that one eye protruded like a soft-boiled egg.

Seeing this, the captives moaned. Some backed away from the cart, while others felt compelled to press forward in dismay.

"It looks like brigands beat him up," Mandan said to one of the men on horseback.

"Instead of climbing down the rock stairs to the waterline, he threw himself over the cliff and dashed himself upon the rocks."

"Lazy coward," said the other horseman.

The prisoners huddled, looked away, while some wailed. Others stood in silence, shaking their heads.

Looking detached, Utho said, "I am surprised you bothered to retrieve the body. Why not let the sea have it?"

Gant remarked in a gruff voice, "My lord believes seeing the battered corpses will deter others from doing the same."

Cade's lips puckered in a pout, and he turned to Mandan. "And now I've lost another worker, Sire."

The abject captives pressed close to the konag. "Please, sir, we are innocent!" one man pleaded. "We did nothing! I am just a poor fisherman. Hear us, save us! We don't deserve this." The fisherman clasped his hands together, showing dirt, calluses, and blood on his knuckles. "We are innocent."

"Innocent?" Mandan lashed out at him. "Your people butchered my father!" He glanced at Utho, and the Brava knew what to do.

Without hesitation, he grabbed the man's head and twisted, breaking his neck as if snapping a grape from a stem. The pathetic prisoner collapsed, and Utho discarded him. The people backed away, aghast.

Cade sighed in disapproval. "And that is another slave lost. We need to keep the prisoners alive, Utho, so they can continue to work."

Mandan huffed, "We are about to set off for war. We will get plenty more prisoners."

Waves crashed at the bottom of the cliffs with an angry roar. Flapping tents and sorting bins had been set up on the grassy, windswept expanse. The Isharan divers wore only loincloths and carried flat pry-knives. Ropes tied around their ankles kept them from swimming away.

෴

Without fear, Mandan walked to the abrupt edge so he could look down the black rocks, while Utho remained protectively at his side. The wet cliffs were studded with moss and fleshy sea growths. Isharan captives picked their way down to the waterline, using narrow steps and occasional iron bars in treacherous spots. The surf foamed around rocks clustered below.

The slaves harvested shellfish in drowned nooks and crannies, filling their nets with the scabrous shells to be sorted in the bins above. Rough waves crashed around the workers. Although they tried to anchor themselves in place, the surf slammed the captives against the rocks. No one took pity on their misery. Mandan certainly didn't.

Lord Cade joined them at the cliff edge. "These workers buy food for their families back in the main camp. If they don't give me saltpearls, then their loved ones have nothing to eat." He smiled. "It is an efficient system."

Gant made a dull sound in his throat but formed no words.

Mandan said, "It is what they deserve."

A wave slammed into the cliffs with a loud boom, sending up a tail of spray. One diver was caught in the undertow and thrown like a drowned rat against the black rocks. Afterward, he floated facedown, bleeding into the water. Cade let out a loud sigh.

Gant observed, without sarcasm, "We will need new workers soon."

21

⁊⁊

THE observation deck on Bannriya Castle had an unobscured view of
the surrounding terrain. Adan stepped out into the bright, gusty afternoon, and King Kollanan joined him wearing a fur-lined jerkin that was too
warm for the Suderran climate. His loose hair blew about, because he wore
no crown or circlet. He looked up into the open sky. "Do you come out here
at night? Have you seen any falling stars lately? And if so, have you decided
what they mean?"

Penda accompanied the two men on the observation deck. Her green ska
rested on her shoulder, teetering to keep his balance. "It could be that the
universe is falling apart." She drew a circle over her heart.

"Sometimes it feels that way," Adan admitted, but he would not let all the
recent setbacks drive him down. Instead, he thought of what he had to live
for—his wife, his unborn child, his people—and how he would find a way
to save them.

Xar let out a fast clicking song, and his faceted eyes sparkled as he turned
toward the line of brown mountains that bordered the deserts beyond. The
ska launched himself into the air and flew up to circle the banners on the top
of the tower.

With a sudden shudder, Penda pointed to the west. "It's coming again.
Another harbinger."

Near the horizon, towering dust rolled out of the mountains like an anvil
of poisonous smoke. Something was approaching them over the high terrain. Adan's throat went dry, and Kollanan gasped, "Ancestors' blood!"

The previous dust storm that came from the Furnace had been a towering
monster of wind and dust, but this was much smaller, a self-contained mass
of blown sand that whipped through the hills. It moved in an unnaturally
straight line, with a clear destination.

"It is coming here," Penda said.

Kollanan scratched his beard. "Does this happen often?"

"Only on the worst of days," Adan answered.

❧

As the dusty whirlwind rolled toward Bannriya, Adan led a group down to intercept it at the edge of the city. A group of uneasy Banner guards stood at the closed gate and thick stone walls. Captain Elcior, head of the Banner guards, reported to Adan, "The gate is secure and the walls should hold against the storm, Sire."

"That's not a natural storm," said the young guard Seenan, who was the brother of the squire Hom, "but it is much smaller than the last one."

"This storm has a different purpose. I can feel it," Adan said. "But we will welcome it and see what the sandwreths intend." To the Banner guards' shocked looks, he said, "It does not serve my purpose to resist Queen Voo now. We are allies and good friends, are we not?" His sarcasm was plain. He knew the queen was flaunting her power, as she had done before, and he did not intend to provoke her. "Open the gate! Let us see what this dust devil intends." Though he tried to be strong next to his uncle—his fellow king—he wasn't as confident as he tried to sound.

Hale Orr shook his head. Kollanan planted his fists on his hips and looked to his Brava, who stood ready for whatever they might have to face.

Thon touched the gate with his fingertips. "I could defend us, if necessary. Queen Voo would be quite surprised." He grinned.

"Not yet," Adan said, though he was glad to know of the dark wreth's supposed abilities. "Let us hear what she has to say."

The gates creaked open with straining ropes and groaning hinges. Swift breezes carried a hiss of airborne sand through the gap. Thon's dark hair drifted about, and he smiled into the blowing grit.

The knotted whirlwind moved down the main road directly toward them, as tall as two men, with diffuse tendrils spreading out. Adan faced it, standing in the open gate.

The dust squall swirled up to the city walls and then paused, as if hesitating. The grains of sand and dust shifted to sculpt an image of Queen Voo's head, with large eyes, long hair, narrow chin. Voo's dusty mouth opened, and the looming visage spoke with a voice of clogged breezes. "King Adan Starfall, my ally! I invite you and Queen Penda to visit my grand desert palace while we wait for your Konag Mandan to answer my summons."

The uncertain face shifted. Voo's eyes were only orbs of dust, and they did not meet the king's gaze. The queen's visage gave no sign that she noticed Hale Orr, King Kollanan, or Thon and Elliel. The blind avatar spoke again. "When you reach the edge of the Furnace, my wreths will escort you."

Adan's uncle stepped forward, confident, even defiant. He raised his voice. "I am King Kollanan of Norterra. I, too, have experience with wreths. I'll accompany—"

The whirlwind of sand and dust went suddenly still, and the grains dropped into a pile in front of the gate.

"I do not think she heard you," Thon said.

"*Cra*, Queen Voo wasn't inside that summoning," Hale said. "It was just a message recorded in sand."

Kollanan shrugged. "Nevertheless, I plan to go with you."

୭

That evening as they all sat in the castle's great room, Koll said, "I came here to learn about sandwreths. If Queen Voo wants an alliance with Suderra, maybe she'll help my kingdom as well."

"It's not an alliance either of us should want, Uncle," Adan warned. "Voo has betrayed countless humans. She is dangerous. But I try to stay in her good graces and prepare in case we must stand against them."

"I didn't say I would trust her! But maybe I can use the queen for my own purposes." Koll's expression sagged. "You saw what the frostwreths did to Lake Bakal, Adan." His face turned ruddy with anger. "You showed me the horrible images of the desert slave camp. Even so, if the frostwreths captured my people, even for hard labor, at least they would still be alive! My daughter, her husband, my other grandson. Instead, the bastards wiped out the entire town. *Because it was in the way!*" He punched a fist into his other palm. "But Birch is still alive, and I shudder to think what Queen Onn means to do with him. Why would a wreth queen want a human child?"

Hale Orr gave his very pregnant daughter a worried look. "It's clear that Queen Voo has an unwholesome interest in your child, too, dear heart." He growled. "*Cra!* You can't go there—she may imprison you and take your baby."

Adan looked at Thon for possible answers, but the wreth man fixed his gaze on the flames in the hearth at the end of the great room. The fire danced and flickered, as if Thon was manipulating it with some strange magic.

Sitting in her comfortable chair, Penda answered, "You may be right, Father. She touched me. She wants this baby. I can feel it."

"She will not have it," Adan snapped.

"She will not," Elliel agreed. "Not if Thon and I can help it."

Adan made up his mind. "I will accept her invitation, and Kollanan will accompany me in your stead, Penda. We will ride out to the desert and see what Voo wants. She will have to be satisfied with that."

The Norterran king nodded. "We will make the best of this meeting without putting Penda in danger."

Adan turned to his wife. "You will stay here where it's safe—far from any wreths."

"I heartily agree," Hale said.

Penda, as beautiful as ever, utterly refused. "No, Starfall, I will not stay here." Before Adan could argue, though, she added, "And I will not go with you either. I don't intend to hand myself over to Voo." She turned to Hale and raised her chin imperiously. "Father, you will join me."

"Of course I will, dear heart. But where are we going?"

"Out among the Utauk tribes, where we will never be found. We can ride with them, wander with them, and I will stay safe."

Hale's grin showed his gold tooth. "*Cra*, now that is a fine idea!"

"Into the wilderness? But how will I find you?"

"Even I don't know where I'll be—that is the point. I need to stay away from the sandwreths."

Adan tried to contain his alarm. "What about the baby? You should stay here and rest. It is only a few weeks."

Penda kissed his cheek. "Utauk women give birth out in our camps all the time. In fact, I'll be more comfortable that way, with my people."

"I want to be with you. I have to be there! For my child."

"It is also your kingdom. Go, speak with Queen Voo and arm yourself with knowledge. Find a weakness." She tried to reassure him. "Don't fear, I will take both skas with me. When the time comes, they will find you."

22

Birch didn't know how long the frostwreth queen would forget about him, but he took advantage of his days of anonymity.

With the drones he was warm, and they gave him meals. Even if the food tasted awful, Birch could feel himself growing stronger. He would live. After everything the frostwreths had done to his family and to him, he would *live*.

He followed the drones through the tunnels into the glacier beneath the palace. By now he understood much of the drone language. They remained full of activity, inspecting storage chambers, moving objects from one place to another—with no purpose that Birch could ascertain. Maybe the drones just wanted to look busy so the frostwreths would leave them alone.

They led him into the vast grottoes filled with thrumming spellsleep chambers, thousands of ice-sealed alcoves with embedded tubes and glowing crystals. The chambers held a whole dormant army.

The drones moved among the cells, chittering as they inspected the frozen warriors, mages, and nobles. They ran small hands over the thin ice windows, melting smudges that refroze.

The entire grotto seemed empty except for the sleeping forms. No wreths were in the vicinity.

Oddly, a pair of drones looked directly at Birch, as if to make sure he was watching. Then they bent over the glowing crystal that sent threads of magic into the sleeping bodies. Unobserved, the drones took out small knives, short but sharp, and with a flicker of movement, stabbed the spellsleep crystal.

Another drone pricked a flexible tube filled with silver blood. Birch's eyes went wide as he saw the fluid leak into the chamber, pooling at the foot of the frozen body inside. The glowing crystal changed color from a bright blue to deep purple.

The drones hurried away from their sabotage, moving as if this were part of their business. One of them muttered to Birch, a word that he understood to mean "break."

He watched the creatures flit along, surreptitiously poking, jabbing, pricking. The group moved from level to level, continuing their subtle, random vandalism.

"Break," the drone repeated, and the group scuttled out of the grotto, continuing their nondescript duties before anyone noticed them.

"Break," Birch agreed, then added another word. "Kill."

23

THE construction sounds around the Magnifica temple were both deafening and satisfying: grunts of effort, shouts of crew bosses, the clink of stonecutters' hammers, the scraping of masons' trowels. Key Priestlord Klovus stood in the shade beneath his awning on a high scaffolding platform that rose like a watchtower above the work site.

Below, he watched crews strain with ropes to raise enormous blocks of stone on ramps lubricated with mud. Bricklayers built archways on the second platform of the great temple, and tile setters adorned them with glazed symbols of godlings from all thirteen districts.

Several clustered neighborhoods had originally been razed to clear the plaza, decades ago, and now the religious markets and temporary sacrificial stations had also been torn down so the work could commence on the titanic temple.

Klovus had been contemplating the Magnifica for much of his life, and now he finally had the power and resources to make the structure a reality. A constant stream of wagons and sledges delivered construction stone, building up the second level of the huge pyramid. The design included a labyrinth of passageways, protected chambers, and interior worship halls, none of which were visible from ground level.

The godling, which currently dwelled beneath the temple square, would permeate the completed temple like blood flowing through veins, and the Magnifica would focus and concentrate the people's faith like a lens, strengthening the godling.

Klovus felt giddy with the possibilities, but his joy was somewhat diminished because this victory had taken so long. The shortsighted empra had crippled the work for years! What had she been afraid of? Now he intended to complete the project in record time. Sitting back to watch from his high platform, he sipped cool water from a goblet as more frameworks were laid.

Soon, the third layer of the tremendous pyramid would begin. A sign of remarkable progress.

Down in the street, he saw a tall man approach his watchtower. Wearing dark purple robes and a square-topped hat of office, the man walked purposefully through the carpenters, masons, water carriers, stone carvers, and bricklayers. Recognizing him, Klovus grimaced.

Chamberlain Nerev was a careful man not accustomed to climbing rickety wooden stairs, but he ascended the thin steps to the observation platform with an intent expression. The key priestlord knew there would be no avoiding him.

Klovus stepped to the edge of the platform and looked down at the top rung of the lashed wooden ladder, thinking how easy it would be just to press his foot against the chamberlain's head and knock him down to the pavement below. But Klovus didn't need to worry about a minister who served an incapacitated ruler.

Huffing, Nerev ascended the last rung and raised his shoulders above the platform level. "Key Priestlord, I must have a word with you. Due to the urgency of the matter, I thought it best to come see you in person."

Klovus stepped back but did not extend a hand to help the man climb onto the wooden deck. "Indeed that is a far better idea than writing me a note."

The chamberlain gained his balance and brushed off his purple robes. Looking around the high platform, he seemed discomfited to find no guard railings or safety ropes.

Klovus remarked, "I'm not certain you are qualified for a position such as this. The scaffolding, I mean."

Nerev immediately pressed his business. "Much of Serepol's treasury has suddenly been diverted to this Magnifica project. I spoke with the finance ministers about the outpouring of funds. This is not authorized."

Klovus placed his fingertips together. "That money should have been allocated to this project many years ago, during the reign of Emprir Daka. We are at last catching up, and that costs money." He drew in a deep, satisfied breath as he surveyed the bustling construction site. "We needlessly lost a great deal of time, and because of that, Ishara is weakened. No wonder Konag Conndur felt confident he could try to assassinate our dear empra. Now we face war with our godless enemy again, Chamberlain, and Ishara is weak because the Magnifica remains incomplete. Our main godling is at only a fraction of its potential."

Nerev worked his lantern jaw, refusing to be distracted. "Over the centuries of our existence, the districts of Ishara developed a solid rule of law. We are civilized now, not the barbaric survivors the wreths left behind in the old world. We have a set of laws that must be obeyed."

Klovus huffed. "The priestlords and our godlings help enforce that law."

"Ishara has a formal leader." Nerev scratched the side of his face. "With Empra Iluris unconscious—perhaps permanently, perhaps only for a short while longer—this must be addressed."

Klovus pursed his generous lips and appeared to be deep in thought, though he had nothing to consider. "For the past year, I have expressed my dismay that Iluris is without an heir or designated successor. That is why we are in our difficult situation. If only she had listened to me."

Stroking his gold chamberlain's medallion, Nerev said, "In the meantime, Ishara must have another empra or emprir, at least in an acting capacity, until Iluris wakes up. We both know that the empra intended for the young woman Cemi to be her successor. For the stability of Ishara, we should install her in that role. I suggest we arrange a coronation ceremony without delay."

Klovus scoffed. The idea was absurd on its very face. "That little girl, a scamp from the streets? The people would never accept her!"

"They would accept her, because Iluris asked them to. You hear the crowds praying to their empra every day. Their chants grow stronger and stronger."

Klovus snorted. "We are paying the price because Iluris did not take her reproductive duties seriously. This is not as dire a situation as you suggest. You worry too much."

Klovus stood on the edge of the rickety wooden platform. The great city of Serepol had other temples that held smaller godlings, which burned bright with the fires of faith, but nothing would match the Magnifica. "The people are being led, Chamberlain. We already sent a naval expedition with the harbor godling to recapture Fulcor Island. They are guided by their faith, and we all know what must be done. Just listen to their prayers!" He closed his eyes and sighed, as if drinking in a cool draught of wine. "Hear us, save us."

"Their prayers are for Empra Iluris." Nerev's words were like the chipping sounds of a stonecutter. "Cemi is the one who should be the next empra."

What would it take to be rid of this annoying man? "I will take that under advisement, but I am busy at the moment. Let me ponder this for a few days."

Incensed, Chamberlain Nerev wrapped his hand around the golden rank chain. "It is not your choice! The question must be brought before the council of advisors." He turned and tried to make a dramatic exit, which was hindered because he had to pick his way carefully down the scaffolding ladder. The poor man had very little sense of balance. Klovus feared it would be his undoing.

ॐ

Inside the empra's tower rooms, Cemi began to feel claustrophobic, but when she received the horrifying news about Chamberlain Nerev, she realized this was also the only place she could feel safe.

An alarmed hawk guard had rushed to the tower chamber, breathing hard from running up many flights of stone stairs. "The chamberlain is dead!"

Cemi pushed forward, startled. "How? How did he die?" She realized the answer didn't matter, because the official reason was almost certainly not the truth. Analera was also there, gathering the dinner tray. Her wrinkled face paled.

"He fell from a window in the palace." The guard shook his head. "His own private chambers are above the plaza in the administrative wing. The window was open, and he was alone in his room. His papers were out on the desk. According to the announcement from the palace guard, Nerev must have been in such despair about the empra's condition that he cast himself to the flagstones below, just like Emprir Daka."

The old servant's voice was filled with scorn. "That is ridiculous."

Vos scratched his crooked nose. "That man did not jump out of a window. He came here to speak with us about the empra's condition only two days ago."

The messenger nodded. "I know that, and every hawk guard knows that. But the story is being spread among the people."

"Emprir Daka did not throw himself out the window either," Cemi said in a low voice. "Iluris pushed him. Daka deserved it, but Chamberlain Nerev did not."

Vos stood close to Cemi, his expression grave. "We know that Nerev wanted to install you as the new empra. That would not serve Key Priestlord Klovus's purposes . . . unless you were willing to be his puppet."

Cemi scoffed. "I would never agree to that."

Vos gave her a proud grin. "We all know that."

Shaken, she sat down on the bed and took the empra's cold hand in hers, trying to draw strength from her mentor. She knew that the hawk guards were faithful, and the people still prayed for the empra's health, but Klovus controlled the godlings and focused Ishara's need for revenge against the Commonwealth. He was also willing to kill to protect his power.

"What chance do I have?"

She stroked Iluris's face. The empra's eyelids twitched slightly as if she were having a dream, but then she went still again.

Analera spoke up to Cemi. "I suggest you increase the number of hawk guards, my lady. You cannot be too careful."

Cemi hated the Commonwealth for what they had done to Iluris, but they were a distant enemy, and a war with them could be brewing for some time. If Cemi were to become empra, she would have to lead Ishara's armies, listen to her generals, direct them, resolve any internal disagreements, and be prepared to fight the continent across the sea, while providing defense against any possible incursion here.

Right now, though, her real enemies were close at hand.

The messenger finished telling his tale and awaited further orders. The hawk guards were more on edge than before.

Captani Vos rested a firm hand on her shoulder, professional yet warm. "We will not let anything happen to you."

Cemi placed her hand on top of his. "At times I feel alone without Empra Iluris, but I'm glad you're here."

She suddenly felt a new chill in the air, an external tingle. A strange sound flickered through the chamber like whispering wind and scraping rocks. The guards stirred, when they sensed it as well. Something moved within the tower room with an invisible rustling that unsettled them.

Cemi rose from the empra's bed. "What is that?"

Before her eyes, the air rippled as if a film of water had formed and dissolved. A presence circled the room, prowling, powerful. To her surprise, she realized she wasn't afraid.

Vos pressed close, his hand on his dagger as the unseen presence drifted over the empra's bed, like a raft of wind.

Through the open window, she could still hear the murmuring chants of people praying for the empra. "Hear us, save us!"

Cemi experienced a strange warmth inside. "I do feel safe," she said aloud.

The shimmering illusion faded away so subtly that a few moments later she couldn't be sure she hadn't imagined it.

24

WHEN the alarm bells rang from the tower, Watchman Klea sprinted up the stone steps to the top of the perimeter wall. Continuous gongs called the garrison to arms, and her soldiers took up their positions. Lookouts stood at the prominent corners, peering out to sea.

Klea scanned the eastern horizon and saw the red-and-white sails of seven Isharan warships heading directly toward Fulcor Island. Her commanding voice boomed across the courtyard below. "To arms. Prepare for the fight of your lives!"

As her soldiers scrambled for weapons and armor, she continued to shout, "We've been expecting this." She felt no fear, only the hot metal of anticipation. Then she whispered only to herself, "And, oh, how I've been waiting for this."

The enemy warships approached at remarkable speed. Though the pennants flapping and snapping from rooftop poles showed that the breezes pushed in the opposite direction, somehow the Isharans were making great headway against the weather. Evil magic, no doubt.

Three Commonwealth warships were stationed here at Fulcor, dispatched after the murder of Konag Conndur. Klea expected more reinforcements, but even she had not anticipated a full-fledged Isharan naval assault so quickly.

Two of the Commonwealth vessels sailed to the eastern side of the island, while the third defender remained docked in the narrow cove below, the island's only safe harbor. The clamor of alarms continued, and sailors rushed down the cliff stairs to the docks, preparing the third ship for departure.

On the west side of the island, a small vessel had recently departed, having delivered supplies and arms to the garrison, along with the news that Konag Mandan was preparing for an all-out war against Ishara. Soon Fulcor Island would be a beachhead for the great invasion of the new world, surrounded by many dozens of warships, but Klea couldn't think of the entire land now. This garrison was hers. She was the watchman, and she would defend it.

Though they were greatly outnumbered, the two defender vessels sailed directly toward the Isharan ships, ready to fight. Decades ago, Isharan block-ade vessels had tried to starve out the garrison soldiers, but Utho—Utho of the Reef—had worked his way out onto the exposed rocks at low tide and taken the anchored ships by surprise, launching fire arrows from a place they had considered safe. Now, Klea's defenders could use those same longbows as they approached the enemy ships and set them on fire.

From the garrison walls, she watched the red-striped sails close in. A flurry of bright dots arced out from her two ships like sparks from a grind-ing wheel. Most of the burning arrows missed because the eager archers had fired too soon, but several struck the lead Isharan vessel. One smoldered in the taut sail. Klea knew her captains would drive forward until they landed several solid volleys of fire arrows, then they would break for safety. Two warships couldn't hope to destroy seven.

Before the lead enemy ship could start burning, though, wooden shutters opened near the waterline . . . and what boiled out of the cargo hold filled Klea with revulsion: a formless shape of wind and clouds, smoke and terror, faces and tendrils, lashing tentacles and battering-ram fists.

"They've brought a godling!" she cried. The soldiers crowding the garri-son's defensive wall shouted in dismay, which soon turned to rage.

The monster spewed from the hold and launched itself across the water, swelling as it pulled up spray.

A swirl of fire arrows struck the warship's hull, but they were snuffed out, causing no damage. Within moments, the godling was upon the first Com-monwealth ship, smashing its prow with a flash of lightning and fire and splintering the wood into smoldering wooden stakes.

Dozens of the sailors tried to flee, their bodies peppered with flying splin-ters. The godling flowed onto the Commonwealth ship, roaring across the deck, ripping up planks until it reached the mast. Lightning crackled up and down the rigging, and the sailcloth burst into flames. The tall mast shivered, toppling backward onto the deck and crushing more of the crew.

Klea stared from the wall, holding her breath.

The godling attacked like a rabid wolf, and the ship rocked from side to side, then the entity plunged down through the deck into the hold. It smashed through the keel and out the bottom of the hull, rocketing under the water until it burst up like a waterspout, spraying waves in all directions.

The second Commonwealth defender tacked to one side, trying to get out of the way, but it was at the mercy of normal winds. The Isharan fleet closed in, trapping the doomed ship among them. As they drew closer, the Isharans began to shoot their own fire arrows.

The Commonwealth ship's sail caught fire, but before the flames could take hold, the godling swept toward it like a fist of whitecaps and thunderstorms. A huge yawning mouth stretched watery intangible jaws, and poisonous mists spewed out to engulf the vessel. The godling smashed through the hull and broke the ship's back.

Unharmed except for a few smoldering spots from fire arrows, the seven Isharan vessels pressed toward Fulcor Island, straight for the harbor.

Sickened, Klea touched the ramer band at her hip and knew she would have to use it.

In the sheltered cove, the third Commonwealth warship was finally manned and ready. Its sails were set, the mooring ropes released, and the crew furiously rowed it out of the harbor cove. With tall cliffs blocking their view of the other side of the island, Klea knew the captain had not yet seen the attacking godling, and was unaware of what they would face.

As the Isharan ships closed the distance, the unleashed entity charged across the waves, plowing a wide white wake. Klea could see that the third Commonwealth ship was doomed as soon as it sailed out of the sheltered cove. She whirled, shouting to her people, "To the walls! Set the catapults. Prepare flaming oil." She ground her teeth together. "Kill all of them! Protect the walls!"

She touched her sword. The ramer would drain her, but she could kill the most enemies with it—when it was time. The garrison soldiers had all the weapons, armor, and supplies they would need for a conventional siege. She swallowed hard, but let no one see her fear. Even a Brava didn't know how to fight a godling storming the walls. One such deity had wiped out their entire colony of Valaera. How could barricades, arrows, and battle axes protect against a thing like that?

The godling crashed into the third Commonwealth warship, sideswiping it and caving in the hull. Without pause, it moved toward the island, leaving the broken vessel to sink behind it. As the roiling, ravening thing came close, it seemed smaller than when it had first emerged, as if waning from the expenditure of energy. But it wouldn't be enough to save the garrison.

The godling waited for the Isharan warships at the mouth of the harbor. The first of the enemy vessels sailed right into the narrow cove, and when the ships ground up against the docks, Isharan soldiers disembarked and swarmed toward the cliffside stairs. The first four Isharan ships filled the available docks, and smaller landing boats were dispatched from the outer vessels, carrying more soldiers.

The last invader ships cruised around the island to hunt down any other Commonwealth vessels. Klea glanced in the opposite direction, saw the supply ship racing away west toward Osterra. She felt a small relief to see that this one at least would escape. The supply ship captain would have seen the attack on Fulcor, and he would take word back to the konag.

"Fly!" Klea whispered. "Tell them what happened here."

The narrow steps leading from the docks up the cliff wall passed through a bottleneck, another natural defense of the garrison. As Isharan attackers swarmed up the steep ascent, their boots pounding on the metal slats, the first ones had to know their lives were forfeit. "For the empra!" they screamed, waving their swords as they raced up.

The top of the stairs led into a cleft beneath the base of the garrison walls, which allowed entry into the fortified compound above. A thick metal barricade blocked the entrance, but for now, the heavy barrier remained open so Klea's defenders could hurl rocks down at the encroaching force. Some poured barrels of oil onto the steep metal and stone stairs, followed by a thrown torch, which ignited the front ranks of the invaders. Isharans covered with flaming oil toppled off the cliff stairs, screaming.

At the cliff gate, the Commonwealth defenders used long spears to skewer anyone who made it to the opening beneath the walls. Although it was a bloodbath, a seemingly inexhaustible force of Isharans continued to swarm from their docked warships. Even though the Fulcor defenders were determined and well armed, their numbers were limited.

Like a storm in black armor, Klea worked her way into entry tunnels beneath the walls and fought beside the other defenders. The Brava was eager to spill Isharan blood, and she became a numbing blur, killing dozens and dozens, but the Isharan invaders seemed driven by a pathological hatred. She could understand that.

Before long, the enemy commanders changed tactics. They sent the godling.

The entity rolled up the sheer side of the cliff adjacent to the metal staircase. The godling did not need stairs. The formless, swirling thing rushed up the flat stone like fire following a rivulet of oil.

Through the open gate, Klea saw it coming and felt an atavistic horror swell within her. The soldiers nearby moaned in panic but braced themselves and stayed in place. Raising spears and swords, they faced the oncoming deity, but Klea knew they couldn't hold the opening themselves. "Close and barricade the gates!"

The defenders didn't need to be told twice. They grunted against the heavy iron-reinforced wooden doors and swung the barrier shut. A howling roar smashed into the barricade just as the defenders jammed in place a crossbar the size of a tree trunk.

The godling struck again with a tremendous crunch. The cliff rock shivered, and several defenders retreated into the catacombs, but the gates held. Outside, the deity became a living battering ram, and it careened its fury with one shapeless arm after another.

Klea watched the thick iron plates buckle, the wooden crossbar crack. Beside her, grim soldiers raised their swords. It was time. She clipped the golden cuff around her wrist and squeezed hard, felt the metal fangs. She ignited the ramer with her determination and blood, and a circle of flame engulfed her hand.

The fighters stood, their weapons ready, their faces gray. The godling smashed into the gate again, and the wood splintered.

"Fall back to the stronghold." Klea cautiously retreated. "We'll make our last stand above, in the walled garrison." The soldiers withdrew. She lowered her voice. "At least we can die in the open where we have room to fight."

More garrison soldiers gathered in the courtyard in front of the high-walled keep, where the Isharans had murdered Konag Conndur. Archers lined the defensive walls as the angry deity continued to pummel the gate below. The iron barricade wouldn't last long, and once it fell, the invaders would rush in after the godling. Klea vowed that they would pay dearly for their victory.

With an explosion below, the gates shattered, and the angry entity surged forward followed by a charge of Isharan fighters. After expending so much energy, so far from home, the thing seemed weaker, but it was still terrifying.

Klea didn't think—there was no time. Extending her ramer like an incandescent whip, she let out a wordless yell and threw herself at the godling. Her weapon bit into the thing, the fiery blade slashing through gelatinous smoke, and a blast of lightning twisted back at her.

Shrieking faces emerged from the shifting mass, and snapping mouths lunged toward her. She slashed again, cut deep with the ramer fire, but the godling knocked her aside. Stunned, Klea tumbled away, while the entity pushed into the training yard, mowing down the first ranks of defenders.

The Brava shook her head and sprang to her feet, turning to attack the godling again, but it had roared past, tumbling toward the barracks.

A squad of Isharans rushed through the shattered gates and surged into the garrison. They fell upon Klea, who swept her ramer across the first three. The purifying fire cut them down as if armor and enemy blades didn't even exist. But more attackers pressed forward, forcing her back.

The godling caused a great tumult in the open yard.

Following the ranks of invaders came one man in a dark caftan similar to the one Key Priestlord Klovus had worn in the delegation with Empra Iluris.

The priestlord looked exhausted, but he shouted orders in a strangely compelling tone, and the godling roared, as if celebrating his arrival. This must be the man who guided the thing.

The priestlord reined in the uncontrollable force, and the godling refrained from destroying the barracks buildings, which it could have leveled in minutes. No doubt the invaders wanted to inhabit the structures once they killed her and her comrades.

With her sword in one hand and ramer in the other, she fought like a fury. She struck down five Isharan soldiers, wading through their bodies as she tried to reach the priestlord. Killing him was her goal. With the man dead, maybe the godling would be cast adrift.

Around her, Fulcor defenders were dying one by one, vastly outnumbered. Trapped on the perimeter walls above, her archers rained down arrows, but Isharans stormed the walls and drove the sentries over into the sea. "For the empra!" they kept yelling.

Klea added her hoarse scream. "For the Commonwealth! For what you did to Konag Conndur." The remaining defenders responded, but in vain.

As her ramer struck down enemy after enemy, Klea slaughtered her way closer to the priestlord in the dark caftan. He saw her coming, and his expression showed fear. She killed another enemy and lunged toward her victim.

With a roar and a whistle, an intractable convulsion of air hit her from the side. She whirled and fought the creature, still desperate to crash forward and kill the priestlord. She had to eliminate that man, extinguish his connection to the godling. But the entity yanked her back, and she spun, slashing with the ramer. She felt hot breath burning her throat, her lungs. Her muscles were shaking, but she kept fighting to the last. "Priestlord!" she howled.

Then the godling pummeled her with blunt tentacles of smoke, fire, and dust. The sheer force threw her against the nearby stone wall, cracking her head.

Stunned, she struggled to hold on to consciousness. After collapsing, she hauled herself back to her knees, saw the priestlord retreating to safety. Her ramer blade flickered and sputtered. She gritted her teeth, forced more fire to come out.

The godling lifted her into the air and slammed her back to the ground.

The fire in her golden cuff snuffed out, along with all her thoughts.

25

L ORD Cade's holding house had a pervasive damp chill that was not dis-
pelled by the fireplaces. Though Utho felt no discomfort, Mandan complained about the cold. The young konag wore a woolen sweater covered by
a fur-lined cape and chose his seat nearest the roaring fire in the dining hall.
Utho took the seat beside him, watching.

Cade's home had thick, dark wooden walls and narrow windows that
blocked the northeasterly breezes and the frequent rains, which gave the place
a brooding air. The vassal lord seemed to enjoy the firelight and shadows for
hosting an intimate banquet. Beeswax candles in branched holders looked
like burning eyes along the table, and hanging lanterns shone from the walls.
A pot of salty fish chowder made with sheep's milk had been served with
warm crusty bread. Platters of steamed rock crabs were offered as a delicacy,
though Mandan found extricating the meat too difficult to bother with.

Cade smiled at his guest. "I hope the food is to your liking, Sire."

"The company is to my liking," Mandan said. "I am impressed with what
I saw today, and I'm glad to have a vassal lord who recognizes our true enemy. You will be of great aid to our war effort."

Utho spoke up. "We have private political matters to discuss, Lord
Cade. Konag Mandan is faced with serious decisions, now that a real war
is upon us."

"Isharan animals," Cade grumbled.

Lady Almeda, the only other person in the hall, sneered. "There are animals everywhere. Isharans are just the most obvious ones."

"Some animals are useful," Cade said. "The slaves harvested enough saltpearls to fund my army, and this holding has far more wealth now than the
dowry fortune your family offered me when we got married."

Almeda set her silver fork on the plate with a clatter. "Don't imagine you
can do without me, Husband! I'm not expendable. That would be another of
your foolish decisions."

Mandan interrupted the sharp discussion, though Utho wasn't sure if it was on purpose or just because a stray thought had passed through his mind. He opened a velvet-lined box that Cade had placed in front of his plate. "I will have my craftsmen incorporate saltpearls into my crown and chains of office. Ah, they are like milk mixed with diamond dust. They are even more beautiful because they're coated with a sheen of justice." He ran his fingers through the pearls, letting them trickle back down with a faint pattering sound. "Work the captives hard to atone for what their people have done."

Almeda fell back to eating in sullen silence. The spiteful woman had caused many problems. Volatile and full of herself, she devoted more energy to personal slights than to the larger political benefit of Cade's county, the kingdom of Osterra, or the Commonwealth in general.

Cade shrugged at the suggestion. "I could have the Isharans do much more work, but they keep dying. With the dwindling work crews, it will soon be problematic." He met the Brava's gray eyes, then remembered to look at Mandan.

The young konag said, "We will get you more prisoners, although I would be happier if they all just died in battle."

"I would prefer they died here after years of useful service," Cade retorted, then lowered his voice. "But it is your choice, of course, my konag."

The paneled door to the dining hall swung open without a knock. Gant stood at the entryway dressed in his full black uniform. His face was a mottled red, as if he'd been out in a blasting wind, but Utho knew it was just the normal flush in his rough skin. "Can I be of service, my lord?"

"Attend me during the meal," Cade said. "Konag Mandan has his loyal Brava, and I will have mine."

With a brusque nod, Gant stood at attention against the wooden wall behind the lord's chair. Almeda looked at him, but seemed to have no opinion about the Brava's presence.

Utho gave an approving nod. "It is good that Gant is here. I have news." The other Brava was a strong fighter, brave and loyal to Cade and to the Commonwealth. Together, he and Gant had helped rescue Mandan on Fulcor Island, whisking him away to the ships while leaving Klea behind as the new watchman. "It is in reference to your previous Brava, Lord Cade—Elliel."

Almeda's face puckered into a scowl as if she had swallowed a mouthful of vinegar. "Bitch."

Gant's brows hooded. "Elliel is no longer in Lord Cade's service. She is disgraced. Her face bears the rune of forgetting."

"She should be dead," Almeda snapped, and Cade glowered at her to be quiet.

"She has taken service with King Kollanan in Norterra." Utho leaned forward on the long banquet table. A log popped in the fireplace, startling them. "But she somehow negated the rune of forgetting and regained her memories. She remembers everything." He paused. "Everything."

"I don't believe her," Mandan said, because he had already made up his mind. "She lies."

Utho gave a somber nod to the young man. "I'm afraid it is all true, my konag, and everyone in this room knows it. She could pose great difficulties. She does not think of the overall benefit of the Commonwealth."

"Who would believe her?" Mandan said. "As konag, I'll say her story is false. I'll denounce her. That will put an end to the matter."

"She has already convinced Kollanan the Hammer," Utho said. "He wrote a letter to Convera Castle, intending it for Conndur." He paused to let that sink in. "Kollanan knows what we did, Cade. He knows what I did."

"It doesn't matter," Cade insisted. "No crime was committed. Elliel was my bonded Brava, and I could do with her as I wished."

Disturbed, Gant grumbled, "That is not what a Brava is for."

Cade looked upset, but Almeda was furious. "We'll send out assassins to find her! They'll cut out her tongue and slit her throat so she can no longer speak terrible things about us."

Cade silenced his wife's shrill voice with a gesture. "Elliel would not have caused problems if you hadn't stabbed her, my dear. All was under control, but you had to ruin it."

"My fault? You caused it because you can't keep your cock where it belongs! I should have used my knife to cut that off instead of stabbing Elliel."

Cade lurched from his chair and slammed a palm on the table with a loud crack. "Elliel would have kept her shame to herself, but you, Almeda—*you* had to turn it into a crisis! You are poison. You're a shrew. If you didn't—"

"Enough!" Utho roared. "I care nothing about your marital squabbles. The Commonwealth doesn't care. The true crisis occurred when Lady Almeda threatened to expose the Isharan prisoners and our saltpearl operations." He was a thunderstorm, rounding on the woman. "And because of your actions, Conndur would have been forced to respond. Sadly, he would not have made the correct decision."

Though a Brava had a lesser rank than any noble, the others fell silent. He shared a paternal look with his protégé at the head of the table. "Fortunately,

Konag Mandan understands. As the war proceeds, he will establish many more camps so the Isharan prisoners can assist us in our effort."

Naked jealousy and anger boiled inside Almeda. Gant, the unattractive replacement for Elliel, loomed behind her. Utho remained deeply concerned about the woman's mental stability, worried that she would blurt out some damning remark to the wrong person. Almeda was reckless and unpredictable. Utho wondered if he would have to take certain measures . . . for the good of the Commonwealth.

An acid silence fell over the banquet table. Uncomfortable with a conversation he didn't entirely understand, Mandan toyed with the saltpearls in the small box, then fell back to eating his fish chowder.

With a polite knock, a shy, willowy young woman appeared at the door. "Mother? Father? Is this a good time to meet Konag Mandan? Could I join you for dinner?"

Utho saw a thin girl with green eyes, milk-white skin, and long red tresses. She was maybe fifteen, with a glow of innocence about her. Her oval face had full lips, a delicate nose.

Although Almeda still wore an expression like rancid cheese, Cade's mood brightened. "Lira! So sorry I forgot to call you. Yes, join us." He stepped over to the door and took her slender arm. "Mandan, Sire, this is my daughter."

The young konag rose from his chair and stared in astonishment as the beautiful girl entered the room. Averting her eyes, she made a formal curtsy. Her gray and blue gown emphasized her slender figure. Mandan said, "I . . . I'm very pleased to meet you. Join us. Please take the chair next to me."

The girl flushed. "My name is Lira. Did I come at a bad time?"

"You arrived at exactly the right time," Mandan said. "I have entirely forgotten what we were arguing about." He spoke sharply to Cade. "Have your servants bring another place setting. We must take care of this beautiful young lady."

Surprised by the konag's unexpected reaction, Lord Cade scrambled to obey. "Gant, see to it." Stalking away as if going to face an opponent, the ugly Brava left the room. Cade continued, sounding obsequious, "Lira is our only daughter, Sire, but she is everything a daughter should be."

Mandan scolded him. "Why did you not introduce her to me sooner? Truly a failure of responsibility on your part." He reached out to take the girl's hand, extricating her from her father to lead her to the empty seat nearest his own. "For years, countless lords and merchants have brought their marriage prospects to me, all of which were unacceptable. If I had met your daughter long ago, Lord Cade, it might have solved all our problems!" He waited for Lira to sit, then took the chair next to her. He was all charm, an entirely different person. "At last I might have found my appropriate wife."

Cade was speechless, and Lira seemed ready to faint with shock. Utho was equally surprised by the konag's reaction, but when he looked at the pale-skinned, redheaded girl, he realized what Mandan was seeing. A royal marriage was exactly what the Commonwealth needed, and Utho would encourage the union, even though Mandan's attraction was for all the wrong reasons.

It was as if the painting in the young man's bedchamber had come alive. The moment Lira entered the room, Utho realized that the girl looked exactly like Mandan's dead mother Maire.

26

Though he disliked the human labor camps, Quo recognized that the sandwreths would need many workers and soldiers for the great battles that were sure to come. He didn't think much of the inferior creatures. Still, his sister had dispatched him to observe and report back to her, and so he rode his auga out to the miserable holding zone in the canyons.

The human dwellings were primitive and austere, with harsh conditions and minimal food and water. Mage Axus had often complained bitterly about the sheer number they lost due to neglect, but Quo argued that such difficulties toughened the remaining workers. That was merely an excuse, though, since the lack of care was simply laziness. Mage Ivun had taken over the work camp, administering it with stern but evenhanded control.

As Quo rode into the main camp, he studied the sullen humans who looked up at his arrival. The camp was filled with a muttering silence. Muscular wreth guards watched over the prisoners who made armor, arrows, shields. The workers looked as if the spark of life had been drained from them.

He slid off the exhausted reptile's rounded back as the mage came forward. Ivun's heavy red robes were embossed with runes that told an arcane tale Quo was not interested in reading. The mage's withered arm, a visible weakness, was a painful reminder of the land's shrinking remnants of magic.

Ivun reached up in greeting, then withdrew his arm in embarrassment and extended his intact hand instead. "You bring the queen's blessing and her glory." It was not a question.

"I come as an observer for Queen Voo." When he tossed his ivory-gold hair, metal bangles clinked together. He wiped dust from his burnished metal chest plate. "My sister wanted me to see the state of the operations for myself."

"Then you shall see."

"I am delighted." Quo's voice was full of disappointment.

Thousands of captives lived here and worked for the sandwreth cause until they were all used up, after which wreth hunters would find more workers. Axus had complained it was an inefficient method, but fortunately, since the devastation of the wars thousands of years ago, the surviving humans had repopulated the land, and there were plenty of them for the taking.

Quo sauntered among the humans, who turned away, shading their eyes. They looked defeated, but Quo chose to consider the mood subservient— appropriate for a created race. His lips quirked as he paused to inspect a stockpile of spears and rounded shield forms that still needed metal plates. The people worked slowly, mechanically, but at least they were working.

Quo turned to Ivun. "Let me address the slaves. I will inspire them."

The mage gave him a skeptical look. With his good hand, he scratched his withered arm and withdrew it deeper into the leather sleeve. "How will that inspire them?"

"I will remind them of what they are and what our purpose is."

The bald mage wrinkled his brow, but he did not argue. Ivun stepped to the red rock wall beside him and slapped it hard with his good hand. A rumbling boom shot out and echoed down the narrow canyons. The sound spread like ripples from a stone thrown into a still pond. "All human work parties come to the center of camp! Present yourselves for an important guest!"

If Quo thought they would come running with excitement, he was disappointed. The slaves at nearby stations shuffled forward and stood blinking like herd animals. Guards riding augas drove work teams ahead of them, forcing the human captives to stumble into his presence.

Impatient, Quo glared at Ivun, who merely shrugged. "They are coming as quickly as they can."

Quo heaved a breath of the hot dusty air and wondered how long this would take. His sister did not expect him back for several days, but he did not like this isolation. It was not fit for a wreth noble.

Although workers still plodded in from the distant mines, he had waited long enough. Quo lifted a delicate hand, expecting cheers from the audience. "Worthy laborers under the command of her glorious majesty, Queen Voo, you have been brought here to help us accomplish the perfection of the world. Although your efforts might seem pitiful and weak, know that your meager accomplishments contribute to building an invincible army against our enemies. You will have a small but vital role in crushing the frostwreths."

He scanned the crowd and saw the shadowed eyes, the slumped shoulders. None of the humans had responded to his words. None of them seemed to care. It annoyed him. Quo realized that these people were simply too stupid to see reality and their place in it.

He raised his voice again. "You may think you have no stake in the coming war, but the only hope you have is for sandwreths to win. If you do your part in exterminating the enemy, if we have our chance to slay Ossus and bring about a better world, then you will forever know the good you have done. That is why your race was created. What better satisfaction can you experience than to serve your precise purpose?"

Quo wanted to coerce some kind of reaction from them. "And we need more of your people. Do what humans do best! Breed! Have many children." He chuckled. "The breeding process is enjoyable, if you do it properly."

Among the captives, he spotted several half-breeds, descendants of lovers the ancient wreths had impregnated long ago. "I may even take some of your women as my own partners, to give you more powerful offspring." He crossed his arms over his chest. "It is a fine way for you to serve the future."

Though the response was only a sullen muttering, Quo chose to hear it as cheers. He was anxious to leave, but he would work with Mage Ivun to make this camp into the productive example that Queen Voo wanted.

They had an army to build, weapons to make, and the future to secure.

⁓

Listening to the arrogant wreth noble, Glik felt a simmering anger that burned outward in a circle. She wondered if humans could tap into the darkness that Ossus exuded into the world—and use it. Around the fringes of her vision, she saw scales, heard a growling sound. She forced herself to blink away the afterimage of a huge slitted eye.

How could the wreths slay the dragon and eradicate Kur's evil when they themselves were the personification of such things, without even realizing it?

Cheth stood next to her, sneering softly at Quo's dictum. "Breed! If he tried to take me, I would twist his manhood from him like I would pluck a squash from a vine."

Glik snickered. "And I am too young. Only twelve . . . I think." She sketched a quick circle around her heart. As an orphan, she had a difficult time knowing exactly how old she was. "Haven't begun my courses yet."

Cheth drew her brows together. "I hope you are right, but do not expect our captors to be kind or fair or to respect modesty."

The other slaves did not show their anger. The survivors had learned how to hide any flare-up of emotions. The wreths could hunt them down if they tried to escape. Glik was familiar enough with the labyrinth of canyons to know she could hide, at least for a while, but how would she ever cross the desert? The wreths would hunt her down. But she didn't give up hope. Cheth and her fellow Brava prisoners held the same attitude.

After the wreth man finished his speech, he commanded the warriors to take him to guest quarters in the stone mansion that Ivun had fashioned for himself. The work teams went back to their endless and hopeless tasks.

With Quo gone, Ivun strolled curiously among the groups. The Bravas continued sparring with one another, and the mage seemed to be counting them. Self-consciously pulling his withered arm up against his chest, he looked at Glik and her nearby companions and nodded to himself.

"I want fifty workers! We march first thing in the morning. Auga teams will lead you to the site." With his good hand, the mage stroked his chin. "We will go north to an ancient wreth battlefield that is still infused with magic. Shadowglass is a resource we require. It will make our weapons invincible."

Glik remembered the blasted scar from one of the climactic clashes in the ancient wars. "The Plain of Black Glass," she muttered.

Cheth looked at her. "You know the place, then?"

"Been there. *Cra*, it is a terrible place."

The Brava woman shrugged. "So is this camp, and I will be happy for a change of scenery."

27

BEFORE departing to seek out the sandwreth queen, Adan had heavy thoughts in his heart. His beloved Penda and her father were departing to lose themselves in the vastness of Suderra so she could have the baby in safety, where Queen Voo could never find them.

Now, before Penda mounted up on her familiar chestnut mare, Adan wrapped his arms around her and pulled her close. He could feel the baby between them and the beating of her heart. Penda's crimson-and-black skirts were loose and comfortable to accommodate the swell of her belly.

She tilted her head to kiss him and let her mouth linger next to his ear. "Don't worry about me, my Starfall."

Adjusting his saddle, Hale Orr called his reassurance. "She probably has more stamina than I do. *Cra*, she'll be fine with me."

"If you hear even the slightest breath of trouble, do everything in your power to keep her safe." Adan filled his voice with hope and concern. "Take no chances."

The two skas flew about inside the stables and landed on the rafters above, bobbing their heads and chittering at the people below. Xar and Ari took flight again, circling, pecking, playing, but Adan could see only his wife.

"I'll miss you."

"If there is any possible way, I will send you a message." She drew a circle over her heart and then over his. "The beginning is the end is the beginning."

He clasped her hand, then released her. Penda mounted the mare, and she and her father rode away from the castle. The two reptile birds darted out of the stables and flew overhead, following the horses toward the eastern gates.

Utauk tribes wandered the known and unknown roads of the land, and Adan knew that Penda and Hale could vanish among them.

In the meantime, though, he and King Kollanan had the opposite purpose. They wanted to *find* the sandwreths.

The terrain became bleak and rocky soon after Adan's expedition left the Suderran foothills and wound its way through the mountains. An escort of Banner guards rode alongside the two kings, mainly for show, since even a hundred soldiers would do little good if the sandwreths decided to attack. Adan was confident they would not. It wouldn't serve Queen Voo's purpose.

As they followed unmarked routes to the edge of the desert, Adan squinted into the heat ripples. The horses plodded along, and they would have to find water for them soon. The sandwreth queen had promised that her warriors would meet Adan's party, but he doubted they would consider the welfare of the animals.

The canyon walls were sharply defined by midafternoon shadows, and the washes and side canyons reminded him of the images from Glik's ska. Somewhere out here, countless human captives were being treated as animals, but the work camp was probably well hidden. He gritted his teeth, tasting dust, and braced himself to maintain his calm when he actually faced Voo again. He would not betray his knowledge of the human work camps. As far as Queen Voo knew, they were friends and allies, but Adan would never trust her or forget his people.

Elliel sat up straighter in her saddle, looking around, warily touching her sword as she sensed something. Thon smiled and raised a hand. "Look, they have found us at last."

Carrying long spears, five wreth warriors rode their augas forward. The stocky two-footed lizard mounts lurched ahead, flickering black tongues. Captain Elcior called a halt of his Banner guards, and the riders faced the ancient warriors, who regarded the two kings and their escort.

The horses whickered uneasily. The lead warrior said, "Follow us. We will go slowly. Your horses are not made for this terrain." He tossed his long hair and turned his auga about. "We will create water when we need to."

They rode for miles with very little conversation. The solemn Banner guards never let down their watchfulness, and the wreth escorts had no interest in friendly talk. Kollanan said quietly to Adan, "Do they intend to ride through the night? We need to rest the animals if we are to keep up with them."

Adan spoke up, calling ahead. "We all need water. You said you would provide it."

The lead warrior turned around. "Soon. Endure a while longer."

As purple dusk set in, the wreths guided the party into a side canyon. The weary, thirsty horses sniffed the air, perked up, and trotted into the canyon. Adan also smelled moisture and saw a seep in the canyon floor lined with green vegetation. A trickle of water bubbled out of the rocks to form a pool.

The warrior said, "We camp here for the night. By morning, we will have augas for you to ride, because the terrain is not suitable for your horses." He looked at the crowded animals drinking from the spring. "Your mounts will be safe enough at this oasis. They will be waiting for you when you return."

The following morning a lower-caste wreth arrived leading twenty riderless augas. "These beasts will take you to Queen Voo," the lead warrior said, then looked at the Banner guards. "Do all your servants wish to come?"

Captain Elcior bridled at the insult. "Servants?"

Adan calmed him before the soldier's pride could cause problems. He whispered, "He doesn't know. To sandwreths, every human is an underling." Even the kings of Suderra and Norterra, he realized.

Adan delegated a relieved-looking Seenan and two other Banner guards to stay and watch their horses, while the rest of the party rode to the desert palace. Kollanan and his companions approached the augas, awkward and uncomfortable. Adan swung into a low saddle, showing the others how to mount the lizard creatures. He glanced at his uncle and raised his eyebrows in amusement. "My pregnant wife rode an auga out on a dragon hunt. I'm sure Kollanan the Hammer can manage."

"Ancestors' blood, I can!"

Taking the reins in one hand, Elliel mounted a reptile's hard saddle. Thon seemed perfectly comfortable sitting astride his creature. "Let us ride! I want to meet this sandwreth queen."

The party moved off into the desert canyons and gravel-filled washes that opened into a sprawling salt pan. The augas bounded along, as if glad to stretch their legs.

After hours of riding, Adan brushed white powder from his reddened face and squinted ahead at what was surely a fevered mirage, but his companions saw it as well: an enormous structure of monolithic rocks, sandstone spires, and spiraled turrets, enticing and frightening.

When the augas reached the high arched entrance, Queen Voo stood there waiting for them. She fixed her spangled eyes on Adan, as if she didn't even see Kollanan, Elliel, Thon, or any of the Banner guards. Her voice held a sharp, scolding tone. "Where is your wife, King Adan Starfall? I requested her to come here. Why would you ignore my words?"

Adan felt a chill even in the hot desert, but he didn't flinch as he dismounted. He stared directly at the queen as if she were his equal, whether or not she believed it. "The rigors of travel might not have been safe for Penda, as she is so close to birth." Right now, it sounded like a good justification.

Voo's offense melted into disappointment. "I forget how fragile and weak humans are. Your wife should have given birth here in my palace. Think of what an honor it would have been."

"I thank you for the offer." He kept his voice flat. As the others awkwardly climbed down from their saddles, he turned to his uncle. "I've brought you an equally important visitor, King Kollanan of Norterra, the kingdom to the north. He wanted to meet you."

"Of course he did." Voo studied the bearded older king, but her greatest interest swung over to Thon. "This one intrigues me. His wreth blood seems more pure than that half-breed." She gave Elliel a dismissive glance. Voo leaned closer. Adan had watched the sandwreth queen look at Penda with similar analytical curiosity. "What are you then? You are not a frostwreth. But how could you be some other kind of wreth?" She sniffed as if she could inhale the scent of his bloodline. She looked into his crushed-sapphire eyes. "Most unusual."

"This is my hair. These are my eyes," he said. "This is me. I came because I hope to find information here. I wish to study the recorded history of sand-wreths and your legends. I want to learn if I am part of it."

Voo turned to the mages standing behind her in the grand entrance. "We have ancient records, but I have not reviewed them in a very long time." She walked around him, curious and intent. "And what is this mark on your face? You are quite handsome, but that design . . ."

"It is a rune of forgetting," Elliel said, sounding defensive next to Thon. "Like mine." She touched her own face.

"You are just a half-breed," the queen sneered. "We know what you are."

Voo showed no further interest, but Elliel continued. "My own people, other Bravas, did this to me . . . but we do not know how anyone could have overpowered Thon and made him suffer such a spell."

"I remember nothing," Thon said, "but I do want to learn who or what I am." He paused. "It has been suggested I may be Kur himself."

Voo laughed. "Suggested by a fool, perhaps! Kur gave the wreths his mis-sion, and then he vanished from the world. He will not return until we have eradicated evil by killing Ossus."

"Ah!" Thon sounded amused. "And Ossus is stirring in the Dragonspine Mountains. Mount Vada split open and belched fire. I was down there myself . . ." His voice trailed off, then he brightened. "Kur must be very pleased if you and the frostwreths are prepared to fight the dragon at last."

Queen Voo seemed to fold in upon herself with anger. "First we must de-stroy the frostwreths. We cannot let them have part of the perfect world."

"Ah," Thon said again.

"Come with me. We will talk further inside." Voo turned with a swirl and led them into the high, dry palace.

The main gallery was a cavernous chamber with an arched ceiling supported by thick stone columns that rose from a floor of pristine sand. Voo glided toward her raised throne, leaving the others to follow her. Her footprints erased themselves in the soft surface, but as Adan and Kollanan stepped after her, their boots sank in up to the ankles.

Before either king could speak, Voo dropped into her sandstone throne and spoke directly to Thon. "How would you fit into wreth history? Can you remember anything of the wars?" She stretched out her fingers, making grains swirl across the smooth canvas of sand, forming shapes. Marching armies appeared and crashed into one another.

"I do not remember them like that," Thon said.

"We keep written records of those wars and our painful history . . . of Kur and his true love Raan, who should have been the mother to his perfect child— until she was poisoned by her treacherous sister." Her expression pinched with rage. "That is what caused all the wars."

On the dusty tableau, armies smashed each other until all that remained was a blasted landscape. Voo observed in silence, then smiled. "And now our race has awakened again, so we can eradicate the children of Suth."

In the middle of the floor, a great bulge arose like a sand dune, which became a mountain range of scales. Finally, the head of a dragon emerged and opened its fanged mouth, drooling dust. "Afterward, we can destroy Ossus." She smiled at Thon. "Will you fight on our side against the enemy? As King Adan Starfall will tell you, I like to have powerful allies."

Adan tensed, not sure how Thon would respond, since he knew about the work camp and what the sandwreths did to their captive humans.

"I am not your enemy," he replied carefully, "but I am not your ally either. I am . . . waiting."

Voo pursed her lips. "You are exceedingly handsome."

Elliel bristled, ready to fight, but Thon didn't flinch. "I am glad my appearance pleases you."

"As handsome as Kur himself, perhaps?" Voo let out a wistful sigh. "You may be right after all."

Though the comment was meant as teasing, Thon took it seriously. "Perhaps I am."

28

PROGRESS on the Magnifica temple was significant, but not fast enough for Klovus. Even after he summoned resources and labor teams from across Ishara, impatience burned within him like indigestion. He wanted to prove his triumph. And he knew how.

Construction crews swarmed over the great plaza. People moved into the site with pallets of mortar and cartloads of bricks. Mule-drawn wagons rolled across the flagstones, carrying water barrels for the laborers, but the workers barely paused to sip a ladleful before going back to their tasks. Wooden rollers were lubricated with a slurry of mud for moving stone blocks, each the size of a cart and requiring dozens of men to move them, block after block, hour by hour.

He wanted more progress than that. Only with the godling's help could he make up for lost time.

When the idea occurred to him, the key priestlord did not hesitate. Now, standing by the scale model of what the completed Magnifica would look like, Klovus clapped his hands and shouted out across the busy plaza, startling the nearby crew bosses. "All work must stop, now! Everything, stop." The exhausted laborers turned to him, blinking with disbelief. He shouted again, "All workers—leave the Magnifica site. You need do no more work today."

"But, Key Priestlord," said Ur-Priest Dono, "we cannot afford to stall. The momentum of all these teams—"

"—will pale in comparison to what I intend to do." He smiled. "Just observe."

Though confused, the priests and workers obeyed his orders. The crew bosses called their teams to halt. Klovus was impatient. "Tell them to hurry."

Gongs sounded to spread the word all around the plaza. Exhausted, grimy laborers dropped their tools, left their mortar and bricks. Hundreds of bewildered, dust-covered workers descended the scaffolding and ramps and retreated to the fringes of the huge construction site.

Klovus licked his lips as he let the energy build within him. He could feel his connection to the Serepol godling, sensed it stirring beneath the temple's sprawling foundation. The great deity was restless, hungry, anxious to do something.

Klovus had not released the main godling for some time. The entity had never been allowed to achieve its full potential, and this was just the beginning. As the Magnifica grew, so did the deity's strength.

Finally, with the construction site empty, a storm of tension hung over the disarray of stone blocks and piled bricks. The second platform of the stair-stepped pyramid was taking shape, and the foundation for the third had been laid out, but it would be weeks before the next level was completed.

The people gathered daily to pray for Iluris, but he would show them the true power of their faith, and manifest exactly what they had given him. They believed in their key priestlord, and that belief allowed him to do virtually anything.

When he was young, Klovus had served as an acolyte, then a minor priest, and finally ur-priest of the harbor temple. Now, because of his strong affinity for the godlings, he was the most powerful priestlord in Ishara. The faith the people used to create and strengthen the entities was connected to his own faith in what the godlings could do.

For hours at a time, Klovus would stand by the spelldoor in the subterranean vaults and sense the Magnifica godling, like a doting parent watching a newborn baby asleep. He would commune with it, nurture it. His thoughts were its thoughts. His wants and needs were reflected in what the godling did. It was his sibling, his shadow, his reflection.

Standing by the model of the Magnifica, he envisioned the huge temple in his mind and felt the godling locked below, attuned himself to it. The entity understood the significance of this construction site, knew what it could do to assist with the enormous task. Then, in the growing hush around the plaza, Klovus called forth the godling.

It stirred beneath the Magnifica's foundation, then emerged from its spelldoor into the real world. Klovus could hear the gasps among the crowd of observers.

The huge temple base trembled and shook, as if the stones couldn't contain the power seeping up from below. The godling was smoke and energy, fire and storm, a mass of emotions, needs, concepts. All the fears, hopes, and unbridled desires of countless sacrifices, prayers for wealth or revenge, for power or peace, were all manifested in a contradictory storm.

The shimmering shadows congealed into a brutish mass that rose taller than three men. Gasping supplicants retreated toward the dubious shelter of buildings around the plaza. Workers from outlying districts had seen their smaller local godlings, but this was the *Magnifica godling*, the main entity in all of Ishara.

The people began chanting, "Hear us, save us!"

Klovus raised his hand and shouted to the godling, "This is your temple, designed by your faithful followers and built by your workers! But you can help. You can make the Magnifica stronger . . . and make yourself strong at the same time."

The spectators could not take their eyes from the rising entity. "Hear us, save us!"

He summoned a crystal-clear mental image of what the Magnifica needed to be. He pictured the components—stone blocks, bricks, structural girders—all laid out in exactly the way the gigantic pyramid must be constructed. The godling could assist.

The indistinct form flowed forward and snatched a cart-sized block of stone as if it were no more than a child's brick, and stacked it precisely in its second-level position. It swirled in and out of the already assembled stones, picking up hundreds of molded bricks, scattering them like leaves in a whirlwind, then laying them down with sharp ricocheting cracks, fusing them into archways, smaller temple alcoves, and sacrificial portals.

As Klovus felt the godling work through him, he twitched his arms and clenched his fists. He watched as the roiling appendages picked up another immense block, and set it in place.

The work crews shouted reverberant cheers of "Hear us, save us!"

Returning to the mountain of quarried stone, the godling laid another block, and another, accomplishing in moments what work teams had taken days to achieve.

The godling thrived on its work, and Klovus swelled with his importance. Directing the deity demonstrated to the people that he was key priestlord, knew that he served and spoke for the powerful entities that protected all of Ishara.

The godling expended great energy, pleased to be released, for it often brooded behind the opaque spelldoor. It wanted to be free, wanted to act, and Klovus gave it a purpose now. More importantly, the people of Serepol witnessed how powerful, how awe-inspiring, how terrifying the thing was, and they knew that the godling, *their* godling, was there for them. All around Ishara, the deities protected their people from natural disasters, served and helped them, but this one was the focus of the land. The Serepol godling *was* Ishara.

Once the huge temple was finished, he hoped, the entity would be strong enough to cross the ocean and reach the Commonwealth, where it could scour the land clean of the godless and leave the old world empty and dead, as it deserved to be.

The increasing crowds watched in awe. Klovus was pleased to note that not once in those hours did a single person mutter a prayer for Iluris.

As the entity moved hundreds of tons of stone, though, completing the second level of the temple pyramid, the key priestlord could feel it diminishing. To Klovus, the godling was noticeably more diffuse, even as it continued to slap down thousands of bricks, build up walls, and shift more stone blocks. Its power, drawn from countless prayers and blood sacrifices, was not infinite.

Klovus could not let the people realize its weakened state. They must never know that godlings had limits.

Fortunately, the basic work of the second level was finished now. Before the fading became noticeable to the crowds, Klovus called the godling to a halt and let it rise and roil like a hurricane in front of the people, who still chanted, "Hear us, save us."

Klovus shouted to the astonished audience: "I hope you are inspired. I now dismiss the godling, because it has shown you what needs to be accomplished here. The godling is your servant, just as you serve its needs. We are Ishara, and we are strong!"

The deity disappeared back into the Magnifica like smoke drifting on the wind. The people stood in stunned veneration.

"Now you must all work harder," Klovus said. "You've seen what the godling can do. Show it what *you* can do!" He had them entirely in his control. "Offer your strength and your sweat! Give of your blood. Present your sacrifices—the priestlords are here to accept them. The more you give your godling, the greater Ishara becomes. Make Ishara strong, and you make yourselves strong!"

29

DISCREETLY leaving Bannriya, Penda and her father headed north into the hills of Suderra. Their saddlebags carried the food and camp supplies they would need.

"I feel like a little girl again," she said as the horses moved along a clear path toward the hills.

Hale Orr glanced at her rounded belly. "You are married to a king and about to give birth to my first grandchild. I can no longer think of you as a little girl."

The skas circled overhead, chasing each other and taking turns landing on Penda's shoulder. Although Ari's heart link remained with the tribe-sister Glik, the blue reptile bird also felt an affinity with Penda. Neither ska showed any interest in Hale, and he pretended not to take offense.

Daughter and father traveled without plan or destination, because they wanted no one to know where they were going. They left the main road and entered the forested hills, following scattered lines of blue poppies, the secret sign that Utauks planted when they wandered the land. They camped alone the first night, building a cheery fire, opting to eat pack food because Penda's father had no inclination to hunt.

"I used to be a good shot with a bow. Alas, bows and arrows aren't my specialty anymore." Her father held up the stump of his left wrist.

She shared out the bread and some cheese. "This is feast enough."

Xar and Ari found a perch in a gnarled oak near Penda's blanket. The sky was clear and the air crisp. Her only misery was spending the night without Adan Starfall. She tried to tell herself each day would get better, although as she rested her palm across her belly, she knew she would think the same thing every single night she was away from him.

Hale Orr had scraped away stones and branches to clear the ground, then spread an extra blanket beneath him, but still he tossed and turned. "*Cra,* you've spoiled me with comfortable quarters in your castle, dear heart. The ground never used to be so hard."

"Your body has grown soft. Your own buttocks should provide ample cushioning."

"Very funny," he said and rolled over.

The next day they came upon an Utauk caravan with wagons, mules, and ponies. Hale recognized a bearded man riding a dappled horse. "Melik! We could use some company!"

The caravan leader looked at the two riders, marking their crimson and black colors before he brightened. "Orr . . . Hale Orr! And is that Penda?" He nodded respectfully. "My queen."

Penda cautioned, "We are just two travelers now. We want no one to remember who we are or where we've been."

"Utauks are good at keeping secrets." Melik tapped his nose. "You're welcome to join our party. We intend to trade with the village ahead, then find a good place to camp nearby." He drew a circle around his heart. "Do you have news to offer us?"

Hale responded with a grave nod. "We have much to share and be shared."

The hill village celebrated the arrival of the caravan, a motley of colorful fabrics, good cheer, and interesting wares for trade. The Utauks sold dripping honeycombs harvested from a hollow tree, packets of dried flowers that could be made into delicious tea, and handmade scarves that the village women adored. In exchange, they purchased wooden and iron tools, needles, and silver jewelry created by local artisans.

The caravan moved on to camp in a nearby meadow. Melik's new wife befriended Penda, asking many questions about her pregnancy because she herself was a few months along with her first child. At the campfire, the caravan leader shared tea and pastries with his visitors. It was time to exchange news and stories.

Melik spoke slowly, as if every word held added importance. "These are dangerous days, Hale Orr. Since you spend so much time within the city walls, you may not be aware of all the whispers around us."

"*Cra*, I hear them. And we have news of our own."

Melik nodded his shaggy head. "Though our tribes are dispersed, Utauks are still aware of what goes on. Our caravans cross the three kingdoms, but I am convinced that some of them have simply vanished." He sipped his tea, then plucked out a floating flower petal in the water. "We have found empty villages, as if the people fled. Where did they go?"

"They were taken by wreths," Penda said. "Enslaved." She raised a hand to call Ari. The blue reptile bird fluttered down and rested on Penda's knee. "This is not my ska. She belongs to Glik."

"The orphan girl? She traveled with us several times."

"Glik was kidnapped, too." Penda touched the mothertear in the ska's collar and played the sickening images of desert canyons, the squalid camp, the hundreds of gaunt human prisoners forced to perform hard labor. Melik and his family watched in disbelief. "Even while this was happening, Queen Voo of the sandwreths came to Bannriya and spoke to my husband and me, claiming friendship, offering an alliance. But she is no friend. The sandwreths have seized and enslaved many humans."

Melik groaned. "That is worse than what I thought."

"Does Shella din Orr know?" asked the caravan leader's wife. "We must spread a warning among all our tribes."

Hale grumbled. "*Cra*, how can any of our caravans defend against this? The wreths are powerful."

Penda said, "We haven't seen Shella since we learned this news."

Melik said, "We passed the heart camp several days ago. We will take you there." He clapped his hands to issue a command to the caravan. "Change of plans! Tomorrow we pack and retrace our steps!"

Hale expressed his thanks. "And we will need Utauk help to hide and protect my daughter. I fear Queen Voo wants to find her."

Though Penda was proud of her family colors, Melik offered her a green and white skirt and a blue shawl, which further disguised the queen's identity. The next day the caravan moved swiftly along the familiar road.

On the way, several young Utauk men and women spread out on the edge of a meadow, carrying a long gossamer net woven from thin threads. Thrashers came across the meadow from the opposite direction, noisily plodding through the tall grasses, startling quail and pheasants. The net bearers rushed forward and flung their weighted nets high. Most of the birds got away, but three were trapped. The hunters extricated their prizes, while others unraveled and straightened the nets before rolling them carefully for the next hunt. Melik proudly accepted the birds. "We can share these in the heart camp. We will be there within the hour."

Penda smelled woodsmoke and heard the camp before they topped a rise and looked down into a dell filled with wagons, horses, and tents. Flying overhead, the two skas greeted several reptile birds that were heart-linked to Utauks in the camp. Three teenaged boys left their chores and ran to meet the approaching caravan. They knew Hale Orr on sight with his gold tooth and his missing left hand, and they soon recognized Penda, the queen of Suderra.

Inside the old matriarch's spacious tent, Shella din Orr sat hunched on a thick woven rug that was a tapestry of countless colors, each strand for a family line, children, nieces, nephews, brothers, sisters, husbands, wives. Thousands of lines were woven into the pattern, and the old woman claimed to know them all. Her eyes were still bright with intelligence. Outside, her burly and bearded grandnephews, Emil and Burdon, stood watch, keeping visitors away to give the matriarch privacy with her guests.

Hale and Penda sat with her, sharing their news. As the old woman watched the images from Ari's collar, tears ran through the wrinkles on her face. With a gnarled finger, she drew a circle over her heart. "Sweet Glik! I knew that girl would get herself into trouble." Her thin lips pinched together. "Is there a way to rescue her?"

Penda shifted, trying to find a comfortable position among the cushions. She felt so ungainly. "Not yet. My Starfall has the armies of Suderra, but we could never survive a war against the sandwreths."

"*Cra,* and that's what it would be," Hale said. "An all-out war!"

Penda shook her head. "We are still searching for a way. For now, Queen Voo does not know that we have discovered her treachery. I just hope my sister Glik can survive that long."

Shella nodded wisely. "She will survive. I know that girl." Her expression and words were filled with sadness. "We have seen signs and received reports from across the land. Utauk travelers in the Dragonspine Mountains bring terrible stories. Mount Vada exploded and the mountains cracked. How can it be anything else but Ossus stirring?"

"Other dragons have been seen as well, like the one the wreths hunted out in the desert. . . ." Penda shuddered. "They said it was only a small dragon."

The matriarch gave a sage nod. "Ossus is made of all the evil and violence from a god's heart. Some portions have leaked out and manifested themselves. When Ossus himself emerges, that will be enough to break the world."

Hale hung his head. "*Cra!* The mountains are cracking like an egg about to hatch."

Shella said, "I expect more dragons will be loosed upon the world."

Outside in the camp, her nephew Emil brought out a small cask of chemical powder. The children gathered around the bonfire and listened to him sing a well-known song about stars falling from the skies, and as he reached the end of his verse, Emil scattered a small handful of the powder into the fire. Bright colors and glittering sparks whooshed up, making the children laugh with delight, although the skas were terrified.

"Do it again!" one girl pleaded. "Do it again!"

Looking put-upon but secretly smiling, Emil reached in and threw another puff of powder, creating a shower of colorful sparks. When the Utauk children kept hounding him, he sealed the wooden lid back in place. "*Cra,* this is rare and expensive powder! You have had enough amusement for one night."

Penda watched with sparkling eyes. She had always enjoyed these light shows as well.

Because it was a clear, dry night, she and her father slept outside near a small fire by Shella din Orr's large tent. Other Utauks offered them cushions and blankets that were far more comfortable than what they had packed on their horses.

Restless, Ari warbled and clicked as she perched on a branch above Penda's bedroll. Xar was more relaxed, poking his snout into his green plumage. Penda lay back, listening to her father snore as she drifted off to sleep.

She missed Adan, worried about Glik, felt the baby stir inside her. She wondered how close she was to true labor. This was her first baby, so she had no idea what to expect. The birth should come in no more than a few weeks. "The beginning is the end is the beginning," she muttered to herself and dozed off.

Deep in her dreams she had a vision of flying skas, thousands of them coalescing into an irregular shape, great wings covered with scales, a sinuous neck, barbed spines and sharp fangs, eyes filled with all the horror and evil ever loosed upon the world.

Penda woke up just before dawn, covered in sweat, her heart pounding. She felt around her on the ground, not sure where she was.

Hale Orr rolled over and wrapped an arm around her shoulders. "What is it, dear heart?"

"Just a nightmare, or a vision. Glik always had dangerous visions."

On his perch, Xar rattled and hissed, disturbed. Through her heart link, Penda felt a strong thrumming, and she heard others in the heart camp stirring. Xar chittered insistently.

With a gasp, she realized that Ari was gone. The blue reptile bird had sensed her frightening dream and fled, or maybe she was answering some other call. High above the camp in the predawn sky, Penda thought she could see Ari streaking away against the stars.

"Come back!"

But Ari flew off and vanished into the first hint of sunrise.

30

⚬⚭

Utho was ready to return to Convera. He did not like being so far from the war plans he had set in motion under the konag's seal.

Mandan, though, was smitten with Lord Cade's redheaded daughter and formally announced that Lira was his betrothed. He wanted to marry as soon as possible. The girl was giddy, and Cade certainly didn't object. Despite the grim procession he had just finished, Mandan was excited to instruct the cultural ministers and the chief legacier about planning the royal wedding. Utho was surprised at his impetuousness, but also relieved that the young konag would finally marry. He encouraged the rushed wedding date, ready to finish the matter and move on to more important things.

On the morning before they were due to depart for home, though, Lady Almeda went missing. She had been on edge for days, snapping at servants, at her husband, and once, in a moment of distraction, she even insulted the konag. Horrified, Cade ordered his Brava to escort his wife to her private rooms, where she could rest until she "no longer felt unwell." Utho was concerned, knowing how much damage the unstable woman could cause. When Almeda mysteriously vanished, Utho feared she had run off somewhere. Would she cause a scandal? Had she been abducted by some rival lord?

Cade did not show sufficient alarm, though. He made a show of being worried for his missing wife, demanded to know where she had gone. He sent out searchers, but it was clear he was glad the shrew had disappeared. Suspicious, Utho met his eyes, searched the expression outlined by his razor-thin beard, but could read nothing there: no alarm, no fear, no confusion. Cade was a hard man, as he had proved with his response to the Elliel incident. Utho usually understood him.

Had Cade done something to his wife, believing it necessary to get rid of her?

Ugly Gant was also unreadable. The other Brava did not confess to Utho whether or not his lord had given him orders about Lady Almeda.

Then, late in the morning, the woman's battered body was found at the base of the saltpearl cliffs. When a rider rushed to the holding house with the news, Cade gathered a party to retrieve her corpse. He showed no apparent grief.

Mandan and Utho rode with them out to the work area above the sea cliffs. Cade's soldiers stood with drawn swords around the fearful Isharan captives inside the camp fence. A dozen terrified slaves were stripped down for saltpearl diving, but all work had stopped when they discovered Almeda's body.

Ropes dangled down the sheer rocks, where climbers worked their way to the waterline. Mandan hurried to the cliff edge, and Utho kept a hand on the young man's shoulder to make sure he didn't slip. They stared down at the pounding surf and watched spray gush around the black rocks. People picked their way over the seaweed-slick boulders. A woman's pale form was caught in a sheltered elbow of tidepools. Her skin was smeared with red, her white garments torn.

"My wife was upset and irrational," Cade mused as he stood next to them. "Easily the type of person who would throw herself off a cliff."

The words sounded rehearsed. "We all saw her moods," Utho said. The ocean breezes made his black cape flutter behind him, despite the finemail lining.

"A shame," Cade said.

"A shame," Mandan echoed. "Poor Lira's heart will be broken. I will comfort her."

Cade frowned in embarrassment. "My apologies for the domestic turmoil, Sire. My wife and I did argue last night, and I'm afraid it . . . concerns you." He heaved a long-suffering sigh. "As a proud father, I am overjoyed that you have chosen our daughter to be your bride, but Almeda is much more possessive. She's the girl's mother and didn't want to give her up. She said . . . she said terrible things about you, Sire."

Mandan's face darkened. "Why wouldn't Almeda want her daughter to be my queen? The queen of the Commonwealth?"

Cade spread his hands. "I often didn't understand her myself. Only great love gave me the patience to live with her day by day."

Though Utho did not believe a word of it, he fashioned an appropriate tale that would be told. "After your argument, Lady Almeda was distraught. She fled your holding house and rode alone up to the coast in the middle of the night." He looked at Cade, waiting for the noble to add more details, but when he didn't respond, Utho continued. "In despair, she threw herself over the cliff."

Cade agreed. "Yes, that must be what happened."

It was a complex and inconvenient way to take one's life, so far from the holding house, but Utho doubted others would question the story. Gant seemed troubled, but he did not speak.

Mandan continued to stare at the crashing waves. He watched the workers gather the bashed corpse and pick their way up the cliff. As he listened to Utho's unlikely explanation, the young man seemed distracted. Eventually, he shook his head. "No, I don't think that is what happened."

Utho frowned in surprise, since Mandan rarely contradicted him. "Truly, my konag? Do you have other information about Lady Almeda?"

"I know these Isharans." He turned toward the scarecrowish captives. "What if Lira's mother came out here to contemplate her decision, and these animals murdered her? What better revenge than to kill the wife of their lord and master? I think they were the ones who threw her over the cliff to the rocks below."

Seeing the intensity in Mandan's eyes, Utho spoke slowly. "That is also a possibility."

"I'm sure that's what happened. Justice must be served. These wretches will face the konag's judgment."

When Almeda's battered corpse was spread on the tall grasses of the headlands, Mandan stepped forward, fascinated. Her skin was torn and bruised. A pink gash washed clean of blood ran down the side of her head.

Gant stood with his arms over his chest, while Cade looked down, showing no emotion. "My dear wife is gone, and now my daughter has no mother when she is about to be married." He adopted Mandan's story and raised his voice to the soldiers who held the Isharan workers at bay. "They murdered her! Somehow, they captured my dear wife and threw her down onto the rocks."

"We will find the killers," Mandan said. "Interrogate them."

The terrified Isharans were all brought together, even the ones who had been harvesting saltpearls at the tide line. They stood wet and shivering. Mandan walked past each one slowly, staring at them, meeting their eyes. Some were stoic, others huddled and wept.

Utho watched the young man, trying to fathom his thought process. When Mandan selected particular victims, he must have noted something in their demeanor or their tone of voice. Perhaps some of them reminded him of members of the empra's Fulcor delegation . . . the people he believed had butchered his father.

"This one." Mandan paused in front of a man with thinning dark hair and a missing tooth. "He is the ringleader. He planned the murder."

The pathetic man recoiled in shock. "I did not! We were held in our shacks all night long. No one escaped."

"Then how did you kill Lady Almeda?" Mandan demanded.

When the man continued to argue, Utho struck him across the mouth. bloodying his lip.

The konag stepped along the line, pointing to three men who looked bruised and scraped, probably from harvesting saltpearls. "And these three helped him. See the wounds? Lady Almeda fought back, desperate to save herself." The astonished slaves protested, but Mandan turned his back on them, his mind made up. "Bind them. They will suffer my punishment."

The captives moaned and wailed, but they seemed paralyzed. Utho assumed they had long ago given up hope of escape, prepared for death ever since they'd been brought here.

The four accused were tied to posts erected in the work area. Cade watched with approval as the soldiers wrestled them into place, and Mandan could barely contain his excitement. Utho would have been disturbed to see the young man's pleasure in such bloody torture, but knowing what the Isharan animals had done to his wife and daughters in Mirrabay, Utho felt no sympathy for them.

Mandan didn't want to get his own hands bloody, so Cade ordered his soldiers to use sharp knives to stab them behind the knees and sever the tendons, then painstakingly flay the skin from their backs. The remaining prisoners were forced to watch.

When the screams grew too loud, Mandan said, "Cut out their tongues so we don't have to hear any more of this." The guards did as they were commanded.

Utho watched in silence for two hours, after which his satisfaction faded to dull disgust. This was a waste of his time. "We must return to Convera, Sire. We are done here." He clamped the ramer around his wrist until the golden points drew blood. He *pushed* and ignited the circle of fire that engulfed his hand. "Many more Isharans need to pay for their crimes."

Gant touched his own ramer, as if considering whether to join his fellow Brava, but Utho didn't wait. He struck swiftly with the fiery blade, executing all four Isharans and putting an end to their misery. The air smelled of blood, burned wood, and roasted meat. Mandan looked pleased.

Cade nodded. "Your justice has been served, my konag." He turned to his soldiers. "Wrap Lady Almeda's body in sheets so that our sweet daughter does not see her mother like this."

"She will be grieving," Mandan said, "but we'll distract her from the sadness of her mother's murder with plans for our extravagant wedding. There will be no delay!"

31

⌘

THE window of solid ice was as transparent as tears, and Birch peered across the white expanse of the north from the high palace tower. When he pressed his palms against the pane, his body warmth did not melt a drop.

A herd of caribou dotted the snow-covered landscape, pawing among the rocks, eating lichens. He remembered once when a caribou herder had brought a few animals into Lake Bakal. He and Tomko had petted them, while their father negotiated for the meat.

Now, he watched the caribou shift uneasily, then bolt as large white shapes bounded after them—shaggy oonuks, several of which carried frostwreth warriors. The pack of wolf-steeds lunged after the fleeing caribou, driving the animals into mad flight.

Birch could do nothing but watch. He heard the distant snarls of wolf-steeds, the shouts of wreths, and the bleating panic of the caribou. The frostwreth warriors hurled crystal-tipped spears to kill their prey while riderless oonuks brought down two large bucks, splashing blood across the snow.

The frostwreths hunted for the meat, but also for practice; most important, they did it for sport. Wreths liked to kill helpless things. Sick in his heart, Birch turned away from the frozen window to find several drones watching him. The drones muttered, speaking their own words for meat, skins, bones. Birch knew the caribou wouldn't be wasted. The drones would use every scrap that the wreths discarded.

Sharp caribou antlers would also make good weapons.

Queen Onn had been occupied with her new lover for days and had no time for Birch, but as he crept past the doorway to her chambers, he heard voices talking rather than the animal noises of sex. He crept closer. He had been growing more confident, tricking the wreths in subtle ways. Birch wanted to learn what the queen planned, because someday he would need to tell King Kollanan. His grandfather was a great hero, and Birch wanted to be just like him.

Peeping around the doorway, he saw Onn crouched naked on the floor, her long hair loose around her shoulders. Irri, also naked, strolled across a large map the queen had fashioned on the frozen floor. She had sculpted the ice into mountains, roads, hills, and rivers, including Lake Bakal and the wreth ice fortress there.

Onn touched the sculpture. "Our fortress should have been a stronghold for our progress south, but Rokk failed me." She stretched her hand over the hills and fashioned a large walled city. "This is a human settlement called Fellstaff, I believe. Their so-called king Kollanan lives there."

"If it is in the way, I can crush it." Like a giant, Irri walked among the mountains, taking in the shape of the terrain. "We will move our armies through their lands and down to the sandwreth deserts. Why not use Fellstaff as our new beachhead, then keep going until we eradicate our enemy?"

Onn stood and turned to the far end of the room, where she hadn't fashioned any landforms. "The deserts are unknown terrain, but that is where the bitch Voo lives." Unconsciously, she touched the scar on her cheek. Gliding on bare feet to the opposite side of her map, she lifted both of her cupped hands and raised a line of rugged mountains. Frozen steam drifted about the peaks like fog. "These are the Dragonspine Mountains." She shifted her hands, and the mountains shook until the range itself split like the rind of an overripe fruit. "Ossus is deep below."

Irri snorted. "We have to kill the sandwreths before we worry about waking the dragon."

She let out a cold chuckle. "We have to worry about everything, so we are not caught by surprise." She stroked a fingernail along her thin pale lips, then spotted Birch lurking at the doorway. She spun on her feet. "Disgusting creature! Are you spying on me?"

Irri stalked toward the boy, and Birch scampered away. Suddenly the drones were around him, whisking him down the frozen corridor. As he fled, he heard the queen chuckle behind him, probably amused to see him so frightened.

The drones moved faster than usual, taking him down corridors and curved staircases, plunging into the tunnels that riddled the glacier like wormwood. Birch realized they weren't just running blindly. From their earnest expressions and wide blinking eyes, he could tell they had a purpose. "You want to show me something?"

"Drones," they said. "More drones."

The light dimmed to blue shadows as they penetrated deeper into the glacier. Birch heard noises ahead as the drones led him to a warm creche filled with humid air and the smells of bodily fluids. There, blue-robed mages tended fleshy sacs that sprouted like flaccid fruit from cracks in the ice wall. The pouches were veined with blue but the membranes were the greenish pink of spoiled meat. The drones observed with a kind of reverence.

The fleshy sacs squirmed beneath the mages' hands as they traced runes on the outer membrane, then followed the webwork of blue blood vessels. One of the sacs split open like yawning lips. A slime-covered figure dropped out and was caught by one of the wreth workers. It was a drone, already full grown. Its arms, legs, and head twitched and quivered. Wreth workers doused it with water, scrubbed the gray skin with rough rags, and placed the shivering form on a cart.

Birch remembered stories about how the wreths had created the human race, long ago. He wondered if the first humans had been born in a warm, smelly creche like this one. The frostwreth creators were powerful and dominating and cruel, as he well knew.

Moments later, two other drones were born from the womb sacs. One came out twisted and misshapen, though—a hand growing from the side of its face and the spine bent in the wrong direction, like a failed pastry from a bakery. The wreth mage grunted in disgust, had one of the wreth workers club the pitiful thing to death, then scraped the mangled body into a bin filled with other bloody refuse.

Turning to Birch and his companions, the mage sneered, "Help clean up this filth, then tend to the newborns in the training chamber."

The drones sprang into action, eager to participate in the work, as if it were an honor. After cleaning the slimy mess from the cold floor, they hurried to follow the newborn drones, with Birch in tow as if he were one of them.

They left the humid creche and moved to a large chamber where young drones were taught basic skills and made to conform. In the large room he saw the newborn but fully formed drones. The older creatures instructed the younger drones because the wreths would not be bothered to do so. The room was filled with a low hum of their strange language, and now Birch could understand enough words to get the gist of what they were saying. He could also speak to them.

Since the first moment he saw the cold sweep over Lake Bakal and kill everyone, when Rokk captured him as a plaything, Birch had hated the cruel frostwreths. Now he believed he could convince the drones to feel the same way. The arrogant wreths would never understand what they were saying.

Thanks to the creche, drones reproduced swiftly. The frostwreths were in the process of making many, many more. Birch wondered exactly how many he would need.

32

UNDER the hot sun, the human captives marched through the canyons, heading to the foothills. The thin sole of Glik's left boot had worn through, but she had no way to repair it. She often felt sand or tiny pebbles irritating her foot, but she would endure. She had survived many ordeals in her time alone.

Inside the circle and outside the circle.

Sitting tall on his auga, Mage Ivun accompanied the fifty workers who were going north to excavate shadowglass. Ten guards led the way on their own augas, their metal-and-bone armor making them look like fierce desert creatures. Reptile beasts of burden towed carts that carried tools for the workers.

The morose group plodded along, leaving the desert and entering dry, scrub-covered hills. Glik had stashed food, supplies, and potential weapons in hiding places around the work camp, but now she was leaving all that behind. She kept her eyes open, looking for an opportunity to bolt and make her escape, but the watchful wreth guards offered her no such chance.

Cheth strode beside Glik, protective and curious. Her black Brava clothing was smudged with tan dust. Glik said, "Plain of Black Glass is ominous." She drew a quick circle around her heart. "You'll feel the power when we get there."

"Enough power for us to kill these wreths and escape?"

"Doubt it." As they walked, Glik described how she had wandered across western Suderra to the craggy mountains. "Was looking for a new ska." She sighed, still felt the grief within her, unable to forget the day when her beloved Ori had flown into a storm and never come back. A burn of tears rose up in her eyes. "Wanted a wild ska, so I went hunting for their eyries. Tracked them by following their flights in the sky." She glanced up at the empty blue vastness overhead.

"Did you find one?' Cheth asked. "I've never understood how you Utauks can keep those reptile birds as pets."

"More than pets. Companions. Scouts."

Urged by the warriors, the augas plodded faster, and the captives had no choice but to pick up the pace, though they were already exhausted from the march.

Glik kept talking. "Found where the skas nest in the cliffs and climbed up there alone. Found my egg . . . and it was filled with love. Ah, Ari, blue as a sapphire, as kind and as clever as any creature who ever lived."

"Where is she now? Did she get away?"

Glik felt the hot tears again, stronger than ever. Somewhere distant, the faint tug on her heart link was still there. "Ari escaped when the wreths captured me. Still feel her, but she is far away." She drew a circle around her chest. "I know she still loves me."

Ivun pushed the group hard for another hour, then called a halt at the base of a brown hill. The wreths dismounted from their augas as the mage extended his withered arm and grimaced with the effort. He closed his eyes, strained with magic until the ground shifted. The dirt slope split open to spill out a pool of muddy water. The augas drank first, then Ivun pushed the spring wider, calling more water. When the flow clarified, the guards drank their fill, scooping with their hands.

Cheth watched them take their time, barely managing to contain her anger. Glik shifted with impatience, but knew that if she complained she would only provoke the wreths into lashing out at her.

Finally, the humans were allowed to drink, taking regimented turns. One man ahead of Glik gulped so much water that he doubled over and vomited it all back up. Mage Ivun scowled at him, and the miserable man did not get a second turn. Glik drank, and felt rejuvenated. She would live another day.

At the end of the third day of forced march, the crew finally reached a line of barren hills that overlooked the glassy scar of an ancient battlefield. The sun set behind them, casting long oily shadows across the slagged jumble of rocks.

Glik felt a chill as her companions stumbled to a halt, looking out at the bleak site. Opposing wreth armies had unleashed inconceivable waves of magic here, obliterating one another and hundreds of thousands of human foot soldiers. Shadowglass was the amalgamated residue of rocks and cities, wreth blood and human bones.

"I can feel it." Cheth touched her heart. "Perhaps some of my ancestors fought and died here."

"*Cra*, seems like half the world fought and died here," Glik said.

The mage raised his voice, forcing the slaves to listen. "Camp here on the fringe. We begin excavations at first light. Rest for now."

When Glik was here before, she'd found the empty pavilion of an Utauk prospector who came to harvest the magic-infused obsidian. His name was Bhosus, according to a journal she found. He had accidently cut himself and bled to death all alone on this ghostly plain. Glik had buried him inside a perfect circle of rocks, then delivered his journal to the next Utauk camp, thus ensuring that his life and legacy would never be forgotten.

Reminded of how deadly the black glass could be, Glik muttered, "We don't want to be out there in the dark."

"Don't want to be out here at all," Cheth replied.

Glik looked across the open landscape as night fell, searching for a way to fight or escape. She tried to take heart, telling herself this place was better than the brutal work camp in the canyons.

Tomorrow she might feel differently.

That night as she lay on the hard ground and listened to the dry wind moaning like lonely ghosts, she stared into the sky. The wreths were silent, so she could not tell whether they slept. The augas grunted, munching on dry grass and thistles.

The brooding magic of the surroundings intruded on her dreams. Even if Ossus did sleep under the mountains, his evil was not dormant. It had seeped out and diffused into the hearts of these wreths, building hatred for one another, and fostering violence among humans.

That was one reason Glik liked spending time alone. . . .

She dreamed of the dragon's huge dominating form. When she snatched Ari's egg from the ska eyrie, she had seen an enormous reptilian eye stirring inside a resinous barrier in the mountains. What was that?

She woke in the middle of the night and looked up to see the stars eclipsed by a tremendous shape, looming over the world with great wings, but when Glik blinked, she realized it was merely a bank of clouds. She felt a heavy ache in her heart, hoping it was just a nightmare.

When dawn came, small shapes flew overhead in the brightening light. She rolled off her blanket and stood up, waving at the skas. "We are here!"

She had no heart link with these wild reptile birds, but Ari sometimes liked to circle and fly free with wild companions. Knowing the skas could sense her, Glik waved again, trying to draw their attention.

The wreth guards reacted differently to the skas. "Little dragons!" they snarled.

Ivun raised his good arm and curled his fingers. Wind whipped up, a howling blast that swept the wheeling reptile birds into disarray. Wreth warriors strung their bows, nocked stone-tipped arrows.

The wild skas pumped their broad wings to fly higher. The wreth arrows streaked upward, higher than seemed possible. One projectile struck a reptile bird's tail, knocking loose a burst of feathers. The ska beat its wings frantically to get away. Two more arrows struck their targets, and a pair of dead creatures tumbled out of the sky.

"No!" Glik lunged toward the warriors, but Cheth seized her shoulder and held her back. Glik moaned again. "No!"

The next arrows missed, but the wreths kept shooting until they brought down three more skas. The feathered carcasses tumbled onto the Plain of Black Glass. Satisfied, Ivun nodded to his warriors. "No more spies."

Sobbing, Glik pressed her hands against her chest, feeling the heart link there as she reached out for Ari. She had been longing to see her beautiful ska, but now she just hoped her companion would stay far away.

33

WHEN one of the warships sailed back into Serepol Harbor, its banners signaling victory, the people rushed to the docks to hear how the enemy had been driven from Fulcor Island. People clustered along the waterfront, filling the warehouse and fish market districts. "Hear us, save us!"

In the open market square, worshippers had gathered, eager to welcome their godling and their priestlord home. Fishermen, carpenters, and merchants usually frequented the harbor temple to make their sacrifices, but the temple had been empty since the departure of the expedition.

The warship approached the main dock, its red-and-white sails stretched tight with enhanced breezes generated by Ur-Priest Xion and his godling. The iron fist of the battering-ram prow stretched forward like a gesture of triumph.

Accompanied by several ur-priests, Key Priestlord Klovus hurried to the docks. He had expected nothing less than complete victory, and he was pleased to see that the hull and sails showed little damage beyond a few smudges of smoke. He chuckled. The battle must have been a complete rout! The harbor godling had done its work.

The other six warships would have remained at Fulcor Island to consolidate their hold on the fortress, as planned. Even so, Klovus would dispatch reinforcements to ensure that Fulcor never again fell into the hands of the godless.

Klovus knew that the harbor godling in the hold would be hungry, and it deserved to be rewarded, after what it had done. The people would feed it with their sweat and toil, their prayers, their blood. He had already dispatched some of his lesser priests to the harbor temple, so they could collect sacrifices.

At the prow of the ship, the captain wore a bandana of rank wrapped around his head. Sailors and soldiers crowded the rails, rubbing shoulders as they raised their hands to accept cheers from the ecstatic crowd. Klovus could

feel excitement returning to Serepol, enough that the people might even forget their concern about Empra Iluris and their prayers would no longer be
misdirected.

Sailors threw down gangplanks so the crew could disembark, and the
crowd welcomed them as if they were close friends. Klovus knew that none
of the returning fighters would want for drink or food, nor would they sleep
alone if they didn't wish to. The ur-priests bowed with respect as the fighters
marched along the pier and into the swirling disarray of the harbor crowds.

The vessel's hull boards groaned and the deck rocked, though the harbor
was smooth. Klovus could feel the restless power contained in its cargo hold.
Ur-Priest Xion stood on the high deck, his caftan tattered, his hair mussed,
his face bruised. He looked drained and exhausted, and glad to be home.

Klovus pursed his lips. So, it must have been a hard battle, then. . . .

Xion remained aboard, quelling the entity in the hold until everyone else
had disembarked. When finally a quiet settled around the ship like a fog of
anticipation, he called down, "My godling is weary, Key Priestlord. We are
both glad to be home where we can rest."

"And where you can rejoice!" Klovus said. "Come, I will escort you to your
temple in full view of the people." He could feel the tingle of the entity as it anticipated going back behind its comforting spelldoor. "After what you achieved
on Fulcor, many people will shed their blood to strengthen the godling."

Worshippers responded well when godlings performed amazing feats on
their behalf. After all, offerings at the Magnifica had gone up more than ten-
fold after the godling there had built an entire level of the temple while the
people watched.

Xion opened the heavy trapdoor and let the wood crash down onto the
open deck. From inside the cavernous hold, a reluctant stirring of smoke
and wind growled, and the deity rose up like a thunderstorm stretching its
legs. Klovus could see that the harbor godling was tenuous, which made him
both sad and uneasy. The entity rolled and lumbered over the warship's deck
and followed Ur-Priest Xion as he descended the gangplank. Klovus was reminded of a dangerous but dutiful hound at the heels of its master.

Though still celebrating the soldiers, the crowd shifted to watch the sham-
bling deity leave the docks and follow the priestlord back to its temple. Klovus
didn't want the people to notice the weary state of the godling, so he shifted
their attitude. "See the tremendous exertion this godling has made for the
heart of Ishara. For the heart of its people! Thanks to such effort and bravery, we now possess Fulcor Island. Our benevolent protector gave of itself to
achieve our victory. And now you can help it."

As Xion led the procession toward the harbor temple, more crowds closed in. Men and women already bared their arms, and ur-priests scuttled forward with blades and collection urns.

Surprisingly, Xion looked at the key priestlord with a flash of suspicion, as if Klovus had usurped something he himself should have done. He added in a shout, "We must give back to the godling that has given so much for you."

Xion entered the open wooden doors of his temple, and the godling boiled inside, where it crawled through the pearlescent shimmer on the far wall, taking refuge behind the spelldoor.

Klovus turned to the enthusiastic people outside. "Give of yourselves. Offer your blood. Feed the godling, so that it may save us again."

Ur-Priest Xion gave him a respectful nod and crossed the temple floor to be with his godling.

Worshippers came forward by the hundreds to give their blood, making the entity strong. Klovus was glad to know that his own godling, the Magnifica godling, was vastly stronger and would always remain so.

☙

The leader of his Black Eel assassins came to Klovus with a fascinating report. "We have a prisoner from Fulcor Island, Key Priestlord."

"I did not ask you to take prisoners." Klovus was nevertheless intrigued. Zaha must have a good reason.

The bland-faced man gave the smallest shrug. "We found her of interest. She is the only survivor."

In the confusion and disarray of soldiers disembarking from the warships, the disguised Black Eels had remained belowdecks to guard the prisoner in the brig. After dark, they smuggled her to the extensive chambers beneath the Magnifica. They met in a large, thick-walled vault sealed by an iron-reinforced wooden door. A hazy pearlescent fog marked the spelldoor behind which the Serepol godling dwelled.

A muscular woman sat bound in a chair in the middle of the chamber. Her black outfit was scuffed and torn, revealing silvery shreds of what had been expensive finemail. Her brown hair was hacked short, and her features were heavy without the delicate lines of feminine beauty. She had a swollen black eye and a split lip. She looked up when Klovus entered.

He narrowed his eyes, recognizing this woman as one of the Bravas who had accompanied Konag Conndur on his diplomatic mission. She must have remained behind at Fulcor, and now she had been captured. Klovus smiled mockingly at the defeated fighter. "Welcome to Ishara."

She tried to spit at him, which only made blood flow from her smashed lip. "Bravas should have been here all along. Ishara was our promised land."

Klovus leaned closer, and his smile widened. "Promised by whom?"

The woman just simmered on the chair. Zaha and the two other Black Eels stood protectively close, but he wouldn't need their assistance.

"Bravas . . . that is what you call yourselves. But what does that mean, exactly?" Klovus asked. "Your features look different from a normal human's . . . those eyes. You are alien somehow." Her face was so battered and bruised, he had a difficult time imagining what she would have looked like under normal circumstances.

"These eyes show my wreth heritage. Bravas are half-breeds. We have some of the powers of our creator race, but we also have a human heart and soul."

"Soul?" Klovus chuckled. "You have no faith. You have no godlings."

"We have our honor and our legacy."

"Indeed?" Klovus said. "And who are you?"

"I am Klea, the watchman of Fulcor Island." Her head sagged. "I was charged with defending the garrison."

"Ah, you failed in that, didn't you? You failed because the people of Ishara *do* have faith. We create our godlings, and they are such a powerful force that your fortress could not withstand even one of them."

"You are liars and you cower behind imaginary beasts," Klea said.

"And we hate you as well," he replied. "Godless worms! How you must envy Ishara. You lust for what we have."

"This land should be ours." Klea strained against her bindings. "We Bravas have declared a vengewar against all Isharans for your crimes."

This woman intrigued him. Klovus slowly circled her chair. "And what crimes are those?"

Struggling against her bindings, she resisted answering. Klovus stepped back, letting his Black Eels coerce answers from her.

They got to work beating her further, breaking her. Despite her defiance, Klovus could tell she wanted to explain herself, to present the reasons for her hatred. Finally, she slurred words from a bashed mouth. "Centuries ago, Brava pioneers established a colony in the new world, but your ancestors brought a godling that wrecked our colony and slew our people. Only a few survivors made their way back home." She strained against the ropes until the bindings groaned. "Since that time we have sworn ourselves to revenge. We protect the Commonwealth and we will eradicate Ishara."

Laughing, Klovus glanced at the Black Eels, who remained expressionless.

"That is a fine ambition!" He leaned closer. The battered Brava smelled of sweat and blood. "That must have been a traumatic point in your history, though few Isharans even remember that it happened. It was an insignificant event to us."

The woman thrashed, trying to break free to attack him. The chair creaked again, and he saw one of her bindings begin to fray. The key priest-lord danced back just as she snapped one arm free and lunged forward. If Zaha hadn't intercepted her, she might have strangled him. The other Black Eels grappled with Klea, holding her down. In the struggle, she managed to break her other arm loose, but the Black Eels subdued her again.

Klovus looked at the throbbing glow of the spelldoor, and an idea formed in his mind. "This woman wants to avenge a wrong that was done to her people long ago." He mused and turned to her. The Brava ceased her struggles and glared at him. "She claims a godling harmed their poor, helpless colony." He gestured to the spelldoor, felt the crackling static power, the presence of the entity roiling closer, full of anticipation. "I offer you the opportunity of a lifetime. Avenge your people. I will let you face a godling yourself, Brava woman. We shall see how well you measure up."

The Black Eels released her, and Klea rose from her splintered chair. She shook herself and turned, wary, ready to fight.

The key priestlord released the godling from its world, and the powerful force flowed out through the portal. Even if the entity restrained itself, it had more than enough wild strength to do what was necessary.

The Brava bunched her fists and drew her lips back in a snarl. The godling spewed forward, and she threw herself at it, thrashing, punching, kicking.

The Black Eels did not interfere, but watched, eager to learn any Brava techniques.

The godling engulfed her, all smoky tendrils and ropes of wind. It swirled and popped, howled and roared inside the stone-walled chamber. Klea's scream of defiance transformed into a cry of pain as her entire body was ripped into tatters of skin. A red mist of blood swirled around the whirlwind, and all that remained of Klea were threads of black cloth and a drifting smear of flesh and bone that settled to the floor like a grisly rain.

34

T HE sandwreth queen was delighted when Kollanan described his attack
on the ice fortress at Lake Bakal. She summoned her mages, nobles, and
warriors to hear the story of how he had led a hundred riders across the frozen lake.

"Thon and I were there, too," Elliel said. The wreth man stood next to her,
and his sparkling blue eyes searched the observers in the room.

"And what did Thon do?" Queen Voo asked, apparently fascinated by the
enigmatic man.

"He did everything," Elliel said.

"I did what I could." Thon's lips curled in a smile. "We defeated them."

"For now." Kollanan went into more detail, describing how his raiding
party had lured the frostwreth warriors out onto the frozen lake, where
Thon had cracked the ice, boiled the water, and engulfed the enemy.

Voo laughed. "It sounds marvelous! I wish I had seen it myself."

"We struck like hornets and stung them. Ancestors' blood, we proved that
humans must be reckoned with!"

Elliel added, "They did not expect our strength."

"They said we were *in the way.*" Koll's voice dripped with the insult.

"This is your war, Queen Voo," Adan spoke up. "My uncle struck a pro-
found blow against your enemies, and now he has come to ask for your
help. I told him your promise."

"Did I make a promise?" Voo sniffed at the suggestion, looking at Kollanan. "What does the king of Norterra have in mind?"

Kollanan stepped closer to her throne that rose above the sand. "You can
help us hit them again. Harder."

Voo leaned forward and rested her hands on her bare knees. "So, you provoked them, got yourself into trouble, and now you need my help?"

Kollanan faced her with a stony expression. "My army has engaged your rivals. Are you afraid to join in? I was told you wanted our help to destroy a mutual enemy."

"Watch your words," the queen warned.

Adan interceded. "You came to Bannriya after the sandstorm and asked humans to fight your mortal enemies. King Kollanan has done exactly that. And is willing to do more."

Mage Axus leaned over to mutter something in Voo's ear, and she tapped her fingernails together. With a knowing smile, the queen looked back at Kollanan. "A stinging wasp may enrage a wild bull. So be it! Onn will have no recourse but to retaliate against you. She will want to hurt you." The queen rose to her feet, towering over them from the raised platform. "It would be a shame to see all your people massacred."

He gave her a perfunctory bow, covering his anger. "That is why I need your assistance. I respectfully ask you to send sandwreth warriors to help defend my kingdom."

Apparently satisfied, the queen mused, "With your blundering actions, you have inadvertently set up a trap for them." Voo stroked her long hair and held up a handful of yellow-white locks. "When last we fought, Onn hacked off a hunk of my hair, and I slashed her face." She chuckled, a sound like broken glass. "My hair grew back lush and full, but she still has her scar." She lowered her voice. "I would be pleased to hurt her again."

Kollanan felt unexpected hope, though he knew how treacherous this woman was. "So, you'll send a sandwreth army north? We could drive out the rest of the invaders."

"An army?" Voo set her lips in a straight line. "Onn and her frostwreths will not expect much from you. When my brother returns, soon, I will dispatch him north with a party of warriors." She snickered. "Once he learns of this mission, I would not be able to hold him back anyway."

"How large a war party?" Koll pressed.

"As many as I choose to send! Onn's people will imagine they are fighting mere humans, but instead they will encounter my sandwreths." She nodded, finished with her decision. "Quo's war party will travel to your Fellstaff Castle when they are ready. It will not be long."

Koll struggled with his emotions as he looked up at the razor-edged queen. This was what he had wanted, but Voo's attitude was strange. She didn't seem to care about the victory, only the exercise.

Adan looked at his uncle with cautious satisfaction. Koll bowed only enough to show thanks without undue deference.

"It will be good to kill some frostwreths," Voo muttered, then cast her gaze around all the visitors. "Stay here tonight. You can depart in the morning."

"That will give you time to gather your histories for me," Thon said, standing on the sand as if he were a mere observer of events. He cocked his head at Voo. "I prefer not to sleep. I slept enough inside the mountain. Instead, I would like to look at your historical records."

Voo quirked a curious eyebrow, but inclined her head.

❧

The intense stars above the Furnace were bright enough to dispel complete darkness. Adan felt isolated in the private chamber Queen Voo had provided him. All members of the human party had been given rooms of their own. Adan would have preferred not to be separated, but she claimed it demonstrated her generosity and warned them not to object.

The tan palace walls were dry and smooth, and the air held a bitter undertaste of dust. As he tried to sleep, warm breezes drifted through the open windows, rustling the gauzy curtains. He found the hush of the desert disquieting: no night birds, no insects, no familiar city noises. It was the silence more than the brooding danger that kept him awake.

Under other circumstances, Adan would have been happy to stare at the stars and mark the constellations. His heart felt heavy as he remembered dispatching such observations to his father. The last time he and Conndur observed the stars together, they had talked about the end of the world.

Now that dark prediction seemed more likely than ever. Conndur the Brave was murdered, and Mandan had taken the throne, bent on starting a war with the Isharans. Adan might well have embraced that war, to avenge what they had done to his father, were it not for the far greater threat these wreths posed. He could never leave Suderra and sail across the sea, especially not now.

As king, he had to shoulder the fate of his people, but as a husband he lay back in the warm desert silence and missed Penda. He wished he could hold her against him, feel the child stir in her belly, and listen to her whisper in his ear about the visions she saw. He hoped Penda had found safety among the Utauk tribes, far from Queen Voo's hungry eyes.

He heard soft footsteps outside his door, a whisper of fabric. He sat up in bed, instantly wary as a slender figure entered the room. Voo's long hair hung loose, and her topaz eyes gleamed as if lit with metallic fire. She had changed out of her leather and copper armor and now wore a tan gown no more substantial than a film of dust.

"Queen Voo," he said with cold formality. "The hour is late. I did not invite you into my chamber."

She chuckled. "This is my palace. I go where I wish." She stepped farther into the room, as if defying him. "And I wish to be here."

"I thank you for your hospitality, but please leave at once." Adan refused to show deference or fear. "You should not be here."

"And you should not be alone," Voo said, then added in a scolding tone, "I asked you explicitly to bring your wife, and you refused." She wagged a long finger back and forth. "Therefore it is obvious that you wanted to be here alone with me, so that Penda could not interfere. You realize that no mere human could ever match the passion of a wreth woman." Voo laughed. "Or better yet, a wreth queen."

Adan, still sitting on the side of his bed, said, "My wife is about to give birth. I wanted her safe. There was no ulterior reason."

"She would have been safe in my palace, as you well know. I should punish you for your defiance." She leaned closer. "No, I think I shall reward you instead. I had many human lovers at the end of the last wars. I will take you as my lover now."

Adan's throat went dry. He grasped her wrist to stop her hand. "I refuse. Penda is my wife. Honorable humans take only one woman."

"I wonder where that ridiculous notion comes from." Her expression was calculating. "I am the sandwreth queen, and my command will excuse you from any impediments of honor."

She tried to push him down on the bed, but he refused to yield. "And I am king of Suderra. I could never ask my subjects to serve with honor if I did not rule with honor." Voo grew frustrated, and he realized he was in increasing danger. As a wreth, she could physically overpower him or call in guards to force him to comply.

Adan would have to be clever. "Penda is a very jealous woman, Queen Voo. Taking me as your lover would endanger our alliance. If I succumb to temptation"—he forced himself to say the word—"Penda would know. No doubt, my wife would find a way to kill me."

Voo regarded him skeptically. "It is good to know human females are strong like that."

"And my people would turn against you. You are our allies." He feared his subjects would also be thrown into labor camps, beaten down, and enslaved. Surely, she would rather imagine a dedicated, cooperative army—even if Adan had no intention of providing one.

Voo stepped away from his bed, and her dust-thread gown swirled. "I admit that if you did make love to me, you would never again be satisfied with your wife."

"Penda would definitely know," Adan agreed, but he was answering a different question.

With a huff, Voo glided back toward the door. "I will leave you for now. At some point I may take another human lover, and there will be plenty to choose from." Her long hair seemed to sag on her narrow shoulders. "At present, the idea has lost its charm."

◦◦

Adan and Kollanan wanted to depart as soon as possible the next morning. Finished with them, Voo was preoccupied and aloof, anxious to discuss matters with her nobles, mages, and warriors. She made no attempt to detain the visitors. They gathered outside the palace, ready to mount the saddled augas. Despite the shimmering desert heat, the queen's manner exuded a distinctive chill.

Kollanan climbed onto his auga without hesitation, satisfied that Voo had agreed to help Norterra. Elliel kept glancing north, as if she wanted to ride back to Fellstaff at top speed.

Thon was delighted with the information he would bring back with him. From the sandwreth archives, Mage Axus had provided sheets of sandwiched crystal etched with wreth letters. Now, the stony mage said in a deep voice, "If you use this knowledge to find your powers, we can use you to help eradicate the frostwreths."

"I found some of my powers," Thon said, "and I have already harmed frostwreths. What I need now is to understand who and what I am. So much about the world is a blank to me." He took the records, which were wrapped tightly in sheets of thin leather, and secured them on the back of the saddle. He and Elliel both mounted up.

Queen Voo frowned at Adan, obviously displeased with him. Her last complaint, though, surprised him. "Why does Konag Mandan take so long to arrive? Did you not dispatch my urgent message to him? Where is he?"

Adan explained, "It is a long journey. My courier might not have reached Convera Castle yet."

"The vastness of the land was not an inconvenience before," Voo said. "Make him hurry. I wish to see this konag face-to-face. How can I build my army without all the humans of your three kingdoms?"

Adan's stomach knotted. "When you speak with my brother, I'm sure you will be able to convince him."

Mounted wreth guards surrounded the visitors to herd them along. Voo lifted her chin. "Keep building your armies for me, King Adan. I will soon dispatch shipments of shadowglass for you to incorporate into your weapons. We have come upon a fresh supply to excavate, and the material will be effective against frostwreths. You might even kill some of them."

Though it set him on edge, Adan knew it was best to appear cooperative. "Thank you, Queen Voo. I will build the Suderran army. As you ask."

Voo dismissed them. "I wish the best for your new child." She smirked. "And for your jealous wife."

35

THE ice flickered away into light and mist, melting the barrier in front of her, and she opened her eyes. Spellsleep drained out of the chamber, out of her blood, her heart, and her thoughts. A name came to the forefront of her mind. *Koru.* It was more than her name: it was her identity.

As she settled into a new permanent wakefulness, her blood ran cold and crisp, her thoughts as sharp as icicles. Dripping water flowed from her hair and down her cheeks. Alive again!

Though countless years had passed since the last time she had awakened, Koru was still young and strong. For a wreth with endless access to spellsleep, able to dodge in and out of time at her own whim, a life span could be virtually immeasurable.

Koru heard a trickling, tinkling sound as the front of the chamber melted away. Thin shards of ice crumbled into puddles that ran down into a drain beside her cell's still-glowing power crystal. Now that she was awake, she no longer needed external magic to keep her alive.

She flexed her fingers, saw the sharp nails, the smooth skin. With a thought she dropped her body temperature, and a sheen of frost sparkled on her arms. She found it beautiful.

Koru stepped out of the cramped chamber. She was naked, unlike many warriors who chose to wear their armor, as if they imagined they would lurch out of spellsleep and plunge directly into battle, still covered with fragments of ice. Instead, Koru had chosen to be more comfortable. She wondered how many others had come here to admire her over the decades—or centuries— since her last awakening. She knew that was why her mother resented her. She preferred that they were not both awake at the same time. Onn couldn't deny her daughter's powers, nor did she agree with her priorities.

Koru's two brothers, Enneth and Grao, had died in battles long ago. They had different fathers, for Queen Onn had many lovers. Koru didn't even know who had sired her, but he must have been strong and intelligent.

Standing free in the grotto's chill air, Koru inhaled with a sensation like thin razors cutting deep into her sinuses. She blinked again, and the world crystallized into clarity. Around her, she saw more activity than expected as wreth mages and workers occupied themselves with other ice cells. The mages clustered around an adjacent chamber, dour and angry.

Koru strode forward, naked, beautiful, and commanding. "What is this? Why is no one here to tend me?"

The wreth man frozen inside the chamber—who should have been preserved for centuries—lay slumped, his mouth open and slack, his eyes glassy. One mage looked up at her with a drawn face. "Mage Gura was dead when we thawed him. The magic failed."

Koru scowled at the news. "How does this happen?" She looked around her and scrutinized the continuing activity in the spellsleep grotto. More mages and lower-caste wreth workers were gathered around other cells with a sense of urgency. One warrior used a club to bash open the frozen barrier and expose the inhabitant. They dragged out more bodies.

Koru was pragmatic. "How many are dead? Do we have a traitor among us?"

The nearest mage looked at her. "Who would betray us from within?"

A second mage touched the rubbery gray skin of Gura's cold corpse and shook his head. "The world's magic has not recovered as much as we hoped. By placing thousands of us in spellsleep, we drew upon a great deal of that magic, and it must have faltered. Perhaps we did not monitor the chambers carefully enough over the centuries. We would not have known anything was wrong until we attempted to waken them."

Koru tried to keep the anticipation out of her voice. "Is my mother in spellsleep now? If she died, that would be a tragedy." Her tone said otherwise.

"No, Lady Koru. Queen Onn sits on the throne, safe and healthy. She instructed us to rouse all wreths from spellsleep."

The other mage added, "We are at last preparing for the final war to eradicate the sandwreths."

Koru straightened. Her back muscles were strong, her arms smooth, her breasts full and perfectly formed, as if the god himself had shaped her. She was a warrior and a tactician. Queen Onn allowed herself too many distractions, but for Koru everything had a clearly defined and considered purpose. "Then it will soon be time to wake the dragon."

A loud shout came from the level below as another wreth was found dead in a thawed chamber. Koru stepped away from the commotion. She was a survivor. She had scars on her body to prove it, and now as she walked naked among the other wreths, she hoped they noticed the scars as well as her beauty.

Koru decided to clothe herself before she went to see her mother.

36

THE smell of turpentine and oil soothed Mandan in his royal chambers. Upon becoming konag he had moved all the maps, his favorite furniture, and the idealized painting of his mother into this much larger suite, which had formerly belonged to Konag Conndur. Again and again, Utho had encouraged him to think of himself as the leader of the Commonwealth.

Mandan would rather have been planning his wedding, dreaming of the joy that was sure to come, but he wanted to finish this painting first. Candles spread warm cheer throughout the room, and cool night breezes came from the open windows that aired out the paint fumes. He stood before the easel and daubed the brush into various tones across his palette. For this particular work, Mandan of the Colors needed a great deal of red.

Over his bed hung the beautiful portrait of his mother. Queen Maire was the most lovely woman he had ever seen, and he remembered how she had caressed him, nurtured him, sung to him. Lira was so much like her. . . .

Mandan was Maire's firstborn, and he was her whole world, just as she was his. He knew that she had also loved Adan, her second son, but the next child, her stillborn daughter, had *broken* her. Maire had never recovered from that grief, no matter how much Mandan loved her and tried to show that he was all she needed. Maire had died of a sleeping sickness—which he knew not to be the true story—on a stormy night. Young Mandan had found her cold body. He remembered shaking and shaking her, but she would not wake up. . . .

Forcing those thoughts out of his mind, he turned back to his painting. The details were coming along nicely, and he worked with aggressive energy. He could recall each Isharan slave he had accused of murdering Lady Almeda, and now painted them with vivid clarity, showing their open mouths, their agony, the beseeching look in their eyes. He also added a shadow of sheer evil from each man's heart.

Choosing a smaller brush, he painted with fine strokes and a deeper red pigment, emphasizing where their skin had been peeled away. They sagged on the wooden spikes after the torture, unable to stand with their knees broken.

This painting would show everyone in the Commonwealth exactly what had happened. Sadly, Utho would not let him display the work yet, because that would reveal the existence of Isharan prisoners who harvested salt-pearls. He would hang the painting later, once open war began. Maybe he would unveil it at his wedding.

Without looking up, Mandan spoke to the impatient visitor in his room. "Isharans! Don't you hate them as much as I do, Lord Goran?"

His vassal lord sat in an ornate chair, sweating and uncomfortable. The two men had eaten together, before the konag went back to painting. Goran was a man with excessive self-importance, not too humble to bring his griev-ances directly to Mandan.

"Of course, Sire! Isharan animals! But that still doesn't answer the question about my personal Brava." His voice had a whiny undertone that grew worse every time he repeated his complaint. "It was important that Klea accompany the diplomatic party to Fulcor Island. Utho made a strong case for it, and I was willing to sacrifice my protection for the good of the land. But why does she need to stay there now? Can you not appoint an actual military commander as the watchman of Fulcor? When can I have my bonded Brava back?"

Pursing his lips in consideration, Mandan splashed a smear of blood across the forehead of one doomed man. "Klea is on Fulcor Island by my command, and she will remain there." He painted more rags on the tortured prisoners' bodies. His anger toward the loathsome enemy was inspiration within him.

Mandan was skilled with paints and brushes. He had learned under the best tutors, though most of his previous work had been in the form of por-traits of people who sat still so he could refer to their faces. Someday, he intended to paint murals of historical battles, the invading armies that had faced Queen Kresca in the fertile confluence of the two rivers, or the raising of the first banners at the founding of Bannriya two thousand years ago.

Initially, for this work he had considered a much more dramatic scene that showed brave Utho with fire streaming from his golden ramer as he struck down the vile captives, but showing such action was beyond his artis-tic abilities.

Goran folded his hands together, fidgeting. "Then I respectfully request another Brava to be provided by the throne. What else am I to do for protec-tion?"

The young konag turned away from the painting and scowled at him. "We must all make sacrifices for the Commonwealth." He looked meaningfully at his painting in progress showing the foreign criminals about to be executed.

Without knocking, Utho strode into his chambers, looking furious. The black boots rang loud on the tile floor. "A messenger just arrived in the throne room. Come with me so you can hear what he has to say."

Already disturbed by the gruesome painting, Goran was startled, jostling his platter with remnants of food.

Mandan let his paintbrush droop. "It's late, Utho. There is a list of the supplicants I will meet tomorrow morning. Can we just add this person's name?"

"*Now*, Mandan!" Utho said, and the young man set down his palette and paintbrush with a clatter and followed the Brava out the door. Goran scurried after them. Without slowing, Utho explained as he took long strides down the corridor. "The Fulcor Island supply ship just returned with grave news." He gritted his teeth as if he wanted to rip out someone's throat.

Mandan was already out of breath and sweating with alarm. "What happened?" Utho didn't reply, and Goran wisely held his tongue as they all burst into the throne room.

The captain of the supply ship stood with a dark felt hat in his hand, kneading it like a baker with a difficult lump of dough. He clearly dreaded what he was about to say.

When Mandan saw the man's expression, his heart fell.

Without formalities, the captain blurted out, "My ship escaped, Sire. We alone made it away from Fulcor. The garrison has fallen! Seven Isharan warships attacked from the sea and then swarmed the island."

Turning white, Mandan glared at Utho. "We left so many troops there, three warships. Klea was supposed to defend the fortress."

Utho replied in a deep, devastating voice. "The Isharans brought a godling."

Mandan's knees felt weak. He stumbled up the dais steps and sat heavily on his throne. "A godling?"

"Just like the one they brought to Mirrabay. Because Fulcor Island is closer to Ishara, the godling was even stronger in its attack."

The supply captain spoke in a rush, as if the panic was still fresh and real in his mind. "The godling sank our war vessels, tore them apart, and then stormed up the cliffs to the garrison. My ship was already sailing away, and we could see the fire and smoke, the soldiers fighting for their lives at the garrison walls. Nobody could withstand an attack like that. And against a godling . . ."

Shaking, Mandan slumped back in his throne. He wanted to strip the skin off every one of the Isharan invaders, then have Utho hack them to pieces with his ramer. "They murdered my father on Fulcor Island. We cannot let those animals have it."

"No, Sire, we cannot." Utho turned to the frightened captain. "Tell your crew to spread news of what they witnessed. I want it heard throughout the dockside taverns, the fish markets, the trading squares. Then sail back down to Rivermouth. We will supply and arm your ship as part of our growing navy."

Reacting to the brusque commands, the captain straightened. "I will fight for the Commonwealth, but . . . what if they bring a godling here? To our shores?"

"I've fought godlings myself," Utho said. "There are things more frightening." He loomed like a statue above the throne, turned to Mandan. "We must respond to this."

Mandan nodded and repeated, "We must respond."

He worked long after midnight with Utho helping him write decrees to reassign forces, commandeer seaworthy ships, and call upon his military commanders to prepare for war.

೪

The next morning, Mandan was miserable and short-tempered, but Utho would not relent in forcing him to his duties. The young man's eyes felt scratchy from lack of sleep, and his body ached as he sat at the long council table listening to reports from droning ministers and military commanders. Servants brought in various courses of breakfast, but he wasn't hungry. He wished wars weren't so complicated.

A colorful Utauk trader talked his way into the gathering, insisting that he had an important message for Konag Mandan. Due to the military council in session, the people assumed the stranger bore some report relevant to the Isharan war. Utauks often had unusual sources of information.

The trader brushed dust from his green-and-tan traveling clothes, adjusting the belt and pouches at his waist. He straightened. "I am Donnan Rah, a member of the Utauk tribes."

"I can see that," Mandan said, his tone sharp. "No one else dresses like your people."

"We are proud of our family colors." Donnan plucked at his sleeve, then continued in a harder voice. "I am proud of my past service for Konag Conndur." He traced a circle over his chest. "The beginning is the end is the beginning."

"Many things are nearing the end," Utho interrupted. "Do you have strategic information for us? We are preparing for war."

"I have vital information about a terrible war. Queen Voo of the sand-wreths commanded King Adan to dispatch an urgent message." He reached into his colorful tunic and withdrew a leather-wrapped wallet, which he carefully unfolded. He presented the message to the young konag.

Mandan was annoyed. "Why does Queen Voo *command* my brother? He is the king of Suderra."

The trader dodged the question. "King Adan considered the message important. The queen of the sandwreths wishes to meet personally with you. Her desert empire has already formed an alliance with Suderra." Donnan sniffed. "Or so it is reported."

Mandan picked up the paper, read the embellished handwriting. Utho stood over his shoulder, scrutinizing the letter. "This is another false alarm, my konag. A diversion."

"Not a diversion at all," insisted the Utauk, sounding haughty. "My people have seen terrible things, inexplicable things—missing caravans, abandoned villages, mountains shaking and bleeding fire. The wreths exert great power, and they mean to wake the dragon." He had a maddeningly superior smile. "That would kill us all. The whole Commonwealth must turn its attention to this crisis."

Utho spoke up without consulting Mandan, who remained seated at the council table. "We have heard the ancient stories. Konag Conndur was so frightened at Mount Vada that he abandoned all wisdom and tried to befriend Ishara. That was his greatest error as a leader. It is what got him killed."

Mandan paled, setting the letter aside. "Such nonsense! Why do you torment us?"

"I know nothing of that, although I do grieve for the konag," Donnan Rah said. "Conndur the Brave was a good ruler, and he paid me well. Believe me, Sire, I have seen the sandwreths myself, and they are dangerous. The frost-wreths have already struck Norterra, from what we know." He grew more serious. "I suggest you respond to Queen Voo's summons. This is not an enemy you wish to make."

Lord Goran, sitting halfway down the table from the konag, spoke up, trying to sound important. "We have other priorities here, sir. There's a war on with Ishara, and the sandwreths are far away."

Anger flashed in the eyes of the Utauk spy. "It will not comfort the people of Suderra to hear how little their konag thinks of them." He drew a circle around his heart. "I will relay the message to King Adan."

Mandan squirmed, trying to think through the consequences as his tutors, and his Brava, had taught him. "Utho, I know my brother will pout if I don't at least send an emissary. Maybe we should not ignore the sandwreth queen entirely." As he looked at the supercilious Goran, an idea occurred to the young man. "Very well, if it's that important, then I appoint Lord Goran as my representative." He nodded to himself, looked at Utho for confirmation, and saw real, deep anger behind the Brava's eyes.

Utho spoke to the annoying lord, but his ire seemed to be directed at the Utauk messenger. "Goran, take an escort and find your way to this Queen Voo. The konag will send gifts with you. Keep her occupied. We don't want anything to do with sandwreths at this time."

At first, the ambitious vassal lord grinned, then he paled. "Me, Sire? I am a poor emissary, untrained in diplomacy. I have my own county to run, and I . . ."

Utho cut him off. "I will make arrangements for you to ride out immediately. We have more important matters to worry about here."

The supercilious lord looked terrified, and Mandan enjoyed his discomfort, glad to be rid of Goran's complaints so they could concentrate on recapturing Fulcor Island.

Mandan also had a wedding to plan.

37

THE journey home from Suderra was long and rough, but King Kollanan rode hard. If Queen Voo was true to her word, she would send warriors to help defend Fellstaff. He hoped they would arrive before the frostwreths retaliated.

As their horses covered mile after mile, Koll kept his concerns to himself. Watching the long road as dark pines replaced low oaks, he knew he and his companions were close to home. The outlying farmlands of Norterra welcomed him with golden grains, bound corn shocks, orchards heavy with apples and pears in late autumn. The farmers went about their harvest, tense and wary as they prepared for what could be hard and violent times ahead.

Koll couldn't wait to see his beloved Tafira. Before he and his companions rode north, King Adan had embraced him, both men acknowledging the silent grief of Conndur's death, as well as the peril that the world faced. "I have to get back to my Tafira," Koll had said. "I need to know she is safe while we wait for the sandwreth reinforcements. I hope Queen Voo does not take too long to send them. Will she keep her word?"

"Yes. She wants to impress you." Adan's heart ached. "And I keep my queen safe by sending her away. . . ."

Now, when he finally saw the fortified city ahead, Koll felt uplifted and relieved. "I feared that we would find the walls shattered, the buildings burned, and my wife . . ."

Elliel shaded her eyes. "The frostwreths must not think we are worth a quick response. If they believe we are so insignificant, we may have a chance."

Thon patted his saddlebag. "With all the historical information Queen Voo provided, I can be more prepared."

Elliel said, "Shadri would be thrilled to help you interpret the documents."

"Yes, the scholar girl is a good research companion."

City guards came to greet them at the main gates, while criers rode through the streets to announce the king's return. The dusty travelers climbed the streets to reach the main market square below the castle, finding a crowd already gathered there. Storm snorted before plodding ahead.

Elliel spotted the Commonwealth banners first. "Another party has arrived from Convera! And a legacier." Koll frowned as he noticed that Captain Rondo and his group of restless escort soldiers had joined the newly arrived procession, like an honor guard. In the square, a legacier in red-trimmed brown robes stood beside a gilded chest that she had opened.

Elliel shouted ahead, "King Kollanan has arrived!" The crowd turned to receive their king, then began to murmur, as if they had been caught in some secret activity.

Standing with his men, Captain Rondo turned to him. "I helped escort the procession into the city, King Kollanan. Their party did make it through the mountains. Some of the roads are passable, though difficult." He looked up at Fellstaff Castle and said in a critical tone, "Queen Tafira has not yet arrived to pay her respects."

"Pay her respects for what?" Koll asked.

"Maybe it's because of her guilt," muttered one of Rondo's men, Sergeant Headan. Kollanan glared at him, and the man quickly averted his gaze and stepped back.

The legacier spoke with an unsettling exuberance as she displayed the contents of the chest for the spectators. She removed a wrapped object and held it up. "By orders of Konag Mandan, we deliver the left hand of our revered Conndur the Brave, who was heinously slain by Isharan animals."

Dismounting, Koll strode into the crowd. "What is this?" His confusion turned to cold hesitation. Conndur's hand?

Elliel and Thon took their places on either side of the king. Distracted for only a moment, the legacier raised her voice. "Conndur's body was dismembered, butchered like an animal, but even that indignity has the power to unite us! We bring this relic so that all our people can remember who he was, and what the Isharans did to him."

Rondo lowered his head in respect, as did his men. The crowd around them murmured in awe, fear, and remembrance.

Koll came forward, full of dread and concern, and faltered when he saw the shriveled, gray skin. "My brother's hand? Why would Mandan send such a thing?"

The king looked at the discolored, ghastly artifact. The fingers were curled like a dead spider. Clenched in pain from when he had been murdered, or was this just the way the decaying muscles and flesh had twisted? A hush fell around him as the others grew silent. He could hear the loud pounding of his heart, his heavy breathing. He wished Tafira were at his side.

The hand was dark, but a white scar line ran from the end of the thumb across the top of the severed hand. Koll remembered that cut, how much it had bled. It had happened during the Isharan war, when he and his brother were moving their soldiers over enemy terrain. One night in camp, when Conn was recklessly using a battle hatchet to split a knotty chunk of wood, the sharp-edged weapon had slipped and cut a gash across the back of his hand. Koll had used a needle and gut thread to sew the wound as Conn winced, while also laughing at his clumsiness. The two brothers had decided that such a wound should not be attributed to a mere campfire mishap, but to a great battle. No one had questioned the story afterward, when the two embellished the tale. Now the memory filled Kollanan, and tears stung his eyes.

"We must show the hand to all!" cried the legacier. "Every person in the Commonwealth must remember how the Isharans murdered our konag. They will look upon this hand and know the foul end Conndur suffered, the pain, the treachery."

Koll, though, shook his head and stepped back. "This is not how my brother's legacy should be remembered." He looked up at the legacier and the procession. "No, this ends here. His pain and suffering is not what I want people to remember." Tears began to pour down his cheeks. "Not my brother . . ."

The crowd stirred, not sure how to react. The legacier and her companions looked weary, as if their long days of marching across the land had worn them out. The woman's voice was dry and rough, no doubt because she had shouted the same story many times along their hard journey. "The people of the three kingdoms must understand how evil and horrible the Isharans are. This is evidence for all to see, for all to remember."

Koll blinked, then closed his eyes to vivid memories of the reckless and heroic deeds the two of them had performed as young men. Koll and Conn. Those thoughts angered him even more. "Conndur's legacy is his life, his triumphs. By doing this, you guarantee that the only thing anyone remembers is the way he died."

The legacier sounded as if she were lecturing a child. "His name has been carved in the great remembrance shrine of Convera. The people have been told his story already. Konag Mandan wants this tragedy to be on the lips of all his subjects. Treacherous Isharans!"

Ah, but Commonwealth soldiers had also done terrible things to Isharans during that war! He thought of how he had saved a village from massacre and rescued the young woman who would become his wife. . . .

"No . . ." Kollanan said, his voice a dry whisper, then he spoke louder. "This is my kingdom, and Conn was my brother. Here in Fellstaff, we will do this my way." He made up his mind before he could reconsider. "We will have a reverent funeral pyre, as he deserved. You have brought me my brother's hand. We will make do." The legacier recoiled, indignant, but Koll stepped even closer. "Bring straw, kindling, and wood—right here in the public square."

Elliel issued orders to the Fellstaff city guard. "Gather the materials. Prepare a pyre!" She pushed the people back, while others swiftly brought armfuls of sticks, construction boards, and logs. Koll spoke not another word as he stared down at the open chest, hypnotized by the severed hand, reluctant to touch it.

Captain Rondo and his soldiers were troubled and hesitant. The legacier's face darkened. "That is not what Konag Mandan requested."

Before long, Lasis rode down from the castle, escorting Queen Tafira in a formal gown adorned with colorful Isharan scarves. The townspeople muttered, looking askance at their own queen, as if the bright dyes were an affront to the dark and sad occasion.

Kollanan's heart brightened as he saw his wife, but he sensed the undertone of suspicion that had surrounded her since he had brought her to Norterra as his war bride.

"Now she arrives," Rondo grumbled, "when her king can protect her."

Kollanan glared at the man. "Why would the queen of Norterra need protection from her subjects?" The captain looked away.

Tafira glided up, taking her place as queen. With her at his side, Kollanan overcame his revulsion and reached forward to take the hard, leathery hand from the chest. Forced to bow to the king's instructions, the legacier awkwardly stepped back, though she seemed possessive of the grim object.

When the pile of wood was laid in the town square, Koll reverently placed the desiccated hand on top. "My brother Conndur was a great man faced with impossible enemies. As konag, he tried to do the right thing and find an ally against the true danger to humankind: the wreths."

The people muttered in fear, although Rondo and his men sounded more skeptical. "And the Isharans murdered him!"

Koll pressed forward, raising his voice. "Conndur's legacy will burn bright. We will remember him by continuing to fight for Norterra and the three kingdoms." He realized he had been so disoriented by the gruesome procession that he hadn't even explained what he had learned deep in the Furnace. "To that end, I have news—sandwreth reinforcements will arrive soon to help us defend Fellstaff. With them fighting beside us, we will retake Lake Bakal."

"But what about the Isharans?" Rondo asked, struggling to maintain his discipline.

Consumed with thoughts of his brother, Kollanan did not give him the answer he wanted. "Alas, after what occurred on Fulcor Island, we cannot count on Isharan help against the real enemy."

He nodded to his two Bravas. Lasis and Elliel clamped their golden ramers around their wrists and ignited the magical fire to light the pyre. The flames roared up to devour the piled wood.

Tafira took her husband's hand as they watched the fire turn the gruesome remnant to pure ash. The king felt relieved, but exhausted as the hot blaze fell into coals. He took the queen's arm. "Come with me back to the castle. I need to be home."

38

⚭

THE *Glissand* cruised toward Serepol Harbor, displaying the prominent Utauk circle on the mainsail. One more run.

Mak Dur stood on deck inhaling the warm salt breezes. The exotic city sprawled in front of him, full of eager customers and possibilities. Docks extended like splayed fingers into the water. Wooden waterfront buildings rose up at the edge of the docks, the harbor temple, whitewashed structures with tile roofs, and the graceful palace larger than any other structure. He was coming back to trade after only a short while away, but he hoped he could make another profitable run. He had departed from the harbor, heading off to the Commonwealth just as the Isharan ships had limped home with their grievously injured empra aboard. Mak Dur had delivered the important news to the naval port at Rivermouth, but now he was back in Ishara with a new cargo of goods from the three kingdoms.

Ever since Hale Orr had commissioned the *Glissand* to sail to Ishara—twice!—for his own business, Voyagier Mak Dur had delivered rare goods to Serepol. They were good customers. Because the Utauk tribes had always been neutral in any conflicts, their ships could travel with impunity even when tensions rose between the continents. Other voyagiers considered the risk too great, especially after the horrific events on Fulcor Island and the imminent war, but that made profits higher for anyone who dared. With a full cargo of Commonwealth goods that Isharans would be eager to buy—perhaps for the last time—Mak Dur wanted to make one final run. He held great faith in tradition. Isharan warships would recognize the wide Utauk circle on the sails and leave them alone.

He was particularly eager to sell a new crate of shadowglass he had obtained from an Utauk prospector, a man with bandaged hands who had traveled overland for months to reach port with his treasure. Mak Dur had paid a premium for the rare material, since he knew the Isharan priestlords used the eerie black glass as windows into the void where their godlings lived. It made his skin crawl just to know the shadowglass was in his cargo hold, but he anticipated a huge profit from it. He drew another circle around his heart.

Pilot boats came out to guide them into the harbor, accompanied by two bulky Isharan warships. The iron-fist battering rams looked like threats, and the bright red-and-white sails reminded him of fresh blood splashed on pale skin. Isharan soldiers lined up on the decks of the escort warships, grimacing at the Utauk sailors like wolves ready to fall upon prey.

Defiantly cheerful despite his uneasiness, Mak Dur called across the water. "We come to trade!" He added in a low voice to his crew, "*Cra,* come on deck, all of you! Wave to them and smile." The others did as they were told, but the Isharans did not seem impressed. Still grinning outwardly, he spoke to his navigator, Heith. "Take care to follow their instructions precisely. Go where they say."

The *Glissand* proceeded to an empty dock at the far end of the harbor, where more soldiers waited for them. The navigator's brow furrowed. "Looks like we're being quarantined."

Mak Dur let out an annoyed sigh. He had hoped they would be able to sell their goods to the public, set up a makeshift bazaar on the waterfront where Isharan merchants could squabble over the merchandise, which would drive up prices, but now he felt uneasy. "If the government of Ishara buys our entire cargo, they can enforce a set price."

The navigator smirked. "Worse, they might just impound all of it."

As the trading ship tied up to the dock stanchions, Mak Dur ducked inside his cabin. He secured his hair with a ribbon and donned a silk shirt, both green, a color that reminded him of the pine trees of Norterra, where he had grown up before heading off to sea. The proud voyagier emerged, careful to wear a cheerful smile as the main gangplank was lowered to the dock. Pretending that everything was normal, the crew opened the hatches and began to bring up the crates from below.

Mak Dur squared his shoulders and stepped down the creaking gangplank toward the line of waiting soldiers. Under his arm, he carried a rolled manifest of the *Glissand*'s cargo, along with suggested prices. He raised a hand in greeting, even though he felt undefined dread, perhaps some innate warning from his Utauk luck.

The Isharan soldiers parted to make way for a priestlord in a blue caftan. A scowl filled the man's entire face. Mak Dur recognized him from when Hale Orr had come bearing a message to Empra Iluris. In a friendly voice, he said, "My gratitude for the military reception, Key Priestlord Klovus! My crew feels exceptionally safe under your protection." He managed to make the words sound natural and sincere.

Klovus glowered at the voyagier's extended hand. "You come from the Commonwealth carrying their unwanted goods. How do we know you don't intend to kill us all?"

Mak Dur forced a chuckle. "*Cra,* that would be terrible for business! Utauks are neutral merchants and messengers—inside the circle and outside the circle."

Klovus was not convinced. "What if I have my soldiers crack open the crates and dump your cargo into the harbor so we can inspect it?"

"Then your harbor would be a mess, to no good purpose. These materials are scarce in Ishara, and so we benefit your land, do we not?" After a brief pause, Mak Dur decided to play his strongest card. "We also carry ten large sheets of pristine shadowglass, polished and flawless."

Klovus's eyes lit up at that. "Ah, we will use that in the Magnifica temple, as windows to observe our great godling."

The voyagier felt great relief. "There, you see? Our arrival is beneficial."

The priestlord's expression became calculating, which immediately made Mak Dur wary. "You can provide one other valuable item—information. We need to know what the godless are doing after their treachery on Fulcor Island. They tried to assassinate the empra, and we expect that is only the beginning of hostilities. What are their war preparations?"

"I am not privy to any war council. No Utauk is."

"But you must have seen their shipyards at Rivermouth," Klovus pressed. "Are they gathering a navy? When will they launch an attack on Ishara?"

Mak Dur spread his hands. "Truly, I know nothing of that, Priestlord. We loaded our cargo in the merchant district of Convera down by the river, then we sailed back here." He realized he had to give the priestlord something. "It's true, the people of the Commonwealth are enraged by what happened on Fulcor. The konag was killed—apparently by Isharans—and his son wants revenge. I would not be surprised if they try to retaliate in some way, but it will take a long time to gather armies and build warships."

He did not reveal that when his ship had previously returned from Serepol, he had reported that the empra remained in a coma, that Ishara was leaderless and in turmoil. He had no doubt Konag Mandan would retaliate. That was why the *Glissand* had to make one last voyage, and now. There was not much time, but they were Utauks!

Klovus considered the ship and smiled. "We will interrogate the rest of your crew to determine if they can provide further details. Perhaps they noticed something you did not."

Mak Dur felt cold. "As I said, sir, we are neutral. My sailors will tell you what they know." He wouldn't have any choice.

The key priestlord raised his voice so all the soldiers could hear his pronouncement. "This ship is impounded. We may need it as part of our fleet."

On the deck, the sailors muttered in dismay. Mak Dur faced down the priestlord. "But Utauks are neutral!"

"No one can be neutral in this war. Your vessel has come here, therefore it is ours. You will not be allowed to leave Serepol."

Mak Dur's heart sank as he looked back at his ship. The worried sailors on deck crowded against the rail.

The priestlord warned, "Your comfort depends on your cooperation. You can be guests, or you can be prisoners." He issued orders to the soldiers along the dock. "Remove their cargo for inspection. I'll want a full accounting." He smiled. "And give me all of the shadowglass."

39

Quo returned to the desert palace with his report about the human slaves in Ivun's work camps. He described the lackluster workers, the angry apathy, the disappointingly low productivity. The queen was not pleased with his report.

Mage Axus strode into the throne room, uninvited. He glowered at Quo. "I have long advised Queen Voo that we should make the humans *want* to fight for us. Treat them better as a means to manipulate them. Since they will not survive the war anyway, we should shape them into what we want. It is to our advantage."

Quo did not respect the troublesome mage. "You bore us with your irrelevant notions. You want to coddle the humans too much."

Axus glowered. "It is foolish to waste resources."

"Humans die easily. There is no way around that." Quo shrugged.

"We can make them die less swiftly. They will work better because they wish to stay alive, and the wreths will benefit because they work for us longer. Make them think we are their benefactors! We—"

"That is exactly what I am doing with King Adan and the army of Suderra," Queen Voo interrupted. She stroked her lower lip as she watched them squabble, not interested in either argument. "Mage Ivun always wants more slaves, more work crews, and it becomes tiresome, but he does indeed produce the weapons and armor I ask for. He attempts to teach his slaves how to fight, though I doubt any are trained well enough to be worthwhile additions to our army. Even if they are slaughtered quickly, though, they could distract a few frostwreths, I suppose."

She rested the back of her head on the hard throne and closed her eyes. "They resent being forced to work, even though that is why their race was created in the first place. King Adan's army seems more tractable, by letting them imagine their freedom."

Quo sauntered up the dais and took a seat on the floor beside his sister's throne. "I encouraged the slaves to breed. That might help." His voice had a humorous lilt, and then he grew more serious. "Humans are more fertile than wreths ever were, but they are also stubborn. Telling them to do a thing makes them defiant, rather than cooperative."

Voo sighed. "It is a flaw in their creation. Fortunately, Kur did not make the same mistake when he created wreths."

Axus strode forward. "We must build our armies, my queen. Hear me, placing humans inside fences and beating them into submission will not create an effective fighting force."

Reflexively, Quo disagreed, but the queen interrupted him. "We will take both approaches. Mage Ivun will continue to run his camp and extract the work and materials we need, especially now that he has begun producing shadowglass. Meanwhile, I will cultivate King Adan, let him think his interests align with ours, even help him arm his soldiers and train them for us. I can manipulate him easily. I will give dear Adan the tools, and he will build a tremendous army. For me. It's much easier that way."

Accepting defeat, or compromise, both Quo and Axus bowed stiffly and took a step back.

Voo opened her eyes and gave her brother a gentle smile. "While you were gone, Adan Starfall came to see me, along with another one of their kings."

Quo was suddenly interested. "Oh? Did their great konag respond to your summons?"

A flash of annoyance crossed her beautiful face. "No, it was a different one. King Kollanan from Norterra. He says he has fought frostwreths."

Quo laughed in surprise. "Frostwreths? They have finally come out of the snow? They have actually been seen?"

She reached down to stroke her brother's long hair and explained about the ice fortress on Lake Bakal and how the humans had the audacity to attack it. Quo found the news delightful. "So frostwreths made a move against humans? Was that a wise thing for Queen Onn to do? It makes no tactical sense."

"It was not intentional. By building their fortress near a human settlement, the frostwreths accidentally stepped on something that bit them. Now King Kollanan asks for my assistance to deliver an even more destructive blow. He asked me to send some of our warriors to go help fight them." She looked at Quo with an earnest, sympathetic smile. "I promised him that I would. I want you to go, dear brother."

He rose quickly to his feet so he could look her in the eye. "I would be happy to shed frostwreth blood, but why should I fight for humans?"

"Fight against the *frostwreths*. And you will do it because I order it. Do not be as stubborn as the humans."

He lowered his head, showing deference.

"Gather a party of warriors—oh, twenty or thirty . . . whatever you think is sufficient. Ride north to the city of Fellstaff, join King Kollanan, and help him destroy the frostwreth fortress. I would be very pleased if you did that."

Grinning and eager, Quo kissed his sister's hand. "That would be my honor. We will let our enemies know that their time has come. The war begins now."

The queen pondered, and Quo could tell she was not yet finished. "That is only part of your task, dear brother. There is something else I need you to do. Something just as important." Voo's expression hardened, and Quo could feel the heat of anger rising from her. "The humans keep ignoring me. Konag Mandan still has not answered my summons. King Adan refused to bring his wife Penda here, despite my specific command to do so. Instead, he has hidden her away somewhere. I want to see her and her baby—it was a very generous invitation—but instead I have learned she has gone to their nomadic tribes. She will give birth soon."

Quo rubbed his hands together, barely able to contain his eagerness. "What do you want me to do?"

"Be alert when you ride through the hills. Extend your magic, scout the wilderness. Queen Penda Orr is out there somewhere, and she cannot be difficult to find." Her eyes blazed like molten copper.

Quo brushed off his legs. "We have taken many humans before—entire villages, crowded caravans—and I sent all of them to Ivun's camp."

"I do not want Penda Orr sent to a work camp! I want her here."

"And what do you intend to do with her?" Mage Axus asked. "I am curious."

Irritation flashed across the queen's face. "I want her and the child simply because King Adan thinks he can prevent me from having them."

40

THE orphan girl stood before smooth pools of vitrified stone like mirrors composed of midnight. Through her visions, Glik knew that the Plain of Black Glass had once been the site of a glorious wreth city, and she had seen its last days through her inner eye, when the wreths had unleashed enough uncontrollable magic to wipe out this entire valley.

As dawn light spread across the ruined terrain, the sandwreth guards led the workers into the dangerous broken area. Augas pulled carts filled with tools for excavating shadowglass. The augas walked cautiously across the black glass, their blunt heads bobbing as they sniffed crannies for rodents they could snatch up. But the Plain of Black Glass was dead, alive only with memories and magic.

"Work with great care!" shouted Mage Ivun. "The shadowglass is precious and powerful." When the dour man frowned, his brows pushed together like colliding folds of flesh.

Cheth looked down at her scuffed black boots, the remnants of her Brava uniform. "It is like walking on razors and sword blades."

"Take tools," grunted a guard, lifting axes, shovels, chisels, and hammers from one of the carts.

Glik received a short-handled pick. Cheth accepted a mallet with a pointed spike. The Brava squeezed the handle until her knuckles turned white, and Glik could tell she was considering how the implements could become weapons. Cheth could probably kill one or two of the wreths, but they would take her down. With his magic, Ivun could knock the entire work party flat . . . and then where would they run?

If Glik tried to race away, her feet would be shredded to ribbons. If she tripped and fell even once, she could slice herself open, like the dead Utauk prospector she had found. She might be free, but she would still be dead and would never go back to her greater Utauk family, not inside the circle, not outside the circle.

The workers spread out cautiously, picking their way. With a light foot-step, Glik hopped from one boulder to another, finding a path. The wind whistled like faint ancient screams from the cataclysmic battle that had oc-curred here. She felt the oppressive sunlight and the weighty haze of time. She said to her Brava companion, "Do you feel it? The blood? The agony and hatred? Shadowglass is the residue left by . . . so much pain and death that it can't even be measured." She drew a circle around her heart.

Cheth looked across the jumbled obsidian. "It seems like such a waste. They are all gone now—their memories, their hopes, their legacies. Humans and wreths."

Glik chose an ebony boulder and struck the smooth black surface with her pick. The shadowglass broke along broad fracture lines, and the tool thrummed in her hand as if recoiling from the magic. The black glass crum-bled into smaller pieces. Sharp finger-sized chunks could be made into arrowheads or spear points; larger flat sections could be affixed to shields.

She nicked her fingertips again and again on the glass edges, and some blood smeared the impenetrable surface. Not much, but she was already in a heightened state of awareness. *The beginning is the end is the beginning.* Mumbling the phrase, she fell into a fugue state, so that she no longer no-ticed the pounding sun, the dry air, the oppressive history that rippled like a mirage from the oily stone.

After a large sheet of shadowglass broke off along fracture lines, Glik peered into the fresh, exposed face of the main boulder. Blackness filled her view, and she was afraid she might fall inside. The rock seemed to be a bottomless pool, an empty window, pulling at her. Visions from history arose around her: the vast battlefield, advancing armies wheeling forward, mages building sorcerous weapons in the fortified city . . . crystals and cannons, gigantic lenses framed with runes. Glik vaguely understood that such machinery of magic had been developed as a means to attack Ossus, but instead the wreths had turned their unorthodox weapons against other wreths.

Glik felt echoes of defeat all around her as a silent thunder of images pounded in her head, tens of thousands of human soldiers forced by their wreth creators to march into battle against a commensurate sacrificial force dispatched by the opposing army.

When the wreths unleashed their magical weapons, obliterating each other, the residue penetrated deep into the world. Glik's eyelids fluttered closed, and she heard skas screaming high in the sky. At the end of that devastating ancient battle, Ossus must have stirred beneath his mountains before returning to a satisfied sleep.

Glik swayed and fell backward, nearly unconscious from the dark forces around her. The unyielding glass struck the back of her head, sending an explosion of dark stars through her vision. With a gasp, she forced her eyes open and lay looking up at the sky. Jumbled shadowglass debris was strewn around her.

Cheth leaned down and grasped her shoulders. "Be careful, girl! What happened to you?"

"Nothing compared to what happened *here*." Just whispering those words exhausted her. Cheth helped her back to her feet.

A wreth guard rode his auga closer, angry that Glik and Cheth had stopped working, but when a shout of pain replaced the clinking of tools, the guard rushed off.

One of the workers had accidentally cut a deep gash in his forearm. Blood spilled out, spattering across the black glass. Mage Ivun lurched forward, reaching the wounded man before the guards closed around him. The injured worker pressed down on the deep cut, trying to stop the flow. The wreths were not interested in treating the wound and let the humans take care of the problem. Cheth, familiar with battlefield surgery, obtained a strip of cloth and wrapped the gash in such a way as to hold the wound closed and stem the worst of the flow.

Ivun's attention, however, was on the puddled blood on the shadowglass. He bent down, tense with anticipation, yet jittery, as if the very idea terrified him. The spilled blood on black glass made the air crackle.

Glik sniffed the air and looked across the ominous landscape. The sensation reminded her of the moments right before a lightning strike.

The wreth mage reveled in it. He swirled the magic around himself and used his good hand to pull back the red leather sleeve of his robe, revealing his shrunken arm. He extended the claw and pressed the deformed limb against the blood on the shadowglass. "There is still magic in the world. Magic we can use!" Ivun drew a deep breath, pressed harder. The human blood on the glass mixed with the mage's leathery skin.

Glik watched his skin engorge with blood and moisture.

As the mage let out a long, rattling sigh, his arm straightened and the hand twisted at the wrist. Ivun flexed his gnarled fingers, bent his elbow, then stretched out his arm as it rejuvenated like a wilting flower given water.

Ivun raised his arm in triumph. His entire body seemed larger now, possibly due to confidence and relief. The bald mage looked at the work crews and shouted, "The magic is here, and it is ours! With this shadowglass we will make an invincible army." He smiled at the battered and bedraggled slaves. "You are blessed to be on our side."

41

Ancient history had never interested Klovus, but the captured Brava's story intrigued him. He had never paid attention to some unwelcome half-breed colony being wiped out by a godling, centuries ago. Obviously, though, Klea had fixated her life's passion on rectifying that injustice. Her hatred for Isharans was as intense as the sun reflected in a polished mirror, and he realized belatedly that understanding the enemy's resentment was as important as turning Isharan hatred against them.

Klovus wanted to know more, and as key priestlord, he had all the resources he might need. He sent a team of priest acolytes into the Serepol archives and museums and dispatched riders with his inquiry to the priestlords in all thirteen districts. "Find any records of a colony built by Bravas from the old world. A place they called Valaera. It will be mostly forgotten now."

He also called his Black Eels. "Monitor the search. No one has looked for Valaera in centuries, and I need to find it."

Zaha was calm, ready to hurl himself into whatever mission the key priestlord commanded. "Shall we kill anyone else who knows?"

Klovus frowned. "No, this isn't a strategic matter. I just . . . need to know. I want to see this place for myself."

He could not forget the defiance on Klea's face when she faced him. If her story was true, then that was why Bravas reviled the godlings. So long ago, the attacking entity would have been only a primordial form of the powerful godlings manifested by the faith of the early Isharan people. As he envisioned that violent night when the fledgling Brava colony had been torn apart, he smiled.

Priests, acolytes, and scholars ransacked old records, pored over faded texts, interpreted legends and folktales. Sooner than Klovus expected, the researchers consolidated fragments of information into a report, and the Black Eels verified the rough conclusions of his scholars.

"We confirmed it, Key Priestlord." Zaha's dark eyebrows drew together. "We found the site of Valaera."

೦౨

In the windswept hills of Khosun District, ten miles inland from the seacoast, lay the remnants of the Brava colony. The key priestlord rode on a sturdy horse accompanied by Black Eels disguised as guides wearing the fur-lined leather outfits common to Khosun.

For himself, Klovus wore a hooded cloak over a plain tunic and trousers, leaving behind his trappings of office. The horses moved across the dry grasses. No roads led out to this empty, forgotten place. Dark scrub oak dotted the shaded valleys, and tall thistles rose like thorny weapons that scratched Klovus's legs.

Zaha rode ahead as if he knew where he was going, though the priestlord could see no distinguishing landmarks on the terrain. This was a wild place. The hills all looked the same, and the population of this district was sparse enough that no settlers had claimed this land. He couldn't imagine why Brava pioneers would have chosen to build a home in this place after sailing across the ocean. He supposed even the bleakest part of Ishara must be a paradise in comparison with the drained old world.

Zaha pulled his horse to a halt on the side of a hill. "This is the place, Key Priestlord." He dismounted and stepped over to assist Klovus, who accepted the assassin's strong grip as he climbed out of the saddle and stood in the rustling grasses.

"How do you know?" Klovus saw nothing.

"If you look closely, you can see the lines. Some bricks, cut stone." He trudged ahead, his boots trampling the grasses. The key priestlord followed, and the other Black Eels fanned out, searching for artifacts in the weeds.

"Look here, it is more obvious," said one of the riders.

Now Klovus could distinguish a straight line, the crumbling remnants of what must have been a wall. "Yes, I can see it's artificial."

"This was once a large structure." Zaha paced off the line of stones, then turned at a corner when he found another part of a wall. "Our scouts searched the terrain. We think there were thirty or more buildings here."

"Thirty?" Klovus was surprised. "So Valaera was a significant village."

"They must have had livestock, pastureland. Crops would have extended through the hills and valleys there."

Klovus tried to imagine the extent. "Our people would not have been aware of the colony for some time. Even now, Khosun District has a sparse population. If the Brava settlement was self-sufficient, it might have taken a year or more before anyone even noticed the invasion."

As he walked through the grasses, Klovus stubbed his toe on a stone block that marked a building foundation. He stepped carefully around it. "It is a good thing they were stopped. The invaders would have brought their wreth bloodline to our pure land."

Zaha offered an opinion, which was unlike him. "One can understand why they came to our shores. Ishara was a pristine place, mostly uninhabited. They left their own poisoned lands to establish a foothold in a better place."

Klovus sniffed. "They meant to take advantage of the fresh magic and the powers here." He seized on a thought and knew he would repeat it often. "Now they intend to do it again! The godless Commonwealth envies our beautiful land. They want to leave their exhausted continent and take ours. That is why they're so aggressive."

Looking at the ghostly shadow of Valaera, he envisioned a once-thriving colony. "But they can't have it! We will tell our own tale of how the Bravas came to our shores without permission, that they meant to seize Ishara and build their own empire here." He nodded, liking the sound of his words. The foundation of his power was in reinforcing the external enemy, turning Isharan anger against the Commonwealth.

He had to do it without interference, so that the loyalty of the people was not confused.

"I see only dust and shadows—and I vow that is all there will ever be."

42

A LONELY silence was different from a merely empty one. Now that he had returned to Bannriya Castle from the desert, Adan saw the shadows differently, sensed the large spaces in his bedchamber, heard the echoing quiet in the corridors. With Penda gone, the castle had numerous associated noises and distractions. In their bedchamber, the wooden stand sat empty without the two skas that always accompanied her.

His uncle had departed for Norterra, but if Adan longed for noise and conversation, he could always go to the meeting chambers, the banquet hall, the throne room. His ministers, advisors, and vassal lords gathered and presented their reports on the training and defensive efforts around Suderra. But such talk was just words, without the warmth of his wife's company.

He also realized how much he missed Hale Orr's cheerful conversation and input at council meetings, trade discussions, and military planning sessions. With longing in his voice, Hale would often tell stories of his life among the Utauks.

Late at night after the people bedded down, Adan climbed to the observation deck to watch the stars. At least here he *expected* to be alone, so the solitude was less painful. He stood out in the dry, clear night, listening to the murmur of Bannriya, looking out at the winding streets, buildings constructed upon foundations that dated back to when the human survivors had founded this first city.

Adan looked up at the stars. He was the king of Suderra, but he was also a husband, and his wife was out there somewhere. Safe, he hoped. That made the loneliness only a little better.

He received word of the approaching procession, somber riders who moved from town to town having traveled all the way from Convera. Apparently, they were carrying part of his father's body, showing it off like some kind of prize.

With twisted tension, he summoned Captain Elcior and five Banner guards to ride out with him. "We need to intercept them before they reach the city. I'm not certain I want them in Bannriya, considering what I think they have. . . ."

The ache in his heart increased as his party galloped through the gates, dressed in leather and plate armor, bearing the banner of Suderra, a red flag on a yellow background. Once beyond the walls, he pushed the horse to a trot.

They intercepted the konag's procession five miles from Bannriya. Twenty soldiers in Commonwealth armor rode at a solemn pace, along with a middle-aged woman in brown legacier robes, two attendants from the Convera remembrance shrine, and a squire from the konag's court. A white horse walked sedately in the procession, his mane laced with ribbons of dark blue, his father's favorite color. Adan knew in the pit of his heart what the small gilded chest contained.

The procession ground to a halt, and the legacier straightened in her saddle. Adan remembered Legacier Naura from his younger years in the castle, when the tutors had made Mandan and him study the stories of prominent men and women from history.

Naura bowed. "King Adan Starfall, we are honored that you came to meet us. Our sergeant wanted to gallop forward each day, rushing to Bannriya, but I felt that the import of this procession warranted a slower pace, so that all people of the three kingdoms could pay their respects and feel the outrage of what was done to Conndur the Brave."

As he wrestled with his emotions, Adan wished Penda could be at his side. He and the queen should have received this painful relic together. He nudged his chestnut mount closer to the white horse so he could look at the gilded box. "They said that you are bearing a piece of my father's body . . . but that cannot be true." He hardened his voice. "Such disrespect could not possibly be shown by loyal soldiers of the Commonwealth or dedicated legaciers from the remembrance shrine."

Naura stiffened at the scolding. "Disrespect, Sire? It is the exact opposite! We share not only the fate, but the physical presence of the murdered konag. Words can say one thing, and tales can grow and change in the telling, but this—" She reached over and rested a hand on the small chest. "Physical reality cannot be denied. This is your father's hand. Konag Mandan has dispatched other processions bearing the sacred remnants of Conndur the Brave to all three kingdoms. Everyone must see."

The Commonwealth sergeant spoke through clenched teeth. "The Isharan animals did more than kill your father, King Adan. This was a blow to the entire Commonwealth!" He nearly spat the words. "Conndur was a wise man who came to them seeking peace, and they . . . they chopped him up!"

Legacier Naura spoke in a more soothing voice. "Everyone feels the pain of the wound, Sire. Everyone deserves to see this." She pointed toward the small chest.

At the fresh reminder of what had happened to his father, Adan felt the grief well up within him again. He tried to speak, but his voice caught. He drew a breath and remembered himself. "What exactly did you bring? And why?"

The legacier opened the chest to reveal gray skin and curled fingers, one of Conndur's severed hands. It could have been any discolored, mummified hand, but the signet ring with its aquamarine stone was distinctive. Adan fought back his disgust and horror. His father had touched his face with those fingers, had used that hand to write down observations of the stars. Tears welled in his eyes, and he turned away. "Close the lid. Mandan . . . my brother sent this to me?"

"Not to you, Sire!" said Naura. "To all the people of Suderra! Once we reach Bannriya Castle, our procession will end. We will display this in your remembrance shrine, or you can construct a special monument in the palace. Supplicants can ponder the hideous fate your father suffered at the hands of the Isharan monsters. You will hold the right hand of Conndur high, and you will call them all to war."

Adan balked. "War?"

The legacier gave him a questioning smile. "Yes. War against Ishara."

His stomach knotted. He was walking a razor's edge here, keeping the sandwreths at bay, diverting Queen Voo, who insisted on having the humans join her own war. The legacier and her companions did not understand, and his brother *refused* to understand.

"Your procession ends now," Adan said, his anger rising. "What would my father think to know that his body was portioned out and sent all over the Commonwealth so that people could gawk? He was Conndur the Brave! He fought in the Isharan war. He ruled the three kingdoms for twenty-eight years. He had a brother, Kollanan the Hammer, and two sons, Mandan and myself. He liked to observe the stars, because he wanted to understand the universe."

As the legacy recitation poured out of him, more details rose in Adan's memory. "He loved to hunt, or to sail a boat on the Joined River down to the sea. He created his own calendar to study the seasons, and he thought he understood them, at least a little. He—" Adan's voice caught again, but he pushed through. "He and I watched the skies together. He gave me the name Starfall, because of a shooting star we saw one night."

He turned to the legacier. "My father's tale is long and will fill many volumes. Historians must know the truthful details of Conndur the Brave. Your scribes are writing it down, are they not?"

"We are, Sire. Most of all, we have chronicled his terrible death and the treachery of the Isharans. Even with his many great works, the murder will be what the people remember most about your father. That is why these processions are so important. The people must see, and remember how he died."

The thought of waving around his father's dismembered hand to whip up hatred sickened Adan. He was working so hard to unify his people against the fearsome wreths. He did want revenge, and he wanted justice, but the last time he had seen his father alive, Adan had beseeched him for help against the wreth threat. . . .

Adan stared at the gilded chest. The lid remained open, the discolored hand curled on a bed of folded velvet. He swung down off his horse, took two steps closer, and slammed the lid shut. "They need to remember, but they do not need to see. I will keep my father's hand with the respect he deserved, but I will not let it become an object of morbid curiosity."

He didn't understand what his brother could be thinking. Why would Mandan send such sickening artifacts? Yes, the Commonwealth should properly remember their fallen konag, and Adan vowed that he would have his own legaciers, minstrels, and tale spinners build and preserve Conndur's legend.

After the eruption of Mount Vada, Conndur had been convinced of how dire the wreth threat was. He had gone to Fulcor Island on a mission, hoping to elicit Isharan aid against a common enemy. Empra Iluris, apparently, did not understand. Neither did Mandan, nor his Brava Utho. After what Kollanan had told Adan about Utho's treatment of Elliel, he didn't trust the man at all. The bonded Brava, who had instructed both princes in Convera Castle, had always seemed a man of monolithic honor, but his actions made Adan doubt everything he knew about him.

Now he turned to his Banner guards. "Captain Elcior, carry the chest with us back to the castle." Adan saw the startled look on Legacier Naura's face, but he waved her away. "Your procession is over. You may go home or come to Bannriya, where you'll be resupplied for your return journey, but you will not continue this abuse of my father's memory any longer."

Adan turned his horse around and rode off at an angry gallop, letting the others follow him. He had been lonely, but right now he wanted no company at all.

43

As Commonwealth warships gathered at the port of Rivermouth, ready to retake Fulcor Island, the young konag admired the graceful lines, the sturdy hulls, the copper sheeting that reinforced the prows. The ten ships were crowded with eager and angry soldiers, and the captains were ready to set sail.

But when it came time for Mandan to board, Utho saw him grow visibly uneasy. His face turned pale and sweaty, as if he already suffered from seasickness. In a low voice, he said, "I am not a battle commander, Utho. You should be the one to command them. You are my greatest general."

Although the konag was right, Utho could not allow that. "And you are the ruler of all three kingdoms, the heart of the Commonwealth. Your legacy is our legacy, and you must inspire your fighters." He added for specific effect, "It is something you can tell your Lady Lira, when she comes to prepare for the wedding."

The ship captains raised the open-hand flag of the Commonwealth and then the rising sun of Osterra. The sailors cheered, as did the Rivermouth spectators, from merchants to fishermen, shipwrights, and simple townspeople.

Instead of inspiring Mandan, though, the rousing enthusiasm seemed to intimidate the young konag. "But if I am to rule, shouldn't I be back in Convera Castle? That is our capital—"

Utho was annoyed by the reaction. "Don't ever let anyone hear you say such things!" He struggled for calm and patience. "You can speak anything to me, my konag, but others might hear your comments as cowardice."

At least Mandan had the decency to look offended. "But my grandfather sent his two younger sons to fight in the Isharan war, because his firstborn was too important to go off to battle."

"Yes, and Bolam stayed home and died of a fever, while Conndur and Kollanan returned." Utho placed a firm hand on the young man's shoulder.

"You will return as well. I'll protect you." He gestured to the ten warships, just part of what would become a breathtaking navy. "We will overwhelm Fulcor Island and throw out the invaders. From there, the garrison will be our base, from which we can launch our full-scale war against Ishara. This conquest will be a vital part of your legacy, and you must be there. We are creating history."

Mandan lowered his gaze, then drew a deep breath. Utho watched the young man fill himself with courage and import, as his mentor had taught him to do. Turning to his warships, the konag lifted his hand in an upraised fist. He shouted, "We are ready to launch! In a few days' time, our ships will reach Fulcor Island to avenge my father!"

A resounding battle cry roared back from the soldiers and crew on the ten ships. As if in a trance, Mandan fixed his gaze forward and strode to the end of the dock, where he boarded the flagship. The captain welcomed him, and the soldiers hammered sword hilts against their shields in a rhythmic beat that could be heard across the harbor.

Utho could tell Mandan was still frightened, but at least no one else saw it.

Within the hour, all ten warships departed from Rivermouth, heading out to open sea. The coastline dropped away, leaving only infinite green water around them. Mandan stood on deck, staring into the salty breezes. The young man confessed to Utho, "I want to be in my cabin, but it's confined and stuffy there. I get queasy."

"Better that the people see you out here, Sire, as the leader of your fleet."

Mandan grudgingly agreed. "Yes, they need to see me."

"It is one of your duties as ruler. You understand why you had to come."

He nodded again. "And you'll keep me safe."

"Yes, as I swore long ago."

Mandan squinted into the winds as if he could see a distant glimmer of the isolated island, though they were still two days away. "I can never forget what happened on Fulcor. My father—" His voice broke, and his expression collapsed.

Yes, Utho had been cruel to stage Conndur's death scene as he had, all the blood he had sprayed on the walls and ceiling, which everyone interpreted as the animalistic glee of Isharan butchers. That desecration had broken Mandan, but it also allowed Utho to rebuild him into the ruler that the Commonwealth, and history, needed.

"This time will be different, my konag," Utho promised. "This time we will not be surprised by Isharan treachery. We will drive them back out."

Mandan's voice had a raw edge. "But how is it possible that they captured

Fulcor from us? You left Klea there as watchman. We stationed plenty of soldiers in the garrison. We left three large guardian ships around the island."

"We thought our defenses were sufficient," Utho admitted, and the guilt dragged his heart down. "With their empra near death, the Isharans should have been in turmoil. We were wrong." He drew a long, slow breath and added, "I was wrong."

"They brought a godling." Mandan paled again. "What if it's still there? How will we fight a godling even with ten warships?"

"The monster will be gone. I'm certain of it."

"How can you be sure? It destroyed our ships and broke into the fortress. Why would it leave?"

"Because a godling weakens when it is away from its homeland. Remember, I fought one such creature in Mirrabay, and it had faded substantially by the time it finished its attack."

Not only had the battle been difficult for Utho, it had driven another Brava—Onder—away in mad panic. Utho controlled his shudder, not letting Mandan see the effect the encounter had had on him. "The godling will be gone, I assure you." His mouth went dry. "Klea undoubtedly put up a terrific fight, as did our three guardian ships. When the Isharans recaptured the fortress, there would have been much damage to the garrison defenses." Utho clenched the rail, willing the attack fleet to sail faster. His hand strayed to the warm gold cuff of his ramer. He wanted to cut and burn every one of the Isharan animals. "This is the time, my konag. Fulcor is vulnerable now."

დ

On the third day just after dawn, the Commonwealth fleet came within sight of the island. The sun rose on the eastern horizon, silhouetting the rocky bastion. The lookout shouted from the mainmast, and the soldiers crowded on deck, ready to fight. They cheered as they saw their target. Similar shouts echoed from the other nine vessels of the fleet. Flags ran up the masts.

Fulcor Island was just a barren rock, windswept and cold. Utho had served there during the previous war, doing his duty, even if it meant leaving his wife and daughters back in Mirrabay . . . to be slaughtered.

Mandan emerged from his cabin, still sleepy, but he had donned his circlet crown and purple cape of office. He wore a belt with a golden buckle around a loose tunic with the open hand embroidered on the right breast, the rising sun on the left. Utho was glad to see that the young man looked the part of a konag.

"I have wanted this for a very long time," Utho muttered. "We finally have a konag who understands our true enemy." He licked his lips, already tasting victory.

"I wish my father were here," Mandan said under his breath.

As the sun rose higher and the glare dissipated from the rippling waves, the lookouts sighted several Isharan ships anchored out beyond the reefs. Another patrol vessel came around from the eastern side of the island.

"Enemy vessels ahead!" called the lookout.

"I doubt there will be more than five," Utho reassured Mandan.

The young konag clenched his jaw. "We will crush them."

"More ships coming! I count seven . . . no, ten!"

"Ten?" Utho stepped back, reassessing. "We are evenly matched, but we will still win."

Then even more ships came around the island, all with red-and-white sails—fifteen at least. Utho didn't know how the enemy had brought in that many reinforcements so quickly. According to the Utauk traders, their empra was incapacitated! Who was leading them?

"We didn't count on facing fifteen ships." Mandan's voice trembled.

Utho fought back his rising dread. All of the enemy warships sailed toward them.

44

AFTER Thon and Elliel returned with King Kollanan, Shadri was eager to see her friends, and anxious to learn more about what they had brought back—a treasure of wreth history and legends that no human had ever seen before.

"I want to help," she said as she leaned her head through the half-open wooden door of the austere castle room Elliel shared with Thon. Breathless with excitement, Shadri pushed her long, somewhat tangled hair behind her shoulders. "I can be useful! I know it."

The Brava woman had dropped her pack of clothes and supplies on the stone floor and was rummaging among the travel garments, pulling them out. Thon had brought in a fresh set of blankets for their bed.

Elliel looked at her in surprise. "You want to help us unpack?"

Shadri looked around the sparsely furnished quarters, and her eyes lit on a rectangular leather-wrapped bundle lying on the table. She stepped into the room. "No, I mean the histories! Is that them? Thon, will you show me your language? Teach me the letters so I can help you translate?"

Thon smiled. "There is much to review. I could use the assistance of a scholar girl." He moved the leather covering aside. The crystal sheets seemed thin and delicate, almost invisible except for the letters etched in several layers, somehow melded onto one another. "So much to peruse and absorb. I do not believe Queen Voo has read them in her lifetime."

Shadri thought of what happened when she pestered others with too many questions. "Some people do not place much importance on learning."

Elliel hung her black traveling cloak and finemail cape on a peg in the wall. "Thon has had enough adventuring for the time being. Now it is time for learning." She leaned close to kiss him on the cheek. "Meanwhile, I have some Brava duties to attend to!"

Shadri considered taking the crystalline histories down to the remembrance shrine so all the legaciers could pore over the records as well, but none of them could read the wreth language either. Instead, she decided the king's library was a perfect place for her to review the materials with Thon, side by side.

Pokle had built a nice fire in the hearth and the room was warm. After Thon set the bundle on the long wooden table, Shadri reverently opened it and picked up the first sheet of thin glassy material. She turned it to the light so the fireplace flames shone through and illuminated the letters. But there was so much more sealed inside the sandwiched crystal.

Thon reached for the sheet. "Wreth blood is required to activate the letters." He removed the dagger at his side and held up his hand. "For the sake of acquiring knowledge, I am happy to prick my thumb." He jabbed himself with the point and let a drop of deep red blood well up. He touched his thumb to the transparent surface. When the firelight reflected through the sheets, letters sprang from the document and into the air, shimmering there. "It is a place to start—so much information, so many stories."

"Read them to me, and I will record every word," Shadri said. She worked in this room often, and she already had a stack of loose, clean paper that Queen Tafira provided for her writing.

Blinking nervously, Pokle arrived at the library with a platter of bread and cheese for them to eat. Shadri and Thon were too busy copying down the words to be interrupted, so the shaggy-haired young man set the platter on the table near them. On his way out, he hovered in the doorway until Shadri looked up and smiled at him. Then, blushing, Pokle scurried away.

She was ready to work long into the night, although it would take days, even weeks, to go through the hundreds of crystal sheets. Shadri marveled at the fresh stories of ancient wreth battles, sandwreth victories, frostwreth treacheries. Thon read legends of the famed warrior Rao, a great commander who had challenged and wounded the dragon Ossus himself. Some documents were screeds against the frostwreth race, the evil descendants of Suth, and how no one would ever forget the horrible crime they had inflicted upon innocent, pregnant Raan, the true beloved of Kur.

As Thon continued to read the hovering letters, Shadri connected a few of the wreth symbols to certain words. While transcribing, Shadri took special care to note the actual wreth symbol for the name of the god. . . .

The following day, while Thon practiced his swordplay with Elliel and helped train the Fellstaff fighters, Shadri continued to sort through the crystalline sheets. She scanned the strange markings she could see, holding them up to the watery sunlight that shone through the windows. She pulled out any documents that seemed to mention Kur, because those might be relevant to the mystery of Thon's existence. She found five more sheets with multiple instances of the god symbol, including one strange artifact with crumbled edges and a yellowish tinge.

When Thon returned to the library chamber that evening, Shadri was excited to show him the exceptional crystal page. "This discolored one looks older than the others, don't you think? Or maybe made of a different material? It must be something special, right?" She pointed down at the etched markings. "Look at the symbol. It mentions Kur over and over again. I wonder what it means."

Thon held it up curiously. "I do not know. Shall we see what it says?" He pricked his thumb again and illuminated the letters with flowing blood. The dark wreth stepped back, reciting the displayed text while Shadri began writing. A strange expression crossed the wreth man's face and he hesitated.

Shadri waited. "What is it? Is it about Kur? Stories of what happened to him? Are there any hints about you?"

Thon read silently for a time until he finally looked at her and explained. "This is an ancient story about Kur and two loves, Suth and Raan. Out of jealousy, Suth poisoned her own sister and made her lose the baby, Kur's baby." His deep sapphire eyes were filled with shock. "But in this version of the story, Kur was heartbroken to the point of despair at what his creations had done. He realized that all of the evil in the world had not been contained within the dragon Ossus. Evil had poisoned the wreths as well."

Thon turned the yellowed crystalline sheet from side to side. The shimmering letters flickered in the air. "This says that in hopeless anguish, Kur withdrew from the wreths." Thon tilted his head, staring at the symbols hanging in the air. "It says Kur worked without rest for one hundred days and one hundred nights to create a magic of forgetting. All he needed was one drop of the blood of Ossus to work the magic. It is said that Suth saw him descend into the mountains to find Ossus, and Kur was never seen again."

Thon set the crystalline sheet down, obviously shaken. "But this record is from an ancient archive. An annotation indicates that it is considered a legend, not true history. But I wonder." He touched the tattoo on his face, then looked up with sudden determination. "Is it possible that the frostwreths know more?"

෨෨

Glad to be back home in his comfortable hall, Kollanan worked his dagger against a block of soft pine, flicking away curls of wood to carve a small figure. He had always told his grandsons that he was merely freeing the toy trapped inside. His sharp blade paused for a moment, stalled by the weight of memory, then he flicked the knife again. He hardly noticed his sore fingers.

Tafira sat near him in a chair before the fire. As he whittled, he told her everything that had happened out in the deep desert, emphasizing that he did
not trust Queen Voo for a moment. "Still, I would be happy if they fought
the frostwreths for us."

He carved wooden arms, sketched lines of armor, and held up a crude
figure of a wreth warrior. He admired his handiwork, wishing he could have
presented the toy to the boys, but Tomko was dead, and Birch a captive. Kollanan tossed the figure into the fire, where the flames blackened it, just as the
funeral pyre had consumed Conndur's hand.

When Tafira spoke, the heaviness in her voice told him she had been
wrestling with her thoughts for some time. "Beloved, I know that my presence makes some of our people uneasy. Do you think I should leave, stay in
a forest lodge in an isolated county? Lord Ogno has extended an invitation.
Shadri could accompany me."

Taken aback, Koll paused as he began carving a new chunk of wood. "I
just came home! I need you with me, especially in these times."

"This Isharan war changes things. I fear that I distract them."

"You certainly distract *me*," he said, trying to make light of her comment,
"and still I'm a good king." With the knife tip, he fashioned one of the shaggy
white creatures the frostwreths rode. "I need you here, my love, and I have
needed you for thirty years. Have faith that the people of Norterra know you
have nothing to do with some evil assassin who killed my brother on the
other side of the world. What would I do without you?"

"I sense resentment from Captain Rondo. We should let him ride back to
Convera. His mission is finished here."

Koll looked up. "He is a well-trained soldier of the Commonwealth and he
will follow orders. Now that I know sandwreth reinforcements are coming, I
want Rondo here for the strike on the Lake Bakal fortress."

Tafira's brow furrowed. "They are soldiers, yes, but only twenty men. Is it
really that significant?"

"Yes, but in a different way. Konag Mandan has been dismissive of the
wreths, primarily because Utho has his eyes set on Ishara and is blind to any
other threats. That is why I intend for Captain Rondo and his men to join us
in the attack. They will see the frostwreth threat for themselves. Then when
I send them back, maybe they will convince Mandan."

Tafira let the matter drop, although her troubled expression told him the
discussion was not over. In deep silence he finished carving the wolf-steed,
then tossed it into the fire as well.

Thon and his two Brava companions walked into the great hall, and

Kollanan could tell at a glance that they had hatched some sort of scheme. Elliel and Lasis wore their black uniforms, freshly laundered, boots polished, as if they were presenting themselves for a formal review. Lasis had his jerkin open at the throat, as if to display the scar where Queen Onn had slashed his neck.

"We have a suggestion, Sire," Lasis announced. "Something you should consider."

Koll set down his knife and brushed wood shavings from his lap.

Elliel said, "There is a chance to save your grandson."

Koll and Tafira sat up straight, giving all their attention.

Lasis got right to the point, as he always did. "When the sandwreth reinforcements arrive, we plan to attack Lake Bakal. Once we do that, it will be open war, and too late for a different strategy. If Birch is a hostage in Queen Onn's palace, I fear his life may be forfeit."

Elliel stepped close to Thon. "Before that happens, Thon and I propose riding north to the frostwreth palace. Queen Onn believes Lasis is dead, but she does not know either of us."

Kollanan stroked his beard. "You expect to sneak inside the frostwreth palace?"

Thon chuckled. "Oh, not sneak inside. We will go to the main entrance and ask to see the queen. I am unlike any wreth Onn has ever seen. Remember how Queen Voo reacted when she saw me?" His bright expression belied the seriousness of the situation. "I have my own goal, and that is how we will get inside the palace. Voo and the sandwreths gave me excellent historical information, and the scholar girl and I have discovered alarming information in those records. It is now imperative that I also review the frostwreth records. I . . . it is possible that I am Kur."

"You considered that before." Koll didn't know what else to say. "You think the frostwreth histories have more information?"

"I must know."

Tafira's brows drew together. "You believe Queen Voo will simply let you in?"

Elliel gestured toward the dark wreth. "Look at him. They will be intrigued, especially if he demonstrates a bit of his power."

"But how will this help Birch?" Kollanan asked.

Lasis said, "While they are inside the frostwreth palace under those pretenses, they can try to find the boy."

"Not pretenses," Thon said, "not at all. I am sincere in my quest to obtain the frostwreth histories."

Elliel crossed her arms over her chest. "It could be our best chance, Sire. We can at least learn about your grandson, perhaps rescue him."

Lasis stroked the scar on his throat. "Queen Onn would recognize me, so I will stay here to guard you, Sire. Elliel and Thon are capable of facing the frostwreths by themselves."

Koll laughed, but the Brava was not joking. Elliel said, "We will learn what we can about Thon, and look for a way to rescue Birch."

"I can keep us safe. I have powers that might gain the queen's respect, or at least her attention." Thon cocked his eyebrow. "Perhaps I can persuade her to release the boy."

"We can be very persuasive," Elliel said. "If nothing else, we may see what war preparations she is making and how soon she might send her armies down to attack Norterra."

"Birch." Kollanan looked at his wife, and Tafira's dark eyes were filled with hope.

"If there's a chance . . ." she said in a husky whisper.

"If there's a chance . . ." Koll said. "Ancestors' blood, go then! Ride together and see what you can do. Once Quo and the sandwreths arrive, everything changes." He turned his knife from side to side so that the firelight licked the blade. He looked at Lasis. "Meanwhile, old friend, you and I will set off on another mission."

45

A FTER she awoke from spellsleep, Koru felt energized to be wearing full armor again. Polished blue and silver plates fit perfectly over her breasts, covered her midriff, spread sharp edges across her shoulders. Her bone-white hair was bound with a thin silver chain. With a gauntleted hand, she rested her crystal-tipped spear of command on her shoulder. Obsidian knives hung at her waist, along with a razor-edged cutter disk that she could hurl and ricochet across the ice to strike down her targets.

Bright sunlight washed over the snow as she watched the continuing war preparations. The frigid air blowing across the tundra braced her exposed skin. She stared into the sharp spray of ice grains, without blinking.

Oonuks bounded across the uneven snow, claws digging into the frozen ground. Their shaggy pelts made each creature look like a coiled blizzard. Studded muzzles wrapped their jaws shut so they did not rip one other apart. It was wasteful to mangle the wolf-steeds during practice. There was enough other blood to spill.

Irri, her mother's new favorite warrior, rode in a plated battle sleigh drawn by two oonuks. He wore a helmet and carried a shield, but left his arms bare to display his bulging muscles. Koru doubted their enemies would swoon with desire from looking at his physique.

She herself was not devoid of desires, but she was not like her mother, who allowed those passions to dominate her, making her capricious instead of tactical. Koru preferred to look at their larger destiny, not follow transient impulses.

Since awakening, Koru had studied the frostwreth armies, taken inventory of their weapons, interviewed the warriors already awake and prepared, and counted those who remained frozen in spellsleep, waiting to be awakened. She was dismayed at how many had mysteriously died in their ice chambers.

Queen Onn seemed to have no plan whatsoever for the coming war. Given the size of her fighting force, she simply assumed they would overwhelm the sandwreths. This lack of planning exasperated Koru. Did her mother have any reconnaissance or intelligence on the enemy sandwreths? Any information at all?

Had she given a moment's thought to their real mission from Kur—to destroy Ossus? At times Koru felt she was the only one who genuinely remembered what wreths were meant to do.

She had studied the written chronicles of wreth history, including their military losses at the end of the great wars. Countless casualties on countless battlefields. Queen Onn chose to ignore those poignant lessons because they were uncomfortable. Koru was satisfied with the potential of her race, and she would make certain her mother didn't let victory melt through her fingers.

Without asking permission, she began to organize the warriors into a true fighting force. Her people were not weak, they were disorganized, and she could fix that. Previously, for their own amusement, frostwreths had challenged each other to test their weapons, engaging in mock hand-to-hand battles. But that was only preparation for winning a duel, not a war. They needed military practice on a grand scale.

Now, full regiments of warriors lined up on the ice and charged forward, led by Irri and other noble commanders in armored sleighs. The oonuks growled and snarled, and the winds blew with the sounds of victory.

Separate from the marching armies, a dozen mages invoked their powers, calling tendrils of magic from deep within the ice. A spiderweb of cracks shot through the glacier. As steam gasped forth, the cracks melted and fused like a scab forming on a wound. The blizzard wall near the palace shifted, a vanguard of howling winds.

Koru felt a deep hatred for sandwreths, yes, but destroying *Ossus* was their reason for existence. Her ancestor Dar had even fought the dragon with her deadly spear. Wounded, Ossus had crawled deep beneath the world. Dar's spear still hung above the queen's throne, and Koru wondered if her mother even remembered the story.

She watched the battle exercises for a while longer, then returned to the frozen palace, where she would engage in another battle—with her mother.

ॐ

Birch remained quiet at the base of Queen Onn's throne. That morning she had summoned him again, claimed to adore him, asked where he had been. He told Onn what she wanted to hear, because it was the only way to keep himself safe. "I have been learning. The drones showed me the palace."

The queen seemed satisfied. "You must be glad to be freed from your bleak existence in that human town."

Sadness and anger tangled in his throat. "That was my home. And my family . . ."

Onn lounged back. "Family is deadly. I told you how Raan tried to destroy her own sister Suth. I think of my hideous cousin Voo, who did this to me during our last battle." She traced a sharpened nail across the long scar on her cheek. "I will make certain she pays a thousandfold for that, and every one of her inferior followers will die."

Not caring about the interruption, Koru entered the throne room, striding across the polished ice floor. She showed little deference to the queen. "Our armies are impressive and strong, Mother. I am overseeing their training."

"I am glad you have taken an interest in our great war."

"Someone needed to," Koru said with biting sarcasm.

Birch pulled his new blanket around him and shrank back as he listened. Koru ignored the huddled boy and kept her pale gaze fixed on Onn. "I do not know if we will be strong enough to complete the mission Kur gave us. We must plan carefully, for our true enemy is powerful."

The queen's eyes sparkled. "I have no doubt Queen Voo means to attack us soon. We need to eradicate our enemy as soon as possible."

Annoyed, Koru gestured to the wall behind the throne, where the broken spear hung, stained with rusty dragon's blood. "I am not speaking of sand-wreths! Our true enemy is Ossus, the dragon at the heart of the world. How will you channel our race to wake the dragon and then slay it? Will you use Dar's spear?"

Onn scowled at the challenge. "The dragon will wait. We must clear the land first, wipe out the sandwreths. We cannot let them taint Kur's perfect world."

"That is not the mission we were given," Koru retorted. "*Ossus* is the man-ifestation of all evil: jealousy, hatred, violence. Destroying the dragon is our true goal. You allow yourself to be distracted."

"Ridding the world of our rivals is not a distraction," Onn scoffed. "I think the long spellsleep damaged your heart and mind."

Koru shifted in her gleaming armor. "All of us were made in Kur's image. When he vanished from the world, he left clear commands that wreths— not one faction or the other, but *all wreths*—were to slay Ossus. Do you not believe the dragon is a greater imperative? Would it not be a better plan for our entire race to fight the common enemy? Even if we all face him together, Ossus may still destroy us."

The queen leaned forward in her frozen throne. "You would let the sand-wreths share paradise with us? You are a fool, Daughter."

Koru struggled with impatience. "It would be wiser simply to slay the sandwreth leaders, kill their corrupt queen and anyone who issues unwise commands. Then we could unify the wreths and prepare for the real battle." Her voice increased in urgency. "Ossus is stirring, and the mountains are cracking. If the dragon wakes before we are ready to fight him, we are all doomed!" She looked at the spear behind the throne. "What is that weapon for if you don't intend to follow the wishes of Kur?"

Onn heaved a great sigh, eager to dismiss her persistent daughter. "I can tell you have thought much about this. You are dedicated, passionate." She tapped her fingernail on the side of the throne and appeared to be considering. She spoke as if the idea had just occurred to her, but Birch thought she might be simply giving Koru something to do, and to get her out of the palace. "We need to learn more about the dragon. Take a war party, as many warriors as you like, even a mage or two, and go to the Dragonspine Mountains. Discover what you can about Ossus and how much time we might have left." She chuckled. "In fact, if the dragon emerges while you are there, this could be your chance to kill him. That would solve our problem once and for all."

Koru flared her nostrils, but she seemed pleased with the command. "I accept the mission, Mother. We need to know. I will ride and find the dragon."

46

THE empra's condition had not changed. Every day seemed the same in the high palace tower, and Cemi felt as if she were teetering on a precipice, waiting for Iluris to awaken, or to die . . . or for Key Priestlord Klovus to make his move. He seemed to have forgotten about them, though large crowds still gathered in the fountain square below, pouring their hopes into the empra's well-being.

Klovus had taken credit for the Isharan navy recapturing Fulcor Island, and he controlled the Serepol godling. He had publicly demonstrated his might by using it to build part of the Magnifica temple.

All the while, Iluris remained asleep and silent. All day, every day, they heard her subjects praying for Empra Iluris. This land loved her. What would happen if Cemi came forth and spoke on the empra's behalf? Who would listen to a girl from the streets, barely sixteen? Especially if the key priestlord tried to silence her?

"Hear us, save us," she muttered.

Analera came to deliver their food daily, sometimes accompanied by other trustworthy servants. Hawk guards were stationed in the corridor outside the tower chambers, while Vos and three others remained in the room. Like a caged animal, Cemi often went to stand by the open windows, staring out at the vast city and looking down on the worried subjects. So much faith out there, so much energy. Maybe the people would listen to her after all. . . .

Though she loved the woman who had rescued her from the streets and trained her in politics and leadership, Cemi longed for unfettered times when she could do what she liked, run at will, see people and places, even flee from angry shopkeepers after she had stolen a meal. Now, during these long days in the tower, she wondered if she would ever leave this room.

At lunchtime a trio of servants carried trays of bread, fruits, and smoked fish as well as hot broth for the empra. Cemi recognized an older manservant named Frenik, a man whom Analera had introduced, accompanied by two new barrel-chested servants with downcast eyes.

"Has her condition changed?" Frenik asked in a whisper. When Cemi shook her head, the old man gave her a comforting nod. "And how about you, dear girl? You look pale and thin."

Captani Vos blocked the two other servants from entering the chamber. "And who are these? I don't recognize their faces."

"They work in the kitchens, Captani," Frenik said. "I'm familiar with them, as is Analera."

"I do not know them," said Vos. He straightened the red cape on his left shoulder and stepped forward to face the newcomers. "What have you to say for yourselves?"

One of the barrel-chested servants held a heavy, steaming pot balanced on a metal tray. "We get interrogated in order to bring soup?"

Cemi caught her breath, noting a dark hardness about the man that did not belong on a meek servant. Instantly alert, she said, "Vos, he's—"

The servant moved with sudden slipperiness and threw the steaming soup onto Vos's face and chest. As the captani recoiled, the servant dropped the pot and swept the metal tray sideways like an ax blade. Frenik turned, confused by what was happening, and the tray slashed his throat. The old man barely had time to flail his hands before he collapsed, spurting blood.

The second new servant also used his tray as a weapon, smashing it into the face of a hawk guard who sprang in to defend the empra. The guard went down with his face caved in.

The first servant careened toward Cemi, who sprang backward and stumbled just as the man whipped a knife from his gray robes and slashed the air where she had been an instant before.

Scalded by the hot broth, Captani Vos lurched toward the commotion, trying to see. "Cemi!" He collided with the attacking guard. A slash from the dagger caught Vos in the chest, ringing against the golden armor scales.

Cemi hit the floor and rolled. As a young girl, she had survived street fights. She dove under the bed and slithered to the far side, where she emerged. The attacker lunged after her.

Hawk guards rushed in from the hall to defend the empra, and Cemi saw the two barrel-chested servants shift their features until they were no longer bland, weary-looking underlings. Now their features had a hard predatory cast, and their dark eyes narrowed with intense focus. Each assassin held two knives as they prowled in for the kill.

Iluris lay still on the bed, as if waiting to be cut to pieces.

Cemi flung a pillow at the nearest attacker. He slashed at it, spilling a blizzard of down feathers. She heard more shouts from the corridor and realized that the palace guard escort had turned on the loyal hawk guards. The clash of blades sounded like the clamor of a blacksmith's shop. She heard screams of pain, grunts, collapsing bodies—but she couldn't worry about the battle in the corridor. She had to survive here, save the empra.

Vos swiped a hand across his scalded face, blinking, defending himself as best he could even though he was still trying to see. Cemi shouted his name, and he spun toward the sound of her voice just as the attacker lunged at her. The captani swung his sword against the man's arm, but his blade rang off the surface, as if the skin had turned to stone.

The fight grew louder out in the corridor, but inside the empra's chamber the hawk guards fell back toward the bed as a last line of defense. Then another group of attackers burst in from the corridor. The four palace guards who had escorted Frenik and the traitorous servants each wore a different appearance now, with murder in their eyes.

Scrambling for a weapon of her own, Cemi retrieved one of the metal platters and held it up as a shield, swinging it to deflect a knife blow. She couldn't believe such a plot had come together so smoothly, and she didn't have to guess who had ordered it.

She stayed at the empra's side, ready to die to protect her. Now that Vos could partially see again, he swung his sword in a vicious side stroke, but the blade's tip whistled through empty air as the nimble assassin sprang back. Two more hawk guards died defending the doorway from attackers.

Cemi held up her metal tray, and Vos planted his boots on the other side of the empra's bed. Five deadly assassins pushed into the chamber while combat continued out in the hall.

With such a loud clamor, surely others would come to help the empra! Priestlord Klovus could not have the entire palace under his thumb. The killers stormed toward her with their long blades, and she had only a metal tray to defend herself and save Iluris.

She knew she was going to die. The empra would be slain in bed, her death explained away that she had finally succumbed to her head injury. Priestlord Klovus would take over and rule Ishara, blaming the Commonwealth for her death. Cemi was sickened to think that such traitors might ever win. She could not allow it!

Empra Iluris *was* Ishara. She was the heart of the land. Even in the midst of battle, she looked so peaceful on her pillow, so vulnerable, her eyes closed, the lids just a delicate veil of skin.

Cemi's burgeoning anger overpowered her fear, and she forgot about her own life. "You will not have her!"

The assassins were not intimidated by a scrawny girl. They looked like hyenas ready to fall upon a wounded antelope.

But as they pressed closer, Cemi sensed a ripple in the air, a shimmer around the empra's bed. Without understanding it, she felt her heart uplifted, filled with a strength beyond anything she had experienced before. The air itself became thick, like flowing water.

A barely seen force flung out and drove back an assassin's blade with such force that it snapped the man's wrist. He staggered away gaping at his bent forearm as the sword clattered to the floor.

With a swelling lurch, the invisible thing pushed forward. Another assassin hurled himself at Cemi and Iluris, only to be snatched in midstride, lifted into the air by unseen hands, and then hammered up into the stone ceiling—smashed again and again, then dropped, until his body sprawled broken on the floor.

Vos shouted, "What is that?" The other hawk guards stared.

"An ally." Cemi didn't care. "It fights with us."

The hawk guards redoubled their efforts against the assassins, but the invisible force was now on a rampage. Cemi felt a breath of cold wind followed by a warm tingle. This entity was on their side, she knew it. It was guarding Iluris.

As the unknown thing attacked, the assassins cried out in alarm. They rallied, standing in a fighting unit, but the entity grabbed them and smashed them together. Bones crunched, blood sprayed.

"It's like a godling!" Cemi said, but this was unlike any godling she had seen. At the moment, she didn't dare question.

Taking advantage of the unexpected diversion, Vos swung his sword and decapitated a distracted assassin.

The melee continued out in the corridor, where several more defenders had fallen. The strange presence gushed out into the hall, looping around and avoiding the hawk guards, selectively seizing the assassins, and popping their heads like ripe grapes.

Before long, the astonished attackers all lay dead. The rippling presence faded, went quiescent. Cemi couldn't tell if it was still there.

Vos looked down at the unconscious Iluris in disbelief, then up at Cemi. "She's safe . . . and you're alive."

"We have a reprieve." She began to move, wrapping sheets around Iluris. If they had a chance to get away . . . "The traitor must be Klovus, but I doubt we could prove it. I didn't think he would be so bold. How will he cover this up?"

"He meant to kill all of us," Vos said. "No witnesses. Then he could spin the reason any way he wished."

"I don't intend to give him that pleasure." Cemi grabbed up the sheets. "We have to move her somewhere that even the priestlord can't find her. How many people in the palace are under his thumb?"

The surviving hawk guards came in from the corridor. Many were wounded, some bleeding badly. Vos took charge. "If the empra is not safe in her own quarters, where can we take her? Is there some place to hide her in the city?"

Bedraggled and in shock, old Analera hurried up from the side stairs in the main hall, accompanied by two familiar servants.

Vos tried to block them, his face ruddy with anger. "The servants betrayed us. They let the assassins in."

Analera shook her head as she looked in horror down at murdered Frenik. "How did this happen?"

"Frenik," Cemi said, "but he was tricked. The manservants with him . . . shifted their features. I think they replaced other trusted servants. Maybe it was some magic from the key priestlord."

"How can we be sure that you are not also imposters?" Vos glowered at Analera.

"You need us," the old woman said. "We love the empra, and I can hide you. There are many passageways beneath the palace, and secret storage rooms used only by servants for countless generations. If we take the empra down the back stairs, we can hide her."

Another shaken servant spoke up. "We would die before letting anyone else harm her!"

Vos grunted, dubious. "Many have died already, including a lot of my men." He struggled to remain calm in spite of the slaughter around him.

Cemi turned slowly in the chamber, searching. She stretched out her fingers and tried to drink in the remaining tingle in the air, to see if their strange benefactor was still there, but the invisible force seemed to have vanished. She looked at the captani, speaking like a leader . . . as Iluris had taught her to do. "We need to move quickly, and we don't have any other obvious choice."

Vos barked orders to the remaining hawk guards to follow Analera. He went to the bed himself, bent over, and, despite his exhaustion from the battle, picked up the frail, motionless empra and held her in his arms as if she were no more than a sleeping child. "You're right. We have to get to a safe place, and if Analera knows one, we'll have to trust her." Others would soon respond to the ruckus, and some of them might well be assassins, too.

For a bent and weary old woman, Analera moved swiftly, rushing ahead. "Come, the back stairs are narrow and dim, but they are safe. Only servants who have worked here a long time use them."

"Careful with her," Cemi said.

Vos walked behind her, showing no effort with his burden as they rushed after the loyal old servant. "I will be as gentle as possible."

Analera and her companions hurried the group along. As they left the empra's spacious chambers, Cemi saw many bodies in the hall, dead hawk guards and smashed assassins. It gave her grim satisfaction to see the carnage inflicted by their unseen protector.

Cemi remembered the horrifying night on Fulcor Island when they had rushed the bleeding empra through the rainstorm. The situation now was just as dire. She sensed the shimmering entity somewhere near, though she could no longer see it.

As the group hurried to the stairs, picking their way around the blood and bodies, they kept their voices hushed. Two of the hawk guards were wounded, looking with dismay at the telltale spatters of blood they left on the floor. Vos called them to a halt, adjusting the limp woman in his arms, and spoke to the man. "Bind your wounds so you do not leave a trail."

One of the guards touched a deep cut on his leg. "We might slow you down, Captani, but we can still fight. If assassins pursue, we will stay here and stop them from following you."

"They can't pursue us if they don't know where we're going," Cemi said. "That is the best solution." She counted them, dismayed to see that only seven hawk guards remained. "The empra needs all the protectors she can get. Enough have died today. We can't lose any more."

Analera opened an unobtrusive doorway that descended into a dim stairway lit by widely spaced torches. The steps were slick with moss and shadows. Cemi followed close behind Vos, looking with concern at her unconscious mentor's face.

The servants led them down and down through the tower, past landings that opened to different floors. In the huge palace, Cemi did not understand the complexity of the interior spaces. When the walls became solid stone, bedrock instead of blocks, she assumed they had gone beneath the surface. The air felt moister, colder.

"There are many choices down here," said Analera. "I know a good empty storage chamber. No one has been there in ages, and we can cover the door-way. No one will think to look."

With a brush of air that raised gooseflesh, Cemi felt the strange presence manifest again, like a brisk wind that blew along with them. She felt a warm confidence. Of all the things she had to fear, this was not one of them. No one else seemed to notice the flitting, hovering presence.

The old servant paused in front of a large, open chamber hollowed out of the rock. It was dusty and dim inside, adorned with cobwebs, holding a few old crates of long-unused supplies, some pieces of broken furniture. Analera spoke in a whisper. "We can bring you cots and blankets, food and water. This is a good place to hide."

One of the wounded hawk guards entered the chamber first, prepared to sacrifice himself in case this was a trap. When he signaled that the room was safe and empty, Vos hurried the empra inside and, after one of the guards threw his cloak on the floor, set her gently down. He rapped his knuckles against the stone. "Solid walls. The seven of us can defend this room, at least for a time." His face was an angry red from the broth that had scalded him.

"Eight of us," Cemi said, counting herself.

Suddenly, the air thickened again, and shimmering ripples flowed around the stone walls and darted over Empra Iluris, as if to make sure she was unharmed. As Cemi watched, the force flowed toward the opening of the chamber and rose up like a sheet of water, blurring their view of the corri-dor outside, and then became more opaque. The entity shifted its physical structure until it assumed the appearance of solid stone—the same color and texture as the corridor wall.

Analera was stunned to see the opening vanish. "Are we trapped?" She pressed the new stone wall that hid the exit. Her hand passed directly through. It was just an illusion!

Cemi tested it herself. Somehow, the empra's mysterious protector, the invisible deity or godling . . . or whatever it was, had created a perfect cam-ouflage. *What else can it do?*

"I don't understand what this thing is," Cemi said, feeling herself start to relax, "but at least I feel safe."

47

With painstaking slowness, the opposing warships drew together around Fulcor Island, held back by the vagaries of winds and currents. Utho watched the inexorable clash with intense interest. For now, the shine was in Mandan's eyes. The young konag had at first seemed terrified of the naval battle, then fascinated, and now he was just impatient. This was clearly not what he had expected a great clash to be like.

The ten Commonwealth vessels were armed to the teeth and full of vengeful soldiers. Their raucous challenges boomed across the water, dispersed by the wind and drowned out by the crashing waves. Utho, though, felt no need to respond.

The distinctive Isharan warships proceeded toward them, seventeen intimidating vessels by Utho's count. As the conquerors of Fulcor, they patrolled the vicinity of the island, a much larger navy than Konag Conndur had ever maintained here. Instead, Conndur had invited the empra there to chat about an alliance. . . .

"What is taking so long?" Mandan leaned over the rail, his eyes bright. The breezes had made a mess of his brown hair, but he didn't seem to care. "I want to smash them so we can take Fulcor back."

Utho explained: "Maneuvering ships on the ocean is not like a cavalry charge, my konag. War at sea is slow and strategic. We can only move where the winds take us, but a masterful captain knows how to work the sails and rigging. Our forces will collide soon enough, have no fear." He squeezed the young man's arm, hesitated, then squeezed harder. "Have no fear."

He could only imagine how Mandan would react in the thick of battle with clashing swords and burning sails, murderous Isharans trying to hack him to pieces. He warned, "Hand-to-hand fighting on deck requires more involvement than watching helpless prisoners being tortured to death. But I will protect you. That is my vow as a Brava and as your friend. My loyalty is to the konag of the Commonwealth. I serve you."

The young man glanced at him with haunted eyes. "Did you not also make my father the same promise? That you would protect him? Why was he not safe with you?"

Utho thought of the shocked look on Conndur's face as the realization slowly dawned that his own bonded Brava intended to murder him.

"Your father . . . gave me another mission." He looked hard into Mandan's eyes. "Be assured that I *will* safeguard the konag. That is my vow. A Brava vow."

Their fleet pressed closer to the stark cliffs of Fulcor. On the fortress walls they could see the tiny soldiers manning the lookout posts. Utho glowered at the invaders, as if his sheer anger could strike them dead. His fleet would have to get past the Isharan ships before the brave soldiers could recapture the stronghold.

Several Commonwealth captains had better luck catching the capricious breezes, and two ships drove ahead of the flagship, fanning out. Six of the Isharan vessels were still outliers far out to sea, and though they had all set their sails and adjusted course, the outliers would not be able to join the fray for some time. The battle would be over before they could try to help their Isharan fellows, and that improved the odds. As a Brava, Utho had unrivaled confidence.

One of the enemy vessels pulled ahead, as if the breezes had been magically enhanced to drive them forward. This unexpected advantage made Utho uneasy. He was certain they did not still have a godling on the island, for the entity would have grown too weak by now. Could Isharan priestlords work their magic and manipulate the weather even without a godling?

The lead Commonwealth ship was guided by a captain with wild dark hair and an unruly beard. He drove recklessly toward the Isharan vanguard and tried to ram the other ship. The two vessels shifted course at the last minute, but the iron-fist prow smashed into the hull boards, sliding and splintering along the side. As they collided, the Commonwealth captain and a dozen of his fighters sprang aboard the enemy vessel. They began a wild melee, hacking with their swords, even though they were greatly outnumbered. The two ships caromed off each other and drifted apart.

While the ships were in contact, Isharan sailors hurled pots of burning oil onto the deck of the Commonwealth ship. The pots shattered, spilling the oil and catching the boards on fire. Flames rolled up the masts and rigging and began to devour the sails.

Out on the open water near a rough line of reef foam, two more ships careened together. The battering ram smashed through the hull of the

Commonwealth ship and lodged inside, locking the two vessels together. The fighting crews seemed evenly matched at first, but the Isharans methodically murdered the Osterran crew, without respite.

From the flagship, Mandan cheered at first, then turned pale as he saw how many of his soldiers were dying, how many of his ships were damaged. A lone Isharan vessel cruised directly toward them, targeting the konag's ship with an outthrust metal fist.

Alarmed by its swift approach, Utho shouted to the captain, "Alter course. Move us out of the way!" His stomach roiled with his need to fight these animals, but he would not put Konag Mandan at risk. On deck, the Commonwealth fighters waved their swords, spoiling for a fight.

More enemy vessels closed in, nearly twice as many as Mandan's fleet. They launched volleys of flaming arrows, trying to ignite the opposing ships. The Commonwealth captains ordered buckets of seawater drawn up, standing ready. Half the sailors aboard were devoted to extinguishing any burning brand as soon as it landed.

One smoldering arrow thunked to the deck only inches from Mandan's foot. He yelped, and Utho swept him to safety as more arrows landed, three of them striking exposed men on the deck. Utho shielded Mandan with his own body, hoping that his finemail cape and chest armor would deflect any projectile. He tucked the young konag between two large crates near the bow. "Stay here. I will lead the battle."

Pale with fear, Mandan crouched in the shelter between crates, no longer interested in the excitement of the battle.

Two more Commonwealth ships were burning, the crews unable to douse the fires in time. Utho saw with angry dismay that four of their ten ships were destroyed or disabled, while the enemy still had a dozen or more on the prowl. With clenched fists, he looked toward the high cliffs and the impregnable garrison above. Fulcor was their goal. He would not be driven away because of unexpected Isharan resistance.

He shouted to the flagship captain, "Make straight for the harbor! Once we reach the island, we will swarm up and recapture the stronghold." If they could make it into the narrow cove, their ships could hold off the remaining enemy attackers at the mouth, sheltered by the sheer walls.

The flagship captain barked orders, and the helmsman adjusted course. Picking up speed, the flagship slipped past two oncoming Isharan vessels without bothering to engage. Utho could only focus on Fulcor now.

More red-striped sails approached from the outlying waters, and the knot in Utho's stomach tightened. How many ships did the enemy have? By his count, the brave defenders had defeated five Isharan warships by now, but they had more vessels to lose than the Commonwealth did. The enemy crews also seemed more adept at extinguishing the fire arrows before a blaze could catch. Arrows flew back and forth like a meteor shower.

The remaining ships in Mandan's fleet closed behind the flagship as they made a headlong push toward the narrow harbor cove. The flagship captain raised signal banners to explain Utho's plan. Two outlying vessels kept fighting, engaging the Isharan ships, while the other four altered course directly toward Fulcor. If they could seize the island, Utho was sure they could hold it.

From his long time stationed there, Utho knew every cranny of the garrison, every cliff face, every defense. He pointed across the water, showing the captain a safe passage between hidden reefs. The strong currents around the island were uncertain, but luckily the ship caught a swift and cooperative flow. The flagship lurched ahead, and the other ships followed them.

The Isharan invaders crowded along the garrison walls above, ready to defend the island. Utho raised a fist in defiance from the deck, knowing the lookouts could spot a Brava even from a distance. Right now, he didn't care if these animals did still have a godling. He touched the ramer at his hip, ready to ignite it at the proper moment.

Two outlying Isharan ships engaged the trailing Commonwealth vessels in the open water, but Utho was intent only on reaching the cove. The flagship and three other warships would be enough. He looked up at the stark walls, the severe defenses installed by generations of Commonwealth fighters. He had thought the Fulcor garrison was impregnable. Now his ships would have to defeat those same defenses. He knew full well that it would be a bloodbath.

As the four Commonwealth vessels reached the narrow cove, the enemy ships held back, concentrating on the stragglers. Utho was perplexed by their strategy. Surely they would be most intent on saving the garrison?

His skin tingled. Was it a trap?

On the fortress walls above, he saw the defenders pulling back, preparing something. He shaded his eyes, trying to see what they were doing. He did not like this. "Beware, Captain—"

He heard a loud wooden thump and creak and saw a skeletal structure, a long wooden arm driven by ropes or springs, counterweights, and tension. At its end was a huge bowl of metal, a basket or crucible of some kind. "They have a new catapult!"

The released wooden arm sprang upward and slammed into the stopping block with an explosive crack. The bowl hurled its contents, a seething mass of chemical fire. Utho stared as the molten sphere hurtled toward the ships. Like a roiling blob of the sun, its crackling fire engulfed the ship just behind them. Liquid fire ignited the sails and poured like acid on the crewmen and soldiers. The deck was awash in a sea of flames.

Crouched between his protective crates, Mandan wailed.

Within minutes, everyone aboard the engulfed ship was either screaming or dead. Utho shouted, "Get us away from the wreck! Do not let the fire spread over here."

From the garrison walls, the Isharans cheered their devastating strike. They creaked back their wooden wheels to pull back the catapult's throwing arm again.

The three Commonwealth vessels avoided the doomed, burning vessel and continued toward the cove. A sheet of black smoke roiled into the sky and the wreck drifted about as it burned to the waterline.

Mandan lurched to his feet, screaming to the captain. "Get us away from the island! The harbor will be a death trap. We need to retreat."

Utho spun. "My konag! They cannot use the catapult on us once we enter the cove! We will be beneath them. It's the only way we can attack and recapture the garrison."

"No, we'll be trapped! That is my command!"

Up above, the giant siege weapon had been reset and locked in place. Utho knew the animals would be filling the basket with more chemical fire. Despite his hatred for Isharans, he understood that he and Mandan and everyone on these ships would die, bottled up like rats if they did enter the narrow cove.

Somehow, Mandan had found his command voice. "Turn about and sail away from the island. We've already lost too many ships. We need to save what we can."

Farther out from the island, the two outlying Commonwealth vessels were engaged on the open water, hammered by Isharan ships. One vessel was already burning, and the second Commonwealth warship had been rammed by an iron fist, its hull ruptured. Isharan fighters charged onto the deck of the sinking vessel.

Of the ten Commonwealth ships, only these three remained.

Utho groaned and gnashed his teeth. He knew what they had to do. Mandan was right. "Yes, my konag. I swore to protect you." The flagship captain was already responding, turning the ship away from the island, trying to retreat. Utho came to the stark realization that even more Isharan ships were closing in to cut off their escape. It was going to be very close.

Mandan pointed to the south. "Sail around the island, Captain! We can get away in that direction." Utho didn't see any Isharan ships there, so south seemed like a good choice.

The other two captains were already racing their vessels out of the catapult's range. With a second loud groan and crack, the siege engine hurled another blazing sphere, but the Commonwealth ships had sailed far enough away so that the deadly fire splashed into the water just to the stern.

Mandan was moaning and sick. Utho had wanted the young man to become seasoned in the horrors of war, a step that had begun when Mandan saw his mutilated father on that stormy night. As konag, he would experience many more such moments.

But this naval battle had turned into a rout.

One of the other two ships pulled ahead, spiraling away from Fulcor Island. Before they had gone far, though, Utho heard a grinding roar and sudden astonished screams as the fleeing ship ran up onto one of the reefs that surrounded the island like claws.

Utho looked at the greenish white line of churned water that indicated more submerged outcroppings. "Hard to port!"

The first ship ran aground, its hull torn open. Many sailors were thrown overboard by the impact, and they swirled in the reef foam, battered to death or swept out to sea.

The captain gripped the rail and gazed out at the water in dismay. "How can we rescue them?"

With the enemy ships closing in behind them, Mandan cried, "We can't stay here! The Isharans are coming."

"We do not abandon our comrades!" the captain said.

Utho looked up, though, and saw the Isharans growing closer. If they got into position and set their trap, the flagship would never get away. Konag Mandan would be captured or killed, and Utho knew what the Isharan animals would do to him.

Though the words tasted like poison in his mouth, he yelled, "The konag is right. Set course away from here and let us hope the second ship follows. We have to find a safe channel out to sea. We need to *go!*"

As swiftly as the winds could take them, they sailed away from Fulcor Island and toward the shores of home, only two ships remaining of their entire attack fleet.

48

THE new sheets of shadowglass drank all light, like glossy tar that had captured the essence of midnight. With the cargo seized from the Utauk trading ship, Klovus now had ten intact sheets of the rare, remarkable material, and he would use it inside the growing Magnifica construction. In the chamber beneath the temple, he ran his pudgy fingertips across the surface, leaving no smear. He would have his devout artisans frame the black sheets and mount them in prominent places. He was in a good mood.

And then the Black Eels reported their failure.

Zaha faced the key priestlord, expressionless. His dark hair hung neat and straight, his brow smooth, his words inflectionless, as if he had killed his emotions before he killed his first victim. "Eight of our Black Eels are dead, Key Priestlord. The empra and the girl Cemi are gone."

Klovus opened and closed his mouth, but his throat was a vacuum of words. "How is that possible?" He wasn't sure he had even understood the man properly. "How could mere hawk guards stand against my Black Eels? Did you not infiltrate the proper stations? Were you exposed?"

"My assassins did everything properly."

"Obviously, you did not!" His shout echoed off the stone walls of the chamber. He reeled and nearly cracked one of the large shadowglass panes.

Zaha continued, undaunted. "I did not participate directly in this operation, but analyzed the scene afterward. The Black Eels successfully entered the empra's chamber and launched their attack. They should have killed everyone there. I examined the scene, the blood, the bodies. Many hawk guards lay dead from sword wounds, but the Black Eels . . ." He hesitated, unable to find the correct words.

Klovus had never seen one of the elite assassins so uncertain before. He was deafened by anger, but restrained himself from striking Zaha across the face, even though he knew the assassin would stand there and accept the punishment and shame. "What are you saying?"

Zaha gave a blunt answer. "My Black Eels were . . . *destroyed*. Their bodies crushed, their bones broken, their organs burst."

Klovus was surprised. "But they can harden their skin. How did that happen?"

Zaha gave a maddening shrug. "I cannot explain, Key Priestlord. I found a large bloodstain on the *ceiling* inside the empra's chamber. One of my Black Eels had been slammed up there and crushed into a pulp by an unimaginable force."

Klovus's mind spun. "Force? What force could do this?"

"I do not know, but then I remembered something." Zaha changed the subject slightly. "When I tried to kill the empra on Fulcor, Key Priestlord, some unseen force drove me back, prevented me from harming her. It was too powerful for me to fight. Perhaps it has returned to guard her again."

Troubled, Klovus looked down at the sheets of black glass, but the substance swallowed questions and gave no answers. Klovus's eyes narrowed. "A bit convenient, is it not, this invisible force that you blame? What could it be?"

Zaha gave another maddening shrug. "Unknown."

Empra Iluris had been in a coma, utterly helpless ever since returning from Fulcor Island. Though the woman was the ruler of Ishara and the people revered her, she had no magic of her own—Klovus had learned that long ago. Iluris couldn't even bear children! He looked at the opaque shadowglass. Had she somehow enlisted the help of a godling? But surely Klovus would know! The wheels turned in his mind. "Where is the empra now?"

Another shrug. "Unknown. She and the others are gone. They must have found a hiding place or left the palace."

Klovus lashed out at him. "Can you provide answers for any of my questions, or are you utterly useless?"

A tiny flicker of anger lit behind the dark eyes. "Black Eels are never useless, Key Priestlord."

Klovus paced the underground chamber. "Where could they have gone?" he muttered, asking the question of himself as much as the assassin. "She's injured, unconscious—a burden. They would have had to carry her from the high tower. Cemi is an ignorant street girl. Could she possibly have planned this, made provisions for escape? They did not know we would attack."

"It does not seem possible, Key Priestlord, but after the death of Chamberlain Nerev, they may have guessed they were in danger."

"Killing her shouldn't have been a problem!" Klovus looked up, thinking of the next crisis. "If we have no answers, then neither should anyone else. Have you cleaned the scene, removed all the bodies?"

"Yes." Zaha's voice now had an arrogant undertone, as if he was offended to be asked such a thing. "We've scoured the bloodstains, removed all signs of a struggle. The empra's quarters are pristine."

"Witnesses?"

"Two servants came into the tower while we were cleaning, and we dispatched them. One minor minister from Ishiki barged in to request a signature from the empra. He was a fool, and he is also gone."

"How should we explain this?" Klovus asked. "To any outsider, she simply vanished without a trace."

"That is indeed exactly what happened."

The torches on the wall flickered. The stone-walled chamber felt oppressive with the weight of the enormous temple above. The hazy, magic-infused spelldoor on the wall remained dormant, but Klovus could sense the godling there, brooding in its own otherworld.

Zaha spoke crisply. "We could have left the dead hawk guards in place, which might have sparked rumors of a conspiracy among the guards, that they assassinated her." He hesitated. "But I doubt the people would believe that."

Klovus heaved a sigh of exasperation. "What else would they believe, then? If we don't give the people something definite, they will make up their own stories. Surely, suspicion will fall on me!" He shook his head. Frightened people would believe anything if encouraged properly. And here in Ishara, a land potent with magic, the people's sincere belief could manifest and become true. "We need to find Iluris before anyone else does. For now, we say nothing. Leave it a grand mystery."

"It is a grand mystery, Key Priestlord."

Klovus traced a fingertip along his lower lip. "Let all the ideas trickle out so long as they don't implicate me, and we will allow the rumors to determine which direction we go."

"Hear us, save us," said Zaha.

"Yes, of course."

❧

The following day, a sweaty, dust-streaked rider rode into the temple square at dusk, where Klovus led the throngs in their worship. The key priestlord raised his hands, encouraging the people to chant and pray.

The rider galloped forward, knocking people out of the way as he carved a passage toward the rising temple platform on his foam-streaked horse. He waved a leather-gloved hand. "Make way!"

Klovus recognized the messenger as an assistant priestlord dressed in green and brown with the markings of Tamburdin District.

The chants faltered, and the crowd noise dropped to a murmur as the rider rushed toward the key priestlord, calling out before he reached the stone steps. "The barbarians have attacked!" His voice was hoarse, as if he had shouted too much already. "Hethrren are swarming Tamburdin!"

In alarm, Klovus turned from the sacrificial altar. Next to him, one of his ur-priests whispered, as if invoking a demon, "The *Hethrren*, Key Priestlord!"

The violent barbarians preyed on hunters, sacked and burned villages, crashed into the defensive walls of the main Tamburdin city. During their last attacks, which were led by Magda, an ugly brute of a woman, Klovus and Priestlord Neré had unleashed the local godling, directing that mass of anger and wild energy to thwart the raid. The godling had driven the Hethrren back into the wilderness, and Klovus had hoped that Magda learned her lesson. Apparently she had not.

Now, though, he realized that the news gave him an opportunity—a glorious distraction from concerns about the empra. Raising his hands, thinking fast, he called the crowds to silence. Arriving at the newly constructed temple steps, the weary priest messenger slid off his saddle, holding on to the horse's mane to keep his balance. The beast itself was shuddering, barely able to remain on its feet.

Klovus stepped down to meet the flushed rider, who blurted out, "Key Priestlord, they burned outlying villages, struck the city walls! Priestlord Neré tried to scare them with the godling once again, but even more Hethrren surged out of the forest. Many hundreds of our people were killed, and she had to call the godling back. She begs for your help."

"Hear us, save us!" the crowd responded.

Klovus understood what a wonderful diversion this was, and it would surely make the people stop whispering about the disappearance of Empra Iluris. Here was an outside threat, even closer than the Commonwealth. "While we prepare our war against the godless of the old world, Ishara is besieged from another side! I must protect us from all enemies. Empra Iluris is gone for now, but pray that she will return."

There, let that be their only explanation. "Hear us, save us!" he said, and the dutiful crowd repeated it.

"As soon as preparations can be made, I will ride south with a contingent of the Isharan army to help defend Tamburdin with their own godling." He swelled his presence. "I, your key priestlord, will confront Magda herself."

He smiled with utter confidence. There was nothing like a battle to distract the attention of a grieving land. The marching army would look impressive as they passed through the districts to confront this new threat. The soldiers would just be for show, however. Klovus had another idea. These barbarians were proving to be most useful.

49

As the pair headed north into frostwreth territory, Elliel realized this was a dangerous, even foolhardy errand. But King Kollanan was willing to take the risk on the slim chance that they might rescue his grandson, and Thon desperately wanted more information about wreth history and about himself.

Their sturdy northern horses were accustomed to the cold, and Elliel added extra layers to her black outfit. They traveled quiet roads, diverting around Lake Bakal and heading directly toward the frozen lands. Patches of snow covered the ground between sparse, leafless trees.

Riding beside her, Thon was so confident and unafraid that he appeared oblivious, but Elliel knew not to underestimate him. As a Brava, she was not defenseless either.

Thon was optimistic the wreth queen would give him key answers. Lost in silence, Elliel thought of how much time she had spent without her past, trying to rediscover her legacy. Unconsciously, she touched her face where the rune of forgetting was still etched into her skin. So much was different now. She was a Brava again, bonded to the king of Norterra. Even so, she could not forget what Utho and Cade had done to her. The konag's bonded Brava was supposed to represent Brava honor for all three kingdoms.

"I can see by your expression that you are pondering important thoughts," Thon said, jarring her out of her reverie.

"It's . . . Utho." Her tone of voice put an entire tale into that one name.

Thon's face was filled with compassion. "That man hurt you, Elliel. There is much I need to discuss with him."

She smiled at him. Thon often surprised her with his warmth. "I hope you get the chance. I have things to *discuss* with him as well." She turned her gaze north. "But let us concentrate on one enemy at a time." What if Thon truly was a disguised god? It seemed impossible, but since meeting him she had already seen so much that seemed impossible. . . .

The cold winds were spattered with falling snow that turned the road white. Her breath was clouded, like white smoke, and she snugged the black cape around her. The horses snorted. Small icicles dripped from their noses, but they plodded on.

As the temperature dropped, the mounts moved stiffly, heaving harder. More ice sparkled around their mouths and noses. The horse hooves crunched through the crust of snow. Even with her extra layer of wool, Elliel felt the biting cold. Her hands were numb inside their leather gauntlets.

As the snowstorm grew thicker, Thon didn't seem affected by the cold. Invoking magic, he diverted the lashing breezes and formed a wedge ahead of them so that he and Elliel could travel somewhat sheltered from the fury.

"This is not a natural storm," he announced. "It is a wreth defense meant to discourage curious travelers."

"I am not discouraged," Elliel replied, but her teeth were chattering. "Are we in frostwreth lands now?"

Thon gave her a perplexed smile. His long dark hair was speckled with snowflakes. "I believe they consider the whole world to be their territory."

Obviously concerned with how cold she seemed, he gestured with an outstretched hand and carved out a wider tunnel in the blowing winds. Silence fell around Elliel's numb ears. Though the cold remained intense, there was some relief now. The horses also took heart and increased their pace.

As the northern forests dwindled to nothing, they reached a desert of snowdrifts punctuated by upthrust black rocks. The snow blew more furiously on either side of them, as if angry that Thon had thwarted it.

When the gray clouds cleared briefly, Elliel glimpsed towers of blue ice in the distance, bastion walls that looked larger and more graceful than the blocky fortress looming above Lake Bakal. She drew in a deep, cold breath. "Do you think they know we're coming?"

"Of course. And I know where they are, too."

Within the hour, something in the air snapped like a string stretched too tight, and the wailing blizzard faded around Thon's protective shield. The winds dropped and became still, the snow settled to the ground, and the white curtain of blowing flakes cleared. The two horses snorted, and Elliel patted her horse's neck as she felt the animal's tension build.

Ahead of them appeared three white-haired wreth warriors wearing ice-blue and silver armor. They bore weapons and angry expressions as sharp as scythe blades. They rode shaggy white steeds, like horses crossbred with wild wolves.

Behind them came five metal-and-leather sleighs that carried bald wreth mages, drawn by a train of small-statured drones who plodded over the snow.

"Halt," commanded one of the warriors.

The two riders reined in their horses. Thon said, "We have traveled far to see Queen Onn of the frostwreths. Please take us to her. She has information I need to see."

The warriors raised their crystal-tipped spears. "You were not invited. Therefore, you are not welcome. You are intruders." The leader gestured to his companions. "Take them and their animals."

Elliel clamped the golden ramer around her wrist and ignited her fiery weapon. She raised the stark orange flame high.

Thon slid from his saddle and stepped forward, ignoring the snarling wolf-steeds. He addressed the armored warriors in a conversational tone. "I made myself clear. We are travelers who wish to see Queen Onn." He gestured toward the palace in the distance. "We will go there ourselves if you choose not to help us." When they did not respond, he lowered his voice. "I can make you move out of our way."

The indignant warriors raised their spears, as if they meant to cut Thon down. The sleigh drones shifted in their harnesses. The mages lifted their arms to summon power from the air. "You are not a frostwreth," one mage growled. "Therefore, you are an enemy."

Thon tossed his black hair. "No, I am not a frostwreth . . . and you do not want me as an enemy." He made an impatient sound, lifted his foot, and brought it down hard on the packed snow.

An astonishing shock wave rippled through the frozen ground. The packed ice shimmered and convulsed. The wolf-steeds reared up, slashed their claws in the air. The mages' sleighs overturned, tossing the occupants out onto the cold ground. When the harnesses snapped, the drones scattered.

Thon brought his boot down a second time, and the surrounding ice and snow melted and refroze to a perfect glassy sheen, a rippling mirror that extended for fifty feet all around them.

Astonished, the wreth mages scrambled to defend themselves. The wolf-steeds bounded away, their claws skittering on the new polished ice. The warriors changed their arrogant posture and dropped into defensive positions.

Standing with arms crossed over his chest, Thon said, "We came to see Queen Onn. I suggest you take us to her."

This time, after only a moment's hesitation, the frostwreths agreed to escort them to the frozen palace.

50

AFTER staying in one place for a few days, Shella din Orr's heart camp packed up to roll over the countryside. Penda and her father traveled with the wagons on an unmarked and unplanned route around the Suderran hills, generally moving north, according to the old woman's whim.

The two rode in the main wagon on either side of Shella. Though the large wooden wheels bounced on the rutted road, the matriarch's seat was padded with so many blankets and furs that she barely noticed the jostling.

Penda wrapped her arms around her belly. In her life among the Utauks, she had seen many young mothers give birth, but she still felt anxious. The saddest part was that she might have to give birth without Adan Starfall if he couldn't reach them in time. When the wagon hit a particularly rough rut, she winced and felt a twinge in her abdomen.

Shella din Orr snapped, "Careful! *Cra,* are you trying to bounce the girl's baby loose?"

"Sorry, Mother," called Emil, who was driving the horses.

Seated on the other side of the old woman, Hale Orr used his short dagger to cut pieces from a fresh apple for Shella. With the next big bump, Hale nicked his thumb and hissed with surprise more than pain. The apple rolled onto his lap, but he caught it with the stump of his left hand.

Shella frowned. "Be careful with sharp things. Don't make me cut off your other hand if you get an infected wound." Her wrinkled lips puckered. "You should have learned your lesson the first time."

Hale flushed at the reminder of how he had lost his hand after an unwise knife fight in his youth. He accepted the good-natured teasing. "*Cra!* I'll try to keep the other one. It's my favorite hand."

The old woman continued, "My policy is to do only one amputation per person. If I cut off both of your hands, I'd be playing favorites among my grandsons."

On Penda's shoulder, Xar watched the trees as they rolled by. The reptile bird had been disconsolate ever since Ari flew away on the night of the dragon dreams. Though Penda had no direct heart link with the other ska, she was sad, not knowing why Ari had disappeared. From a distance, she could not sense the blue ska. Had the young reptile bird gone to search for poor Glik, or had Ari just fled?

Xar ruffled his feathers, tucked his wings close, and rested his head against Penda's long dark hair. "Tell Ari to come back," she whispered to him. "I worry about her."

Xar clicked an answer.

Shella leaned forward and squinted through a milky film of cataracts; Penda never knew how much the old woman could actually see. "I want to go north again, before it gets too cold."

"Is there something you need to see one last time, Mother?" Hale asked.

Her face pruned in a scowl. "One last time? Don't rush me to my death! My legacy fills four volumes already, and I expect to fill at least a fifth. Mind your own story and do something significant with your life."

Hale chuckled. "My daughter is all the legacy I could possibly want."

"Indeed, she is." Shella reached over to give Penda's belly a gentle pat. "But she is not done yet, either."

The road wound through a section of forest where the maples had died from a blight, leaving skeletal trunks and naked branches that looked like a frenetic charcoal sketch. Squinting, Shella shuddered violently enough to rattle her bones.

Penda also felt a surge of uneasiness twist inside of her.

Emil called the horses to a halt. "Forest spiders! Look at them all."

"Hundreds of them," said Burdon, the other grandnephew.

"Harmless creatures," Shella replied.

Penda knew that was true, but she still felt a strange dread inside her. Something wasn't right.

"*Cra*, we used to roast them when I was a boy," Hale said. "You need to cook them slowly so the bodies don't pop, but after you pluck off those sharp legs, they're very tasty."

Penda and her father climbed down from the wagon and walked toward the Utauks who stood by the curious trees. The forest spiders had used the framework of dead maples to string their webs from branch to branch. A cat's cradle of lines caught tiny droplets of mist, leaving patterns like silver threads bound up in the air. Spiders the size of walnuts hung motionless, waiting for insects to be trapped in the sticky strands.

Hale propped his wrist stump against his hip. "Never seen patterns like that before!"

"Not natural," Penda said, and her skin crawled. The ska sprang from her shoulder and flew into the air, circling away from the interconnected threads.

Each large and sturdy web was strung with circles, perfect circles unlike anything seen in nature, hoops within hoops that made the webs look like archery targets. A forest spider sat in each bull's-eye center, as if they expected praise for their unique web work. The Utauks muttered in awe, unsure whether this was an ill omen or a cause for hope.

Penda drew a circle around her heart. "The beginning is the end is the beginning." Her father echoed the words, as did the other Utauks.

⁊❧

The wagons established a new camp many miles from the eerie, dead forest. Penda slept outside near the remnants of a glowing fire, huddled under blankets to keep warm without Adan beside her.

Xar woke her in the middle of the night when he landed on her chest and tugged on the covers. He hissed and chittered in her face. She sat up in alarm, but through their heart link, sensed only excitement rippling through the ska's emotions. "What is it?"

The reptile bird hopped into the air as she pushed her blankets aside. He let out a jangling, clattering sound, which was answered from up in the night sky. Unable to see in the low campfire's glow, Penda listened to the response. It was another ska—Ari! The two reptile birds swirled in the air, dancing and playing in flight, and then both landed beside Penda.

"Ari, you're safe!" She stroked the blue ska's head, ran her fingers down the pale feathers. Ari clicked and thrummed. "Where have you been? What have you seen?" She touched the collar and removed the mothertear diamond.

Grumbling and still half asleep, Hale rolled over in his bedding and rubbed his eyes with the flat of one hand. "*Cra,* can't you control your skas?" Then he realized Ari had returned. "Ah, both skas? Where has the little one been?"

"I am about to find out." She activated the mothertear diamond, and images poured out—desert canyons, high rock walls . . . and the wreth camp filled with desperate human prisoners. Penda gasped. "She followed the heart link and found Glik."

"*Cra,* a lone ska couldn't rescue those poor people." Hale bent closer to the ominous images in the air. "Look, there are many more human slaves now."

Penda gritted her teeth. "And more wreths. Even a mage."

In the images, the angry sandwreths shook their fists when Ari swooped low to see better, as if they considered the reptile birds a threat. The mothertear also showed a party of lean, arrogant wreth riders arriving at the camp on augas, nobles and warriors, haughty in their armor. The lead male had a pointed chin, large eyes, and a sneer engraved on his face.

Penda recognized him. "That is Quo, the queen's brother." A foul taste filled her mouth, like rotting meat mixed with sulfur. "He dined with me and Adan, calling us allies . . . and he is directly involved with the horrible camps! He knows! He may even be in charge of them."

"He counted on our ignorance, dear heart," Hale said.

"But we know what's going on!" She stroked Ari, who seemed unsettled by her failure to save her human. "With these new images, we know more about the camps. Good job, Ari." The reptile bird accepted the praise. "But I don't see Glik in those images."

"I wish we could ride in and free all those prisoners," Hale said. "But even with the Utauk tribes and the Suderran army, would that be enough?"

"Against the sandwreths? We would be massacred. No, my Starfall is right—our greatest defense is the fact that they think we are oblivious. We must look for the right opportunity."

Penda touched the mothertear again and leaned close to Ari. She spoke directly to the diamond, recording a message of support, if the ska ever found the girl again. "Glik, my dear sister, we know where you are. We know about the treachery of the sandwreths. Please don't give up hope! Adan Starfall and I will come for you. We are trying to find a way."

Hale leaned next to her. "And the Utauks will help."

"We will come for you," Penda repeated and drew a circle around her heart.

51

⚘

AFTER Elliel and Thon rode off to the north, Kollanan prepared for war at Fellstaff.

Each day, while his soldiers drilled, he gazed beyond the city walls, expecting to see an army of pale warriors coming for revenge. Weapons and armor were distributed across the kingdom, preparing villages and towns. In separate counties, Lords Bahlen, Alcock, and Iber were building strongholds in abandoned wreth cities, reinforcing walls and defenses to protect their people.

With a bittersweet pang, he remembered quiet and peaceful days with Jhaqi and the grandsons, but such days would never happen again. In some far-distant future, he hoped that he and Tafira, and all of Norterra—no, all of the Commonwealth—would find stability and peace. But the wreths wanted to end the world before that.

Queen Voo had promised a large group of sandwreth warriors for the offensive on Lake Bakal, but Koll feared the enemy would attack before any reinforcements arrived. In the meantime he needed to know what was happening at the ice fortress.

Taking Lasis as his companion, he headed north toward the devastated frozen lake and the frostwreth fortress. After two days of hard riding, they topped the ridge and looked at what should have been a thriving village on the beautiful lakeshore, with docks extending into the water, fishing boats drifting across the waves.

"All of it is gone," he whispered, struck anew by the painful proof that his daughter's whole village had been wiped out.

He and Lasis kept hidden among the silver pines. Not long ago, his raiders had damaged the fortress, started fires in the outlying buildings where the drones lived, and killed many wreth warriors before galloping away. They had stung, and hard.

Now the wreths were reconstructing their defenses. Ahead of them, many wreth workers cut gigantic ice blocks from the lake and shaped them to rebuild the walls. Mages fashioned new sheets of ice to patch the ominous stronghold and to make it larger than before.

"It looks as if we never even attacked," Koll groaned.

"They will not forget what we did, Sire," Lasis said. "With the sandwreths to help us, we can tear down those walls."

Around them, among the frosted pines hushed from the cold, Kollanan heard bushes rustling, saw figures moving in the snow. Immediately on his guard, the Brava swung down from his saddle and prepared to defend his king. Storm shuffled from side to side, and Kollanan reached down for his war hammer. "We do not intend to fight," he warned Lasis. "If the frostwreths see us, we will ride away as if demons are chasing us."

They tried to identify the furtive sounds. Arrogant wreths would never creep through the forest to ambush them, but these watchers were stealthy, furtive. "Come out!" Koll's normal voice sounded loud in the forest.

The Brava stood in front of the king's black warhorse, his sword drawn.

Small figures crept out and stared at the two men. They had soft features, like mere sketches of people rather than finished works of art. Six of the creatures showed themselves, but he sensed many more lurking in the tree shadows.

"Drones, Sire," Lasis said, then stepped forward, lowering his voice. "I know them. They helped me survive after Queen Onn . . ." He swallowed hard, and the white scar on his throat jumped.

Koll dismounted and rested the hammer against his shoulder, but the drones did not seem intimidated. They came forward, mumbling in a language he didn't understand.

Lasis sheathed his sword, extended both hands. "After Queen Onn dumped my body outside the palace, these creatures saved me, helped me to get home to you, Sire."

"I know," Koll said. It seemed the diminutive creatures showed little loyalty for their abusers. He stood next to the black-garbed Brava. "I am King Kollanan. Are you friends or enemies?"

The drones gathered around the two men as if they were a great curiosity. They held up their hands to demonstrate they bore no weapons or ill intent.

"King," one of the drones said.

Another said, "King of Norterra."

They also muttered and whispered, coming closer to Lasis. The Brava said, "These must be survivors from the night of our attack. Their shacks burned, and many of the creatures scattered." He had wonder on his face. "Maybe they took a chance at freedom, hiding in the pine forest."

Taking a risk, Koll extended his hammer toward the blocky ice fortress on the other side of the frozen lake. "Those are my enemies. The frostwreths killed my people, and I want to tear down those walls. I came here to figure out how we can do it."

The drones chattered to one another, then moved about like frenetic ants. Kollanan couldn't understand why they kept shifting positions. They cleared a wide patch of snow, like a blank canvas. One of the drones pointed toward him. "King Kollanan of Norterra." He pointed at the fortress. "Frostwreth enemies."

Moving with one mind, the drones plucked twigs from a silver pine trunk and stripped off the side branches to make sharpened implements. Working in concert, they drew a detailed sketch in the snow, marking the lakeshore, the outbuildings, followed by a precise representation of the frostwreth fortress. The drones pointed with their sticks, indicating the main arched entrance, as well as other openings and sidewalls. They drew the higher level of the structure, showing rooms and chambers.

Amazed, Koll followed their images, able to see where the fortress walls were thickest and where the gates might be vulnerable. Lasis scrutinized the drawing. The drones made another sketch that indicated underground vaults.

Koll stroked his frost-encrusted beard. "This is much more than I hoped to learn."

Lasis said, "I agree. We do not need to ride closer to the fortress itself, where we might be captured."

"Tafira will be glad if I don't take a greater risk." Koll turned to the drones. "Thank you."

The creatures bolted into the trees like pigeons scattering in the courtyard.

❧

Shadri would have preferred to spend every evening poring over the sand-wreth chronicles Thon had brought from the southern desert. The stories were amazing, and there was so much to learn!

But Pokle invited her to his favorite tavern in Fellstaff, insisting that she go with him. Ever since the young man had been rescued from Lake Bakal, he had worked in the castle stacking wood and keeping the fireplaces lit. Pokle clung to her as an unexpected friend, and she saw him as someone she could talk to. He listened as she tried to teach him, and although he seemed fascinated by the sound of her voice, she couldn't tell if any of the knowledge sank in.

Once he got an idea into his shaggy head, though, he was stubborn and hard to convince otherwise. "But they're having goose pie tonight! You've got to come. It's delicious."

"The castle kitchens feed me just fine, don't they?"

"Not like this." His eyes shone. "And the chamberlain paid me enough walking money that I can buy you dinner. Please?"

Seeing the hopeful look in his eyes, Shadri wondered why it meant so much to him. With a start, she realized that Pokle wanted to impress her, wanted her company. Was he flirting with her? She tried to wrap her mind around that idea. In her studies, she had learned about history, mathematics, music, human anatomy, and any other subject that caught her fancy, but when it came to romance, she had experienced little. "Well, you did say please, didn't you?"

The tavern was noisy and the ale was sour, but the goose pie was as delicious as promised. One pie would have been large enough for them to share, but Pokle insisted on demonstrating his largesse by buying two. Once he sat across the rough wooden table from her, however, he didn't know what to say. They ate without talking, awash in the background noise, until Shadri picked up the burden of the conversation. She chattered about the legacy stories she had read, new documents she had found in the Fellstaff remembrance shrine, some of the wreth tales Thon had translated, even the myths that might explain what the dark wreth really was. Pokle was relieved to listen to her, as if he found the movement of her lips reassuring. She thought he looked like a mooncalf.

As she continued talking about whatever came into her head, Shadri stopped in midsentence, interrupted by a burst of humorless laughter from the far side of the great room. Out of their formal Commonwealth uniforms, Captain Rondo and his men called for a second round of ale.

"I know about Isharan cuisine," Rondo said to his men and, by virtue of his loud voice, he also spoke to everyone else in the great room. "If you've tasted it, there's a flavor you can't identify. They use foreign spices, some of which are poison to normal men."

Shadri frowned, having eaten many of Queen Tafira's recipes herself. The flavors were exotic, and she found all of the food delicious.

"Back in Ishara they add human blood to the cooking. That's how they make their stews," Rondo continued. "In their temples where the vile godlings live, all the people slash their arms and give their blood. I hear Empra Iluris drinks goblets of it chilled on a warm summer day."

His companions grumbled. Some laughed in disbelief, but others in the tavern listened. Seeing he had their attention, Rondo continued, "Now, for special delicacies, Isharans use the blood of babies. That's why their pastry dough is always red."

Shadri knew of no such thing, even though she had studied Isharan culture, but many of the listeners nodded, as if they frequently visited Isharan bakeries.

Rondo raised his fresh tankard and gulped down half of it. "But the blood of brave Commonwealth fighters—ah, that is what they consider the best! I bet they stole some of Conndur's blood when they butchered him!" Then he asked rhetorically, but poisonously, "I wonder what Queen Tafira uses it for? I hear she has outlandish dinners."

"Plenty of Commonwealth blood to be had for people like them," said Sergeant Headan.

The tavern patrons grumbled at the absurd story. "Beware what you say about our queen," said a broad-shouldered carpenter, rising half out of his seat.

Headan also rose, drew his sword out of its scabbard, glaring at the carpenter. The trained soldier could easily best the other man, who stood his ground for a moment before slowly seating himself again. "She has always been good to us," the carpenter muttered. Other customers in the tavern agreed.

"How do you know what she is really thinking?" Rondo asked. "She could just be biding her time."

"For thirty years?"

Shadri saw that other tavern patrons were nodding as if they agreed. She pushed away her half-eaten goose pie, which no longer tasted right to her. "Let's go, Pokle."

The young man seemed disappointed and confused. As far as she could tell, he hadn't even heard the men talking. She tugged his arm. "I will let you walk me back to the castle."

He brightened at that, and the two of them left the tavern as Captain Rondo began to tell another outrageous and provocative tale.

52

ELLIEL and Thon stood before the throne of the frostwreth queen. The scar on Onn's cheek both marred and enhanced her beauty. This woman was exceedingly powerful, no question about that. An ancient spear was prominently displayed on the wall behind the throne.

The queen seemed fascinated by the two outsiders who had dared to come to her, but they were aware that the slightest provocation could turn her capricious amusement to fury. "You are here of your own accord, knowing your lives may be forfeit. Even my drones are more intelligent than that."

Beside Elliel, Thon was caught up in his own concerns, his deep desire to glean what information the frostwreths might possess about him and how he fit into the universe. "I need to learn what you know about wreth history, and what you remember."

The incredible palace was sculpted out of a living glacier, its towers and walls raised up so that the structure loomed as high as a crystalline mountain on the plain of snow. Elliel had also seen the sandwreth palace, which was just as imposing. Unlike the deceitful sandwreths, these people did not hide their murderous intentions toward humans. Was that preferable?

Frostwreth warriors stood along the ice-block walls, shifting their spears and regarding the two visitors. Irri, a muscular male warrior, stood closest to the throne, as if he considered himself Onn's personal protector, or her personal possession.

If frostwreths intended to sweep down and eradicate the gadfly humans, Elliel feared Norterra was doomed. Even with the help of Thon, could she convince Onn to release Birch? Was the boy still alive?

The queen rose in a liquid motion, looked down at Thon. "And what sort of being are you? You are unlike anything I have ever seen." Her brow wrinkled. "A sandwreth creation? A spy?"

"No, I am most certainly not that," Thon said. "I came here to review your histories, so I can learn the answer for myself."

Onn turned her attention to Elliel, raking her gaze up and down the black finemail cape, her chest armor, her sword. "You are another Brava half-breed, a female. Females are usually wiser." She mused for a moment. "I brought a Brava here as a toy not long ago. I killed him when I was done with him."

Elliel responded mysteriously: "Bravas are not so easy to kill."

Cold blue fire ignited behind the queen's eyes, but she dismissed Elliel and stepped closer to Thon. He remained motionless as she touched his dark hair, his silvery scaled chest plate. "Handsome but . . . unsettling."

"I wish to see your historical records. It is important to me." He flashed his perfect teeth, as if to convince her that what was important to him must be important to her as well. "We have a different purpose as well. You have taken a young human boy. We would like him back."

Elliel was startled he would be so blunt. She spoke quickly: "As a gesture of respect. We make this formal request of the queen of the frostwreths." She paused a beat as Thon continued to stare at her. "Does the boy still live?"

"Birch is a dear child, endlessly interesting, though he requires a good deal of watching." Onn's pale eyes shifted toward her standing guards, and a frown flickered across her features. "I wonder where he has gotten to. . . ." She shouted to anyone who could hear her command, "Bring the human child here! I want to show our guests how well I take care of my wards." She turned back to the visitors and sniffed. "What is he to you? The mere fact that you ask about him means he must be someone of importance."

"I did not know the wreths considered any humans of importance," Thon said, again surprising Elliel, but he exactly played upon the queen's mood.

Soon enough, a group of agitated drones escorted a gaunt boy into the throne room. He stood with shadowed, downcast eyes, dressed in patchwork clothes, scraps tucked into other clothes, overlarge trousers held up by a short length of rope. He looked up at Thon and the Brava woman, but did not recognize either of them.

Elliel felt a warm rush to see the child, despite his miserable condition. She bent down and took him by the shoulders. "It's all right. We're trying to get you home." She lowered her voice, careful not to say Kollanan's name. Somehow the boy had kept his identity hidden. "Your grandfather will be glad to know you are alive."

When Birch looked at her, his eyes welled up with tears. "Is he coming for me?"

Elliel rose to her feet and said to the queen, "It would be a great display of generosity and kindness if you let us take him."

Onn seemed scandalized. "Birch is one of my most prized possessions!

He sits at the side of my throne. Why should he want to go back to mere humans?"

"Because they are his family and his home. Surely you can understand that?" Elliel was not sure of such things at all.

"I honor him by keeping him." Onn paced in front of her throne while the silent guards watched, ready to attack. "No, he is mine. Why should I be generous? You will not deprive me of his company." Onn lashed out at the silent drones. "Take him away, deep into the tunnels. He is not going anywhere." She also turned to two of the powerful wreth guards. "Be sure the boy does not get . . . lost."

Elliel felt dismay as Birch was whisked away. She could tell there would be no changing the queen's mind. Maybe they would require more extreme measures.

Onn's face took on a calculating expression. "The child is interesting, but has little knowledge. I shall keep both of you here, as well. My mages will enjoy extracting information."

Elliel backed away. "You will not." She clamped the gold ramer in place and called forth the fire.

Thon stood unarmed and seemingly relaxed, but his voice sounded ominous. "You disappoint me, Queen Onn. We came here with a reasonable request."

"I alone decide what is reasonable," Onn said.

Elliel stood close to Thon with her ramer raised, shining the intense orange fire against the blue-white cold of the palace. Onn seemed amused by the glow of heat shining on her pale skin.

Irri strode forward, swelling in size with the opportunity to protect his queen. More wreth warriors advanced, raising spears and swords. Elliel stood ready to fight, the fire crackling. She was confident she could kill Irri, but she could not kill them all.

Onn sat back on her throne as if hungry to watch the unfolding battle.

Enigmatic and silent, Thon studied the enemy warriors closing in. He had battled them before at Lake Bakal, but that was at a distance, not hand-to-hand. He seemed perplexed to be facing actual opponents. Elliel didn't know what he would do, or what he *could* do, but she had faith in him. She had seen the immeasurable power that Thon possessed, whether or not he understood what he was.

"I had hoped the wreth race would be powerful, honorable, and worthy," he said. "Alas, I find you lacking."

Irri's deep-throated laugh sounded like a growl. Raising a hand and invoking an invisible force, Thon lifted the armored warrior off the floor, his reinforced boots dangling in the air as he kicked out. As Thon held him suspended in the air, the helpless warrior slashed the emptiness with his sword but could reach no one.

The startled frostwreths hesitated. Thon pressed Irri against the frozen wall near the stained spear. The surface of the ice blocks melted and reformed. Horizonal streams of water folded around him to encase Irri in a frozen cocoon.

Queen Onn looked at the trapped and struggling warrior in astonishment. More warriors charged forward, cocking back their spears. Thon gestured toward the mirrorlike ice floor, which suddenly liquefied, and the charging warriors sank in up to their knees. With a second gesture, Thon refroze the floor, trapping them in place like insects in amber.

Two trapped warriors hurled their spears at him, but Elliel's ramer destroyed the weapons in midflight. More warriors paused at the edge of the throne room, waiting for a command from the queen.

Onn looked at Thon, amazed. "What are you?"

"That is what I am trying to discover. I was sealed beneath Mount Vada in a chamber made of crystal. Someone put me there, long ago." He touched the intricate tattoo on his face. "I know nothing of my past. What can the frostwreths tell me? What are your legends about Kur? And the dragon?" He stepped up to the dais, and the queen backed to her throne. His tone changed and he demanded, "Did *you* do something to me?"

"I have never seen you before," Onn said. "Our history says nothing about a wreth man sealed inside the mountain."

"Why was I there? Who am I? What is my purpose?" His questions became louder. "If you know, you must tell me."

Elliel was surprised he did not ask her directly if he was Kur. Maybe he didn't believe in the possibility enough.

"I do not know!" Onn said.

"Then help me find out. Queen Voo provided me with all of their legends and records. I request that you do the same."

Onn calculated it was a small price to pay. "You may see our records." Her voice became smoother. "Once you understand us, perhaps you will help us achieve victory."

"That depends on what I understand about you, and what I am."

Irri continued to struggle against his frozen bonds. The warriors trapped in the floor could not pull their legs free. Elliel was sure Queen Onn could easily melt the ice with her own powers and free them, but she didn't dare use her magic while Thon remained there. She issued more orders that echoed through the throne room, and soon worker-caste wreths hurried in with stacks of thin crystalline sheets, even a few crumbling documents written on old parchment.

Two mages accompanied them. "These were stored in our palace, untouched during the years of our dormant spellsleep."

"I will need them all," Thon said.

Onn did not argue, intimidated. "Take them and leave."

A hundred additional warriors arrived, ready to defend their queen. They crowded at the threshold, inside the throne room.

Elliel felt strong beside Thon as she continued to hold her crackling ramer, pouring power into the fiery blade. "And the boy. We will take him with us."

"No!" Queen Onn shrilled. Her pride was ignited. She snatched the ancient spear from the wall behind her throne and held it. "The boy stays here with me. If you ask again, I will have him killed right now."

Elliel could see that she meant it.

As he looked at the documents, Thon was delighted with the treasure trove of information, but Elliel just wanted to get away. Even with Thon's power, she knew the battle could turn against them in a moment. "We should leave." She glanced around, ready for the flash point. "We can't fight them all."

"I don't wish to, and I choose not to." He turned, bearing his prized documents. "We will go now."

Elliel kept her ramer ignited as they retreated. The ominous frostwreths watched, but made no move to prevent their departure.

53

THE two surviving Commonwealth warships limped back toward Osterra. The sails were singed and torn, the decks damaged, but the konag
was alive. The other eight ships in the strike force had been sunk near Fulcor
Island.

Mandan spent most of the return voyage in his cabin with the doors barricaded, as if afraid that Isharan murderers would somehow steal aboard and
attack him in the night. Utho remained on guard outside the door, giving
him some sense of safety. Mandan had never doubted his Brava's strength,
but he had underestimated the evil of the Isharans.

On the last night of the return voyage, praying that they would soon reach
the Rivermouth shipyards, Mandan huddled on his hard pallet, listening to
the uneasy creaking of the hull.

They had seen no sign of Isharan pursuit since they fled Fulcor Island, but
Utho would not let the crew lower their guard. Lookouts on the tallest masts
used far-seeing tubes to keep watch, but they spotted no red-striped sails
pursuing them. Nevertheless, the fleeing warships sailed with all the speed
they could imagine, as if their lives depended on it.

Mandan remained in his dark cabin, listening to the sounds and feeling
unreasonably cold. He had seen dark clouds at sunset, and he was terrified
that a thunderstorm would churn the waves and thrash the ships. Lightning
and thunder would make every moment a waking nightmare.

He moaned to himself, all alone. He had slept only a few hours in the days
since the disaster, but sheer exhaustion finally drove him into a sleep filled
with stark images of his father's mutilated body. He would never forget the
inhuman viciousness of the act. How could such hateful people exist?

The young man woke up screaming, and even though he had barricaded
his cabin, Utho snapped the latch and shoved the door open. Thunder
cracked in the sky, and Mandan felt queasy. His bunk swayed as the ship
rode the choppy waters.

"There is a storm at sea, my konag, but you are safe. The captain says there is nothing to fear."

"There is always something to fear," Mandan said.

"Not while I am here."

A bright flash of lightning seeped through the window hatch, and the subsequent boom of thunder made him cringe. Utho held him in an iron grip, which was at first comforting and then stern. "You must not be afraid of a mere storm. As konag, you have to bring the Commonwealth together and be a brave leader. Fear the Isharans and what they can do! After this naval defeat at Fulcor, we must return with ten times the force and exterminate them. We will build an army for this vengewar with soldiers from all three kingdoms."

"All three kingdoms. . . ." Shuddering, Mandan leaned against Utho's muscular chest, felt the reassuring leather armor, but the Brava pushed him away and held him at arm's length.

"You are Konag Mandan of the Colors, and you write your legacy with your actions. You survived at Fulcor Island—twice!—and you have learned. You must learn!"

"I will," Mandan said, determined. Another crack of thunder startled him, but he steeled himself, did not react. In the lantern-lit cabin Utho gave a slow approving nod.

"We expected to capture Fulcor Island, Sire, but even defeat—temporary defeat—provides fuel to feed the fire. As I told you before, a vengewar is not a quick thing, but it is necessary."

"What are we to do? As soon as we reach Rivermouth, all the people will know that I could not recapture Fulcor Island. What about Lira—"

"You couldn't do it this time. Next time, though, we will crush them."

Hearing the confidence in the Brava's voice, Mandan pushed aside his doubts.

◈

The following morning, after the lookout sighted the misty coast of Osterra, Mandan sat in a chair on the deck, which was still moist from the previous night's downpour. He eyed scorch marks on the scrubbed planks, scars where arrows had gouged the deck. The marks of battle. Utho called them the marks of survival, not of defeat.

"We sank several of their ships," Mandan said. "I only wish we could have taken some Isharan prisoners for Lord Cade. It . . . it would have made a fine wedding present for my father-in-law."

"Set your priorities, my konag. When we conquer the continent, we will secure more than enough slaves for our needs. And there are things more important than your upcoming wedding." Utho gave him stern instructions. "You need to write a letter to the kings of Suderra and Norterra. The Commonwealth must be united, and the fate of our entire land now rests in how we respond to the enemy. We know from the last Utauk trading ship that Empra Iluris remains in a coma, unable to rule." His gray eyes hardened. "Therefore, Ishara is weak, leaderless, in turmoil. Now is the time to strike. We cannot miss this opportunity!" Mandan nodded, agreeing completely, and Utho nudged him into action. "Write all that! Tell your brother and your uncle. Now is our chance. We need to stand together."

The young man called for fresh paper, ink, a quill. Thanks to Utho, he had so much anger he could barely find the words to write. He struggled to compose the letter as he sat outside in the deceptively bright morning.

Utho nodded down at the paper. "Write, Sire. Issue your commands. You rule the three kingdoms, and this is our war. They all have to obey you. Call them to action."

"But . . . but King Kollanan sent that terrible letter about what you did to Elliel. What if he doesn't heed me?"

Utho's face grew as dark and stormy as the previous night's clouds. "You are the konag, Sire. He is only a king." That seemed to be all the answer he would give.

As Mandan worked through the first few sentences, the words began to flow better. He read his first draft, but found it inadequate, so he tore it up and rewrote the document in stronger, clearer language. He was the rightful konag, issuing a royal command.

When he felt satisfied with the document, and after Utho approved it, he wrote identical letters to Adan and Kollanan.

This war against Ishara would consume the resources of the Commonwealth: the ships, soldiers, weapons, armor, food, and supplies. The three kingdoms, which had been allied since the time of Queen Kresca, would need to merge their armies into a single force capable of crushing the enemy that had committed such horrible crimes. Norterra, Suderra, and Osterra could have no other priorities. They would stand together under Mandan's rule. He was the konag, and they must obey.

Mandan signed and sealed his letters. As soon as the warships landed at Rivermouth, he would dispatch riders across the land to deliver them with all possible speed.

54

Key Priestlord Klovus traveled with part of the Isharan army to Tamburdin District. Before he left the capital, he issued public announcements and spread quietly insidious rumors about the danger of the Hethrren, which would help distract the people from thinking about the silent empra, although many still prayed for her every day. The spectacle of marching troops caught their attention, at least for a while.

Days later, they arrived in Ishara's southernmost district. The main city had been turned into a veritable fortress with thick walls. A handful of surviving soldiers manned the watchtowers on the wooden stockade. Klovus thought they looked more frightened than confident.

Countless mining and logging villages had been massacred, the survivors fleeing to the main city to hide behind the high walls. The barbarians had ravaged the land, pillaging, thriving on destruction. The town leader and the troop commander had dispatched numerous scouts to monitor the Hethrren movements, many of whom never returned.

The city itself—little more than a wilderness outpost, really—was crowded to the breaking point with refugees from ravaged areas . . . refugees who should not have been there at all, if the soldiers and the Tamburdin priestlord had done their jobs properly.

Klovus knew what the barbarians were like. In his previous visit here, he had seen their loathsome leader Magda, a woman who had more in common with a shaggy forest beast than a human being. She maintained her rule by letting the Hethrren clans unleash their violence. Klovus wished all that destruction could be turned against a proper enemy. Ah, what a fine weapon these Hethrren would be if he could manipulate them! If not, their entire race should be eradicated, torn limb from limb.

As the army contingent entered the city gates, Klovus was most disappointed in Priestlord Neré. The local priestlord had the godling and she had the faith of her people. Given such power, Klovus didn't understand why she allowed a single Hethrren to remain alive.

He would save them if their own priestlord could not do it herself.

He basked in the cheers as the people of Tamburdin celebrated his arrival. Several hundred Isharan soldiers flowed into the city, reinforcing their desperate defenses. Klovus would let the military commanders discuss strategy, review past battles and failures, and propose new attempts to control the outside threat.

Meanwhile, he had other business. He went directly to the rustic temple.

In Tamburdin, the hardy people lived close to nature, at the mercy of wild animals, storms, falling trees. Their temple was built from dark logs stripped of bark. Inside the worship area stood wooden carvings of fierce forest animals—a wild stag with sharp antlers, a roaring bear, a snarling wolf that could rip its prey open, a great eagle with talons spread. Blackened beams came from trees struck by lightning, and some of nature's power remained within the wood. That power, combined with the faith of the people, manifested in the strength of their godling—a strength that Neré had failed to use.

The priestlord waited to receive him. She was thin and small-statured, her long brunette hair done in tight braids. Her brown-and-green caftan bore symbols from Tamburdin District. Neré's expression showed clear relief upon seeing him. "You received my message, Key Priestlord. I am glad you came yourself."

Klovus said with a bitter undertone, "Your failures demanded that I come."

Ignoring her abashed reaction, he stepped to the heart of the temple floor and reached out with his mind, opened his heart. He could feel the throbbing power there, sensed the angry local godling ready to lash out.

"Your godling wants to destroy Tamburdin's enemies," he said to Neré in an accusatory tone. "Why don't you let it fulfill its purpose?"

"I have! But it is so furious and uncontrolled that I could not let it range far. We defended our city, but Magda attacks our outlying villages and towns. I can't let the godling range across the entire district and leave our city vulnerable."

"You can and you should," Klovus said. "The godling wants to be released. This is why the faith of the people created it! Their prayers and sacrifices gave it form for a purpose." He brushed her aside. Against the far wall of lightning-struck logs shimmered the misty spelldoor. Klovus extended his palm to the crackling ant hive of energy that lurked just behind the magical membrane.

"I saved the city, Key Priestlord," Neré insisted. She tossed her braids over her shoulders. "That was my mission. But if the godling were to get loose and rampage through the wilderness, how would we ever call it back? Nothing could stop it. How could we ensure that the godling would return to this temple and protect us again?"

Klovus scowled. "You are not a fit priestlord if you cannot control your own godling. It is not an unruly child throwing a tantrum—it is your partner. It is a product of your faith and the people's faith."

"Hear us, save us." She bowed in surrender. "I can bring followers here, Key Priestlord. We have many urns of blood waiting, and the worshippers are ready to sacrifice, if we need more. I will join you in your mission." She looked up at him, clearly subordinate. "Together, you and I will strike the barbarians."

"*We* will not strike the barbarians," Klovus snapped. "I will go alone. I do not need your distractions."

෨෨

The people maintained their faith, even if Priestlord Neré had been afraid to let the godling achieve its full potential. Klovus would not be so reticent. He would use the deity to knuckle under the remarkably strong barbarian tribes to do his bidding, but if his plan went badly, then the wild, unchained godling could still rage among the Hethrren like a dog in a henhouse. Either way, the problem would be solved.

No one knew where the barbarians had come from. The original settlers of Ishara were descendants of survivors from the wreth wars. The Hethrren were also human, as far as Klovus could tell. Were they a separate group of refugees who had come here from the old world? Or had they broken off from early Isharan colonists many centuries ago?

Two hours past midnight, after his entourage had bedded down in the main government house of Tamburdin City, Klovus went back to the temple. The streets were quiet except for patrolling soldiers, but the city slept restlessly. Only a few lantern-lit windows shone orange into the night. The key priestlord had already given instructions to the city guards, and at the right time they would clear a path and open the high wooden gates. An impatient godling should never be asked to wait.

At the temple doorway, Priestlord Neré greeted him with a bow, unsettled. "I wish you would let me fight at your side, Key Priestlord." Her voice held no demand, no insistence. She seemed broken and accepting.

"I wish you deserved to fight at my side. I will tether the godling to my mind and heart, and we will achieve what you failed to do."

Inside the rustic temple, smoke from burning torches added an acrid tang and a primal power to the air. The formidable animal carvings looked ready to attack.

At this time of night, with the population sleeping, the godling would be at a lower ebb, but its worshippers had made their sacrifices, prayed to it, chanted "Hear us, save us!" The entity would be strong enough to protect him when he issued his ultimatum to the main Hethrren camp.

Neré stood beside a bronze chute that fed into an opening in the wall. Two large urns stood on either side of the altar, filled with dark blood from the recent sacrifices.

Without bothering to chastise her further, Klovus lifted one urn and poured the thick red liquid into the chute, and Neré added the contents of the second urn. The blood, the prayers, the beliefs, and the unconditional need were exactly the power source the godling required. The spelldoor throbbed as the misty silver barrier folded and unfolded into an unseen realm, and the bright entity pushed behind it, eager to be released. Every drop of the blood drained down the polished chute, and Klovus felt his connection strengthen. The deity was ready.

"Release the godling," he said, and Neré dissolved the spelldoor, letting the writhing mass of power, energy, and anger blossom forth like gouts of smoke. The Tamburdin godling drew energy from the dangerous forests, the unkind wilderness, and manifested with fangs and claws, sharp horns, and thick fur. A tornado of predatory instinct, it rolled out, leaving black marks on the wooden floor and pressing against the tall ceiling beams.

Neré flinched away, and Klovus grimaced in disgust at her weak reaction. No priestlord should ever fear her own godling! Her control had not kept up with the rising anger and desperation of the populace. The people of Tamburdin made their godling strong, but Priestlord Neré balked at using the weapon she had.

Klovus turned his back on the swelling, shapeless form that had been created by the worshippers. He did not doubt the godling would follow him. Neré remained in the temple watching her godling go, but Klovus didn't give her a second glance.

Outside, he had arranged for one of the soldiers to saddle a horse, a sturdy chocolate-brown mare. The horse snorted, uneasy with the frenetic force of the godling looming behind, but Klovus patted its neck and climbed into the saddle. He settled himself, took up the reins, and nudged the mare off through the dark streets toward the stockade wall. The godling remained dark and formless, but it sizzled with occasional lightning flashes intermingled with red eyes like a wolf's caught in the firelight. Klovus governed it, reeled it in.

"Follow me," he said under his breath. "Soon you can do what you were made to do."

In the houses along the streets, shadowed faces pressed to the windows of darkened buildings as they passed. The mare's hooves clopped on the main street, an even pace. When dogs began to howl, crouching in alleys or doorways, the godling instinctively lashed out, but Klovus pulled it back. He called ahead, feeling the mare restless beneath him. They needed to be outside, soon. "Open the gates!"

The guards swung the barricade wide and sprinted out of the way. The key priestlord pushed the horse into a trot and rode out of the city with the godling at his heels like a monstrous hound.

Klovus headed down the road, leaving the stockade walls behind. He rode for hours and miles into the forested hills, where he knew the Hethrren had their primary camps. He would find the barbarians, or they would find him. It didn't matter which; the end result would be the same.

The godling simmered after him, wavering back and forth and leaving a smoking path in the grasses. Though he was alone in a land infested by bloodthirsty barbarians, Klovus felt no fear, no vulnerability. The godling was tethered to him, always at his beck and call, even as it stretched away to explore its boundaries. The horse continued along, and the godling rushed into the pines, rocking the boughs, creating a storm in the high trees.

Klovus traveled all night. Near dawn, as deep red light seeped from the east, he heard shouts from the forest and the approach of horses. His mare snorted. He was alone on the road, a pudgy bald man in a blue caftan. He halted his mount at a wide clearing and waited, hearing the hoofbeats grow louder. Soon enough, fur-clad warriors galloped toward him bearing clubs and swords. They let out a wordless howl upon seeing their victim.

Keeping his uneasy horse under control, he faced them and shouted, "I demand to see Magda." He felt the powerful godling lurking in the trees.

The Hethrren rode up, hideous-looking men with some teeth crooked, some sharpened. Their long hair was braided and knotted beneath metal helmets. "Magda will eat you alive," one of the men growled.

With a thought, Klovus summoned the godling, letting the thing show itself. "She would find me an unpleasant meal." He needed to clench the barbarians in his iron grip, and thus he had to terrify them.

The entity flowed back to him, crashing through the boughs. The pines shook with a rushing sound, intimidating the riders. Their dark horses

pawed the ground, backing away. His own mare trembled but remained under control.

With his heels, he nudged his mount into motion, making the barbarians
accompany him. He didn't know how far away their main camp was.

After he spoke with Magda and learned what the Hethrren really wanted,
then he could determine how best to use them.

55

HIDDEN beneath her palace after the assassination attempt, Empra Iluris lay motionless and pale, but safe for now. Cemi and the hawk guards made her as comfortable as possible. They had no doctor with them in their secret, sheltered place, but none of the court physicians had been able to help anyway. Cemi could not tell if her own care helped at all, but she did it for Iluris regardless.

She, Captani Vos, and six hawk guards remained inside the camouflaged chamber, though searchers must be trying to hunt them down. Tense days passed, and Cemi, feeling safe for the time being, wondered what would happen next. The hawk guards stood vigil, ready to give their lives to protect the empra and her designated heir.

At first, Cemi didn't let herself think beyond mere survival, but now they had to consider a larger plan. How long could they simply cover themselves in shadows? What would happen if the empra never awakened? Palace guards had participated in the assassination attempt, and killers had infiltrated the serving staff. They had no allies and didn't know whom to trust.

"We cannot hide forever," Cemi said, her words startlingly loud in the silent chamber. "We have to prepare for what to do next."

"I know," Vos said. The two had grown very close in their enforced isolation. When Cemi looked at the captani, she noted the crooked shape of his once-broken nose, which added a counterpoint to his otherwise handsome face. "My hawk guards and I will fight, as will you, but our little group is not enough to stand against the key priestlord and his forces. If they find this place, they will kill Iluris, kill you, and dispose of all loose ends."

Cemi looked to the masked chamber opening and felt a thrill of macabre mystery. "We aren't entirely alone."

Their strange guardian had remained in place, hiding them. If she focused, Cemi could peer through the hazy illusion, but outsiders would see only solid rock. She still didn't understand what the entity was.

Only old Analera and a handful of trusted servants knew where the empra and her protectors were hiding. They had sworn their loyalty, and they understood that the smallest accidental revelation could mean the life of Iluris. Loyal Analera came every day smuggling food, water, plentiful candles, and chamber pots. An empra deserved far better conditions, but they were safe until they could develop a strong plan.

Cemi recalled what she'd endured on the streets in Prirari, the dark and filthy places she had hidden when pursued by gangs. There had been a ruthless one-armed man named Lero, who kidnapped street children and forced them to rob drunkards. Once Cemi blossomed into womanhood, men had wanted to force themselves on her, but she still kept her virginity, despite the efforts of one aggressive man who tried to tear off her skirts in an alley. Cemi had found her knife in time and castrated him. He wouldn't be taking anyone's virginity.

Cemi was good at surviving, and she would do so now. But Empra Iluris would want her to find a way to save the throne, too.

After two weeks of relative quiet, the mysterious guardian dissipated, fading into the air and leaving only a filmy shimmer across the opening. The tunnels outside were silent, and no one came.

Taking turns, hawk guards ventured out as scouts but did not let themselves be seen. Since they were the empra's personal protectors, they would surely be targeted. Cemi could not guess how extensive the plot was.

She went over to sit by the pale, fragile woman. She said to Vos, "If Iluris awakens, she can stand before the people and reclaim her authority. But they would never accept just me. . . ."

"You are stronger than you know," he surprised her by saying. "When the assassins came, I believe that *you* were the real target, Cemi. Not the empra."

She looked at him in disbelief. "Me? I am nothing. The attack was meant to finish the job and kill Iluris."

Vos slowly shook his head. "Oh, they would have killed the empra, to be sure, but right now you are more important. Everyone knows you were Iluris's chosen successor. You are a much greater threat to Key Priestlord Klovus."

Cemi sat down on a water barrel, feeling the weight of what he had said. As she considered the idea, she knew his words were true.

Vos continued: "If Klovus felt he could manipulate you, he would put you on the throne right now. But he knows you would not be his puppet."

"Never!" Cemi said.

"Therefore, you must be eliminated. Without you, Klovus will be the obvious mouthpiece for the empra." He leaned closer, his face filled with worry for her. "The key priestlord benefits from having Iluris alive but incapacitated, because then he can make all the decisions in her name. You are the one he needs to be concerned about."

Cemi swallowed. "That's why he killed Chamberlain Nerev." If it came to a direct challenge of leadership, could a sixteen-year-old street girl ever command the loyalty of an entire land? She didn't think so. Not against a powerful and ambitious man like the key priestlord.

Suddenly, two hawk guard scouts hurried into the chamber, alarmed as they passed through the faint field. "Searchers are coming through the tunnels again. We may have to kill them." The men looked at the thin camouflage over the opening. "They will probably find us."

Vos and Cemi rose from the empra's side. If they were merely casual searchers, the hawk guards would make swift work of them, but then the searchers' absence would be missed, and more would come. Cemi got ready to fight. The other tense guards fell into a hush.

Cemi suddenly felt a lurch in her heart, a fire running through her veins and her thoughts. The air shimmered and thickened in the chamber at the same time as a ripple of self-contained energy thickened across the entrance to the chamber. The entity hardened, shifted color, and once again became a perfect mask of a stone wall. Then, on the inside, it shifted to blurry and transparent, so that Cemi and the others could see out into the corridor.

Within moments a party of Isharan soldiers strode along, clearly hunting for something. The suspicious men poked into alcoves, giving a cursory search. The protective presence remained in place, shielding the refugees, and the soldiers walked past the camouflaged stone wall without a second glance. Vos and the guards let out a quiet sigh of relief when they were gone.

Cemi felt drawn to the shimmering entity that had protected them. She stepped close, sensing the crackle in the air and energy like the echo of a thunderstorm. Tentatively, she reached out to touch the field. Her fingertips tingled, but not painfully. She pressed her palm harder against it and felt a warmth inside, a connection.

Could this strange protector be a new godling manifested by the constant prayers for Empra Iluris? Every day, the people chanted and sacrificed—not just to the godling in Serepol, but also to the empra herself. She suspected the new godling was tethered to Iluris and, by extension, to Cemi, too.

She pressed harder with her palm, enjoying the thrumming reassurance, and knew the entity would protect them. *Are you a new godling?*

The searchers had long since vanished down the corridor, but the invisible guardian remained in place. Cemi whispered, "Thank you," and felt that it understood her. She also sensed it was curious, even a little frightened about its situation. Maybe it did not understand what it was.

"I'll tell you stories, if you stay," she promised. "Once I explain what I know, you can protect us better." The warm tingle inside her was the godling's way of acknowledging her words.

Vos looked at Cemi with awe. She smiled, glad she could impress the handsome guard captain. At last, Cemi allowed herself to feel genuinely safe.

∾

After bringing a basket of smoked fish and fresh apples through the blurry camouflage field, Analera distributed the food. During their weeks of restless hiding, the old servant also brought them news from outside. The old woman told them of rumors spreading throughout the city because Empra Iluris had mysteriously vanished. Some raised the question of foul play, with Klovus the obvious guilty party.

"Priestlord Klovus rode away to Tamburdin with part of the Isharan army," Analera said. "The Hethrren barbarians have stepped up their attacks." She grimaced. "I am quite happy to have that man gone."

Cemi looked at Analera as thoughts spiraled out, possibilities she had not guessed before. "This may be our chance." She glanced at Captani Vos, who nodded. Flushed, he rose to his feet, barely able to contain his excitement.

"If Key Priestlord Klovus has gone to Tamburdin," Cemi said, "we have to take advantage of the opportunity. At least spread word through the streets, find out who our allies are." She tried to think of what Empra Iluris would have done. She searched through her memories of classes, the lectures of statecraft. For Iluris, she needed to find some way to hold the land together, otherwise her mentor would have no throne when she finally awakened.

"Should we bring the empra out to the people?" Analera asked. "Show them that she is still alive? We can reveal the assassination plot."

Cemi wanted that more than anything, but she was wise enough to understand the great risks and drawbacks. "What they will see is an unconscious woman near death. They will think the empra is weak, and they will be fearful."

Vos interjected: "We know that Klovus is behind those assassins, but we have no proof. His men have been searching for us constantly." He looked up at the shimmering entity that provided camouflage. "Without our guardian, we would have been discovered weeks ago."

Cemi said, "We don't know how many secret allies Klovus has. This conspiracy might run through the army as well as the palace guards. If we show ourselves but have no allies, the empra and all of us might well be killed before we could speak a word to the people."

"But you can't just hide, my lady!" Analera said, then intentionally added, "Excellency. The people do not know what to think. They have heard nothing of their beloved empra, have not seen Iluris except for when you rushed her through the streets after returning from Fulcor Island. Even you, Cemi, have not stepped forth to claim your place."

"I wasn't strong enough," Cemi said.

"My hawk guards will help you," Vos replied. "*I* will help you."

Cemi thought of what she might do, even trapped here. Iluris would have told her to think and see *differently*, to find unexpected resources where others saw nothing. "We must plant seeds. Analera, you have contacts in the city, in the craft districts, the markets. You speak to other servants, traders, shop owners, craftspeople, commoners."

"Oh yes, Excellency. Every day I hear people expressing their fear for the empra, praying for her to come back. You heard it, too, from the tower windows."

"Praying for her . . ." Cemi said and thought of the shimmering force that protected them. "Have them keep praying, but also tell them that the empra is with the godlings, that she is guarded by them against the treachery in her own land. And when she is strong enough, she will return." She bit her lower lip, smiling at what she had suggested. "Yes, spread the rumor. Let her people tell the story."

"Oh, yes." The old servant's thin lips broke into a grin. "It will be like ripples from stones thrown into a pond. They will talk, and others will talk. The story will take hold while the key priestlord is gone."

"Tell as many people as you can," Cemi said. "Compile a list of our most trusted supporters, people we can contact when it is time, but do not write it down."

Analera responded with a somber nod. "I would not put such people at risk." She touched the side of her temple. "I will know. I will remember who is still loyal."

"Good," Cemi said, taking both of Analera's hands in hers with a grateful smile. "While the key priestlord is in Tamburdin with Isharan troops, it's time for us to quietly raise our own army."

56

WHEN Elliel and Thon returned from the north without a young boy huddled on their saddle, King Kollanan's heart broke again. He hung his head, squeezed Tafira's hand. "Ancestors' blood, what have they done with the poor child?"

Without dismounting, the two reined in their horses at the gates, where the king and queen met them. Elliel looked down at Koll from the saddle. "Your grandson lives, Sire, but the frostwreth queen refuses to release him. She considers Birch a pet."

Kollanan wrestled with his emotions. Birch might be alive, but Queen Onn knew the child's value as a hostage . . . if wreths even understood such things. When the sandwreth reinforcements arrived to attack the Lake Bakal fortress, how would Onn react? Now that the diplomatic overture had failed, would she simply send his body back for revenge? How much did she value him?

"Does she know that he is the king's grandson?" Koll asked.

Elliel considered. "I don't think so, Sire."

"I do not believe she makes much distinction among humans," Thon said. "I used my powers to intimidate them, but Onn threatened to kill the boy if I used greater force. I . . . I am sorry I was not able to accomplish it."

Tafira looked up at the distraught riders, noting the exhausted horses, the scuffed tack, the rumpled clothes. "Thank you for trying. It was a brave attempt."

"Were the wreths preparing to strike?" Koll asked. "How much time do we have before they retaliate?"

Thon fidgeted in his saddle, as if distracted by the towering walls of Fellstaff. Elliel said, "Thon's powers will make Queen Onn think twice about attacking us. I don't think she's ever seen anything like it."

Thon said, "The frostwreths are building a huge army in the north. They consider the sandwreths their mortal enemies, but humans seem to be no more than a nuisance to them."

Elliel nodded. "I agree. Norterra did not seem to be her greatest concern."

Thon brightened and turned back to the king. "We did accomplish one thing." He patted two large wrapped packages slung behind his saddle. "The frostwreths offered all their historical records."

Elliel's smile was filled with pride. "You gave her no choice."

Thon responded with a sheepish grin. "The scholar girl and I will learn as much as we can about who I am and who the wreths are."

❧

The castle's private library was lit by a warm fire. Pokle added logs twice an hour, mainly as an excuse to see Shadri. With candles in sconces as well as the watery sunlight from the windows, the young woman found the place warm, cozy, and conducive to learning.

Shadri wished she could read the wreth language herself. Stacks of sand-wreth documents remained for study. She and Thon had translated and transcribed only a small portion of them.

Standing before the long library table, Thon magnanimously spread out the sheets he had just retrieved from Queen Onn. "Now, with both sets of records, we have the history of the wreth race . . . my race? Soon, scholar girl, we will know more about the wreths than anyone else in the world."

Shadri tapped the crystal sheets and looked at the handwritten papers beside them, where she had transcribed the other legends, including the apocryphal tale of Kur hiding inside the mountain to forget his sorrow. "I doubt either version is the true history. Were these accounts written contemporaneously, or are they legends set down much later?"

Thon picked up a sheet, held the transparent crystal up to the candlelight, watched the flame flicker through the etched writing. "What is true history and what is a false story? How would we know? I don't remember any of it personally, nor do you."

Shadri pondered and then asked a question that would have horrified any legacier. "Does that ancient history truly matter to us now? Humans survived for two thousand years after the wreths destroyed the world and abandoned us. We built ourselves up, created our own cities. We have records of those terrible first centuries, while we healed the world. As stewards, we tended the scarred fields and replanted the forests so that two thousand years later the land is recovered, almost healthy. That is what matters more to me."

"And now the wreths are back," Thon said. "I do not believe it is cause for celebration."

"Neither do I." Shadri picked up one of the crystal documents Thon had brought back from the north, then pulled out a fresh sheet of paper. For so long she had wandered the three kingdoms with her meager journals, writing in cramped letters and filling each page with as many words as she could possibly fit. Now it seemed extravagant to have so much paper, but she was writing history, documenting vital new information. She felt pride in her heart to have such important work. "To business."

Thon ran his long finger across the crystal surface as if his mere fingertip could draw truth from the document. "If you are ready, Shadri?"

She adjusted her blank paper, flexed her fingers, and dipped the quill in ink. "I am ready."

Thon pricked his thumb and spilled a drop of blood onto the crystal sheet before his innate healing abilities stopped the flow. The stain on the crystal-line sheet interacted with the markings, catalyzing them to display layers of text that hung in the air.

Thon narrated a story about some of the last wreth battles, in which the exhausted and decimated armies battled in the mountains. Most of the human foot soldiers had already been wiped out, parts of the landscape turned to black glass by magical explosions and outpourings of blood.

In the crags of what were now called the Dragonspine Mountains, Queen Voo had her final confrontation with Queen Onn. They battled on the mountaintop with the ground shaking and lava flowing, the world itself crushed and broken around them. The two clashed with crystal spears and sharpened swords, symbolizing the age-old conflict, their need for revenge.

Thon paused as he read. "I found an account of the same battle written by the sandwreths, and it is a different story." He let out a rude snort. "Each faction sees through only one eye."

He finished reading about how Voo had slashed Onn's face before a great eruption shook the mountains and drove the two apart. The frostwreths swept their wounded queen to safety, while the sandwreths retreated across the blasted land. Both races went dormant for two thousand years.

"I wish they'd just stayed gone," Shadri muttered. "And left us alone."

Thon selected another random sheet from the stack and read an important story about a pair of wreths who had actually battled Ossus. One huge army was led by Dar from the frostwreth faction—although oddly the text simply said *wreths*, without distinguishing whether they were the descendants of Raan or Suth. Dar wounded the enormous dragon with her spear, and Rao, "one of the greatest wreth warriors," fought beside her. Ossus was injured, and the dragon tunneled deep under the mountains, where it remained buried ever since.

"I think I must have been sealed inside Mount Vada long before Dar and Rao battled the dragon," Thon said. "I don't remember it."

Shadri ran a finger along her lips, curious. "So, Dar was a frostwreth, and it is apparent from other documents that Rao came from the sandwreths. In this story, the two are fighting together, joining forces against a common enemy."

"Ah, a novel concept! Though I am sure both races would deny your interpretation. They seem to have forgotten that point now."

"Whether or not it was ever true," Shadri muttered.

Thon said, "Dar's spear is mounted behind Queen Onn's throne, and it still has the blood of the dragon. I saw it myself. That gives evidence the story is at least partly true."

Shadri was more skeptical. "Anyone can hang a bloodstained spear on a wall and tell a story. And it seems preposterous that a dragon can be so large that its buried body makes a mountain range. If Ossus is truly that big, how would the wreths possibly defeat it? Even if they all worked together?"

Thon regarded her skeptically. "You know how much evil exists in the world—look at what happened to my poor Elliel. We know what the Isharans did to your Konag Conndur. We saw how the frostwreths wiped out the people at Lake Bakal. The dragon is the embodiment of that evil. Kur must have had a plan for it all." He scratched his dark hair, his brow furrowing. "It feels strange to speak of him that way. If I . . ."

"So the story goes," Shadri said. "Kur purged himself of all evil thoughts and used them to manifest the enormous dragon. But that doesn't make sense. If all the evil in the world is wrapped up in a dragon buried deep beneath the mountains, then why is there still evil loose in the world?" She raised her hands in frustration. "Why is there violence and anger and revenge? We see it everywhere! Why do people still do terrible things to one another? Why do the wreths still hate their rivals? The evil is not buried away!"

"I do not think all darkness remained sealed inside the dragon," Thon said. "How could one dragon encompass it all? Perhaps evil is inherent in us . . . or in you. Maybe you are born with it. It is as if in purging himself, Kur removed a bucket of water from a stream, yet the water keeps flowing."

"Then what hope is there?" Shadri asked. "If the wreths are inherently flawed and therefore we humans—their secondary creations—are also flawed, then killing the dragon will not stop the evil."

Thon ignored the hovering letters that shimmered in the air. "True. The stream will keep flowing."

Shadri leaned close and asked, "Can you feel the evil in yourself? You aren't human, and I'm not entirely convinced you're just a wreth either. If you are Kur, then there's no evil in you. . . . If you purged all that darkness from yourself, do you experience hate? Do *you* feel violence?"

"I do not know what it would feel like. . . ." He shrugged again. "Maybe we all need hardness and softness, strength and weakness, in order to be truly strong."

With a wave of his hand, the letters in the air disappeared. He was much more interested in the discussion with Shadri than in reading documents. "Maybe a single dragon cannot contain all of the dark powers of a god. What if the evil from Ossus is leaking out into the world . . . and has done so for centuries?"

Shadri was caught up in the idea. "Or maybe Ossus is gone, but still lives inside every one of us. If all the evil in the world were safely buried away, if every person—every wreth and every human—was entirely good and pure, then how would you even measure evil? Would it even exist?"

Thon remained silent for a long moment. "I do not know." He picked up another sheet and pricked his thumb, reopening the wound. "Let us content ourselves with legends instead of philosophy. Sometimes that makes more sense."

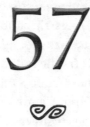

57

A PROCESSION of augas came over the hills, twenty of the beasts striding two abreast. The reptilian beasts plodded forward on muscular
legs, dragging wooden sledges piled high with remarkable obsidian material.

Adan was reminded of an Utauk caravan. Leading the procession was
the stern wreth mage Axus, followed by three other wreths from the worker
caste. The augas ground to a halt as Adan came out to meet them. His Banner guards remained alert, taking up positions behind him, but he felt alone
without Penda or her father.

Mage Axus did not dismount, but turned his deeply lined face down toward the king. "Queen Voo commanded that I deliver this shadowglass and
provide instruction in its use. Shadowglass is a potent substance." Other
wreths worked to detach the harnesses from the beasts. As if a spell had been
broken, the sledges sagged onto the ground.

Adan looked at the piled black sheets that drank all the light of day. Other
boxes carried shards and fragments. His father-in-law often wore a pendant
of black glass hanging from his ear as ornamentation, and the load from
even a single sledge here was worth a fortune. "You have brought me a great
treasure."

"Not treasure—a war chest. As Queen Voo explained, this shadowglass is
to be used to enhance weapons for your fighters. With such armaments, your
army may survive when we battle the frostwreths. The queen wants you to
kill as many of them as possible."

The worker wreths lifted sheets of the obsidian. Axus continued, "Use the
shadowglass to make your shields impervious to frostwreth magic. Larger
fragments can serve as projectiles." His stony face creased in what might
have been the attempt at a smile. "Smaller shards can be used for arrows
and spears that will pierce frostwreth armor. Longer shards can be inlaid on
swords to enhance the blades. Shadowglass fuses well with steel."

Adan walked past the mounted wreth mage, studying the nearest pile of shadowglass. Tentatively, he touched the intriguing stone, expecting the black surface to feel hot under the open sun, but it was cold and eerily slippery. He withdrew his tingling fingertips and looked at them as if they had been burned by magic. His glassmakers and stonemasons would be fascinated by the shadowglass. "How fragile is it?"

"Shadowglass is dangerous, not fragile. Queen Voo is convinced that your Suderran army will serve us well in the final war. You will be rewarded for it. Some of your people might even survive." His voice grew deeper. "Voo watches you, King Adan Starfall. The queen is counting on you, and she will know when your army is ready."

Adan felt a chill, but he met the mage's deep amber eyes. "Thank you for this powerful gift."

The ominous mage nodded. "Voo has faith in humans. She is impressed that your race survived after the ancient wars. Some sandwreths disagree with me, but I suspect that humans may be more than they seem."

Once the heavy loads were unhitched from the augas, the worker wreths mounted the reptile saddles again. Mage Axus nudged his auga and bounded off. The worker wreths turned their now-unhitched mounts, and the entire pack thundered off toward the hills and the barren expanse of desert, leaving the sledges behind.

꒰꒱

An Utauk caravan arrived in Bannriya carrying the usual assortment of spices and craft items, but the caravan leader, a bearded man named Melik, also brought the best possible news. The man brushed road dust from his colorful cloak. He grinned, bowed, raised his head, and grinned again. "Your wife sends her greetings and her love, King Adan." He drew a circle around his chest. "The beginning is the end is the beginning."

Adan reflexively did the same. "Where is she? How is she? Is the baby born yet?"

Melik's bushy brows drew together. "She and Hale Orr have hidden themselves among the Utauk tribes, Sire. It is not safe to tell you any further information."

"Her location is secret even from me? I am her husband."

"Penda says you are also in contact with the sandwreths. Who knows what evil magic Queen Voo might use to extract information from your mind?"

Adan felt a hard knot in his gut. "So answer my other questions—is the baby born yet? How is Penda?"

"She still has time," Melik said, "and she is in good health and good spirits, except that she misses you."

"Except for that."

"We parted ways more than a week ago, but she asked me to bring her message to you if I ever returned to Bannriya."

Though the caravan leader had said little of substance, the mere contact from his beloved wife made Adan giddy. "Thank you, Melik. Bring your wares to our kitchens and castle staff. We may find some of it useful."

Melik had a twinkle in his eye. "I charge high prices, Sire, especially when I know that you feel obligated to buy something."

Adan laughed. "I expected nothing less!"

Because of the encounter, the king was smiling as he entered the council chambers for the day's session with his advisors, but when he looked at the sour faces and heard his commanders issue their reports, the warmth in his heart quickly faded.

"Shadowglass is an interesting substance, Sire," said Lenon, his most experienced military commander, a man who had put down a brief rebellion a decade ago. "The armorers and swordsmiths experimented with samples of the stuff. It does indeed fuse well with steel."

On the table lay samples on display—a sword, a handful of arrows, a shield, even a metal helmet. Adan picked up the sword, which had been inlaid with patches of shadowglass. He turned it from side to side.

One advisor, Elfas, held up a bleeding thumb he had been nursing. "Careful, Sire. I nicked myself on the stuff."

Adan stepped closer to the open window and lifted the blade into the sunlight. The glass was as black as a lonely night. He swung the blade slowly forward, and then in a backstroke, swift and sure. The sword whistled with a low, mournful sigh. He picked up the arrows, each one tipped with a sharp triangular fragment of shadowglass. The edges were like razors, each tip a dagger. "How many of these can we make?"

"Thousands," said Lenon. "It all depends on how you want to distribute the materials the wreths gave us."

Urgar, another military advisor, spoke up. "If the material is as powerful as Mage Axus says, we should create as many weapons as possible. Equip our army and build a large stockpile. Can we ask her for more shadowglass once we've used all of the first shipment?"

"Possibly," Adan said, "as long as we keep convincing her that we are doing her bidding."

"Why are we doing her bidding?" growled an unsettled vassal lord. "Now that we know what those wreths are all about and how they intend to enslave us or let us be killed on the battlefield, why help them at all?"

"Because Voo is watching us," Adan said. "We'll use this shadowglass to arm our soldiers, as she requests. I want her to keep thinking of us as allies."

"But why do it, Sire?" pleaded Elfas. "It is foolish to build such a huge fighting force for her benefit! Why accept these weapons?"

Adan made his voice as sharp as one of the shadowglass blades. "Because this substance is deadly to wreths—*all* wreths." He looked around the table. "That means we can use shadowglass against sandwreths, as well."

Around the table, the others smiled as understanding dawned. Lenon nodded, because clearly the thought had already occurred to him. Adan touched the obsidian surface on a displayed shield, feeling the cold that reached all the way to the core. He had a lot of work to do and much blood to shed so he could make the future safe for his child. . . .

Before the end of the meeting, a courier arrived after riding hard and changing horses along the way. He was breathless when he delivered the folded message from Konag Mandan. With a sense of foreboding, Adan broke open the wax seal, not overly mindful of the ornate "M" on the konag's stamp. He read with widening eyes.

"It is not unexpected," he said in a hoarse voice. His brother had declared outright war against Ishara. In an impetuous and poorly planned strike, Mandan had lost many ships in a naval attack against Fulcor Island—an attempt to recapture the garrison, which failed miserably. Now he wanted revenge even more than before.

Adan read the message aloud to the disbelieving council members. "The konag demands that we send all the military resources of Suderra to join his war against Ishara. He commands that I offer up my entire army, march our soldiers to Convera, where they will be dispatched across the ocean to fight." His tight grip wrinkled the edges of the letter. "He orders me to leave my kingdom defenseless! At a time like this!" He shook his head, barely noticing the gasps of astonishment and angry disbelief. "I want to avenge my father as much as anyone, but . . . but my entire army? I cannot. I cannot!"

With the sandwreths watching everything he did, Queen Voo would never let him send away what she considered to be *her* army.

58

A HUMAN emissary and his party from Konag Mandan arrived at the edge of the desert. After a long journey, the man and his four dusty escort soldiers looked plaintive and lost.

Queen Voo found them disappointing. She had expected something more extraordinary from the great ruler of the three kingdoms. She had demanded to see Mandan himself, as a gesture of respect, and this mere emissary was not at all satisfactory.

A wreth patrol had spotted the humans stumbling through the rocky canyons. Per Voo's instructions, her scouts surrounded the konag's party, then herded them to the sand palace.

When the sunburned and inadequate emissary was brought before her throne, Voo tried to be polite. After all, King Adan had proved useful and interesting in certain ways. And she had him under her thumb. She had sent him shipments of shadowglass so he could prepare his army for her. Perhaps this Konag Mandan could be useful as well, provided he learned to show respect.

The nervous emissary had a long face, narrow nose, and sparse beard; his thick brown hair was disheveled from rough travel. Because the wreth patrol had rushed the humans here, the man had not been able to make himself presentable, but Voo was happy to keep him off balance. His garments were heavy and ornate, featuring brocade, thick cuffs, gold buttons—showy, perhaps, but entirely impractical for desert travel. Even so, the man had a pompous and self-important air, as if his costume earned him intrinsic respect. In Voo's eyes, it did not. She wondered what messages he might bring and what excuses he would make.

Wearing drawn expressions, his human escort soldiers stood behind him, trying to look intimidating in their flimsy armor. Voo's guards had not bothered to disarm them; perhaps it calmed them to think they had some chance of defending themselves. Every man among them looked out of his depth.

The escort soldiers had carried a weighty chest into her throne room, some kind of gift, she supposed. Either they were weak, or the chest was filled with a heavy burden. They wallowed in the soft sand of the floor as they stumbled forward.

Voo lounged on her throne, showing the tan skin of her thigh and calf. She wore only scant armor that left her midriff bare. She did not desire any of these men, but she wondered if they found her enticing.

Standing before her on the clean sand floor, the emissary brushed dust from his heavy garments and cleared his throat. "It is my honor to introduce myself to you, Queen Voo of the sandwreths. I am Lord Goran, designated representative of Konag Mandan. He sent me in response to your invitation."

He bowed from his neck rather than kneeling or prostrating himself on the sand. She didn't know what sort of gesture she had expected, but this disappointed her, too.

Goran continued: "We rode long and hard to see you."

Voo wondered if their konag considered himself her equal. She leaned forward on her throne like a predator sensing its next meal. "King Adan of Suderra shows respect by speaking to me in person when I call him. He understands my power and he knows his place. My instructions to Konag Mandan were quite clear. I commanded him to come to me in person, and yet he sent . . . you." She nearly spat the last word.

Goran bowed again, and his escort soldiers shifted uncomfortably. They stank of fear. "My deepest apologies, Queen Voo. Konag Mandan is currently engaged in a terrible war. Defending the three kingdoms against Ishara commands his complete attention." Goran remained awkward, a poor diplomat. "Under other circumstances, he would have come here himself, but he sent me, one of his most respected vassal lords, in his stead. I have his countenance." The simpering man pressed his hands together and bowed a little deeper, as if he began to understand his dire situation. "I hope you find my presence acceptable."

Voo scowled at him. She still felt frustrated that Adan had refused to bring his pregnant wife, despite Voo's clear invitation. Sooner or later, Quo would find Penda wherever she was hiding out in the wilderness. But at least King Adan and King Kollanan had come to see her in person, rather than sending some insulting substitute. "I do not find you acceptable."

Fourteen wreth warriors stood around the throne room, holding their weapons ready. In mere seconds they could cut the escort party to pieces. Voo had only to lift a finger.

Flushed and sweating, Goran scuttled to the ornate chest his soldiers had delivered. "To show his generosity, Konag Mandan sent this gift for you." He lifted the wooden lid to reveal mounds of gold coins, chains, jeweled rings, and loose gems. Oily white saltpearls were scattered among the treasure like the remnants of a hailstorm. "He scoured his treasury to find beautiful and worthy items for you. He hopes that you and I will have fruitful discussions, and that at some point you will visit him at Convera Castle."

Voo stepped down the dais and glided across the sand floor, leaving no footprints as she approached. Goran seemed proud of the treasure he had just offered. Without looking at him, she sifted her hands through the coins, chains, and gems. She held a saltpearl between thumb and forefinger, then flicked it across the room. With two fingers, she pushed the entire chest over and dumped the contents onto the sandy floor.

Her expression grew stormy. "I hoped to find something else hidden at the bottom, but all I see are jewels and pretty metals . . . things that I can create anytime I wish." Goran blinked at her, not knowing what to say. Voo raged. "Do you think to impress a wreth queen with shiny objects? We are your creators! When I have need of you, you must obey."

Goran didn't seem to understand what she was saying. "But Queen Voo, uh, Majesty . . ." He spread his hands. "I'm sorry, but I do not know the proper way to address you. Konag Mandan meant this treasure as a great honor. He sent this chest hoping you'd accept it as a gesture."

"A gesture? Very well. I will return his gift with a gesture of my own." Voo looked at the overturned wooden chest and sized up the pathetic man. "Go back to your konag with a message from me." She touched the wooden chest. "You may have difficulty fitting inside, but I will help."

Concentrating on the quivering human, Voo used her magic to bend his arms, until his bones snapped. Goran gasped in terror, and his eyes bulged with pain. She broke his leg bones, folding him up, shoving him down. With the flick of a finger, she cracked his spine. Goran screamed.

The human soldiers drew their swords and yelled, but they were vastly outnumbered by the wreth warriors around them. Voo told them not to kill the escort, though. Instead the horrified humans were forced to watch as she bent, twisted, folded, and compacted Goran's body. With magic, she tucked his head down to the center of his chest, and turned it, reshaping him, while keeping him alive. In the end, the broken and compacted Goran fit inside the treasure chest, though not an inch of space was wasted.

She closed the lid on his agonized face and stepped back to regard the pale, horrified soldiers. "You may take him back to Convera Castle, so that they may all glimpse my power. Then tell Konag Mandan that the next time I issue an invitation, I expect it to be properly obeyed."

59

U THO was reluctant to leave at such a crucial time, but he had Brava business to attend to. He made certain that the konag had issued the proper instructions for the vengewar, and the glamorous royal wedding plans continued apace. Then, leaving Mandan in the care of his inner council, Utho packed his saddlebags and rode off.

Utho promised he would be back in a week, but he could not tell anyone where he was going, since the training villages were not marked on any map. Long ago, after the massacre of Valaera, the Bravas had vowed never to be vulnerable again.

Departing from Convera, he rode west through the trees, following main roads into the mountains where traffic had dwindled since the eruption of Mount Vada. He knew exactly when to leave the main route and head off on what looked like a game path into the tall stands of beech trees. The forest floor was strewn with layers of sweet-smelling brown leaves. He turned north at a thin stream and followed the bank until he found another trail that led him to a cluster of buildings surrounded by pines.

As he approached, he expected to see Brava children practicing with wooden staffs and blunted swords. Instead, the settlement was eerily quiet. His horse whickered, and the silence made him alert. He touched the sword at his side.

When he found Onzu, however, he saw that his old training master had merely put the students to work on daily chores instead of mock battles. The eleven Brava children had smooth movements and a lissome flexibility, even when they were pulling weeds. Every child here would become a black-clad warrior once he or she became proficient in necessary skills.

Many of the children sported purple and yellow bruises as if they were regularly beaten by a stern master, but Utho knew they were the marks of relentless rough-and-tumble training. No student of Onzu's, regardless of skill or talent, emerged unscathed from a day's session. The wizened old warrior insisted that a sore body promoted humility; he also wanted to hammer home the realization that no Brava was ever immortal. "We will all fall to an opponent one day," Onzu had said. "Death will claim each one of us, but I want my final opponent to be old age rather than some fighter on a battlefield."

Each qualified Brava went out as a paladin to defend the land or to bind their services to a patron. Many came back to live in the training village for a year or so, performing necessary work for the Brava people before they departed for their larger duty.

Utho had a sudden flash of one other Brava paladin, the young man Onder—one of the sons of Master Onzu, though the family bond was not strong—who had faced a rampaging godling alongside Utho at the fishing village of Mirrabay. Onder's courage and training had broken that day, though, and he had fled, disgracing himself. The Brava had been banished, his memory stripped away with a rune of forgetting applied by Utho himself. That young man had been trained here, by Onzu.

Master Onzu knew what his son had done, and what Utho had done, but they did not speak of it. The old master had a calm, strong grasp on what was necessary.

Today, Onzu had put the children to work in the community gardens. Some excavated potatoes from dirt mounds, others harvested tomatoes and beans. The children looked up as Utho rode in. One boy set down his shovel.

The training master sat on a rock observing the work, ready to offer criticism. His smile showed a broken tooth from where he had let his defenses slip in a battle—once. "Utho! Come to do your Brava duty? There are no women here waiting for a man. The last one rode out two weeks ago."

"And I'm sure you did your own duty." Every Brava had an obligation to continue the half-breed bloodline, but Utho had no love for any of those women. After losing Mareka, Utho had also lost his capability for love and romance. All that remained for him was duty, his vow to protect the Bravas, the Commonwealth, and the konag. "I came for a more serious purpose." He assessed the children of various ages who had stopped their garden work to listen, but realized they were all too young. "None of your students are ripe yet, but I would ask you for your help."

Onzu stiffly rose from his rock. Utho knew the old man exaggerated his physical ailments because that made opponents underestimate him. "I assist where I can, Utho. You were one of my best trainees." He snapped at the bruised and weary children, "Get back to work! If you don't maintain our gardens, we will starve." He snorted. "At the very least, we'll have to go to the next village and buy food." The children returned to their chores, but they continued to eavesdrop.

Utho ignored them. "This village is isolated, but you must know that Konag Conndur was murdered by the Isharans, and that the Commonwealth is now at war." Nearby, his horse snuffled at the plants growing in the garden. One of the students shooed the horse away. "Conndur foolishly attempted to forge an alliance with the Isharan animals. They killed him for it. His greatest mistake was trusting them in the first place."

Onzu seemed surprised by his harsh tone, but Utho did not back down. The entire Commonwealth had to be engaged in this great war for their very survival. Utho's empty void could only be filled with revenge. He had spread the call for capable fighters, and Konag Mandan had decreed that any seaworthy vessel was to be conscripted into the Commonwealth navy to rebuild the fleet. But Utho also needed the Bravas.

"It is our vengewar, Onzu—at last. We need all our people from across the three kingdoms, including paladins and bonded Bravas. If you send out the word, they will come."

Onzu scratched the side of his nose, and a troubled look crossed his face. "Why me, Utho? You are bonded to the konag himself. They will listen to you as much as they listen to me."

"They respect me, but they revere you."

Onzu laughed, but he seemed uneasy. "I do not argue when one of my students speaks the truth."

"Our only goal must be to punish the Isharans. The blood of Konag Conndur is only one more reason to hate them. We will swarm over their continent, reestablish our colony there, let the Bravas thrive in a new Valaera."

The old master looked wistfully at the idealized statue of a Brava man near his own dwelling. "Just like the dream Olan had for our people when he led them across the sea. . . ." He narrowed his eyes, enhancing his wrinkles. "I am isolated here, as you say, but I am not deaf. I know that our paladins have discovered entire villages that are simply empty, including one of our Brava settlements. We cannot account for that . . . but I know it has nothing to do with Isharans."

Utho was surprised. "Some settlements emptied out after the eruption of Mount Vada. Many towns were evacuated, and the countryside is still in turmoil. I am aware of this."

"Not that," Onzu said with a snort. "Not that! I mean small mountain villages, particularly in western Suderra, entirely abandoned. A Brava training settlement empty, silent . . . all of them gone. Taken, if you ask me."

Utho felt a chill. "What are you saying? Who can defeat Bravas?"

"Indeed, who can defeat Bravas?" Onzu repeated while nodding. "You know the answer—the wreths! They have returned, and they see us as a resource for their own wars."

Utho's face twisted in disdain. "Wreths again? We have heard rumors, but the *Isharans* attacked us on Fulcor! Konag Conndur was heinously murdered. That is where our true military conflict lies. We must do what is necessary for the Commonwealth."

"Oh, I am not as pliable as your young konag, Utho. Never underestimate a threat. I taught you better than that." Taken aback, Utho began to speak, but Onzu held up a hand, silencing him as if he had struck a blow. The training master continued, "You cannot deny what is happening. We should summon the Bravas, yes, but our most pressing enemy may well be the wreths. Our people must be prepared for a tremendous battle—not across the sea, but right here." He held up a gnarled finger. "And you know what the wreths want to do. None of us will survive."

Utho was angry. "Legends! Conndur let himself believe them, and now he has been murdered because of that folly."

"Some legends are true," Onzu said. "You are blinded by your vengewar. What if it is not the Isharans we really need to fight?" The trainer stepped closer to Utho, who could not help but back away. "What if we have to fight dragons?"

60

❧

THE konag's decree was terse and provocative, and Kollanan took offense at the wording. Yes, Mandan was the ruler of the three kingdoms, but he was naïve and unproven, far from being prepared to lead. Though he was a year older than Adan, he was not at all seasoned enough, especially in a time of war. Mandan had been aloof and dismissive when he heard the warning about the wreths, merely parroting the words of Utho. And now Kollanan knew what sort of manipulative man the Brava was.

Reading this impertinent decree now, Koll felt a chill, realizing that his own warning letter about Utho written to his brother had fallen on deaf ears. Conndur would have taken the message more seriously, but Mandan was entirely under the Brava's thumb.

Keeping his anger in check, Kollanan instructed the courier from Convera to wait in the antechamber. The man was exhausted from fighting his way over the nearly impassable mountain roads.

The king called Lasis, Elliel, and Queen Tafira to join him in his reading room, and Shadri followed. The hearth was cold, and the sunshine of a late-autumn day came through the open windows. For years he had mounted his war hammer on the wall here, never intending to use the weapon again. But times had changed.

Kollanan rested his elbows on the wooden desk and held up the letter. "The konag commands me to gather every capable fighter and dispatch them on a forced march to the coast. He wants the Norterran army to join the larger Commonwealth forces for an immediate attack on Ishara."

Normally implacable, Lasis drew in a quick breath.

Elliel said in an acid voice, "Those words were put in his ear by Utho."

The queen placed her hands on Koll's shoulder as she leaned over to read the letter. Her face paled. "But we do not have an army to spare. We are building all available defenses against a frostwreth attack." She looked up, her dark eyes wide. "That would leave our entire land vulnerable."

"The sandwreth reinforcements should be here soon to help us," Elliel said. "We need our armies here, so that we all fight together."

"We simply cannot send our fighters away," Lasis said, crossing his arms over his chest. "It would be foolhardy."

Kollanan set down the letter, agonized. "Mandan is still the konag, my brother's true heir, whether or not I agree with him." His heart sank as he realized that Adan must have received a similar letter in Suderra.

"Would a token force be sufficient?" Tafira asked. "A hundred fighters, perhaps, to fulfill our obligations to the Commonwealth?"

Koll shook his head. "With the signing of the Commonwealth charter, the three kingdoms agreed to fight as one, swore to follow the konag as the ruler over all of us. If I defy this decree . . ."

Shadri's eyes shone with a new idea, and she blurted out, "Well, then, that is your answer, Sire! The three kingdoms vowed to protect one another since the time of Queen Kresca, didn't they? We all know that, right? It is explicitly stated in the Commonwealth charter. Remember the fifth section? Think of the exact words." She was breathing hard, her cheeks flushed.

Elliel looked at her. "You memorized all the words to the Commonwealth charter?"

The young scholar frowned in surprise. "Mostly. I have read it many times, as part of my studies. I don't know that I could recite it all from memory, though. We may need to refer to an actual copy if we are to invoke that part of the charter."

Lasis and Elliel responded with perplexed expressions. Kollanan stroked his beard, searching his memory. "We have copies here at the castle and at the remembrance shrine. Please refresh my memory, girl. What is it you suggest?"

Shadri grinned with excitement. "Konag Mandan's decree does not invoke any specific clause, so can you not turn the demand around? The Commonwealth charter, section five, states that if any one of the three kingdoms requests assistance under grave circumstances, the other two kingdoms must respond. Invoke that obligation, Sire."

Surprised, Kollanan looked at Tafira, who offered an intrigued smile. He said, "I believe that part of the charter refers to seeking aid in the event of a natural disaster, a flood or a famine."

"Implicitly, not specifically," Shadri said. "The authors and original signatories of the charter could not conceive of an outside enemy, since the wreths had vanished and Ishara had not yet been settled." Her smile widened. "The words are the words."

"The words are the words," Koll said, stroking his lower lip.

The scholar girl continued. "Write to Konag Mandan, invoke section five, and tell him that you require the Commonwealth military to save Norterra. Your kingdom is facing a grave threat, as specified in the charter. The frostwreths have already destroyed Lake Bakal, and we know Queen Onn is building terrible armies. You have plenty of evidence, plenty of witnesses. Without question, our kingdom needs military assistance. By the terms of the Commonwealth charter, the konag is required to send aid if you request it, isn't he?"

Elliel smiled. "That's very clever, Shadri."

"Not just clever, she's absolutely correct." Kollanan's eyes brightened. "I agree. Norterra needs the help of all three kingdoms more than ever before. Help me write a proper response, quoting the appropriate words from the charter. There can be no doubt."

"Could we send Captain Rondo and his soldiers with the courier back to Convera? To ensure the message is delivered?" Shadri suggested uneasily. "They are just causing trouble here. I've heard them talking . . ."

Kollanan dismissed the idea. "No, I want them to join the fight at Lake Bakal so they can see the frostwreths with their own eyes. Once they've faced the real enemy, they will not be able to deny the danger." He scratched his thick beard, then shook his head. "Afterward, I will grant them leave to go. When they return to Convera, they can help convince Mandan."

"If they are willing to open their eyes," Tafira said.

Together, Shadri and Tafira helped him shape and temper his words as he wrote out his response and his request invoking the terms of the charter. When the letter was ready, Koll summoned the courier into his reading room. The man had refreshed himself and awaited a response, though he was not looking forward to the arduous journey back. The king looked down at the folded message before handing it over. "I cannot do as Konag Mandan asks. Rather, this is a formal request for him to assist my kingdom in our defenses. I've already enlarged the Norterran armies, but we cannot spare any soldiers for a war across the sea while we face a full-fledged attack from the wreths here in our own land."

The courier was aghast. "Sire, you cannot refuse the konag's command! After what happened to Conndur the Brave, we have to attack Ishara!"

"Ancestors' blood, Conndur was my brother, and I despise what the Isharans did to him, but my kingdom is more important than revenge. Conndur would have rushed to help Norterra if I'd asked! Norterra's existence is at stake." He pushed the letter into the courier's hands. "This is a formal request, per the terms of the Commonwealth charter. He is required to help us."

The courier squirmed. He looked down at the letter in his hands. "I cannot deliver this to the konag."

"You will. It is my command as king of Norterra. Konag Mandan is bound by the Commonwealth charter. The defense of the three kingdoms outweighs a discretionary aggressive attack." When the courier still hesitated, Kollanan barked at him: "We will give you provisions and a fresh horse. Ride! It is imperative that the konag receive my request as soon as possible. We need him to send his army here."

The courier scuttled down the corridor, clutching the letter.

After he had departed, Elliel said, "If Mandan sends Utho to lead his armies, I intend to fight him."

"We will have enough enemies to fight, do not fear," Koll said, his heart heavy. He had provoked his nephew, and he didn't know what the young man would do.

"This will not end well, beloved," Tafira warned.

With a sigh, he rested his bearded chin on her head as he held her close. "Sadly, you are almost always right."

◈

The sandwreths finally arrived from the south. Only twenty of them, Kollanan saw with deep disappointment. They rode augas, sixteen armed warriors with metal and bone armor, three dour mages in rusty leather robes, and Quo, with honey-gold eyes and long bleached hair. "My sister sent us to you. We will help you destroy the fortress of our enemy."

Koll and his queen stopped in front of them, accompanied by a crowd of awed curiosity seekers. "Welcome. We had hoped for a larger force from Queen Voo."

Quo snorted as if he had been insulted. "How much more would you need? You do not understand the power we can wield." His dull-eyed auga flicked out a long tongue. "Your human army can assist us. Are you not willing to fight as well?" He smiled. "In ancient times, humans were quite good at fighting and dying on the battlefield."

61

In the thick forest just outside the Hethrren camp, the restless godling stirred. Klovus kept the entity under control with his bond, letting the thing out and then reeling it back in, like a fish on a line.

The uneasy barbarians realized that the godling responded to the key priestlord's summons. They were terrified of it, and therefore terrified of him—exactly as Klovus intended. He drove back his lingering resentment. At any time, Priestlord Neré could have done the same thing, using the Tamburdin entity to destroy the enemy camps. Klovus had no patience for a priestlord who was unwilling to use her power.

The Hethrren riders had taken him through pine forests across the hills and ridges and into the deep wilderness. The barbarians had built a towering bonfire in the center of a clearing, as if the conflagration might intimidate the godling. Now he sat in their camp, facing their leader—such an ugly thing!

Magda had a square face, features devoid of any art or grace. Her dark, wiry hair was matted—intentionally, Klovus thought, or perhaps through utter lack of care. Her body reminded him of a barrel filled with muscle. Her large breasts were squashed under leather chest armor, and a wolf pelt hung as a cape on her shoulders.

The barbarian woman squatted on a fallen log that she seemed to consider a throne and held a knotted club with a rounded, twisted head varnished with the blood of victims. She leaned forward and grinned. One of her front teeth had been filed to a sharp point. "You dare to come to us, soft man." Her voice was like a continuous belch. "What do you want?"

Though she disgusted him, he did not flinch. His connection with the roiling deity made him incapable of fear. "If I were a soft man, I would simply let my godling rip you all apart. But I wanted to look you in the face, Magda of the Hethrren. I wanted to see if you are worthy."

Magda made a hacking sound that he interpreted as a laugh. "Worthy of what? We take what we wish."

Klovus brushed the front of his caftan. The roaring bonfire cracked and popped, sending sparks into the air like wayward stars. "I will decide whether or not to let you and your people live, depending on what you say to me tonight."

The barbarians huddled close, looking at their visitor as if he were a meal about to be served. A dozen or more children were interspersed among the adults, looking at him with wide eyes and feral expressions; with long tangled hair, clad in furs and holding sharpened weapons of their own, they looked like miniature versions of Hethrren.

When he considered Magda's attitude not to be deferential enough, Klovus drew the godling closer to remind them of its power. The trees stirred and crashed; boughs cracked; splintered branches flew into the air and tumbled down into the bonfire, releasing a gush of coals. Startled, the barbarians looked out into the forest. Magda rose from her log, held her club as if it might be a useful weapon against the deity.

"Sit down," Klovus snapped to her, "and listen to me."

She whirled toward him with her club raised, and in an instinctive response, the godling stormed out of the forest into the camp. It manifested itself like a thunderhead of primal energy, a maelstrom of predator eyes and snapping fangs. When the Hethrren shrieked like children, Klovus allowed himself a smile. "I said *sit down!*"

Magda obeyed this time, although she continued to squeeze her twisted club as if strangling it.

He let the godling continue stirring on the outskirts of the firelight for another moment, then directed it to retreat to the trees. "I could destroy you all now. You know that."

Magda grunted. "We are too many. You may destroy these here, but thousands of Hethrren throughout the forest will avenge me. They will kill every one of you soft pale people."

Klovus surprised her with his suggestion. "I would rather come to a different accommodation. The Hethrren may be useful." He laced his plump fingers together, showing the gold of his rings. "You prey upon Tamburdin lands. You raid and burn villages. You attack the city and steal what you can, but you never conquer." He narrowed his eyes. "Are you lazy? Why don't you take over the city and declare yourselves rulers of Tamburdin?"

"We *are* the rulers of this place," Magda said. "We go where we wish and take what we want."

"Then you run away and hide in these primitive camps." Klovus gestured around him at the clearing, where the Hethrren spread blankets and piles of their loot.

"Hide?" Magda was insulted. She seemed to have forgotten the godling already. "City people hide behind their wooden walls, trapped the way we trap animals—and they do it to themselves." She rumbled her deep laugh again. "Cities are too small. They would confine us. The Hethrren run free."

Klovus placed his elbows on his knees. Now was the time to negotiate. "But what is it your people *want*? If Tamburdin City is too small, then what would be big enough for you?" He knew what he would offer, but he waited to hear her answer first.

"We want conquest! We want treasure, and we want to collect the tears of the defeated." She pounded her club on the ground.

"I see your ambition, Magda. I know the strength of your people and the damage you can cause." He raised his eyebrows. "Even Tamburdin District is too small for the Hethrren. You are meant for great things."

The barbarians muttered in agreement. As Magda considered, the expression on her squarish face made her look as if she had gas. "We are already achieving great things under my rule."

"I can offer you more than that," Klovus said. "Tamburdin is not enough. I can grant you an entire land, three kingdoms." He smiled. "The Commonwealth across the sea—a continent for the taking."

"Across the sea? We have never looked upon the sea."

"My people are at war with the old world. We need warriors, and you have proved yourselves in my eyes. I am Ishara's key priestlord. Be my mercenaries. We will grant you weapons and armor. We will provide ships and send you as a massive invasion force against the godless."

He felt the godling in the forest, gave it a burst of energy. The swelling entity knocked down several trees, and the loud booms intimidated the Hethrren. Klovus raised his forefinger. "If you attack us here, we will squash you. But in the Commonwealth, nothing could stand in your way. They have no godlings, only their armies and their swords. Are you afraid of them?"

This time, Magda didn't flinch. She looked intently at Klovus. "We would conquer a land, and you would give us the weapons to do it? Then we can enslave the defeated people? Take everything they have?"

"With my blessing," Klovus promised. "But you have to leave Tamburdin. Come to Serepol, and we will put you aboard ships and turn you loose on the old world." His offer was serious. The Hethrren were an enormous fighting force, but undisciplined as an army. He was happy to let them burn out their energies across the three kingdoms. They could create as much havoc as they liked, so long as they were safely far away from Ishara. Klovus rose to his feet and stood before the brutish woman, meeting her eye-to-eye.

Her features were orange in the light of the bonfire. "Your offer sounds good, soft man." The shaggy and obscenely muscular Hethrren crowded close to listen. They pounded their weapons and made loud noises. "An entire land and all the weapons we need? That is acceptable to me and my people."

As Klovus felt victory swell in his chest, Magda poked him in his round belly, then reached down and grabbed his crotch. "Your own weapon is soft and unthreatening, but I can fix that." He recoiled, but she kept her hand there, fondling. Her leer showed off her sharpened front tooth. "The Hethrren have only one way to seal such a bargain. I take you as my lover tonight. If you satisfy me, then our agreement is final."

The idea nauseated Klovus. Legends said this woman fornicated with bears, and she smelled as if she did exactly that. Magda stepped back and sized him up, challenging. "I've had far better men, but you will do. Come with me so I can see if you have any hardness inside you, or if you are entirely soft." She added with a sneer, "We can go under the trees for privacy, if that is what you need."

Despite the bile rising in his throat, Klovus knew he would have to do this. Back at the Serepol temple he had taken many lovers, most of whom were young women who offered themselves as sacrifices to earn favor with the godling. Some were eager; others clearly didn't want him, yet they gave their bodies for the deity through him. Right now, this was a distasteful sacrifice Klovus would have to endure, but he always did what was necessary.

Magda was already striding away on her thick legs, pulling at the bindings of her leather vest. Klovus followed, mentally preparing himself for a horrible experience. He wondered if this was how young women felt when they offered themselves to *him*.

Out in the forest, the restless godling churned, radiating disgust. But Klovus drew on it for strength and did what he had to do.

62

THE sandwreth war party wanted to charge off and strike Lake Bakal as soon as they reached Fellstaff. Quo was incensed that King Kollanan didn't have his army ready and waiting for their whim. Queen Voo's warriors gathered inside the castle's banquet hall.

Koll showed firm patience. "This is war. I need to gather my vassal lords and their soldiers, and we must discuss strategy for our attack on the enemy fortress." He immediately sent riders to summon extra military forces. After the messengers were dispatched, he said, "When they arrive, we have to plan and coordinate."

"That is what a weak person would say." Quo sneered at the suggestion. "We do not need plans. We should surprise them. My mages can simply melt the walls and bring the fortress tumbling down."

The arrogance annoyed Kollanan. "It will take more than that."

"For you, perhaps. My sister told me to assist you, and I will demonstrate how powerful we are. Afterward, the armies of Norterra will join us in the final war." His grin looked like a sharp slash. "Then you will be able to kill many more frostwreths. Your people will enjoy that."

Knowing about the secret human work camps, Koll would never be tricked by false sandwreth promises. But if he could use these warriors to fight a different enemy and benefit Norterra, then he would do so. He worded his answer carefully. "Our alliance is still a matter for consideration."

Prowling inside the great hall, the bronze-skinned wreths gathered close to the blazing fireplace, claiming the north was too cold. Koll noticed that they avoided the mysterious Thon, though, casting occasional glances in his direction.

This was the time for the long-awaited strike. Before the day was out, Lord Bahlen and his Brava arrived with fifty soldiers, most of them taken from his construction work in the ancient ruins. Cleff, the mayor of the town of Yanton near the wreth city, brought a dozen townspeople and farmers who tried to look like warriors. Mayor Cleff grinned nervously, and seemed too overwhelmed to speak much.

Lord Ogno arrived with another seventy soldiers, riding hard from his distant county. Reveling in memories of his first attack on Lake Bakal, the burly man was ready to smash heads. Several other vassal lords—Teo, Alcock, Vitor—also brought fighters from their local militias.

Despite the impatience of the sandwreth war party, Koll quickly gathered an army ten times larger than the initial strike force that had stung the frozen fortress. This time, he knew they would do more than sting.

On the second night of gathering his army, he joined Quo next to the roaring fire. "While waiting for you, my vassal lords and I developed lines of attack, based on possible vulnerabilities I saw during my detailed reconnaissance of the fortress. I share our strategy with you, so you can support the full assault."

Quo was uninterested. "If you must."

"He must," Thon interjected, which drew a surprised and annoyed look from the sandwreth noble.

On the large wooden table in the great hall, Kollanan laid out sketches of the fortress's architecture and defenses, details provided by the feral drones at the site. Despite his standoffish demeanor, Quo became fascinated, and his three mages—Inod, Ulla, and Aoron—came close to study the drawings.

Despite his condescending tone, Quo showed a grudging respect. "I did not expect such excellent information. How did you obtain it?"

"I have spies." Koll gave no further details.

Quo did not want to waste more time. "This is all we need. Your armies are ready. Shall we depart tonight? How long will it take to travel to Lake Bakal?"

"Tonight?" Ogno spoke so explosively that food came out of his mouth. He wiped a hand across his lips. "My riders just came in! The horses are exhausted, and so are my men. They need a good rest."

"I forgot how fragile humans are," Quo said.

Kollanan said, "It would be in our best interest to wait a day. Lords Iber and Alcock are sending more soldiers." He felt as impatient as Quo to charge in among the evil frostwreths with his war hammer raised high . . . but he also wanted victory, and he wanted to keep his people alive. "I promise we will leave as soon as possible. We have the same goal." He did not intend to keep these sandwreths around any longer than absolutely necessary.

๑๑

When the full army was finally gathered, they rode north out of Fellstaff at dawn: five hundred human soldiers, twenty sandwreth fighters, three Bravas.

And Thon. Riding in the vanguard nearby, Captain Rondo was dressed in full Commonwealth armor. The captain made no secret that he resented Kollanan's orders to join this assault, but the king insisted that he and his men needed to see the wreth threat for themselves.

The riders surged along the road, filled with the fresh energy and bravado of a new war. Villages to the north had once been bustling commercial centers, but after the frostwreths killed the residents at Lake Bakal, many people had fled their homes. Scouts located an abandoned farmstead with large stores of grain and bales of hay, and the army camped there for the first night before riding off again.

On the afternoon of the second day, the large group of soldiers reached the rise above the mountain lake. The king, his vassal lords, the Bravas, and Quo's party gathered to view their target. Ahead of them, the lake remained frozen, and a wash of snow still covered the hillsides. The frostwreths had stacked and fused more ice blocks to build an outer curtain wall, and they were in the process of erecting another large square tower that gleamed in the low sunlight.

"Ah, they have been busy," Quo said from the back of his auga. "An impressive structure."

"It will be difficult to bring down the entire fortress," said Mage Inod.

A second mage, Aoron, shrugged. "We could destroy it in pieces."

"We will do it in pieces, so long as we destroy it." Quo shifted on his scaled saddle. The reptilian mounts were sluggish from the cold. "I wonder if your reconnaissance is still accurate, King Kollanan."

Impatient with the wreth's arrogance, Koll gripped his hammer. "As you said, if we knock it all down, the details won't matter."

One of the sandwreth warriors extended his spiraled spear. "They have mages!"

"Along with teams of their own workers." Quo shook his head. "They should not have killed all of the humans in this village. A waste of good labor. You are right to be annoyed, King Kollanan. Your people could have been kept alive. Wiping out the town was not a wise or efficient thing to do."

Kollanan seethed at the comment, but did not respond.

The sandwreth noble continued to look around, curious. "I hope to see some of their drones. I hear they are an interesting species. The sandwreths should make some of our own."

Koll didn't spot any of the feral drones among the thick silver pines, and hoped that they were hiding from the army. His vassal lords rode among their troops, preparing their separate companies for the main charge.

The augas snorted. The wreth fighters raised their spears and knives. The three mages sat like clenched thunderstorms, and Koll could feel them exude a crackle of power.

Quo lifted his hand, curled his fingers as if dredging up magic. "Your army is impressive in its own way, King Kollanan, but my people are ready, and I have no interest in waiting. Follow us and fight to the best of your abilities! Destroy the frostwreths wherever you can!" The wreth man grinned as if this entire expedition were a mere lark. "Let us see how well your Norterran army can fight!" Quo shouted commands to his war party.

Alarmed, Koll said, "Wait! We must have a coordinated strike. My army will split into divisions and attack the fortress from different directions. We can all—"

Not listening, the wreth noble gestured forward, and the twenty augas thundered over the rise, picking up speed as they loped toward the frozen lake and the towering fortress.

Left with no choice, Koll cursed out loud and called his combined soldiers. "Ride! Now!"

Howling a disorganized battle cry, the army surged forward.

63

IT was a harsh night on the Plain of Black Glass. The slaves continued to excavate the obsidian rubble under the light of a full moon. Glik was so sore she could barely move; her hands had been nicked in a thousand places, and her arms were a web of small scabs.

The shadowglass absorbed the silvery light of the moon, and Glik felt as if she were walking on a void beneath her feet. The patter and clink of tools rang through the night like insect chirps. Even after weeks of hard labor, the workers had excavated only a small part of the ancient battlefield.

Cheth and her fellow Bravas worked together, suppressing their anger. They fell silent whenever the sandwreth guards were nearby, but spoke in quick quiet voices when they were alone, using some kind of code.

Glik pried loose a thin layer of the glass, careful not to crack it because the sandwreths would beat her if she damaged the material. She didn't know why this eerie obsidian was so important to wreths, but every time she touched the black glass, she felt her fingers throb. Invisible power thrummed from this blasted area, a reservoir of magic.

Suddenly, a Brava man cried out in great pain. Glik had never heard such a sound from one of the half-breed warriors, not even during intense combat practice. "I am cut! Ah, it is deep! Help me before I bleed to death."

Glik looked up in alarm. Cheth was working near the injured man, and two other Bravas rushed to help.

"Help me! It hurts." The Brava sounded so strange.

A trio of guards stalked over, leaving their augas behind. When one wreth guard bent over the man who lay writhing on the ground, the supposed victim lunged up with a razor-edged chunk of shadowglass in his hand. His swing caught the wreth guard just beneath the chin and chopped into his neck. Blood spurted out.

Now Glik understood that the injury was a ruse! Cheth dove in to tackle the second wreth guard and seized his spear. As the two fought, the weapon's shaft snapped, and Cheth shoved the pointed end through the guard's chest. So, this had been planned!

Two other Bravas fell upon the remaining guard and tackled him to the ground. They smashed his head on an uneven block of obsidian, and his blood and brains stained the oily glass.

"Run!" Cheth bellowed to the haggard workers. "All of you!"

More sandwreth warriors rode in on their augas, easily outnumbering the escapees, but the Bravas ran together so they could stand and fight. After disarming the wreth guards they had killed, the Bravas now carried weapons, and they would fight to the death if necessary.

The mayhem gave Glik the chance she had been seeking all along, and she was ready. She could not help Bravas in hand-to-hand combat, but she could escape. If she got away, she could find the Utauks, spread the word and a warning—and send help. In a second, she was off.

Under the moonlight, while other slaves bolted toward the grassy hills beyond the melted battlefield, Glik instead ran deeper into an area of rubble on the plain of obsidian. Even though the terrain was far more dangerous, the wreths wouldn't expect her to hide there. She picked her way along as fast as she could go.

The sounds of combat echoed behind her, the clang of steel, the clack of wooden shafts. Glik scrambled over boulders, but she did not dare stumble. The soles of her shoes were already sliced. One fall, and Glik could cut her own throat. She was barely able to see the obsidian jumble in the moonlight.

Behind her, a fog of blue lightning rippled out, a webwork of bright lines. A Brava shout turned into a scream, and this time the pain was real. Mage Ivun entered the fray, releasing some of the magic that simmered beneath the demolished battlefield.

Glik kept running, making her way to the heart of the ancient battlefield. She rounded an obsidian outcropping taller than she was, large enough to block out the moon. Twisting her foot on a rock, she slipped, caught herself on a sharp edge, and hissed in pain. She held her sliced palm against her chest and kept running.

Suddenly, she came upon a flat, perfectly circular pool of shadowglass. It looked like a hole that plunged into infinity. The blackness was absolute, refuting the full moon high above. Glik halted at the edge and stared, unable to tear her eyes away. *Inside the circle. Outside the circle.*

Blood from her wound dripped onto the black glass, and immediately she felt dizzy. She thought that if she plunged forward into the obsidian mirror, she might keep falling forever and ever. The strange surface rippled and shimmered, as if she had disturbed some dark presence within.

Paralyzed, Glik stared as images formed beneath the black glass. Caught up in the vision, she drew a circle around her heart over and over. The blood from her cut hand smeared her shirt, but she didn't see it, didn't realize it. Her whole world drowned in the pool of shadowglass.

Then the blackness *blinked* and became the color of copper stained with blood. An eye, a slitted *eye*, filled the entire obsidian pool. To Glik, that horrible eye seemed as large as the world, baleful, once hidden but now looking out into the world—the eye of a dragon, but ten times larger than any dragon she had ever imagined. Ossus!

Glik's teeth chattered, and her muscles locked. She could not tear herself away from that staring orb. The reptilian eye blinked again, and the images shifted.

In the circular pool of obsidian, the dragon's eye was supplanted by something formless and powerful . . . a primal entity, a force balled up and tangled, waiting to be released. It was distant, not Ossus, but something else . . . something that even the dragon feared! The dragon in the shadowglass shattered into a million smaller creatures. Skas!

Glik's knees gave out, and she moaned. Through her heart link, she yearned outward, missing Ari. Countless ska images filled the petrified pool, and she thought for certain they would burst out into the real world, and the huge flock of chittering creatures would protect her from the wreths.

She swayed in place and continued to draw the circle around and around her heart. "The beginning is the end is the beginning is the end is the beginning." She slumped forward, and when she pressed her cut hand against one of the rocks on the shore, the pain startled her.

Gruff voices rang out behind the rocks. "There is another one. Kill it!"

Glik scrambled to her feet to see two wreth guards raising their spiraled spears. She had no place to run.

Before they could hurl their weapons, a figure crashed into one warrior, knocking him aside. Cheth! The Brava woman was streaked with blood, her clothes torn and slashed. "Leave the girl alone!" She slashed the air with a broken, bloodstained spear, driving the wreths back.

Cheth jumped to stand beside Glik, but when four more warriors arrived on their augas, the girl knew they were both doomed. She hunched over, still spasming from what she had seen. "A dragon! I saw Ossus in the pool. And something else, something that might be even more powerful."

Cheth growled, "Right now, I care most about these wreths." She wrapped both of her hands around the spear shaft.

Mage Ivun appeared next to the wreth warriors. "Hold!" Lines furrowed his brow. He raised his deformed hand, which was withered again, as if he had used up the restorative magic. "Dragons? You see dragons?"

Glik pointed to the obsidian pool. "There, in the shadowglass."

The mage pushed past the wreth warriors, ignoring Cheth, who stood menacing with her broken spear. He peered into the empty black pool, then gave Glik a piercing glare. "You see dragons?"

"Ossus. I am certain of it."

He turned, his red leather robes swirling around him. "Come with me."

Glik had no choice but to obey.

64

A NGRY and unsettled by Master Onzu's attitude, Utho spent the night in the guest dwelling, but departed the Brava training village early the next morning. In the back of his mind he knew that Commonwealth armies were gathering, soldiers being trained, ships refitted in the Rivermouth shipyards. It was happening.

A vengewar is not a quick thing, but it is necessary.

Ishara needed to be torn to shreds, left in rubble, so the Bravas could reclaim the land and establish their colony. The betrayers from ages ago would suffer justice, as Brava honor required. Konag Mandan would follow Utho's advice in a way that Conndur the Brave never would have, and at last it was on the verge of happening.

Every Brava should have celebrated the prospect, yet Onzu was worried about wreths? About a legendary dragon?

Instead of heading back to Convera, Utho rode in the opposite direction.

He clenched his gauntleted hand and urged his horse to a gallop, following damaged forest roads into the Dragonspine Mountains. The terrain still smoked and simmered. The eruption of Mount Vada had made Conndur believe in the legends of buried dragons and vanished gods. Because of that, Utho considered him a gullible fool. But he knew that Onzu was not a fool, and if his mentor was convinced . . .

If Utho continued to deny the danger even in the face of overwhelming proof, then who was the real fool?

If a man sat in a burning house and refused to believe the fire existed, his resolute defiance would not save him.

Utho ground his teeth together and leaned forward on the horse, staring ahead into the smoking, angry mountains. He rode harder. He had to see for himself, to convince himself that it was not real. If anyone but Onzu had challenged his beliefs . . .

The smell of sulfur and smoke made the horse uneasy. On the slopes of

Mount Vada, the trees were dead, the vegetation covered with layers of ash like a pestilent snow. Yellow scum covered streams and standing pools of hot water that bubbled up from heat beneath the ground.

He passed through a village of empty, ruined homes. An inn had crumbled as boulders and fire swept through in the wake of the eruption. Those towns had existed for centuries, but with the ground shaking and lava flowing, people throughout the mountain range had evacuated, many of them fleeing to Convera. They had hoped the konag would save them, that the walls of the capital city would shelter them against the end of the world.

Now those refugees ate the food, crowded lodgings, and drained Convera of resources. Fortunately, many of them had joined the army, swelling the ranks. They were terrified of dragons and wreths, so Utho would turn them against the Isharans, an enemy they could truly fight.

His horse picked its way along the obliterated road. The ground was buckled in places, and trees had fallen across their path. Pines and aspens lay like scattered broomsticks.

Utho kept working his way up the eastern slopes. The acid stink in the air burned his nostrils, but he kept going. His thoughts collapsed to a pinpoint of focus. He looked at the restless mountain ahead of him, its conical shape now damaged, a good portion of it blasted away. Scarlet lava still leaked out like heated iron from a blacksmith's forge.

When the terrain became too broken and uncertain, Utho stopped at a boulder field. Taking his horse through it would surely result in a broken foreleg—and a dead horse. He wrestled with his anger and uncertainty, then dismounted and tied the animal to a standing dead tree. The horse shuddered with fear, covered with still-falling ash. Protected by his gauntlets and boots, Utho set off on foot and climbed over the rough, hot boulders.

He breathed hard with the effort, but kept climbing. Fumaroles exhaled steam from the ground. Could it truly be the breath of a dragon? The boulders vibrated beneath him, and he heard the patter, then rumble as more giant rocks slid down in an avalanche. Dust joined the smoke that lingered in the air.

After he climbed to a hanging valley partway up the slope, Utho stared at a hellish landscape of hissing steam and boiling mud pots. This was as good a place as any—he had reached his destination. He listened to the inherent rumble beneath the ground, the growl of thermal areas, the cracks that let poisonous fumes escape. He knew he was the only human within miles, because everyone with common sense had gone away.

"Dragon!" he shouted. "Ossus, are you there?" He pulled off his gauntlet and tossed it on the ground before grabbing the golden cuff of his ramer. In an abrupt gesture he pressed it around his wrist and felt the satisfying spike of pain as metal teeth cut into his veins. He pulled forth the fire, and a circle of flames engulfed his hand, then extended into a blazing lash. He raised his arm high, like a beacon or a threat.

"Ossus! Where are you?" He stood with the ramer flaring, crackling, drawing attention. "I am sworn to protect the Commonwealth and serve the true konag."

He waited for a response. The ground rumbled with a crack of rock, but he couldn't tell if the buried dragon heard him.

"We will fight our mortal enemies, and we do not care about you. Stay asleep, dragon! Hold your evil beneath the ground."

He still ached to remember the recent failed naval attack at Fulcor Island, how many ships had been sunk, how many sailors lost, how much innocent blood shed. "Our war is against Ishara. Leave us alone!"

He held his ramer high, and the ground shook. Boulders the size of houses slid down the slope, crashing and thundering as the mountainside cracked. Red lava sprayed out like fresh blood.

These mountains were full of power. Utho could sense it. Perhaps the dragon did exist at the heart of the world, fashioned out of Kur's evil thoughts and emotions. That was the legend, but Utho did not care about legends.

Onzu would scold him for his single-minded obsession. Just as the wreth factions wanted to destroy each other, so Utho's drive was to eradicate the Isharans. If fed and channeled properly, maybe his vengeance would be even stronger than a dragon.

With a great upheaval, the ground buckled, and Utho clutched a boulder that shifted toward him. He leaped out of the way, extinguishing his ramer. The ground cracked again, and superheated steam screamed out, blasting his black armor. Swirling his finemail cape over his face to keep from being scalded, he staggered away from the thermal field, climbing over the rocks.

He stubbornly pushed against the idea that Ossus had actually heard him and responded. This natural disaster was simply that: natural, an instability in the world like a storm or a blizzard.

But if it was indeed a dragon, then Utho and his Bravas would have to deal with it . . . later. He just needed more time.

Returning to his terrified horse, he untied the reins and climbed back into the saddle. He felt inexplicably exhausted, shaking, but not from fear. He was *Utho*, and fear had no place within him . . . not when a vengewar was about to begin.

He pushed the horse hard, heading back toward Convera and his konag.

65

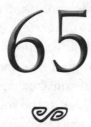

As the reckless sandwreths charged toward Lake Bakal, they ignored Kollanan's shouts behind them. Seeing Quo's war party launch the impetuous attack, Koll's own soldiers roared with impatience. Lords Ogno, Vitor, and Teo turned to their king, squirming for permission to lead their divisions on the multipronged strike. The plan was already falling apart.

Koll threw caution to the wind. He raised his war hammer and shouted, "We can't let the sandwreths do all the fighting!" He kicked Storm into motion, and the black warhorse galloped forward.

The army streamed ahead, enthusiastic and bloodthirsty. He led the advance along the snow-covered road, thundering toward the fortress looming above the remains of the frozen village. The bitter grief of that town's significance made him ride harder.

Ahead of the human army, twenty augas ranged across the rocks and through the silver pines as they made a straight line for the wreth fortress. The towering structure shimmered, the blocks of ice glowing from within. Quo let out a wild cry, which all the sandwreths repeated.

Amid construction piles of cut ice and braided ropes, the frostwreth workers rushed to the massive walls in alarm. The great gates were restored after Koll's first raiding party had battered them down, and now he couldn't wait to wreck them again—permanently this time. His army was ten times larger now, and the sandwreths promised to leave only rubble.

Restless but well trained as Commonwealth soldiers, Rondo and his escort party drew their swords. The captain looked skeptically at the towering ice fortress and the reckless charge. He shouted across to Kollanan, "This is not what we discussed, Sire! What about the battle plan, our separate divisions? We were supposed to attack together!" The military captain's face reddened. "Do we ride in and hope we can fight whatever they throw against us? That is not enough!"

Koll was also furious at impulsive Quo. "It is unexpected," he said. This wasn't his choice, either, but he could not control the sandwreths, even though he needed them. "Ride!"

The augas had surged ahead of the galloping human cavalry. Ogno and Vitor split their forces into two prongs as the army reached the lakeshore, spreading out to attack the half-constructed second tower of the fortress. Ogno's primal challenge was as loud as the shouts of a hundred soldiers.

Elliel and Lasis ignited their ramers and raised the fiery blades. On the other side of the army, in Lord Bahlen's division, Urok also lit his golden cuff and created a blazing whip that sent sparks flying into the air. Bahlen's professional soldiers were joined by Mayor Cleff and determined townspeople from Yanton.

As the army closed in on the looming ice fortress, frostwreth warriors emerged from the high gate carrying long spears and transparent swords. They rode enormous wolf-steeds, fire-eyed animals with claws like hooked daggers. In eerie unison, the frostwreths shouted a challenge that echoed like a thunderclap. A burst of arctic wind swooped across the landscape, battering Kollanan. The human forces staggered against the cold wave, then pushed forward again.

Around the base of the new fortress wall and the half-constructed tower, near the crumbling hovels where drones had once lived, human soldiers faced hundreds of frostwreth workers who fashioned weapons out of construction materials. They moved forward with clubs and prybars, each fighter as powerful as any human warrior.

Koll gripped his war hammer, ready for his first victim as they charged headlong into the enemy forces. The king of Norterra prepared for the fight of his life.

He hoped their temporary sandwreth allies were as powerful as Queen Voo promised.

∾

As the cold wind blew against her face, Elliel was ready to kill. Her ramer blazed like a torch leading the way. Nearby, Lasis raised his, as well. The two Bravas would not try to slip quietly into the fortress, as they had last time in search of the king's grandson. This was a frontal attack. Lasis swung his ramer blade, cutting a long arc in the air in front of him.

Riding close to Elliel, Thon seemed intent and fascinated. His deep blue eyes sparkled. He had chosen to fight in this battle today, with the forces of Norterra, which gave him the opportunity to release his enigmatic powers.

In her time with Thon, as she learned to love him and taught him about emotions, she had also instilled in him a sense of justice. And all the villagers murdered here demanded justice. Despite the thousand questions that lingered about the dark wreth, Elliel didn't doubt what he could do.

Enemy warriors guided their furry oonuks to form a line of defense in front of the fortress, flanked by armored frostwreths on foot. Behind them came several pale mages in heavy blue robes.

"Wreth warriors are difficult foes," Lasis shouted over the rising din, "but we must beware of the mages!"

"I will take care of the mages," Thon said with a shrug. The three separated from the ranks of human soldiers that thundered behind them.

Riding ahead of the main army onto the frozen gray lake, Quo laughed as he pressed toward the main fortress gate. On the ice, the lead frostwreth warrior pushed his wolf-steed toward Quo's auga. When the oonuk slashed with long claws, the auga kicked out with one muscular foot and disemboweled the beast. The wolf-steed pawed at the spilling red entrails and tumbled.

The frostwreth rider was thrown onto the snow-covered rocks, but he sprang to his feet and drew his weapons. Quo slashed at him with his bloodied spear, but the frostwreth blocked it. The two clashed and parried. Around them sandwreths engaged in their own duels, reptilian mounts tearing at white wolves.

Elliel and Lasis rode in from the side, striking down Quo's opponent with their ramers, then moved on. Offended, the sandwreth noble shouted, "I did not require your help, half-breeds." He wheeled his auga about and rode into the fray. "But this frees me to kill others."

A towering frostwreth warrior closed in on the Bravas, drawn by their ramers like a moth to a candle flame. Elliel wondered if she had encountered him before in Queen Onn's throne room. His wolf-steed pawed at the air, which terrified Elliel's horse, but Lasis swept past and slashed a smoking line across the white fur. The beast roared in pain.

Elliel slid out of the saddle and dropped to the ground, letting the panicked horse gallop away. Planting her boots apart, she faced the warrior mounted on his injured oonuk. Drawing on the magic in her blood, she slashed her ramer fire like a whip.

Her opponent, an ugly, long-jawed wreth with scarred runes on his cheeks, blocked her ramer with his spear shaft and drew a curved dagger in his other hand. Lasis joined her on foot, and together they faced off with the mounted wreth warrior.

They both engaged in a flurry of ramer blows that drove their opponent back, breaking the spear shaft and searing his skin. They knocked the warrior off of his injured wolf-steed, and he seemed surprised by their combined strength. While Lasis engaged the oonuk as it wheeled toward them, Elliel cut another smoking wound down the warrior's arm. Within moments, Lasis joined his blade with hers. The two of them drove the wreth warrior back hard, and Elliel cut off his head.

Looking at the smoking corpse, she asked, "Did we stain our honor that two of us fought a single opponent?"

The other Brava wasn't concerned. "We must defeat these creatures. That is the only rule."

Together, they engaged another warrior, a fierce wreth woman with spines like icicles protruding from her shoulder plates. Her hair was braided as tight as a fist and seemed frozen solid with a sheen of ice. In each hand she held a short sickle-tipped weapon.

As Quo's sandwreths approached the fortress gates via the lake ice, the three blue-robed mages stood shoulder-to-shoulder, raising their fists. Working together, the mages summoned a howling white wall of ice chips and snowflakes, which rushed across the shore to engulf the oncoming sandwreth war party. Quo's own mages defended themselves with spells, etching runes into the ice that blazed with fire. Together, Inod, Ulla, and Aoron created an explosive boom that sent structural flaws and fissures through the palace's foundational blocks.

At the rocky shore, Eliel saw Thon dismount and stride out onto the thick, gray ice of the open lake. Alone on a clear area, he knelt to concentrate, then raised a fist and brought it down like a hammer. A crack split the ice, and dark, cold water welled up like a gash in Lake Bakal. The fissure widened like a lightning bolt, zigzagging across the solid lake all the way to the fortress. Quo and the sandwreths dove out of the way, astonished by what Thon had done.

The amazing dark wreth dipped his fingertips into the fresh water, making it boil and froth. A wall of steam built up as a smoke screen, disguising the surge of an unnatural wave of lake water that rushed forward like surf crashing against the shore.

The frostwreth mages stood together at the gates, unsure of Thon's magic. His wave rolled forward, building and building as it drew more water from the lake. The pale mages raised their hands to defend themselves as the wall of water lurched like a striking viper. They drew on their defensive magic, which froze the wave solid into a half-shell barricade rising in front of them.

Thon sat back on his heels, seemingly unconcerned as the rival mages strained against him. He plunged both hands into the crack in the ice, immersing them, and summoned an even larger wave that hurtled toward the frostwreths at incredible speed. It raced over the top of the first frozen shell and plunged down to engulf the mages. Then Thon reversed his magic and froze the water solid, encasing the enemies in a solid mound of ice.

Quo and his sandwreth warriors hooted insults at the failed mages, then swung around to engage enemy fighters who attacked them. The pale warriors managed to kill two sandwreth fighters and an auga before Quo rallied his companions and drove them back.

His sandwreth mages continued their work, now that Thon had neutralized the others at the base of the fortress. Inod, Ulla, and Aoron summoned a scouring wind that picked up dust and pebbles. With their magic, they converted it into a tornado that pummeled the fortress walls.

Angry at the deaths of his two warriors, Quo picked up hand-sized stones and hurled them at the fortress, enhancing his throw with magic so that the projectiles shattered the wide main window. Meanwhile, his mages' continuing abrasive wind chewed at the frozen walls, scouring holes, tunneling channels, weakening the foundations. One section began to crumble, and the ice shattered and fell down in an avalanche.

Then, the hemispherical cocoon that had engulfed the frostwreth mages shivered and cracked. One pale mage smashed through the frozen shell, shattering the ice into long daggerlike shards. He flung sharp weapons that whistled through the air.

The ice daggers impaled two of Quo's mages. Inod and Aoron grasped at the deadly projectiles, which melted as the mages collapsed onto the frozen ground. Another shard struck Ulla in the head, stunning her.

Quo cocked back his arm and hurled his spiral-shafted spear. The weapon flew true and plunged through the frostwreth mage's chest.

Intent on his target, Thon glided forward, sealing the fissure in the lake ice before him. He reached the front wall of the frozen fortress, where the blue-white structural blocks were already cracked and pitted. Thon placed his hands on his hips and looked at the high, glistening structure.

"Ice is easily turned back into water," he said aloud. He touched the primary foundation blocks at the bottom of the immense walls and simply dissolved them. The melted ice flowed out, and with a loud rumble the entire fortress began to fall.

◈

Hundreds of human soldiers crashed into the construction site near the new tower, where frostwreth foot soldiers faced the Norterran army. King Kollanan rode in, swinging his hammer, reminded of his younger days with his brother in the Isharan war.

Even though he smashed his hammer into the forehead of one warrior, the enemy rocked back, stunned but not dead. Koll had to follow through with another blow to the temple, and finally the wreth fell. He decided that the enemy must have incredibly thick skulls.

The frostwreths were powerful, but Kollanan's army vastly outnumbered them. Even if it took five human soldiers to bring down a single warrior, they did so, again and again. His soldiers fought in a great melee, biting like bears this time, rather than stinging like wasps.

Lords Ogno and Cerus seemed to be having a competition. The two men rode forward, hacking any frostwreth they saw. Bahlen's troops, which he easily identified by Urok's blazing ramer, circled around and attacked the construction site from the rear, where some workers had retreated into defensive positions.

Shouting encouragement to anyone who could hear him, Kollanan smashed right and left. His arm was sore, but he drew strength from gaining some vengeance for all the people lost at Lake Bakal.

Then a wave of unexpected figures entered the mayhem. They darted in, frenetically attacking the wreths with small weapons of their own. The drones! Amid roars of surprise, Koll saw the wreths retaliate, killing many of these surprising allies.

Storm reared up, dodging a long spear. Suddenly, a drone dove in front of the spear, sacrificing himself to save the king. The poor creature was skewered, but his body weighed down the frostwreth's weapon, enough to give Kollanan an opening to bring down the war hammer with a furious crack, splitting the enemy's skull.

Above the din of the battlefield, he heard an ominous rumble and turned toward the great fortress. In a slow-motion, astounding collapse, the ice structure began to fall apart, its façade tumbling down.

Quo and his surviving sandwreths raced their augas away from the devastation. Thon jogged along the shore as if he felt invincible, with the fortress still crashing down behind him.

Captain Rondo bellowed to the fighters around him: "We'll all be crushed! Ride for your lives."

"Well, we are in it now," Sergeant Headan growled, "thanks to King Kollanan."

Soldiers wheeled about and ran from the crumbling fortress. Some frostwreths raced toward it, as if intending to use magic to shore up the walls, but the damage was too great.

Koll watched with satisfaction as the entire fortress collapsed into a mountain of shards and rubble, destroying everyone and everything inside.

66

WITH Utho gone on his own quest, Konag Mandan felt adrift. His sweet, perfect bride Lira was still far away in Lord Cade's holding, though he had summoned her to Convera with all due haste. It was time for her to adjust to her new home.

Soon, the Commonwealth would celebrate their wedding, and the hearts of all three kingdoms would beat harder, stronger. Less than a month now, and the city of Convera was abuzz with preparations. Mandan had an army of advisors, protocol ministers, and admired planners of state, and he knew they took care of all the details, even though his beloved would want some say. She would be here soon.

But right now, Utho was gone, and the castle seemed empty and cold.

Mandan entered the elaborate hedge maze with its complex corners and curves, the blind pathways that tried to distract him from the one true route leading to the apple tree in the center. As boys, he and Adan had come here often, challenging each other, tormenting each other.

Adan was a soft and compassionate ruler, and now his people in Suderra loved him, but it was easy to make people love their king during peace and prosperity. These dark and dangerous times demanded a more determined ruler, though, and Konag Mandan was that ruler.

As he walked along the twisting gravel pathways, looking at the walls of shrubbery higher than his head, he shuddered at the memory forever burned in his mind: that night on Fulcor Island, the thunder and lightning of the storm, the clash of swords and the shouts of Isharan betrayers. He had called his father's name, pulled open the door to his chambers. He smelled the sickening stench, saw the blood—so much blood!—and the mutilated body. Mandan's throat still felt raw from his endless screams.

Now he wandered the maze, a place with warm memories of happier times. After years of repetition, Mandan knew the correct turns, avoided the blind ends. The hedge maze reminded him of his own situation, the decisions he faced, the blind choices, the unpredictable outcomes.

Long ago, his father had assigned a succession of tutors who trained him in statecraft, geography, history, economics. Mandan had been a passable student, but as he'd recently discovered when he went to see the towns devastated by Mount Vada, the facts and concepts in his head bore little relationship to reality, to the suffering of people, to the true cost of lost lives and homes.

Convera City was still crowded with refugees from that devastation, their eyes red, their skin as gray as the ash that fell from the skies. They had flocked here seeking help, food, shelter, believing the end of the world was at hand, that the dragon would awaken and destroy them all. Utho insisted that the legend was exaggerated, but Mandan had seen the cracked mountains with his own eyes, smelled the smoke, felt the ground shake beneath his feet. . . .

His Brava had already been gone for more than a week on his mysterious mission. Every day advisors came to Mandan, demanding that he make immediate decisions of great consequence, and he tried to do what he believed was right. But without Utho to shore him up he felt like a table with wobbly legs. Mandan did not know how to run a war by himself, and he couldn't wait for the Brava to return.

Reaching the heart of the maze, Mandan sat under the apple tree and listened to the birds, ignoring the world. He wished he could just immerse himself in his paintings or think about the lovely Lira. But he knew he had to go back.

Frowning, Konag Mandan retraced his steps through the maze and entered the castle. People would be waiting for him. Mandan stalked into the throne room, startling a bedraggled party that had gathered in front of the empty throne. Their hair was matted, their eyes haunted. They wore jerkins embroidered with the open hand of the Commonwealth; others carried the limp banner of Osterra.

Mandan snapped, "Who are you? Where did you come from?"

"Sire, you sent us with Lord Goran to meet the sandwreth queen," said one of the intense men, stammering.

Quaking with fear, two of them brought forward a heavy chest and set it at the foot of his throne. "Yes, now I remember." He looked down at the chest. "Was that not filled with treasures to appease Queen Voo? Why did you bring it back?"

The man seemed to shrink from Mandan's words. "Queen Voo was not appeased, Sire. She was offended that you did not come to her yourself, as she requested."

Mandan scoffed. "Who is she to demand my presence? I am the konag of the three kingdoms."

"And Voo is the queen of the sandwreths. She has . . . great power."

Another man dropped to his knees and broke down weeping. "Impossible power!"

Incensed, Mandan covered his confusion with indignation. "Where is Lord Goran? I want to hear the report from him."

"Lord Goran is . . ."

The weeping man blurted out, "He is not dead." His voice became a wail. "She did not kill him!"

The escort soldiers stared meaningfully at the closed chest, and Mandan stepped down from the throne and seized the lid, expecting to find his spurned jewels and gold. Instead, there was a man folded up and somehow crammed into the box, which was far too small to fit a human body. Goran was broken into a thousand places, rearranged and stuffed into every corner so that his tortured face looked up from the center of the chest.

Mandan recoiled as if he had stumbled upon a nest of spiders. Though Goran's bones had been shattered and his internal organs burst and rearranged, his face was still active, his eyes wide and ready to explode with agony. Goran's mouth opened and closed with a wet sucking sound in the middle of his chest, unable to form words.

One of the escorts spoke. "Queen Voo said that the next time she summons you, she expects you to come yourself."

Goran continued to mewl and gasp, making gurgling sounds inside the box.

Mandan staggered two steps away, but the fractured thing kept making noises from inside the chest. The sound would stick in his nightmares for years.

He yanked the dagger from his belt. Utho had taught him how to defend himself, and now he lurched to the open chest, raised the blade. The folded-up man continued to choke and whimper, and Mandan plunged in the knife again and again until the sounds stopped. His stomach roiled.

Servants hovered in the doorway, looking at the mess on the floor and the bloody horror inside the trunk. Mandan choked out an order. "Clean this up! Take the chest away. I want this room pristine again."

Shuddering, he made his way back to the throne and slumped forward, resting his elbows on his knees and his head in his hands. He groaned, "Where is Utho?" He didn't understand these wreths. Why had they returned from oblivion? He had scoffed when Adan and Kollanan had warned about the ancient race. But who could have imagined this . . . this horror?

He clamped down on his revulsion. None of that mattered now in the face of the new war. The Commonwealth army was already gathering against Ishara. Every vassal lord in the three kingdoms was expected to provide fighters, weapons, and armor.

Less than an hour after the mangled body of Goran had been taken away, a new messenger arrived, delivering a reply from King Kollanan of Norterra. The courier swallowed hard.

Mandan snatched the message, tore it open, and read the words in his uncle's bold hand, unable to believe what he saw. "He refuses? But . . . he cannot defy an order from the konag. I am the ruler of the Commonwealth!" He crumpled the paper in his hands. "Kollanan has betrayed me."

"He did more than refuse the decree, Sire." The courier's voice shook. "King Kollanan sends a formal demand for you to dispatch all capable soldiers to come to his aid and defend Norterra against the wreths."

"Wreths!" Mandan squawked, reminded of the horror of Lord Goran. "Why do wreths continue to plague me? I didn't even believe in them until recently." He lurched from his throne, tossed the folded paper to the floor.

The messenger said, "I saw that Kollanan was gathering a great army. He sent word for his vassal lords to dispatch soldiers to Fellstaff."

"Did you see *any* wreths?" Mandan demanded.

The messenger looked away. "No, Sire, but I did see a substantial army."

"Norterra's army . . . is my uncle perhaps planning to use it against me? Would he actually march on Osterra to overthrow the rightful konag?"

The courier blinked as if he had never considered the suggestion.

Mandan's thoughts whirled as he drew one conclusion after another. "Was Kollanan jealous of my father? Does he want to take the Convera throne from me?"

"I . . . I cannot say, Sire."

According to Utho's teachings, Mandan needed to project the image of a powerful leader, but he just wanted to run away and hide in the hedge maze, where no one could find him.

Without his Brava, the young konag did not know what to do.

67

HEADING back to Serepol, Klovus and an escort of Isharan soldiers rode well ahead of the unruly Hethrren hordes, who would march up to the capital city in their own time. Klovus needed to reach Serepol long before the Hethrren arrived, so he could prepare the ships that would take the barbarians across the sea to the Commonwealth.

Long riding lay ahead of them, though. They were still five days away from the capital. Beside him, the company commander shaded his eyes and looked ahead. "We will reach Prirari by late afternoon, Key Priestlord."

"That is good news," he said. "Hear us, save us."

"Hear us, save us."

Klovus longed for good food and a comfortable bed. After several days in the saddle, he ached all over, and he felt grimy with road dirt and sweat. "The people of Prirari don't believe in immersion, but maybe I can command them to draw a bath for me." He brushed at his face, felt grit on his soft skin. "Moistened cloths won't be sufficient."

The marching barbarians would be a week or more behind them, and he didn't imagine that Magda would hurry. The barbarian leader had promised to keep her people from pillaging the countryside on their way north. He hoped she would remember.

The Tamburdin godling had coerced the Hethrren into compliance, but what Magda had required from Klovus was far worse. Every time he thought of coupling with her under the trees, he was nauseated. She had pawed him and criticized him during the act, demanding that he thrust harder, and then finally rolled him off her, pressed him to the ground, and climbed on top so she could do what she wanted.

Now, as he swayed in the saddle, Klovus squeezed his eyes shut. She had complained about his unthreateningly small manhood, but afterward Magda had laughed and dragged him back to the bonfire, giving him barely enough time to don his caftan. "My new lover!" She held up his hand and

clasped his wrist like a manacle. "He promises us a whole continent to conquer." The Hethrren let out raucous jeers.

Magda had leaned close, whispering in his ear with a breath of rotting
meat. "Next time will be even better."

It had taken all of his composure not to summon the godling to smash her
into a puddle of bone splinters and flesh. But Klovus had achieved his goal.
That was his sacrifice for Ishara, just as whimpering young women sacrificed
themselves to him.

Magda had sent out her call, and the barbarian clans came riding in from
the unexplored hills beyond Tamburdin. She promised Klovus that she
would gather her people and march to Serepol. The Hethrren were tanta-
lized by the prospect of pillage and conquest.

The company leader jarred him out of his thoughts as he pointed ahead.
"There it is, Key Priestlord! We are an hour faster than I expected."

Klovus wiped perspiration from his brow and saw the stately buildings
of Prirari ahead of them across the grasses. This district was filled with orchards and grazing meadows, known for its cider, cheeses, and grains. With
calm weather and natural bounty, Prirari was one of the gentler districts,
and their resident godling reflected that. Such a kind deity might be nice for
the populace, Klovus thought, but in these changing times, a gentle godling
was not what Ishara needed.

He urged his horse to a faster pace and the escort followed, their armor
and tack jingling. Klovus needed to go to the temple first and speak with
Priestlord Erical, and then he could relax and enjoy a fine dinner.

The Prirari temple was a lovely work of architecture, with a sloping white
roof and triangular glass panels. Graceful arcs and arches made the temple
look like a white lily. When Klovus entered to meet the beatific priestlord,
he felt as if he had stepped into a cool, safe embrace.

Erical greeted him with a bow and a welcoming smile. He was handsome
and soft-spoken, dressed in a blue-trimmed gray caftan. He had a large
frame, but bowed his head and stooped his shoulders so as to look less imposing. At the wall near the temple's altar was a sheet of mounted shadowglass. Within the mysterious substance, glints of light shimmered from the
godling's void, warm multicolored glows like a knotted aurora.

Klovus briskly instructed the priestlord to prepare. "The Hethrren tribes
are marching north, and they will come through Prirari District within days."

Erical recoiled. "Priestlord Neré barely holds them in check down in Tamburdin."

"Neré does not do enough to control them, but I have resolved the issue,"

Klovus said. "The barbarians are violent and destructive, but now they are devoted to our cause. Their leader is my ally, and she is leading the Hethrren up to Serepol, where they will board naval ships and storm the Commonwealth." Chuckling, he expected Erical to respond with equal delight.

The other priestlord was concerned, but resigned. "Better the barbarians attack those who harmed our beloved empra." He bowed. "I agree, Key Priestlord. It is a hard choice you made, but a good one."

"I made the decision for the good of Ishara. At present, the empra is incapable of leading her people, and I have reluctantly stepped into the role so we are not vulnerable when the godless attack, as they surely will."

"I heard that Empra Iluris disappeared," Erical said. "That she has gone to hide among her people, or that she has ascended to the realm of the godlings." He glanced at the shadowglass window. "But I commune with my godling daily, and she has not informed me of this. Is it true that Iluris vanished?"

Klovus avoided the subject. "I have been preoccupied saving our land, but I intend to investigate the empra's disappearance further when I return." Not interested in further uncomfortable questions, and anxious for a meal and clean garments, he turned to go.

As he left the temple, he called over his shoulder, "The Hethrren will pass through Prirari on their way to Serepol. Magda has promised that her people will not engage in plundering, pillaging, or raping, but they do need to eat, and there are many Hethrren. Our districts must provide them with the food they require, because they will be our crusaders. I encouraged them to move as swiftly as possible so as to cause no undue harm to the land."

"Hear us, save us," Erical muttered.

"They may well save us." Klovus brushed at the sleeves of his caftan. "I leave Prirari in your hands, Priestlord Erical. Let me be the steward of the rest of the world."

⟡

Three days later, after Klovus and his company of soldiers had gone, Erical received word that a barbarian army was approaching. They marched across the landscape like locusts. Fields were shorn and then trampled, storehouses raided. The Hethrren ate all available food, cut down orchards for firewood, made camp wherever they chose. Some villages used their local godlings to divert them and protect themselves, though Magda and her uncouth followers seemed to defy the lesser deities.

Inside his temple, Erical ran his fingers over the shadowglass. He could see his beloved godling swirling there, the most beautiful thing ever to exist in the universe. "You know what is happening," he whispered to her. "You must be strong. We have to save our city." He shuddered at the thought of those barbarians sweeping through the streets of Prirari and disrupting the lives of the good people here.

Attuned to him, his godling swirled in a slash of color, brightening with anger. Erical wanted to calm her, but the people were uneasy—and what the people felt, so did the godling. She responded and magnified those emotions.

Ever since the first reports of Hethrren had trickled in to the city, the temple sacrifices had increased—urns of blood, baskets of fresh fruit, bushels of bread, gold coins, anything of value—and the godling grew stronger. Now Erical had to decide how to use her. Key Priestlord Klovus had explained his plan and had told Erical not to provoke the unlikely mercenary army, but he wouldn't let the barbarians harm his followers either.

"They are coming, and we must face them." He pressed his palm against the shadowglass and felt the godling without needing to activate the shimmering spelldoor. He had never been forced to bring this godling into battle before. "You will awe them. You will terrify them. I may need you to fight, but I will try to find another way."

He looked at the offerings piled in the temple. Perhaps there was an alternative to outright battle . . . a chance that might still hurt Prirari, but not cut so deep. "I always need you, but soon I will need you more than ever. We will save the city together." He hoped the godling could feel his confidence.

Erical's personal love was worth as much to her as all the prayers of the people. And he felt the godling's warmth surge back into his heart. His thoughts sparkled, brightened.

☙

When the Hethrren army proceeded across the landscape, some followed the roads, while others spread out into fields, orchards, and pastures, wherever they wished. From behind their city walls, the Prirari people saw the smoke from distant camps. It was an army large enough to devastate any city, should the barbarians choose to wield their strength.

Lines of mounted Hethrren came forward carrying clubs, spears, and swords. As Erical watched them draw closer, he knew that he must not fail.

Getting ready, he activated the spelldoor and released the glorious godling. She emerged like a pillar of smoke mixed with rainbows and lightning, dazzling colors that would make even a blind man weep. She was an ethereal column that undulated like a serpent of storms, a river of beliefs that manifested faith and goodwill. This godling had protected Prirari ever since the farming town had become a city, preventing floods, diverting forest fires, helping the people prosper.

Erical left the temple and walked with the godling behind him, majestic, beautiful, and exuding as much power as could be created by fears and imagination. He felt invincible.

Outside the walls of Prirari city, the Hethrren closed in, whooping and cheering because they saw much wealth and minimal defenses. But the priestlord intended to stop them, or at least divert them. Erical sensed that his godling was uncertain, yet not afraid.

Emerging from the city gates, the priestlord walked toward the oncoming barbarians and the stocky woman who rode at the fore. Some young children rode in front of their parents in the saddle, or trotted along beside the ragged columns. Both men and women had babies strapped to their backs, mixed throughout the barbarian army, although it did not seem to affect their warlike posture.

The swirling godling hovered behind him and flowed closer, rising up like a cobra to defend her priestlord. Magda urged her horse up to him, dubious but not frightened by the entity. She held a twisted club in her hand, ready but not threatening. Not yet.

Erical faced her. "I am the priestlord of this district. Key Priestlord Klovus told me that you would pass through our land, and that you have sworn not to pillage or destroy our homes."

Magda snorted. "Yes, my lover made me promise that, but our people must eat, and you are required to give us food."

"We will feed your armies so you can be on your way."

"Good. Then open the gates of your city so we can ride in."

"You will remain outside," Erical said. The godling swelled and looped up like a ribbon of anger and defiance. The aurora colors brightened, and a panoply of scarlet eyes lit like fresh flames in the shapeless head of the godling.

Magda's horse reared, forcing her to grab its mane. "We must eat! You are required to give us food."

"And so I will."

The godling stood as a guardian, intimidating the front lines of barbarians who looked hungrily at the city, but were afraid to pass the angry deity. A few of them even seemed ready to challenge the godling, but they would not need to.

Priestlord Erical raised his hands in signal, and horse carts emerged from the city, all loaded with fruit, piles of bread, kegs of fresh cider, wheels of cheese, hams, smoked legs of lamb. "We will feed you," Erical said, "and you will be satisfied. However, you will not enter my city."

Magda looked skeptical at first, but as wagon after wagon emerged piled with the supplies Erical had taken from the city storehouses, from merchants and farmers, she grunted. "Perhaps it will be enough."

"And then you will be on your way," Erical said.

The godling flared, and sparks crackled up and down her serpentine length as she twisted and shifted like a contained tornado.

Magda scowled back at her thousands of Hethrren and clenched her jaw. "Yes, then we will be on our way."

Erical felt a swell of relief, coupled with the godling's satisfaction. The people watched from the city, and when they understood that he had negotiated a painful but necessary solution, they all prayed, "Hear us, save us!"

The entity grew stronger, more colorful, more beautiful—and more threatening.

Magda and her Hethrren rode away the following day, as promised.

68

Dispatched by her mother from the ice palace, Koru led her frost-wreaths in search of the dragon. Ossus stirred in his deep underground sleep, which caused the Dragonspine Mountains to buckle and break. She just needed to find him.

Riding oonuks, her war party included twelve warriors and a pair of mages, a male and a female named Elon and Mor. All were eager to face their destiny after centuries of spellsleep, though Koru was disappointed that Queen Onn saw fit to send only fifteen on such a crucial mission. Her mother gave so little importance to the very reason for their existence!

Elon and Mor, both bald and unattractive, clutched their mounts' thick white fur and rode along with the party as if enduring a punishment. The warriors were fully armed, bred for combat, and entitled to victory. Koru had trained with them to hone her abilities. Her own armor felt like a protective shell that covered her shoulders, breasts, abdomen. Crystal-scaled boots reached to her knees, but left her thighs bare.

Far ahead, a black line of snowcapped peaks undulated across the landscape. Her party had been riding south and east through the frozen wastes for days, and she could see the pall of smoke in the air where the dragon's hot exhalations boiled up from the side of a mountain.

Koru yanked on the spiked reins to draw her wolf-steed to a halt, and considered the mountains. "There lies Ossus." She gripped a spear with an elongated tip of cold crystal. "If we can make the dragon show himself, perhaps we can kill him."

Leran, one of the warriors, laughed a deep-throated challenge. "You have always been ambitious, Koru. You think you could slay Ossus yourself?"

"Of course not. That is why I brought the rest of you along."

Leran touched his polished armor. "Dar wounded Ossus long ago. We can finish the job." Their mounts pawed the drifts of dirty snow.

Koru wanted to know how Dar could have been so brave, so powerful. On further study of the legends and historical records, she learned that another great wreth warrior, Rao, had fought at Dar's side against Ossus. Maybe it had taken both of them to inflict the wound that drove the dragon underground.

But she had discovered that Rao was a descendant of Raan—one of the *sandwreths*. Had Dar and Rao fought together, as allies? Had they worked to defeat the dragon—as Kur had commanded them to do—rather than trying to kill one another? That might be the only way the wreths could slay the dragon.

Annoyed with Onn's narrow-minded vision, Koru raised her spear. She was impatient with her people, frostwreths as well as sandwreths. Their petulance and prejudice were delaying the god's return and the restoration of a perfect world. With a huff, she prodded her oonuk into motion. The great white beast bounded forward.

Koru's party rode hard for days, heading toward the heart of the smoking mountains. When she found roads and abandoned villages, she remembered her mother's pet boy child, a reminder that the humans had built their own civilization while the wreths were dormant.

With the recent eruption, an incredible amount of ash, smoke, and debris had spewed into the air, obliterating these villages on the slopes. Now the wolf-steeds prowled among burned and ruined barns, warehouses, inns. Gray ash covered the ground, softening the harsh skeletal outlines of the town. Pawing at a fallen, charred beam, the beasts uncovered two blackened bodies. Koru looked down, trying to imagine the lives these poor creatures had. The oonuks tore the blackened flesh from the bones and feasted.

Moving beyond the town, the war party picked their way among jumbles of black volcanic rock. The ground thrummed and vibrated, but the shaggy wolf-steeds climbed boulders and leaped across fissures, bearing their riders.

The most prominent mountain stood like a grand throne, but its top had been sheared off in the recent upheavals. Mount Vada looked like an open wound, its peak gone, the side split. Thin rivers of orange lava streamed down like the spilled blood of a dragon. Was Ossus still bleeding from the wound Dar had inflicted with her spear?

When the war party reached the steeper slopes, they paused again. Without speaking, the two mages slid off their mounts and stood side by side, spreading their arms and splaying their fingers as if catching the air. Elon and Mor bent down in their blue robes to touch the hot ground. The blistering rocks sizzled their palms, but the two mages did not flinch.

"The world is in pain!" Elon said. "The ground in upheaval."

Mor said, "These mountains are filled with power."

Koru lifted her spear. "Then we should release it." She glanced at the determined frostwreths around her. "We will not have a better opportunity than this."

"We can sense the anger." Mor's voice was even rougher than her partner's gruff tones.

Elon lifted his hands from the hot rocks, stared at his blackened palms, then used his innate magic to heal them. "At the end of the wars, the power in the land was nearly spent, but much of it remains here in the Dragonspine Mountains. We can feel Ossus stirring."

"Then shake him awake!" Koru and the others also dismounted, telling their oonuks to follow. "We will join in the effort."

The mages' expressions did not change. Mor said, "We will borrow your power." She slammed her palms against the mottled rock that had recently been belched out of the mountain.

Koru felt a weakening inside, as if her own life and strength were flowing into the world.

Mor shoved the ripples down into the ground, and Elon did the same.

Koru dropped to her knees and pressed her hands against the searing rock as well, ignoring the burn. The ground shuddered, the slopes writhed. Koru felt a slash of pain through her heart as the world reacted. They called the dragon.

When some dark presence deep below lunged out, she lost her balance and fell backward. The other wreths sprawled as the earth heaved. Mount Vada bucked in convulsions.

The two mages continued their silent onslaught. Fumaroles vented hot gases with a shrill whistle. Geysers sprayed feathers of superheated liquid high into the air, and the jets rained hot pebbles down around them.

The ground roared, and then Mount Vada split open again. Lava squirted out in a scarlet plume, and smoke and ash became a fierce blizzard. Enormous slabs of blackened rock slid away to reveal a chasm in the mountain.

Something huge and black moved within the darkness, clawing its way out.

Koru scrambled to her feet and grabbed her spear. At first she saw jagged and angular wings, black scaly skin stretched between long ribs, and then came a pointed snout, horns and spines, fiery eyes. The creature screamed and shoved itself free from the confines of the mountain.

A dragon exploded into the smoky air as lava continued to spew out. Flapping its great wings, it pushed itself into the sky. The wreth warriors scrambled for their weapons, some shouting in challenge, others with fear-cracked voices.

Then, before the dragon could circle around once, a second terrifying figure began to emerge from the fissure—another dragon just as monstrous as
the first.

"How can there be two?" Leran cried. "There is only one Ossus!"

The first beast flew above the rumbling mountain, lashing its barbed tail.
Koru said, "Ossus embodies all hatred and violence. Maybe that cannot be
contained in one form. The two dragons must be fragments of Ossus."

The ground shook again, and the rumbling grew louder. Smoke and
fumes filled the air as the second giant reptile struggled to break free of the
mountainside. The head emerged, stretching a serpentine neck. Fire sputtered from its long tongue, gasping out of a cavernous throat. With muscular back legs, the second dragon lunged out and flapped one huge wing, but
its other wing was stunted and malformed. Though it strained against the
tough, scaly membrane, the other wing remained weak, bent.

The first dragon screamed into the air with a world-shattering sound. It
flew high into the sky and arced away from the mountains to spread its evil
across the land. It soared away.

But when the second dragon finally took wing, it could not fly far.

As Koru and her war party gathered their weapons, the monster spotted
them below. In pain, struggling to fly, it dove toward them to attack.

69

As the Utauks piled dead wood for the communal bonfire, Penda and Hale Orr took seats outside next to the old matriarch. She liked to watch the heart camp's nightly blaze. Shella din Orr was surrounded with pillows and cushions, covered with colorful blankets.

Penda was also propped on pillows, so that she felt less ungainly. Her belly seemed to grow more enormous every day. Other Utauk women—including one who had borne eight children of her own—kept Penda company during the uncomfortable rides as the wagons traveled across the landscape. The mothers gave her advice, told her stories, and emphasized how wonderful childbirth would be. Penda had seen women give birth before and knew that it was a messy and painful process. She just wanted this over—with Adan at her side.

But she was also the queen of Suderra, and she turned her thoughts to other concerns. "We know what the wreths are doing, Mother. *Cra*, we've got to do something about the slave camp where Glik is being held."

"Just knowing that the wreths cannot be trusted gives us an advantage," said the old woman. Her voice whistled and clicked as she formed clear words in spite of having only a few teeth. "They think we are all happy to be their friends."

Hale cracked a stick in his fingers. "*Cra!* That advantage does us little good unless we can use it. We should do something to free those poor people."

"You want to make the Utauk tribes into armies?" Shella remained skeptical. "We have never been good at war."

"We will all have to fight if it is the end of the world." Hale's voice did not have his usual bluster and optimism. He was weary and concerned for his daughter and her baby. "Utauks strive to be neutral, and we surround ourselves with a tight community, but we are not helpless."

A pair of teenagers lit the kindling, and soon the flames caught on the bonfire's larger logs. At smaller cookfire rings around the camp, pots heated water to boil vegetables. Birds caught in the nets and hares hunted down by archers would be roasted for all to share.

Three camp skas swooped overhead in aerial combat as the twilight deepened. The reptile birds liked to dodge and loop, harrying one another, but this time they seemed edgy and unsettled. They collided in the air, snapping with their long snouts, genuinely vicious. Loose feathers drifted down.

Penda looked up in shock. Their distressed owners ran out, waving at the sky. "Come back! Stop that." One of the skas returned wounded, seeking refuge with its human partner. The reptile birds continued to harass one another, while their masters yelled at them.

Even when most of the pet skas were brought under control, they remained brooding and restless, hissing at their human partners, who felt distraught through the heart link. Two of the camp skas refused to obey their masters and flew overhead, letting out loud mournful sounds.

Penda drew a circle around her heart and pressed a palm against her chest. She could feel Xar's agitation, too, through their heart link. Earlier, she had bound him to his resting post with a leather thong, but now Xar flapped his wings and strained to break free. Seeing how the other skas had attacked and fought, she didn't want him up there where he could be hurt.

She levered herself up from the cushions and went to stroke Xar's pale green feathers, cooing and humming to settle him. She saw turmoil in the reptile bird's faceted eyes. "Calm down. It'll be all right." Xar nudged her with his head, insisting that she continue calming him.

Stars had begun to twinkle through the deep blue overhead. Sadly, she wondered where Ari had flown off to. After recording her message into the mothertear diamond, she had released the young blue ska again, which had flown off to find the orphan girl. If Glik did receive Penda's message, she might draw hope. . . .

Penda untied the leather thong and placed Xar on her shoulder, stroking his feathers, then made her way back to where Hale and Shella watched the growing bonfire. The matriarch reminisced about when she had once seen a dragon, back as a young girl. When Penda had first heard that story—as had all Utauks—it seemed an unlikely tale, but now Shella's words rang true.

The ska flapped his wings, and she struggled to soothe him. "Easy, Xar." She also pressed through the heart link, but his agitation continued to increase.

Hale watched her struggle with her pet. "What is wrong with him, dear heart?"

"It's not just Xar—look at all of them." She indicated the sky with a toss of her head.

"Something in the air," said Shella din Orr.

"*Cra*, something in the whole world!"

Just as Penda lowered herself back to the cushions near the bonfire, her abdomen clenched and her muscles tightened in a spasm. She doubled over, and Hale lurched over to grab her arm.

Penda drew a deep breath, trying to find air. It was an early labor pain; she knew it. She had felt them before, but they were mere twinges. This was a more intense shock wave that went from the base of her legs, through her womb, and all the way into her heart.

The pain was more than a mere cramp, though, and it was not just inside of her. Something was happening deep within the earth, a distant pain that surged into her senses. Xar rattled a hiss in his scaly throat. He strained his wings, but Penda held his leg, preventing him from flying away. She was terrified for him now. Something about the skas . . .

Although the labor spasm passed, the pain in the world kept growing. The ground beneath the camp started to shake from a distant rumbling. The stacked logs in the bonfire shifted, sending a shower of sparks into the air. Cookpots swayed on their tripods above the smaller fires.

Shella din Orr clutched the pillows and cushions at her sides. "I can feel it. Something . . . tearing!" Other Utauks shouted.

Around the camp, the agitated skas broke free of their masters, squawking, clicking, and hooting. They flew into the air, harrying and pecking one another, desperate to escape. Their owners yelled after them, some in dismay, others in anger.

Hale Orr didn't care about skas, though, as he knelt in front of his daughter. "Is it the baby's time?"

A shudder passed through her again, another clenching of muscles, but then it faded. "No, not yet. It's just an early pain. *Cra*, it can't be time." She shook her head and insisted, "It cannot be time!" With one hand she drew a circle around her heart. She pulled in a deep breath, imposing her will upon her own body. "I have to send a message to my Starfall. I need him to find me."

Just then some of the humans heart-linked to their skas swooned and dropped to their knees, dizzy. One fell backward to the ground and lay with eyes open, teeth clenched as if having terrible visions.

Penda squeezed her eyes shut, sensed something powerful, terrible . . . huge scaly shapes with great wings and lashing tails, a breath of fire.

Xar broke free of her fingers and flung himself into the air, but Penda snatched the leather thong still tied to his foot, afraid to let him go. The other skas were going wild. He flapped and slashed, trying to break free, but she held on. "No, Xar! Please stay with me."

Eventually, the ska surrendered and let her draw him back to her, but he watched as the other agitated reptile birds fled into the dark sky as their dismayed human partners ran after them, called out, but to no effect.

Old Shella watched the skas fly away. Tears sparkled in her eyes.

"Will they come back, Mother?" Penda asked, feeling the heartache of what the other partners were experiencing.

"They may, or they may not, child. I think it means that more dragons are coming."

"Are skas afraid of dragons?" Penda asked. "Is that why they escaped?"

Shella considered for a long moment, staring into the burning bonfire, then shook her head. "It may be that the skas are *connected* to them."

COLD white steam rose from the rubble of the Lake Bakal fortress. Broken frostwreth bodies littered the site of the disaster, and drones scurried over the debris, picking and sorting through it.

The complete destruction gave King Kollanan a sense of vindication.

Tempering the victory, however, were his many losses, dozens of soldiers slain in the fierce battles, and others caught in the collapse of the ice-block walls. Battlefield surgeons tended the injured, heating sword blades in new fires to cauterize necessary amputations. Others tended the dying, leaning close and listening to the last words so all those lives and legacies would not be forgotten.

Koll leaned against his warhorse. Storm's black hide had an angry-looking scrape and several deep cuts that would need to be tended. Other mounts with broken legs or deeper wounds had to be put down.

Bleeding from a dozen injuries, Ogno strode up to the king, coughing hard and spitting a glob of phlegm and blood to the side. "Cerus is dead, Sire, but it took two frostwreths to kill him. I stabbed one of them in the back, but I was too late." The big man held up his hand, befuddled by the blood there. He frowned when he noticed that his index finger had been hacked off. "My wife is going to be upset," he said, then wandered off.

Kollanan stared at the shattered fortress in awe. The structure had covered a large part of the lakeshore, and he tried to take heart in wiping out the frostwreths. His triumph here was indisputable, but it did not bring back Jhaqi, Gannon, or little Tomko. And Birch was still held prisoner at the northern palace.

Lasis and Elliel approached him, their ramers extinguished, their swords bloodied, their sturdy capes ragged. They looked drained. "We did not take a count, Sire," Lasis reported, "but Elliel and I killed many of them. Urok also slew his share."

Koll looked around, searching for the other Brava. "Did he and Lord Bahlen survive?"

Lasis nodded. "We saw Bahlen tending to the wounded."

Elliel's cinnamon hair was matted with blood in the back where someone had struck her, but she seemed unaffected by the injury. Her green eyes brightened. "We hunted down and dispatched any enemies who escaped the collapse, even if it took ten soldiers against each frostwreth warrior."

"A few escaped, though." Lasis gestured to the fortress rubble. "We saw them bounding away on wolf-steeds." He tugged at his tattered cape as if it offended him, then removed the ruined garment and tossed it to the ground. "Queen Onn will know what we did to her fortress."

Thon came up to them, smiling but obviously drained. "I should have done that last time, but I was not confident in what I could accomplish." He marveled at the destruction. "The sandwreth mages provided substantial assistance in the overall battle."

"As did my warriors," Quo said, riding his auga up to them. He wore a superior grin, but his attitude seemed oddly deprecating. The injured reptile moved sluggishly. "I did lose two mages and five warriors. Seven casualties total." He frowned. "Perhaps I should have brought a larger war party after all."

Koll saw with disgust that the wreth noble had slung the body of a drone across the auga's saddle. The small creature's eyes were round and open, the dead expression blank. The king scolded, "Those drones fought at our side."

Quo looked down at the corpse and pushed the side of its smooth head, which lolled away from him. "Their assistance was not significant."

"They were still our allies. Did you kill it?"

"It was already mostly dead. I wanted to bring a specimen to my beloved sister. Voo will find the creature fascinating. Perhaps she can learn how to make drones of her own. If the frostwreths can do it, then we will be able to do it better!" He was oblivious to Koll's anger. "If we can create armies of our own drones, we will have many more allies in the coming war. Along with the human fighters that you and King Adan provide us, we will surely crush the evil frostwreths who plague you so much."

Koll struggled to keep his anger in check. "Norterra has not agreed to an alliance yet."

Quo jerked his chin toward the icy ruins. "I kept my part of the bargain. We destroyed the enemy fortress, as you requested."

Thon stepped forward. "You *helped* destroy it."

Quo was not swayed. "It is still a complete victory. The fortress is gone.

The cold-bonded spell will dissipate, and you can rebuild the town." His grin grew more pointed. "The frostwreths were . . . in the way."

Kollanan registered his sarcasm, but he was not amused.

Elliel turned to the king, ignoring Quo. "We have our large army here right now, Sire—and we have the sandwreth reinforcements. This is the most powerful we have ever been. If we take our army north, we can strike the frostwreths before Queen Onn is able to prepare. We can press our victory."

"That might also be our chance to rescue Birch," Lasis added.

Kollanan longed to agree, but he knew it was the wrong decision. "Our army is not sufficient against the frostwreths. They have thousands in the army they are building. You reported that yourselves."

Quo said dismissively, "Do not count on our further assistance. My sister gave me another mission, and we must be off." Additional sandwreths rode up on their augas, including Ulla, the last surviving mage. Dark spatters of blood stained her rough face and her red leather robe.

Koll turned in surprise. "You are leaving? We still need your help here. Queen Onn will certainly retaliate!"

"My party has done its work and paid a high price." Quo looked at his lone mage, his surviving wreth warriors, some of them injured. One riderless auga stood next to the others. "I helped you out of courtesy. It gave me a chance to observe how your people fight. I am impressed, particularly with your half-breeds." He glanced toward Elliel and Lasis. "But we must complete a task for my sister. We are loyal to Queen Voo first."

"What task is more important?" Koll demanded. "After this, Norterra is now vulnerable—"

Quo took offense, and his warriors gripped their weapons. "You might call yourself a king among the humans, but you have no part in sandwreth business." Then the capricious wreth noble chuckled. "This has been amusing! Thank you for the opportunity. It is always a good day when one spills the blood of an enemy." He adjusted the drone corpse across his saddle and nudged his auga into motion. The sandwreth war party rode away from the battlefield around Lake Bakal.

71

ᘒ

EVEN after the wreths recaptured her, Glik could not break free of her
visions. *Inside the circle. Outside the circle.*

In the frozen pool of shadowglass, she had glimpsed the mind and heart
of the dragon, feeling its hatred and evil. She had also seen an equally terrible
force, just as powerful as Ossus and able to wreak as much destruction. Glik
understood the dragon, but this other thing was beyond her comprehension.

Half unconscious, she drew a circle over and over and over, mumbling
her mantra. She was so trapped in the fearful visions that she could barely
see the moonlight, the jagged outcroppings of shadowglass, and the wreths
around her.

Sharp pain jarred Glik out of her catatonic daze.

"What do you see, girl?" The voice was angry, full of command. Mage
Ivun shook her. His hand had shriveled into a claw, tight leather and sinew.
As if from a distance, she realized that he must have expended much of his
magic reserves to quash the escape attempt. She hoped he would continue to
wither away.

"Leave her alone," Cheth shouted, then grunted in pain as the wreth warriors pummeled her to the ground.

"Tell me what you saw!" Ivun pushed Glik forward, shoving her face close
to the still pool of obsidian. "*Tell me!*"

But the mage had shattered the connection. Though she remained frightened, the looming visions had vanished. Now when she stared at the smooth
black surface of the pool, she saw nothing, not even a hint of her own reflection.

"It's gone," she said in a hoarse whisper. "I don't see the dragon now, but
there was something else, too."

Ivun leaned over the shadowglass. Peering down, he placed the palm of his
good hand on the impenetrable surface and bent so close that Glik thought
he might kiss it. He swiped his hand over the black glass, then in frustration,

pounded it with a fist. Ivun's clawed fingers dug into her shoulder. "There are no visions here! You drained them all. You took them for yourself."

"I—I did not want them."

"And yet you have them." With his intact arm he lifted her up. "You will come with me." Ivun looked at the wreth warriors who still held Cheth. "Take that prisoner back to the camp and round up any others who escaped. I want them all. We have much work to do here."

The mage glared at Glik with close-set eyes the color of honey lit on fire. "I will find a way to extract what you saw so I can share your knowledge." His voice had its own reptilian hiss that was so unlike the roar of the dragon she had heard in her mind.

"I *need* the knowledge."

Glik could barely walk as the mage dragged her along. Her knees and hands were bleeding; her clothes were in tatters. When she stumbled, Ivun ordered one of the warriors to dismount from his auga. He lifted the orphan girl like a discarded package, dropped her into the saddle, and climbed up behind her. Surefooted even on the jumbled shadowglass, the auga loped off toward the camp.

Ivun's pavilion was braced with supports of iron-hard wood and large bones lashed together. The night was hot and still, and the moon hovered overhead, shining pale light across the bleak terrain. The Plain of Black Glass sucked away all noise, all wind.

Glik did not want to help her captors, but she was shaken by what she had seen. If Ossus awakened, he could destroy them all . . . but that other roiling force was no ally. She stammered as she described what she could recall of her visions for the demanding mage.

Although Ivun listened with interest, he was intent on his own preparations. "Not good enough. I need to see what you saw, sense what you sensed."

"I've already told you all I remember. I don't have anything more!"

"You have it inside you," Ivun insisted. Reaching into the sleeve of his leather robe, he withdrew a shard of shadowglass with a razor edge.

Glik scrambled away from him as he clamped his withered hand around her wrist, squeezing tight. She feared he was going to slice her open, maybe rip out her heart. She struggled, but the mage was much stronger than she was.

He dragged her over to a small table on which he had set an unevenly shaped bowl, also fashioned out of shadowglass. He drew her toward him, turned her hand up, and slashed her forearm with the black dagger. Blood welled up. She gasped from the pain.

He tossed the shadowglass knife away and held her arm over the basin to catch her blood. As the bowl filled, Ivun watched with keen interest. "Shadowglass knife. Shadowglass bowl." He looked at her with blazing eyes. "Shadowglass visions."

When he'd captured enough blood, Ivun released her and drew his withered arm against his chest, as if he had expended all the physical energy he possessed. Using his good hand, he rubbed the shadowglass bowl, turning it slowly as he peered into the pool of blood, which shifted from red to black and then sparkled with stars.

"Is this what you saw?" he demanded, then added a louder hiss of command. "Look, girl!"

Glik nursed her cut arm, but was drawn to the blood in the basin. When she stared into its liquid surface, it stared back at her with a reptilian eye. "Yes! It's Ossus."

"It is Ossus." Ivun's voice was filled with hunger. The slitted powerful eye blinked in the basin, then widened. A different blackness swirled around it . . . the other powerful force. "What is that?"

On the starry surface, a bubble rose and burst, splattering red droplets across the mage's face. Ivun knocked the bowl off the table, spilling blood onto the floor of his tent. "We know Ossus. We must awaken him and destroy him. But that other force . . ."

Glik interrupted him with a hard retort. "Are you afraid of it? Maybe it will destroy all the wreths so that your god will never come back."

She could see he was shaken as he wiped the blood from his face. "Afraid? I do not know enough yet to be afraid. But it is wise to have respect for things you do not understand."

He casually tossed her a strip of cloth from the belongings strewn about his pavilion. She wrapped it around her bleeding arm. "Once you understand a thing," Ivun said, "then you can destroy it."

72

⨏

As Mount Vada continued to rumble around the frostwreth war party, the stunted dragon careened through the air, ungainly but still terrifying. Because of its malformed wing, the monster struggled to fly far from the crack in the mountainside.

Koru ducked as smoking rock shards and thick ash fell around them. She gritted her teeth and waved her spear. This was what she had wanted. The stunted dragon was not Ossus, but it would be good practice. Her wreth warriors scrambled as they made preparations to fight the monster.

The first dragon had flown away, abandoning its crippled sibling. The second dragon seemed outraged at its own inadequacy, and the deformity seemed to make it even meaner. It thundered toward the wreth war party, as if blaming them for its misery.

Koru's two mages hurled magic like a crashing wave crest through the air. Buffeted by the turbulence, the lumbering dragon hissed, and its eyes blazed an orange brighter than the lava itself. Its gaping jaws were ready to snap up the wreths, regardless of their armor.

The oonuks bounded away in panic, but Koru grabbed one as it lunged past. She threw herself onto its back and wrestled its head around, forcing the beast toward the dragon.

The warrior Leran shrieked a challenge and raised his spear in one hand and a crystal sword in the other. Exuberant, he ran over the shifting ground as fast as the wolf-steed. As it passed, the stunted dragon's good wing swept Leran into the upthrust boulders, smashing him with such force that his head and ribs split open. He lay twitching like a squashed insect.

Koru dropped off the oonuk's back and landed with her feet planted apart. She ducked as the dragon swooped over her head with a breath of sulfur and hate, trying to break and batter her. Reaching up, she slashed at the leathery skin between the vanes of its good wing, and her spear point sliced the tight membrane.

In pain, the dragon reeled upward, trying to gain altitude with its mal-formed wing, and a wide ragged hole ripped open in the other. Together, her warriors threw numerous spears. Several stuck like splinters in the scaled haunches, and one pierced its ribs.

Separating, the two mages climbed onto high rocks at the edge of the new fissure. Lava flowed in a molten brook, spewing fiery droplets that solidified in the air and pelted down in hot rubble. Elon and Mor pushed with their magic in unison, reaching into the mountains themselves and drawing on the power that ran hot and furious to the surface. The mages flung boulders at the dragon, like loads from a dozen catapults. The rocks pummeled the monster, and one projectile broke the tip of its stunted wing.

The angry creature plummeted to attack again, and Koru's warriors scat-tered, seeking shelter. The dragon caught one of the wolf-steeds in its talons, lifted it into the air, and tore the beast in half before flinging the bloody pieces aside.

Elon and Mor summoned another volley of hot boulders, but their efforts agitated the unstable mountain. Burning stones rained down on Elon. One scored a black furrow across his bald skull, and he collapsed and rolled.

Mor was standing closer to the river of lava, calling on the deep magic, when a jet of superhot molten rock showered up and incinerated her before she had time to scream. The volley of boulders hurled by the mages now broke from their trajectories and crashed down, barely missing Elon, who writhed in pain on the ground.

Another boulder dropped from the sky and crushed a wreth warrior who challenged the oncoming dragon. The monster snapped him up in its jaws.

Koru was panting so hard that the hot air seared her lungs. Their god had given all wreths the mission to destroy Ossus . . . yet this wasn't Ossus, merely what she had guessed was a fragment of him. Even though this small dragon was injured and malformed, it might still massacre her entire war party.

But Koru swore she would not fail. She had to make an example and force her mother to see how enormous the true threat—the wreths' true mission—really was.

She faced the damaged monster, ready to fight as she had never fought before. When its wings could no longer hold the behemoth aloft, it crashed to the ground and became an even more fearsome juggernaut. A mountain of scales and fangs. The dragon lurched forward on clawed feet, charging the war party.

Two warriors stood together to face it, showing no fear as they hurled their crystal-tipped spears. One weapon caromed off the dragon's scales, and another pierced the membrane on the malformed wing. When the monster roared, one warrior threw his last spear down into its gullet. The weapon lodged in the soft pink flesh, but the dragon crunched down, snapped the shaft, and spat out splinters. It swept its enormous barbed head from side to side and seized both warriors in its jaws.

Though wounded, Mage Elon climbed to his feet, his skin smoking. Angry at the death of his partner, he launched a hail of projectiles borne on a buffeting assault of wind.

Koru rallied her surviving warriors, only eight of them now, for a final push. Two had retrieved their oonuks, and the others were on foot. "Even if we kill just a fragment of Ossus, we have struck a blow for victory. We know the mission Kur gave us." She heaved a scalding breath. "The mission he gave *all wreths*!"

Imagining the frostwreth armies and the sandwreth armies, she was dismayed by how the two factions were weakening each other with hatred rather than joining against an insurmountable enemy. Where were they now? They should be here!

The stunted dragon lumbered toward them, knocking aside slabs of rock. The ground shook, and Koru couldn't tell if the mountain was ready to erupt again, or if it was merely signaling the approach of the monster. Koru held her spear, and drew strength from knowing it was modeled after Dar's weapon from times past.

When the dragon stormed closer, her warriors threw yet another volley of spears, and two pierced its hide. The dragon lifted its triangular head, and trumpeted in pain and outrage. Pounding both wings, it somehow lifted its massive body aloft again. Koru ducked as waves of air buffeted them.

Looking up, she hefted the spiraled shaft of her spear and thought about her ancestor Dar. This was not just any spear, and Koru was certain it would fly true. She could smell an oily reptile musk, the stink of the dragon's passage as it thundered overhead.

Koru drew back her arm and hurled the weapon with all her might and determination. It streaked upward and plunged into the softer scales at the base of the dragon's throat. The leaf-shaped tip sank deep, and blood spouted out, smoking in the air.

The dragon thrashed and writhed as it fought to stay aloft in spite of the new wound. Cheering, Koru ran along with her warriors, chasing after the monster and ready to hack it with their swords if it crashed to the ground.

The struggling dragon made it to the smoking cauldron in the side of

Mount Vada. With a gasp of surrender as if it actually sought the embrace of the molten fire, the dragon plunged into the lava-filled fissure. It writhed and smoked as it sank, its scales catching fire, its blackness breaking into thousands of pieces that seeped into the liquid rock.

Standing as near to the edge as she dared, Koru stared, uncertain of her triumph. "The dragon is dead. We killed it."

His skin still smoldering, Mage Elon strode up to her, shaking his head. "We killed one of them. That manifestation of the dragon may be dead, but now its evil can seep back into the world."

"There is already enough evil in the world." Koru feared that evil had tainted the wreth races as well. "We have to kill every dragon, *every* manifestation, until Ossus is finally dead. Then at last the world can be made perfect."

73

THE Hethrren hordes marched without urgency, but their movement was inexorable. By the time they approached Serepol, word—and some measure of panic—had traveled through the city.

Key Priestlord Klovus tried to make many preparations. When he spoke of his plan, he demonstrated immense outward confidence, although in his heart he was terrified. He had spread the "good news" among the people, but even his greatest supporters among the priestlords were anxious about their supposed allies. Though Serepol was far from Tamburdin District, stories of the barbarians had spread via merchants and travelers journeying north.

"Hear us, save us!" Klovus shouted to the people, making it sound like a celebration. "Our new Hethrren friends are coming, and we must show them grace and hospitality. In the harbor, Isharan navy ships are even now being made ready to deliver our vengeful force to the enemy. The Hethrren will be our sword against the godless." He raised his hands to encourage a loud cheer, prodding the people into the proper response. Klovus had trained them not to doubt him.

When he received reports of the bizarre rumors spreading about Empra Iluris, however, he was at first amused, then annoyed. "How can they believe such ridiculous things?" he had asked his Black Eels.

Zaha responded with a blank but steely gaze. "She is missing, Key Priestlord, with no explanation. Would you rather they all believed that you assassinated her and disposed of her body?"

Klovus flushed. "We should spread rumors of our own that Commonwealth spies kidnapped her when she was recovering from her injury. Say they took her away and tortured her to death in their own dungeons."

The Black Eel seemed hesitant. "We could spread that rumor, Key Priestlord. My companions could take different forms and tell the same story out of many mouths for added veracity." He paused, then added, "I cannot guarantee anyone will believe it, though."

"They will believe anything," Klovus snapped. "Obviously."

✍

The Magnifica temple grew taller and more imposing each day, and Klovus was pleased with his dedicated workers. Traders and suppliers, burly laborers and delicate artisans poured their sweat and skill into erecting the enormous structure. But he wanted to show more progress before the barbarians arrived, so he again summoned the godling in order to use its strength and majesty to help assemble the temple.

The dust-coated, sweaty laborers backed away to the edge of the temple square and stared in awe and anticipation. Klovus reached into himself, pulling with his heart and mind—as well as the faith of the people—and called forth the Serepol godling.

The thing roiled out, eager to please, a barely contained avatar of Isharan strength. Klovus directed it as he had done before, and the godling reached out with titanic arms of smoke and lightning, lifting up house-sized blocks of stone and raising them to the half-finished third level of the stepped pyramid. It hefted cartloads of bricks and slid them into place. Though the effort drained him, commanding the towering entity also gave Klovus power.

Tapping into the Magnifica's design in the key priestlord's mind, the godling could envision and understand the shape of its future home. The city people were both terrified by and enamored with what the deity could do. They watched, they *believed,* and their inner strength powered the godling.

Klovus and the godling worked together for hours, completing another significant portion of the enormous structure. When he was finished, the godling was discernibly weakened and more diffuse. Klovus had let himself get carried away, absorbed in the glorious work, and now the entity had done too much. He himself felt exhausted.

Barely able to stand, he turned to the crowd, and they all cheered. Deep inside, Klovus could feel the godling draw another glimmer of strength from their renewed excitement and faith. With great thanks, he dismissed the godling, and it retreated weakly into the temple behind the spelldoor to simmer in its own void and gradually recover its energy.

The key priestlord also wanted to go back to his own quarters and rest, eat a fine meal, perhaps take a perfumed hot bath. He felt too weary to take advantage of any female supplicants who might want to offer their bodies as sacrifices. He shivered, recalling what Magda had done to him. . . .

Before he could retreat to privacy and relax in peace, though, he received a surprise message from a scout who rode in. The news was expected but still unnerving. Klovus had thought he would have more time.

The Hethrren had arrived.

When he watched the oncoming throng from a tall watchtower on the out-skirts of the city, his heart quailed. A hundred fur-clad riders cantered in the front lines, followed by a vast army that ignored roads and trampled the landscape. Magda, a mound of muscle and skin, wearing a wolf pelt over her bare shoulders, raised her twisted club as if it were a scepter of office.

Bracing himself, Klovus rushed out to meet the vanguard before they reached the city. Even from a distance, Magda's grin was so wide he could see her crooked teeth. Though dressed in his fine blue caftan, the key priestlord clutched his gold chain of office, suddenly forgetting his confidence as the Hethrren leader galloped toward him. He felt weak from his long efforts at the Magnifica, and the godling was recovering, so Klovus was on his own.

Magda pulled her horse to a halt just before the front hooves trampled him. "I brought my people as you requested, lover. Are you happy to see me?"

Klovus paled but forced himself not to flinch. "You offered to fight the godless, which benefits us both." He nodded to reassure himself. "As we agreed, I will provide your people with weapons and ships. We've been pre-paring for your swift departure ever since I arrived back in Serepol."

"We want you to be ready for us. Mount beside me." Magda reached down to grab his hand, then chuckled. "You can mount me later."

Klovus felt the familiar nausea return. Reluctantly, he struggled onto her sturdy horse. Magda had to lift him bodily in front of her, and he was neither small nor lightweight. The other Hethrren riders glowered at the anxious-looking city people who stood outside their shops and animal pens. Behind the front line, the main army kept marching toward Serepol.

"I showed you my camp, lover. Now show me your palace." Magda leaned forward, and a vile smell wafted out of her mouth. "I've never slept in a fine royal bed before."

"I am a priestlord, not a king," Klovus said. He gritted his teeth and forced himself to agree. "I will take you into Serepol. You and this first line of warriors. I assume they are your generals? The others need to camp outside the city, though. We will provide food and supplies while we finish preparing the ships. It should not take more than a day or two. Then you can be on your way to victory."

As he sat on the saddle in front of her, Magda wrapped her beefy arms around him. "Why so eager to be rid of me?" She dug in her heels, and the horse lurched forward.

Citizens of Serepol scattered out of the way as the Hethrren riders pushed into the city. Behind them, the main barbarian army let out a loud cry and picked up their pace.

"Stop!" Klovus looked back in alarm. "We must obey the forms."

"We are leaders. We make our own rules," Magda said.

As they rode into Serepol, Klovus tried to steer her toward the Magnifica temple. "In this great structure, we are building a home for our greatest godling. You can see how immense it will be."

"I can see it is not finished. Your godling can have it." Magda pointed toward the high palace. "That is where your empra rules?"

Klovus swallowed hard. "That is the palace, yes."

"Do you have rooms of your own there?"

He had indeed claimed chambers in the palace as he assumed more and more duties with Iluris gone. "Yes."

It still maddened him that he didn't know where the empra had gone, but his searchers had found nothing. Rumors were widespread, ridiculous, and unhelpful. It was almost as if someone wanted to create confusion and concern.

"Then that is where I shall be, with you. Find rooms for my"—she looked around at the shaggy riders who cantered beside her—"my generals as you called them." She laughed. The bearded men and women stared from beneath hooded brows, assessing the homes, the shops, the places to plunder.

Klovus wanted nothing more than to slide off the horse and run. Unfortunately, the exhausted godling was too quiescent to offer him protection right now. "This is not what we agreed."

"We didn't settle all the details."

As the unruly force rode on into the city, Klovus realized that part of the front ranks had already dismounted and made their way into taverns or restaurants, taking whatever food or drink they needed. He could hear scuffles and shouts of dismay behind him. "You must control them!"

Magda cuffed him on the side of the head, and his ears rang. "They traveled a long distance on your command. They have needs, and you promised to provide them." She leaned closer and growled in his ear, "I expect you to satisfy me as well."

His stomach knotted.

People were emptying the streets, rushing into buildings, shuttering windows, barring doors. The Hethrren pushed toward the palace, but Klovus managed to divert them down the main streets that led to the open harbor. "Let me show you our warships. You will find them impressive."

Magda pursed her lips. "Yes, I want to see these ships that we will ride across the sea."

Her words gave him only a small amount of relief. He tried to catch his breath, but the animal stink around Magda made him gag. She had covered her skin with old grease, which she said drove away the bugs, and the wolf pelt on her shoulder smelled as if it had not been properly cured. "Will you sail with us, so you can watch my Hethrren win a great victory?"

He blinked. "No, I am needed here. You will command the armies that conquer the old world."

She huffed. The Hethrren rode down to the docks and spread out to inspect merchant stalls, sniffing and frowning at the fish sellers. Some vendors closed up and fled; others tried to haggle with the strange new customers. One Hethrren grabbed a scrawny potter who complained when he broke a small glazed pot. The barbarian picked him up by his neck, held the potter with his feet dangling off the ground, then tossed him into his own pile of pots, shattering many more.

People gawked at the shaggy barbarians. They clasped their hands and raised their arms, beseeching the key priestlord. "Hear us, save us!"

Knowing he had to keep up appearances, Klovus shouted from horseback in front of Magda, "These are the Hethrren, our new friends. They will stay for just a brief few days, before they sail off to crush our enemies."

The people seemed guardedly optimistic. Magda laughed out loud. "Hethrren do not know ships."

"Our captains and sailors will bring you across the ocean." Klovus pointed toward the harbor. "The voyage takes only a few days, and then you can run free across a whole continent."

Out in the sparkling water, dozens of Isharan war vessels filled the docks, their red-and-white sails tied up to yardarms; even more ships were anchored out in the open harbor. Klovus tried to calculate how many ships would be needed to ferry all of the barbarians across the ocean.

"The fleet is being supplied now, as you can see." Klovus indicated where people worked aboard the warships. "You'll have all the weapons you need."

Magda grunted. "We have had a long journey to reach Serepol. Perhaps we should not depart so soon."

Behind them, the unchecked Hethrren army entered the streets and moved through neighborhoods, terrorizing shops, taverns, stables. Magda said, "Your city looks comfortable. We may stay here for a while."

74

W HAT are you?" Cemi whispered to the rippling, insubstantial presence in front of her.

Though the guardian force had dissipated into near transparency, she could still sense it there, in addition to the power that clung to the stone walls and permeated the foundation of the palace. The force, the entity—the godling?— was connected to her as well.

And if it truly was a godling, a young and inexperienced deity created by all of the faith and concern for Empra Iluris, then the thing needed to be nurtured and strengthened.

She experienced a surge of energy inside her as the godling responded to her nearness. The air twisted like currents in a stream, and she reached out, felt the invisible touch.

Vos stepped up beside her. "Without our protector, we would never have survived the assassination attempt. We would have been discovered and killed long before now."

Cemi nodded. "Our enemies have many advantages over us. They have numbers, resources, weapons, and opportunity. Yet we still live." She reached out, spread her fingers, and felt the godling wrap itself around her. Her voice grew harder with determination. "We have been saved for a purpose, and it was not just to hide here." She looked over at the pale and fragile Iluris, still lying motionless. "We are destined to do more. I wanted to protect the empra until she woke up and took back her rule. But now . . ." She had a difficult time facing it. "I have to do what she would want."

"You know what she would want," Vos said. It was not a question.

Analera delivered regular reports about the secret efforts to build support throughout Serepol. Each day she found more and more people who believed the story that the godlings protected Empra Iluris, that she would come back when the time was right. It was not hard for even the lowest ditchdigger to realize that there was corruption in the city, that there were those—including

Key Priestlord Klovus—who were not to be trusted. Now, with the astonishing reports of a barbarian army arriving and even being welcomed into the city, the mutterings grew louder. People whispered strong prayers for the empra to come back. "Hear us, save us!"

"Tell them to keep praying," Cemi had urged the old servant that morning. "Their beliefs will strengthen this new godling, their protector. Our future depends on them, on their faith."

Analera had nodded. "They understand, Excellency. In their homes, in shadowed alleys, in public gathering places, they all pray for the empra's safe return."

Cemi reached out. If she could make the new entity more powerful, then her small group might have a better chance. Although they were trapped underground, she could sense the prayers outside increasing, because she felt it through the godling.

Beside her now, Vos said, "That godling is our shield, and you have a connection to it. How can we make it stronger than our enemies?"

Beyond the prayers of the people, Cemi thought of another way to make the godling stronger. The priestlords did it all the time. "Captani, give me your knife."

He was startled. "What do you need it for?"

"I need it," she said, then softened her voice, "please."

He handed her his razor-sharp dagger. She looked at the gleaming edge, then slashed it across the ball of her thumb. She held up the cut, the blood that welled forth. "All of your hawk guards will need to do the same."

The new guardian entity shimmered around her. "We all make sacrifices," Cemi said. "By giving up something important to us, we shore up the godling." Blood ran down her palm and along her wrist, but the godling whispered around her like a warm breeze, taking the blood, making it vanish, sealing her cut.

Voss took the knife and slashed his own hand. "I'm glad there's something we can do while we wait."

75

⁓

Uᴛʜᴏ returned to Convera, uneasy after what he had seen in the Dragonspine Mountains. He was a Brava, and his character was made of steel, and he would set a course and not waver—that was always his strength. But Onzu had made him wonder if it was also a weakness. Did his absolute focus on the vengewar make him blind to everything else?

When he reached the castle, he sensed the anxiety in the court and realized instantly that something dreadful had happened. Striding up to the nearest court guard, he demanded, "Why are these people so tense?"

The man snapped to attention, but he looked ill. "It's Konag Mandan's emissary to the sandwreths. . . . Queen Voo was . . . not satisfied." He explained about the horrific fate of the emissary folded in a box, still alive.

Utho ground his teeth. "Wreths again! Was it a parlor trick? Or some kind of torture?"

"It was magic, sir. Wreth magic! Voo says she expects Konag Mandan to come in person next time she summons him."

Utho was offended. "Mandan is not her slave. He's the konag of the Commonwealth."

"I know, sir, but what are we to do if wreth armies invade the three kingdoms? King Adan and King Kollanan already—"

"Wreth armies are not our concern! Tell me, have the Isharans attacked us again? Or do we still have time?"

The guard blinked. "Isharans? No, but King Kollanan insists the wreths—"

"I've heard enough about wreths for one day." He stalked past the guard, making his way to the konag's chambers. He had been gone for so long, Mandan would want to see him immediately. He hoped the young man had not made unwise decisions in his absence.

Unconcerned with the sweat and dust from his long ride, Utho strode down the corridor to the spacious royal apartment. He remembered when Conndur the Brave had lived in these same rooms, which held a few war mementos, but not many, because Conndur was not a man overburdened with nostalgia. Upon taking the crown, however, Mandan had changed the chamber.

Now three easels stood with paintings in various stages of completion. The air smelled of turpentine and firewood, and the konag's brushes and palettes lay in disarray on a table. One wall was entirely covered with maps.

He entered without knocking and found Mandan standing before one of his easels, staring at the canvas. He blinked his empty eyes and didn't seem to see Utho. He held his paintbrush over a palette filled with black, gray, and red pigments. The painting was a sketchy and distorted version of Conndur's mutilated body sprawled on the blood-soaked bed. "I cannot get it out of my head, Utho. I thought that maybe if I painted it . . ."

Utho yanked the canvas from the easel and turned it to face the stone wall. "That only sharpens your memory of it—sharpens it into a dagger that stabs your heart."

"I wish he wasn't dead. My father would know what to do!" The young man's voice was raw. "No one accepts me as the konag. Why won't they obey my orders?" Near his bedside a small table held a crumpled letter. Mandan grabbed it, held it up. "I sent my decree to Suderra and Norterra, as you said, and they don't listen. My own uncle defies me!"

Utho took the letter and read with disbelief. "Kollanan demands that you send the Osterran army to him?"

Mandan shouted, "But he can't refuse."

"You are correct, he cannot refuse." Yet Kollanan had done exactly that, dismissing a formal declaration of war and a call to arms, citing some obscure clause in the charter. The fate of the Commonwealth was at stake!

Utho knew the real reason, and it was not about wreths. It was because Elliel had told the Norterran king all about Lord Cade, the saltpearl operations, and what Utho had done to her. She had corrupted Kollanan.

Mandan was uncertain. "We can't let him get away with it, can we?"

"No, my konag, we can't."

"I bet my brother will say the same thing. Adan hasn't even answered." Mandan walked over to the empty easel, stared at his paints, and knocked them aside in disgust. "Our courier said that Kollanan was building an army. I believe he means to march against us."

Utho was alarmed by the thought. He hadn't imagined that, but it was possible.

A polite knock on the chamber door interrupted them, and Cade was there with his beautifully dressed daughter Lira. When he saw the redheaded girl in a seafoam-green dress, Mandan's entire demeanor changed. He smiled, and his eyes shone. "Lira! I did not expect you in Convera until tomorrow."

She blushed and gave him a formal curtsy. A necklace of saltpearls shimmered like stars against her pale skin. "My konag, when you commanded me to come to the castle, we hurried as fast as we could."

Cade gave a respectful bow. "My daughter was anxious to see Convera. There are so many wedding plans to be made. Are you certain the date is firm? Three weeks hence seems a bit rushed."

Mandan took the girl's hand and kissed it delicately. "You brighten even the darkest night." He looked harder at her father. "And yes, the date is firm. I am counting the days."

Lira giggled. Utho turned his steely gaze toward Cade, and a message passed between the two men. Serious matters were at hand.

"We will have the largest wedding in the history of the Commonwealth, my love," Mandan promised. "I'll appoint a committee with ministers and tailors, jewelers, painters, florists. Everyone will prepare the castle, all will be perfect. And you will be my queen."

Lira looked as if she might swoon, and Lord Cade swelled with importance. Utho said, "Yes, there is much planning. It is best, my konag, that we send the girl off with her ladies-in-waiting so that we can discuss important matters."

"Lira shall have everything she wishes," Mandan interrupted.

"Everything she wishes." Utho looked at the giddy girl, wondering if she might be another tool to keep Mandan in line, or if she was just a distraction. He glanced at the painting of Lady Maire on the wall by the konag's bed. Was the striking resemblance not obvious to everyone? Even Cade didn't seem to notice.

"We will have a long life and a great legacy together," Lira said with a shy smile. "Tell me more about our wedding."

"All the important people will come," Mandan said, then his expression darkened. "But not King Kollanan . . . and probably not Adan either."

Lira was disappointed. "They are the other two kings of the Commonwealth. Is this not an important occasion?"

Utho took the girl by the shoulders and turned her out into the corridor. "We should find the ladies who will help you prepare. You must be weary."

"But I just arrived! I want to spend time with my—"

"The ladies will be delighted to see you." Utho glanced at Cade. "Your father will remain with us."

With a longing expression, Mandan watched the young woman go. As soon as the three were alone, Utho closed the chamber door and explained to Cade what Kollanan's response had been to the war decree. The konag grew surly again. "This cannot stand! King Kollanan must be punished for his refusal."

"Kollanan the Hammer is no longer fit to be king of Norterra," Utho said. "He should be removed in favor of a leader more loyal to the Commonwealth." He looked at Cade with the implicit suggestion that it might be him.

Mandan blurted out, "I need to demonstrate that I am the ruler and they are my subjects! There can be no doubt." He picked up a short-bladed knife next to his half-eaten supper and threw it at the wall. The knife stuck into the map of Norterra, its tip piercing the name of a town. "There, that is as good as any! That village will bear the brunt of my anger. I want soldiers to march there and destroy the town, just to show King Kollanan that he cannot defy me."

Cade, perhaps drunk on the thought that he might become the next king of Norterra, walked to the wall and studied the map. He removed the dagger and placed his finger on the marked town. "Yanton."

Utho had never heard of the place.

Cade squared his shoulders and faced the young konag. "As you know, Sire, I possess a large standing army. They have been drilling to fight the Isharan animals, but here . . ." He reached up to indicate his own holding on the northeastern coast and traced a line across the map. "My troops could march directly above the Dragonspine Mountains and come down into Norterra. We could find that town and . . . and do as you command."

Mandan brightened. "That would be a wonderful wedding present to me from the father of my bride."

Cade bowed. "It would be my honor, Sire."

Utho agreed. "That would be an acceptable gesture, Cade. You and I will lead the army and eradicate Yanton. King Kollanan will not misunderstand the message we send. He must heed the konag's decree."

Mandan paled. "You've been gone for so long, Utho! I need you here. I can't be a strong konag without my loyal Brava." Utho was about to argue, but he saw how crestfallen the young man was. "Stay here and help me prepare for the larger war. Lord Cade can lead his soldiers . . . for me."

Utho glanced at Cade, who nodded. "Fear not. I know what to do."

76

ℰ

RIDING their augas toward blessedly warmer terrain, Quo and his sand-wreths searched for Penda and her unborn child, the primary reason Queen Voo had dispatched them on the mission.

He and his war party had fulfilled his sister's promise of aid. He cared little about King Kollanan or Norterra, but Quo had gladly accepted this mission because he hated the frostwreths so much. True, he had enjoyed killing the enemy and had been thrilled to watch the collapse of their titanic ice fortress. Perhaps if the humans did become allies, they could be turned into shock troops against the enemy. That would make this exasperating effort worthwhile, he supposed.

As a gift for his sister, one of the riderless augas carried the stiffening drone corpse across the empty saddle. A preservation spell kept the body from rotting too quickly, but after several days of riding, Quo lost interest in the small creature. He was glad to leave the unpleasant snow behind.

As the augas galloped into the rolling countryside, Quo looked ahead. Somewhere out here, Penda had gone into hiding. He didn't know why Queen Voo was so interested in the baby, a mere human and thus virtually worthless. Humans had offspring all the time, but he knew his sister better than anyone, and she could be mercurial. When she wanted something, for whatever reason, it became an all-consuming obsession. He would capture Penda and take her back to the sandwreth palace in the warm, beautiful desert. Then Voo would be happy.

The augas loped along the foothills. Circling high overhead were the black specks of wild skas, the little dragons that some humans kept as pets—what folly! They clearly did not know what the skas were. Because the soaring reptile birds had their eyes on the entire landscape, however, they were the perfect spies. He turned his gaze up into the blue emptiness. The creatures were wise to keep a safe distance, but it wouldn't be enough.

Locating Penda would require intense magic, and only one of his mages remained alive. Now Ulla glanced at the wheeling skas, then indicated a stand of trees in the winding grassy hills. "Here. This is a good place."

The augas ground to a halt, flicking out their black tongues to taste the air. Ulla slid down and stood in her red mage robes. As the reptile birds circled far above, the bald woman scanned the ground, nudged the grasses with her foot, and bent down to pick up a pebble. She inspected it, held it in her palm.

The remaining wreth warriors sat on their mounts with weapons ready. Shifting restlessly, they waited for Ulla to complete her purpose.

With her empty hand, the mage shaded her eyes and looked up at the high-flying skas, selecting her target. She rolled the pebble between her fingers, pulled back her hand, and threw it into the sky. The stone soared upward. Ulla curled her fingers and pushed with magic to create a breeze that accelerated the projectile.

Quo squinted, but the rock was so small and the skas so high that he could not see anything.

One of the flying specks jerked and began to fall. Ulla's satisfied smile deepened the etched lines in her rough face. The reptile bird swirled as it plummeted. It was a long time falling all the way to the ground.

The mage climbed onto her auga and raced to where the ska had struck the grassy slope. Quo and the others urged their reptile mounts after her.

The ska was a broken mess of orange scales and feathers. Quo remained in the saddle, looking down, but Ulla jumped to the ground and bent over the dead creature. She picked up the broken body, inspected the lolling head. Her small stone had struck the ska directly in an eye and bored through the skull—a perfect shot directed by magic. Quo congratulated her, but Ulla was too busy to accept compliments.

She removed a small limestone bowl from her saddle pack, a shallow basin little more than a hand's breadth in diameter. With a dagger of crystallized bone, she sliced open the ska's belly and pulled out the entrails. She placed them in the stone bowl and flattened the ropy guts along the bottom. She squeezed the ska's body until blood filled the bowl up above the entrails.

"This ska sees what all skas see," Ulla said. "One of them will know where Penda Orr has gone."

Wanting a better view, Quo slipped out of the saddle and came forward, but the mage was so focused on her spell that she did not notice her audience.

The blood in the bowl shimmered, brightened, and shadowy images formed on the surface. When they became sharp and clear, Quo could discern Penda's face. She was a beautiful human with long dark hair, brown eyes, and elfin features that even a wreth might find attractive. "There she is," he said. "But where?"

The blood image made no sound, but Quo could see that Penda was obviously speaking. Ulla rotated the bowl as if turning a knob, and the image receded until they could see Penda sitting on a wooden stump. Given the obvious state of her pregnancy, the woman would give birth soon.

"We may have only a few more days," Quo said.

Ulla raised her eyebrows, wrinkling her shaved scalp. "I thought Queen Voo merely wanted the infant. Does it matter whether or not it is inside the woman?"

Quo considered. "It makes no difference. We will take it, one way or the other."

The mage continued to turn the bowl, and the view drew back to show a larger camp, as if the observer rose higher and higher. Quo looked down on a gathering of wagons, horses, people dressed in colorful garments. Utauks. That was what those tribes called themselves.

Finally, from a great height, Quo could see familiar landforms, and he knew where to find Queen Penda Orr. He smiled and nodded. "We must ride hard. I wish to reach them before they move to a new location."

Ulla dumped the bowl with its bloody entrails on top of the gutted ska. She wiped stained fingers on her leather robe, and the fresh blood vanished into the runes.

Quo and his sandwreths headed out to find the Utauk camp.

77

STANDING at the clear ice window and surveying the frozen world, Onn watched a bedraggled group of frostwreths ride toward the palace. They seemed battered, wounded, their wolf-steeds limping along, but she could not tell who they were.

Her lips curved in a cold smile. It must be Koru and her troublemaking party. They had gone to prod the dragon Ossus beneath the mountains.

Onn was weary from a long night of rough lovemaking. Irri's stamina was unparalleled after centuries of spellsleep, and now she reaped the benefits. If all warriors were as strong as that one, her army would be invincible against the sandwreths.

Impatient for the riders to arrive, she dispatched Irri to receive the party and find out what they had to say. Later, Onn would sit high in her throne, look down on Koru, and listen to her failure. It was time for her daughter to fall in line with true frostwreth priorities.

On her way to the throne room, she commanded her drones to bring a meal. On a whim, she also called Birch, so the boy could sit at her side. He seemed quiet and dull, as meek as the drones. Maybe she should have sent him back home to Norterra, as the two emissaries had requested.

Onn wore a gossamer gown of white silk and a diamond-studded belt. Because her mind had turned toward thoughts of war, she donned a sword at her hip, a stout blade of milky white metal. She waited on her throne and dragged a sharp-nailed finger across her lower lip. What was taking the party so long?

Drones entered the chamber with ornamental trays of food: cold fruits, frozen meat sliced so thin it was just a film of red fibers. Birch accompanied the drones as if he were one of them, even carrying a tray. Annoyed to see how her pet had lowered his standards, she snatched the tray from the boy's hands. "You are not a servant! I commanded the *drones* to bring me food. Why do you follow them like a simpering slave?"

For a moment she saw an unexpected flash of defiance before he made his expression dull and unreadable again. "They take care of me," he said. "You sent me to them."

"Sit near my throne, down on the lower step. That is where you belong, until I give you leave otherwise."

Birch dutifully did as she told him. She inspected the food on the tray he had carried—a plate of silver icefish covered with frozen crystals but still wriggling. With her fingers, she slurped two of them, then set the tray aside to see what other delicacies the drones offered.

Finally, Irri returned to the throne room, his blue and silver armor studded with spikes, his hair combed long and free like a comet's tail. She noticed a scratch on his cheek from where she had marked him during the throes of passion.

One of the drones offered Irri a sampling of food, which the warrior ignored. His expression was stormy and alarmed. Behind him came several injured, defeated-looking frostwreths, but it was not her daughter's party. Instead, they brought far worse news.

◈

By now Birch had managed to hide several sharp knives about the frozen palace, where the frostwreths would never find them. Sometimes, he was brave enough to carry one on his person. He had taught the drones how to make weapons, too.

Now, as he followed them into Onn's throne room, he tucked a small scrap-metal knife into his waistband. The blade was barely as long as his finger, but he could hurt one of them if he had to. Day by day, he grew more bold. On their way to the throne room, he had even snatched several of the icefish and some of the berries, knowing the queen would never notice.

He watched intently as Irri ushered the bedraggled wreths into the throne room, and the disheveled newcomers shuffled forward, six warriors and one noble, scuffed and injured. Birch had never before seen the wreths *shaken*. They looked stunned, defeated.

One of the warriors spoke. "We escaped from Lake Bakal, my queen." He bent, wincing as a long gash on his pale bare arm broke open, oozing blood.

Birch perked up when he heard the name of his village.

"Our fortress is destroyed," said the lone noble. "We watched it collapse as we rode away to the north."

Onn rose from her throne, as if she hadn't understood. "No, my fortress there is being expanded and reinforced."

"It is only rubble, my queen," said the defeated noble. "We were attacked."

The bleeding warrior gave more details in brisk military fashion. "King Kollanan came with an army, much larger than the force he brought earlier."

Onn stared in disbelief, then said in a mocking tone, "Human soldiers again? Why did you not eradicate them?" Birch looked away, hid his smile.

"They were joined by a war party of sandwreths." The injured warrior paused to let the word resonate against the ice walls. "*Sandwreths,* my queen—warriors, mages, and a noble."

"And more half-breeds," said another warrior, "along with that dark-haired one who came here and demonstrated his power." He looked at Irri, who growled in annoyance at the memory. "They brought down the walls, my queen—killed everyone inside, massacred our army."

"That is not possible," Onn said. "Even the sandwreths cannot be so powerful."

The noble looked at her, his mouth slack. "And yet it occurred."

Irri struck the floor with a deadly pike. He glowered at the survivors. "King Kollanan has allied with the sandwreths!"

"Obviously it is only the first of their strikes against us," the bedraggled noble said.

The drones stood motionless with their trays of food, but Birch's heart swelled to know that his grandfather had caused such harm to the frostwreths. Someday, he would do the same.

"Sandwreths!" Queen Onn screamed toward the vaulted ceiling. She drew her frozen sword in a rage. "Sandwreths!" She leaped down the steps of the dais and went wild.

The drones could see what was coming, yet they did not move. Lashing out blindly, Onn hacked the small creatures to pieces. The ice blade sliced their flesh as if they were no more than soft cheese.

Birch flinched as blood spattered his skin. Each one of those drones had been his friend. He pulled his new wool blanket tighter around him, afraid to make a sound, but he began to feel more anger than fear. Queen Onn fancied herself capable of slaying the giant dragon at the heart of the world, yet all she killed were helpless drones. He could not hate her more.

Looking down at the carnage, Onn panted hard as she turned to Irri. "I had a mind to ignore those humans. They were not worth my while, but now I cannot brush them aside, especially if they are helping the sandwreths. I must send a swift and unequivocal message."

Irri's lips quirked in a smile. "Let me be your messenger, my queen. I will not disappoint you."

"Good. Find some of these humans and kill them." She looked at Birch for a long moment, considering him, then turned away. "Any ones will do. Deal with the pests, so that they no longer interfere with our war."

78

THE city of Serepol shuddered as their new allies swarmed through the streets. The key priestlord began to realize the enormity of his error.

He might have to summon the godling if it had recovered enough, although the crowds seemed to spend more time offering prayers and sacrifices to Empra Iluris.

Klovus followed Magda as she barged into the empra's palace. The barbarian leader admired the ostentation, the marble pillars, the gold leaf and inlaid jewels, but she had no interest in the artwork or cultural treasures.

The brutish woman looked around the empty throne room and let out a loud hooting call, then grinned as she listened to the echo. Laughing, her Hethrren companions tried the same trick until the throne room resounded with their bestial noises.

"Please!" Klovus said. "This is our palace."

"I see only an empty throne," Magda said. "Where is your empra? I need to know if she is worthy of commanding us."

"Empra Iluris is . . . absent. She has other priorities." Despite his search parties, no one could find where Iluris had gone, but he could never admit that to Magda.

"What are her priorities if she leaves her city without a leader, her land without guidance?" Magda playfully punched him in his soft biceps. "It is a good thing we came here. You obviously need my Hethrren. Your people look soft and lost."

Klovus was forced to show indignation. "Ishara is strong." He'd had many conflicts with Iluris, but he would much rather be sparring with her than with these barbarians. He almost regretted commanding Zaha to assassinate her.

The hawk guards had disappeared from the palace at the same time as Iluris vanished, and Klovus feared that they were planning some kind of rebellion. But how? An uneducated girl, a comatose woman, and a handful of guards? Iluris might even be dead by now. What if that was what her scant followers were trying to hide?

He was far more worried about the Hethrren. His personal guards, stationed in the palace and on the streets, were outnumbered. The barbarians continued their unruly behavior, but since Klovus had declared that they were allies, soon to depart across the sea, the city patrol didn't know what to do, other than to stop the most egregious infractions.

Magda sniffed and looked around, then made up her mind. She crossed the polished stone floor, climbed the dais, and threw herself into the empra's throne. Her bearlike body barely fit.

The key priestlord quailed in disgust. "Please don't, Magda! You must—"

She slapped the arm of the throne with her thick hand. "What does an empra do all day? Sit in this uncomfortable chair? Ridiculous! No wonder she vanished."

Klovus found himself making excuses. "An empra has many ministers, countless treaties, trade negotiations among the thirteen districts. Our treasury is vast, but the money is required for roads, sewers, canals. We have to store grain in preparation for times of famine. We—"

Magda lost interest in the conversation. "You worry so much about the future that you forget to live. At least take time to enjoy coupling—especially with me." She let out a guffaw and punched him again. "Now that you have had me, lover, you will find every other woman insufficient. We must try it tonight on a fine bed. I've never had that before. Where does your empra sleep?" She crushed him against her.

He managed to squirm away. "Alas, our time is short. You agreed to sail to the Commonwealth, and our ships are nearly ready. We should discuss our war plans. I have maps of the three kingdoms, a list of targets along the Osterran coast."

"I agreed to that, but I did not say when we would go. We have never seen a city like Serepol, and we want to explore it. What better time to enjoy it than before we go off to war?" She glowered at him. "You would not try to stop us, would you?"

Klovus did not think he could stop them. "So long as you tell your Hethrren to restrain themselves." He had only one viable threat. "Or do I have to summon the godling?"

"We are not skilled in restraint." She sighed as if the look in his eyes pleased her. "But we will make the attempt."

Claiming urgent business, Klovus retreated before he could be forced to entertain Magda in one of the spacious palace beds. He escaped to the safest place he could imagine—the Magnifica temple, where construction work continued, but at a slower pace, because many of the work crews were with their families, trying to defend their homes.

Klovus went to the underground vaults, where he often communed with the godling and felt its power. Now, he sensed the terrible, restless entity that lived in its own place between realities, but it watched over Serepol, and it watched him. He could summon the godling and turn it against the barbarians, but then he would not be able to launch such an immense army against the Commonwealth. He still hoped he could herd the barbarian horde onto the ships and dump them upon the godless shores. He had to walk a fine line.

Soon enough, though, he might have to take drastic action. The new shadowglass panes shimmered against the far wall. He opened himself to the godling, his godling.

Zaha and three other Black Eels joined him. "To ensure your safety, Key Priestlord, several of us were in the palace disguised as guards, watching you. If the barbarians tried to harm you, we would have stopped them."

Klovus was exasperated. "Why didn't you stop the entire army?"

"Black Eels are effective assassins for individual targets, but we are not an army." Zaha's calm was maddening. "We believed this was what you wished. Did you not invite the Hethrren to come here?"

"I want the barbarians to ransack the old world, but while they are here, we need to keep them under control." Klovus went to the newly installed shadowglass on the wall, which let him see the godling growing more powerful and more angry in its realm. He leaned close and whispered to the obsidian surface. "I can sense that you hurt as much as I do." The entity thrummed and throbbed, ready to protect him. Thousands of the barbarians could not harm him, if the entity stood in their way.

"We will make the people pray harder," Klovus said, speaking to the entity as well as to Zaha and the Black Eels. "To us, not the empra." These Hethrren needed to be reminded of who held the power here. He had let Magda bully him, but he had been shortsighted and weak.

Through the bond, Klovus felt the godling swell inside him. These barbarians needed to expend their destructive energies across the sea, not here in Serepol.

Yes, he would have the people sacrifice. They would pray and strengthen the godling even more because it manifested their will. Klovus could use the people's faith to make the Magnifica godling invincible. He would evict the barbarians before they could cause permanent damage to Ishara. He would make them fear him.

But when the godling was whipped up with such powerful fury, Klovus wasn't sure he could control it.

79

RETURNING exhausted but victorious to Fellstaff Castle, King Kollanan ordered wine barrels rolled out and food stockpiles released in a great feast for the soldiers and vassal lords.

Soldiers and lords crowded the main hall as kitchen workers brought in cauldrons of hot soup, cartloads of fresh-baked bread, and platters of roasted vegetables with Tafira's Isharan spices. The noise of conversation was as loud as the sounds of battle. The celebrating fighters bragged about their prowess, showed off their wounds, and sang songs for their fallen comrades.

Carrying a large book, Shadri wandered among the soldiers and talked with them. She wrote notes as she collected stories and names of the fallen soldiers so as to preserve their legacies. The scholar girl looked weary with her long, straight hair hanging loose, but she didn't stop her quest. She insisted the project was as important as translating the wreth historical records with Thon.

Elliel and Lasis joined the king and queen, accompanied by Thon, who looked beatific after what he had accomplished. Koll was wary about celebrating a complete victory, but his wife reminded him, "The enemy fortress has fallen and many wreths died. Take a moment to be pleased with what we've done."

"Agreed, but I won't let them swagger too much. Ancestors' blood . . ." He did let himself smile as he remembered the thunder of crashing walls and the screams of dying frostwreths. "I had hoped Quo and his party would stay to help with our defenses. Sandwreths are unreliable allies, at best."

Lasis said, "I don't like to rely on those creatures, Sire. We know they have enslaved humans, even as they pretend to be our friends. Wreths!" He spat out the word, then looked at Thon, who responded with a bland smile.

The king grew serious. "If Quo and his sandwreths had not charged recklessly into battle without a plan, others might have been saved. Cerus is dead, as well as nearly a hundred of our soldiers."

Overhearing them, Lord Bahlen strode up, carrying a hunk of bread in his hand. "Cerus would have been in the thick of the hottest battle, no matter what happened. I might have died myself, if Urok hadn't protected me."

His bonded Brava stood at his side and gave only a quiet nod in acknowledgment.

Bandages wrapped Bahlen's left forearm and more bound his ribs, but he shrugged off any questions, claiming that his injuries were too minor to be of note. "I brought all my able-bodied workers for the fight at Lake Bakal, Sire, but much work remains to fortify my old wreth city." He bowed slightly. "I beg your leave to return so I can make the ruins defensible and protect my people."

Mayor Cleff and his Yanton townspeople clung together, many of them in shock. "Four dead. I will have to tell their families when we get home. Four dead . . ." Cleff forced an uncertain smile. "But the rest of them lived, and they can tell the stories. We have all earned a grand legacy."

Shadri bustled over with her book in hand. "The queen and I saw what Lord Bahlen has done in the old city, Sire. He is making great progress."

"Not enough progress," Bahlen said. "The eastern perimeter wall has gaps. We don't know how much time we have, now that we have attacked the frostwreth fortress."

Elliel considered, glanced at Thon. "We can assist him if you wish, Sire."

"Yes, *we* can," Shadri said, lifting her book. "As soon as I gather more stories from these soldiers."

"I will join them in the wreth city," said Thon. "The place . . . resonates with me."

A frown of doubt wrinkled Kollanan's brow. "I may need you here at Fellstaff if the frostwreths return."

"Then I can come back. It is only a few hours' ride," Thon said. "But for now I am required to go to Lord Bahlen's city."

"Why is that?" the queen asked.

Thon spread his hands as if the answer were obvious. "Because Elliel is going there."

Pokle pulled a firewood cart into the great hall and loaded the fireplace, making the blaze roar, even though crowds already filled the chamber with warmth and boisterous noise. Ogno pounded his beefy, bandaged fist on the table and offered a loud toast for the fallen Lord Cerus.

One of other soldiers added in a hoarse voice, "And my brother Nathan! He died saving me from a wreth warrior. A cheer for him, too! Long life and a great legacy."

The others echoed, "Long life and a great legacy!" Someone named another fallen warrior, and then the fighters named more, until the hall resounded with names and memories. Koll felt uplifted by such bravery and loyalty, yet weighed down by the cost in blood. So many dead, so many other lives affected.

Shadri scribbled down the names as they were called out, and Koll saw the city's legacier Thooma and others doing the same. As king, he vowed that his slain heroes would not be forgotten, no matter how long this war lasted.

The main feast arrived, three stags that had been roasted all day over the coals in the castle kitchens. As the fighters ate, some remarked on the unusual seasonings Queen Tafira used—peppers and spices crusted over the meat to diminish the gamey flavor. Some of the outsiders reacted favorably, while others frowned in distaste.

Amid the noise and cheers and stories, Captain Rondo presented himself to the king, formal and grave despite the celebration all around him. He was respectful, as a soldier of the Commonwealth army should be, but the respect did not penetrate to his eyes. "King Kollanan, I took part in your attack on Lake Bakal, as you insisted. Since it is over, I must make a formal request."

Koll stroked his beard. Beside him, he could sense Tafira's sudden tension. "A formal request, Captain? Now that you've seen the frostwreth threat with your own eyes, I hope your attitude has changed."

Rondo remained ramrod straight. "My loyalty to the konag does not change like the clouds in the sky. My escort soldiers remained in Norterra at your insistence, and three of my men died in your attack on the ice fortress. I shall never forget that."

"Many people died, Captain." Kollanan grew more wary by the moment. "It only emphasizes the danger the wreths pose."

"The fortress was destroyed, and the frostwreths defeated, Sire." Rondo inhaled deeply. "Therefore, your hold on my soldiers is done. We know the roads are open over the mountains, particularly the northern route. My men can ride home . . . and there is no reason your armies cannot march with us. Konag Mandan has summoned the soldiers of Norterra to join the war against Ishara. His orders outweigh your local squabbles." He added the last word seemingly under duress. "Sire."

Tafira squeezed Koll's hand so hard his bones creaked. With a mighty effort, he kept his temper in check. "The konag is also bound by law to send troops to defend any one of the three kingdoms when such aid is requested. I have made that request, and reminded him of the terms of the Commonwealth charter.

I am still waiting for his response, but in the meantime I consider your men to be only the first of the reinforcements I expect him to send. You should make yourself at home."

Rondo's face reddened, but he did not look surprised. "So you refuse to let my men obey our rightful konag? The Commonwealth is at war with Ishara, King Kollanan—for the murder of your own brother. Will you commit treason against the konag?"

Kollanan knew there was great tension among Rondo's soldiers, but he also felt that young Mandan—almost certainly under the influence of Utho—was not acting for the good of the three kingdoms or of the human race. His judgment was clouded. Rondo's attitude was only making Koll more stubborn.

"My war is here in Norterra, Captain."

He had hoped the escort troops would become his allies after seeing the frostwreths, but they seemed to be blind to facts that did not fit into the framework of their already-formed opinion. He had intended for them to convince Mandan to send help to Norterra, but now he feared the opposite. Because they lived in the barracks, the escort soldiers were aware of Kollanan's military preparations, the size of the Norterran army, their weapons. If he sent Rondo's men back to Convera, they would bring vital intelligence with them.

With that invaluable information, petulant Mandan might well issue even more forceful demands that the entire Norterran military be conscripted and sent off to Ishara. He could not let Captain Rondo and his men act as spies.

Koll's wife took his hand. A spark of anger flashed deep in Tafira's eyes. Her voice was dry and sweet. "Why start a new war, Captain, when one has already landed on our doorstep? You prefer vengeance over survival?"

Rondo sneered. "Of course you would speak to protect Ishara. I know where your true loyalties lie." He swirled his blue cape as he turned to leave. "Just as I know where mine are."

80

STANDING on the observation deck of Bannriya Castle, Adan thought not of the end of the world, but of Penda. He spent his days meeting with war ministers and the commanders of his army divisions; he inspected and inspired his foot soldiers and his cavalry; he received reports from the armorers incorporating shadowglass into their blades and shields. He learned how his vassal lords were building up defenses and training fighters across his fifteen counties—exactly as Queen Voo expected him to do. But he wasn't doing it for *her*.

Now Mandan had demanded that he send the Suderran army to fight in the new Isharan war, but Adan would not march his only defenses away, if for no other reason than fear of retaliation from Queen Voo. She considered the army hers, and the sandwreth queen was a greater danger than his capricious brother. . . .

Alone after dusk, Adan wanted a moment for peaceful thoughts as he watched the awakening stars. He hoped Penda was safe, confident that Hale Orr and the Utauks would protect her. But he still missed her. Penda was a bastion of strength, a sounding board who gave him a balanced perspective and made him a much better king. Adan did not lack for reports, reconnaissance, encouragement, or sobering frankness from his numerous advisors, but his wife was worth more than a thousand advisors. He felt as if he had abandoned her, leaving her alone when they should have been together, closer than ever before. It had been too long since he last heard from her, so he didn't even know if their baby had been born yet.

He mapped out the star patterns in his mind, tracing lines from one bright point to another, as he and his father used to do. A shooting star sketched a quick bright line across the night, and he smiled, wondering if it was an omen, perhaps a message. That thought came with a bittersweet pang as he once again realized that Conndur the Brave would never get to see his first grandchild. . . .

His brother had declared war against the Isharans, rallied all three king-doms in the name of revenge. If not for the clear wreth threat, Adan would also be demanding Isharan blood, but Conndur had told him so many sto-ries about the grueling and ultimately pointless war thirty years ago. Would this be any different? Adan could not leave his people vulnerable.

He also knew Mandan well. If he responded with a blatant refusal to pro-vide the requested soldiers, then his brother would be forced to respond, prob-ably in a petulant way. He wished he knew how Kollanan had answered, for he had surely received the same decree. For now, with the long travel times across the continent, and the damaged roads in the Dragonspine Mountains, Adan decided he could justify a little longer delay. He would not answer yet.

Against the silent night, he heard a flutter of wings, and the clicking and warbling that marked the creature as a ska. It circled with a flash of pale green feathers, and he raised his hand. "Xar, it's you!"

The reptile bird swooped past him as if teasing, perhaps annoyed that it had flown so far just to find this human. Xar landed on one of the star-watching benches, turned his faceted eyes toward Adan, then preened himself.

Adan stepped closer. "Did Penda send you?" Xar skittishly moved away as the king reached for him. The reptile bird jerked his head forward, poking with his scaly snout, but Adan didn't flinch away. "You've been with her, haven't you? Do you bring news?"

The ska made a humming sound and strutted along the bench. Adan spotted a strip of paper banded to his leg. Since only Utauks could access the mothertear images from the collar, Penda had chosen a more primitive way to send him a message. He reached for the ska's leg. "Now don't you skitter away! You know she sent that message for me."

As if surrendering, the ska lifted his head, aloof. Adan fumbled with the knot on the tiny string, while Xar clicked, impatient with the king's clumsi-ness. Finally, he unfurled the note. In the dark under the stars, he couldn't read the tiny letters, so he lit a nearby lantern. When the flame grew strong and steady, he held the strip of paper close and read words as tiny as the sharpest quill could make them.

"Starfall, our baby's time is near. First contractions started. Only a few more days." His heart leaped and he tried to calculate how long it had taken Xar to fly to Bannriya. How much time remained? "Utauk camp near Nor-terra border. With Shella din Orr." She described the rivers and the valley, giving directions on where to find her. "If you come to me in time, we will both welcome our new baby. I love you."

He skimmed the message again, then glanced at the ska. "You did well,

Xar. Now we have to go." He snatched the lantern and rushed to the door. There would be no more stargazing tonight.

He ran through the halls, shouting to rouse Hom. "Pack my things! We leave within the hour." The reptile bird flew after Adan, following them down the corridors.

The squire bustled after him, bleary-eyed. "Is it a long ride, Sire? Where are we going? Am I coming along?"

"Yes, and we'll bring your brother Seenan, even Captain Elcior. We are going to join the queen."

"The queen?" Hom brightened. "Oh, the queen! Is it the baby?"

As the boy threw necessary traveling clothes into a pack, Adan roused the Banner guards and sent orders for horses to be saddled. All his soldiers had been trained for going to war, and they responded without hesitation.

The night was still dark, hours before dawn, when the small party galloped away from Bannriya. At last Adan was doing something he wanted to do. He hoped he would not arrive too late.

81

Two more Brava riders came to the training village on war mounts, grim and ready for battle, as if the fires of vengeance had been stoked within them. Master Onzu extended a traditional greeting to the visitors as they came out of the forest, and the children clustered closer, curious.

Tytan, a male Brava with shoulders so broad they made his head look small despite his thick neck, sat with his heavy black cape behind him; his polished ramer was at his belt and a large broadsword hung from his right hip. The black-garbed woman beside him, Jennae, wore a perpetual sour expression that would have made her unattractive even with more elegant facial features.

Tytan looked down from his saddle. "We have ridden hard and will stop here only a few hours. We are on our way to the war."

Jennae looked at Onzu as if disappointed to find him here. "You may join us if you like. You always talk of your prowess in battle, and the vengewar could use you." She frowned at the young trainees, then looked back at the bald master. "Are you packed?"

"I heard Utho's call for Brava fighters, but we have other callings as well." Onzu gestured to the children. "The fate of the next generation is in my hands."

"If you had trained them faster, they could join us now and fight, as Bravas should," Jennae added. Her horse snorted as if in agreement.

The big warrior sniffed. "Why not bring the children? They can still fight. They are young but they are Bravas."

Jennae muttered, "Unless your training is weak. It doesn't always take." She looked away as heat flared in Onzu's cheeks.

He knew they were referring to his son Onder. "I wasn't there. I do not know what he experienced or why he did what he did."

According to the stories, Onder had panicked under the onslaught of the godling that attacked Mirrabay. The young Brava had run for his life, leaving Utho to fight the ravening deity by himself.

"I was present when he received the rune of forgetting," said Jennae. "Onder did not deny the accusations. He accepted the tattoo, and he walked away broken, with no memory and no longer a Brava." Her voice had no sympathy, and Onzu couldn't tell if she was challenging him or accusing him.

"We know Utho tells many stories. Sometimes they mean nothing," Tytan said, sounding oddly conciliatory. "We will need food and water, but we cannot stay the night. We can ride for miles in the hours of sunlight that remain."

"We will provide what you need," Onzu said. "But I stay here."

The Brava children watched curiously as both visitors swung down from their mounts. Onzu gestured with his chin, and two of the oldest boys grabbed the reins and led the horses off, hitching them to a post near the wooden statue of the ancient Brava pioneer Olan.

"Let us eat and be on our way." Jennae strode toward one of the main dwellings. The two Brava riders were sweaty and weary from their long ride.

Onzu barked at the gawking children, "All of you back to your chores. And if you have no assigned gardening or firewood gathering, then train! You can never stop getting better."

Joining the two visitors in his dwelling, the master prepared a quick and hearty meal. He removed smoked sausages and ham from the larder, along with old bread and some late-season apples. Tytan and Jennae wolfed down the food. Onzu filled their goblets from a water pitcher.

"Utho has called all able-bodied Bravas to prepare for the all-out invasion of Ishara," Jennae said. "We have broken our terms of service with sworn lords because the vengewar takes precedence." She gave him a hard glance. "*All* Bravas."

"Yes, I heard Utho's tale," Onzu said. "But perhaps you have not heard all the tales. Remember the wreths and the dragon Ossus. You must be aware of the stirring beneath the Dragonspine Mountains, the eruption of Mount Vada?"

"We also remember Valaera and the slaughter of Bravas," Tytan said, spearing a large slice of ham with his dagger. "That is more personal than an ancient myth."

"Utho didn't believe me either," Onzu muttered. "What did you mean that he tells many stories?"

Tytan pursed his lips, unsettled. "There was a letter . . . sent by King Kollanan." He looked at Jennae, who was clearly displeased that he would reveal such a thing. The burly man laced his fingers together and rested fists like rocks on the rough table. "Kollanan's letter was intended for Conndur, but it arrived after the Isharans murdered the konag. Mandan received it instead. Utho called it a distraction and he convinced Mandan to dismiss it, but word leaked out anyway."

"I place no stock in the message," Jennae said, biting one of the apples in half, core and all. "We have priorities other than the wild tales of yet another disgraced and fallen Brava."

Onzu set his sausage and dry bread aside as a flash of Onder crossed his mind. The eager young man had gone out to become a paladin with bright dreams of an enduring legacy for himself. Onzu had never seen his son after his downfall, with the complex tattoo on his face, the rune of forgetting. . . . "What other disgraced Brava do you mean?"

"How many do you know?" Jennae quipped, challenging him.

"Elliel," Tytan answered.

Onzu was surprised. "The woman who murdered children up in Lord Cade's holding?"

"That is what Utho claimed," Tytan replied.

"That is what she did," Jennae said. "Utho's word is good enough for me."

"King Kollanan's letter said otherwise." The big Brava man was obviously not happy with the knowledge. "Elliel has since found a way to overcome her rune of forgetting, and now she accuses Utho of using her as a scapegoat. She says that Lord Cade ravished her and that Lady Almeda threatened to expose their secret Isharan slaves who harvest the saltpearls."

"Not much of a secret," Jennae said with a snort.

Onzu was confused. "What does Elliel have to do with that?"

"King Kollanan says that she has regained her memories," Tytan said. "That Utho concocted the story of her slaughtering the children, but it never happened. He just wanted Elliel's memory gone. He wanted to give her a shame so great that she would never look closely for answers." The big man was upset by the idea.

Jennae rose to her feet. "Enough of this! We are warriors, not old washer-women exchanging gossip."

A knot formed in Onzu's stomach as he remembered the hard and grim Brava man he had taught. Utho always had a dark edge, and his ethics were somewhat dependent on circumstances. "King Kollanan sent the letter? Is the word of a Commonwealth king not worth heeding?"

"The call of Konag Mandan is stronger." Jennae's face became more unattractive as it grew pinched and determined. She stepped away, ignoring the scraps of food on the table. "We have to leave, Master Onzu."

"For that I am glad," he said, using his words like a lash. His thoughts continued to spin. "If Utho fabricated that story about Elliel and branded her with the rune of forgetting, how do we know he didn't do the same to Onder?"

The Brava woman looked at him, and her entire body became a sneer. Even Tytan showed no sympathy now. "There were many witnesses at Mirrabay. Onder's cowardice is undeniable."

The old master had feared as much. "Yet if there is this question posed by Elliel and supported by the king of Norterra, should you not consider it? The code of honor runs through our veins stronger than any blood and burns brighter than any ramer. If Utho would betray one of our own, is this a man you would follow to war? What if he's manipulating Konag Mandan?" He raised his voice, and the tension in the room increased. "Does Brava honor mean nothing to you?"

"The vengewar means more, and Utho brings us that, at last," Jennae said. "A true Brava would feel the same call and not talk about wreths and dragons."

Her words were like a slap, and Onzu's hands strayed toward the cuff of his ramer. Jennae flinched for her own weapon, but Tytan stopped them both. "We will save our fighting for the true enemy. Our horses should be rested now." He strode toward the door. "Thank you for the meal. We ride off to Convera."

The two Bravas stalked away, striding to their horses. When they rode off, Onzu felt that part of his core was crumbling inside.

82

THE two great rivers in the land, the Bluewater and the Crickyeth, tumbled in from the north and west, converging to form a wedge of land on which the city of Convera had been built. Fertile farmland spread out along the river valleys, and boat and barge traffic dotted both rivers.

Utho stood at the apex of the bluff above the confluence. He watched the two waterways flow together to form the Joined River, which led to Rivermouth and the sea. His great fear had always been that someday an Isharan fleet would push its way up to the confluence and lay siege to Convera. No Brava could allow that to happen. For generations his people had devoted their lives to serving the konag and defending the Commonwealth. Utho would do no less.

It angered him that Mandan could not count on his own people.

Now, of all times, the three kingdoms must be united, must be strong. The army ranks should have swelled with fighters from Suderra and Norterra, but Adan had remained silent, and Kollanan had openly defied the decree. The king's remarkable demand for Commonwealth reinforcements against the wreths only made Utho—and Mandan—angrier.

Yes, Commonwealth troops were being sent to Norterra, but not to assist King Kollanan.

Lady Lira and the young konag spent much time discussing wedding preparations—the music, the minstrels, the gowns, the feast. It seemed to go on and on. Utho wished Mandan would devote as much energy to his war plans.

The Brava stood on the high point of land listening to the wind and watching the flow of the water. Some things just took their natural course. The Bluewater and the Crickyeth inevitably flowed to the sea, and the vengewar against Ishara was likewise inevitable.

Utho turned and stalked back into the castle.

Cade's army marched at a steady pace on their way to the targeted town in Norterra. His ugly Brava Gant rode at the front, following his bonded lord, as he was required to do. His sword would serve for most fighting, and he could always use his ramer in extreme circumstances.

A storm brewed inside the Brava, though, as the ranks of soldiers continued their advance. To show off his military force, Lord Cade was resolved, even eager, to carry out the konag's orders, but Gant had misgivings. Though his expression remained unreadable, emotions were turbulent inside him.

Cade glanced at him with a roguish grin. "You are so silent, Gant. Don't you have any jokes for me?"

"I do not tell jokes, my lord."

"Of course not! Bravas aren't known for their sense of humor."

"True, my lord."

The handsome lord looked back to admire the troops streaming behind him, his strong jaw outlined by his razor-thin line of beard. "This is so much better than simple training exercises back at the camp."

Gant stared forward. "Attacking the Norterran town will be no mere exercise."

Five hundred mounted soldiers made their way overland. Gant didn't know what sort of defenses King Kollanan could mount against this surprise attack, but Cade's army was surely enough to devastate one insignificant town.

"It will be a stinging rebuke, a lesson to teach Norterra, that the actions of their king have consequences. Years of peace and cooperation have made the people of the three kingdoms complacent. Now that we face a real enemy, we cannot let people disobey their konag willy-nilly."

"There is indeed an enemy," Gant said, chewing on his words. "But King Kollanan asserts that it is the wreths, as does Adan in Suderra. Are we wise to ignore what they say?"

"The two kings are cowards. When Konag Mandan calls his people to arms, we must fight. Remember what the Isharans did to Mirrabay *and* how they butchered poor Conndur. You were there on Fulcor yourself!" He nodded, as if he found his own words convincing. "Ishara is obviously our true enemy."

"And yet we are marching in the opposite direction," Gant pointed out.

Cade gave him a sour frown. "You begin to annoy me. Is that part of your duties as my bonded Brava?"

Gant shrugged as they rode along. "Bravas fight, and we obey our bonded lords, but if King Kollanan speaks the truth about the wreths, then he did in fact make a legitimate request for mutual defense, according to the Commonwealth charter. I am not a politician, but I believe Konag Mandan should have taken the request seriously. He could have attempted to negotiate, rather than launch an immediate attack." He lowered his voice. "I do not see how this will turn out well."

Cade laughed. "You imagine we might fail? Look at our army! Kollanan will not expect us, and Yanton can't possibly stand against an invasion. The Norterrans will simply capitulate, and then we can all fight against Ishara." When the Brava gave no acknowledgment, Cade made a rude noise. "Why do you argue with me? I thought all Bravas hated Isharans."

"We hate the Isharans, but we also love truth, and we love honor. In this instance, I do not see how those three add up."

"You are a challenging man, Gant." Cade urged his horse to a faster pace, which made the troops behind him work to catch up. "Even Elliel was a better conversationalist, and she was certainly prettier! Did your mother drop you on your face when you were a baby?"

"If she did, she never told me of it," Gant said, taking no offense. "I spent my childhood in a Brava training village. My mother visited only occasionally."

"I can see why." A lascivious gleam came into Cade's eyes. "But Elliel . . . quite a stunning woman, those green eyes! And her luscious hair exactly the same color as the thatch between her legs." He sighed. "I have vivid memories of that night, though frankly, I expected a Brava to be a better lover."

Gant clenched his muscles, tried to keep the words inside, but they came out anyway. "Perhaps you should not have taken her against her will."

The lord looked at him in surprise, then made a dismissive gesture. "Who would credit the whining complaints of a spurned lover? She had to fabricate stories after Lady Almeda stabbed her in a jealous rage."

"Whining complaints . . ." Gant ground his teeth together so he would not say more. No Brava, no matter how insulted or spurned, would falsely accuse another. Gant had not met Elliel personally, but he knew who she was, knew her heritage, her training. No Brava woman would lie about rape. Ever.

After taking her place in Cade's service, Gant had researched Elliel. Wherever he rode around the counties, he made inquiries about how Elliel had supposedly lost herself in a blood rage and murdered children. He was not surprised to learn that the tale was entirely false, yet she had been marked with the rune of forgetting.

By now, Gant knew what sort of person Lord Cade was, although the Brava had been unaware when he'd accepted the bond. In previous years, Gant had been a solo paladin in Osterra, serving the people wherever he saw a need. In the wake of Elliel's supposed disgrace, Lady Almeda had demanded a male Brava—preferably an ugly one—and he had been pressed into service.

Gant had learned so much more since then. Some of the tasks Cade requested of him danced on the very edge of honor. The Brava was bound to obey, but there might come a point when he would have to refuse.

As the large army marched into Norterra, he wrestled with his loyalties. Every Brava knew of the generations-long blood feud with the Isharans, and he had fought alongside Klea and Utho during that horrific night on Fulcor Island, but he did not dream of large politics.

After Gant's long silence, the lord spoke again, sounding conciliatory. "I'm glad you are with me. I didn't want to do this without my bonded Brava, but I am capable of killing if need be." He gave his predatory smile again. "As my dear wife recently learned."

Gant stiffened. He had never asked the lord directly. He had, in fact, once feared that Cade would command him to murder Lady Almeda. When she had been found dead, however, Gant knew that she had not taken her own life. He was aware that Cade had ridden out that night in secret and returned exhausted just before dawn.

The army marched onward, heading toward the spot on the map that Konag Mandan's dagger had pierced.

When Utho entered the konag's war council room, he encountered a flurry of tailors and seamstresses and brightly dyed fabrics. Standing on display, maidservants had been dressed in ornate gowns that made them look beautiful, but also intensely awkward. Bakers set out a display of cakes, pies, and small pastries on a long table against the stone wall.

Utho brought a summary of the private soldiers, horses, weapons, and supplies that Cade had taken on his march across the north. He felt warm and sweaty, having just ridden in from Rivermouth, where he had overseen the arming and supplying of four more ships for the Commonwealth navy. He also brought a rolled map of the Isharan continent, sparsely detailed, since it was all they knew of the strange land. After studying the coast, he had marked preferred landing points for the invasion, in addition to the primary strike in Serepol Harbor.

But Konag Mandan was far more engaged in his wedding plans than he was with the vengewar.

Utho stopped, his hand clenching as he absorbed what he saw. The young konag walked among the servant girls, inspecting the different styles of gowns, which were unlike anything they would ever again wear. Tailors and seamstresses proudly showed off the knotted braids, draped lace, ornamental ribbons, and intricate beadwork. Lira stood beside him, ethereal and smiling as if she floated on a rainbow. She marveled at the colors of the fabrics. Mandan urged her to taste an almond pastry topped with jellied fruit.

A sick anger took hold of Utho. His voice cut through the chatter like a scimitar. "Have you forgotten your murdered father so soon, my konag?"

With a gasp, Lira set down the small bite of powdered cake she had been tasting after the almond pastry. She looked skittish and pale.

Mandan spun about, startled and looking guilty, but he recovered himself. "I am planning my wedding, Utho." He smiled at the young woman. "The most important day in my life."

"The most important day in your *reign* will be when the Isharans fall." The Brava paused to think of his own dear wife and daughters, and he forcibly stopped himself from pointing out that wives and marriages could vanish in an instant. Because of the Isharan animals. He stalked farther into the room. "With war preparations commencing, Sire, and with Lady Lira's father on an important military mission to Norterra, we should postpone the wedding until a better time."

Mandan blinked as if he had trouble understanding the words his Brava had spoken. Utho knew the young man would not be happy with the delay, but he would listen. He had never pushed back against his mentor's advice before.

"No," Mandan said. "This is my wedding. The entire Commonwealth will celebrate. It will unify us in a time of troubles, and it must happen as soon as possible."

The response astonished Utho, but everyone in the room was listening, and he could not chastise the konag. He chose his words carefully. "It is not an opportune time for such an event, Sire. Better to wait another month, preferably two."

Mandan still refused. "I have waited for this date, as has my beloved Lira." He looked at the willowy young woman, and she fawned over him.

"But the bride's father is not here," Utho said. "Lord Cade should attend his daughter's wedding, especially a grand royal wedding such as this."

Mandan actually looked angry at Utho. "Then he had better finish his mission and return. There is time."

With great effort, Utho emptied himself of rage, adjusted his thoughts. He could not lose control here. Before he spoke again, Mandan actually cut him off. "The date of the wedding will stand, Utho. All has been perfectly planned, so many intertwined parts. Our guests will arrive, and the wedding will be a bright spot in these dark times. I have spoken."

Utho saw the hardness in the young man and realized that Mandan clung to this one thing because it was an event he could control, an event he could understand.

"As you wish, my konag," he said, but in his mind he would never forget that Mandan had defied him. "Your wedding will be a day to remember."

83

As the empra's chosen successor, Cemi had never imagined she would live like a rat in tunnels beneath the palace. The hawk guards remained alert, ready to defend the helpless woman on her pallet. Iluris's condition had not changed, and the men were edgy, impatient, and uncomfortable.

From Analera's outside reports, Cemi knew the rumors were spreading, that the people were even more desperate for their empra, now that Key Priestlord Klovus had let a powerful, unruly force of barbarians into the city. The prayers for Iluris increased, and the strange new godling felt the strength and the faith coming from outside.

Cemi said, "It's comforting to know the people still love the true empra."

"Klovus can summon the Serepol godling to demonstrate his power," Vos said, "and we can show only a sleeping woman who should have died weeks ago." He looked drained from the constant tension as he sat at Iluris's side, stroking the woman's cool, dry arm. He spoke in a low voice so his fellow guards would not hear. "We must seriously face the possibility that our mother may never awaken."

By now Iluris's actual injury had healed, and she no longer wore bandages around her hair. Cemi had brushed the empra's ash-blond tresses, laying the strands out over her shoulders. Though they fed her broth and tried to keep her strong, it was obvious the woman was wasting away.

"She's not dead," Cemi said. "That is our spark of hope. When she wakes, she will know what to do. The people are ready to rise up in support as soon as she comes back." It wasn't a good enough answer, and she had realized that weeks before.

"Or it is time for you to rally the people." Vos looked down at the motionless form, her closed eyes. "Your godling is strong." The entity remained with them, a shimmering presence in the air, but for now it had withdrawn around the vault opening.

In the stone tunnel outside the isolated chamber, old Analera appeared and ducked inside carrying a cloth-covered basket of food. "Only apples today and some old bread." She sounded exasperated. "The Hethrren have ransacked the kitchens, taken the ready supplies, and made it impossible for the cook staff to create large meals. Such a mess." Her face pinched in disgust. "I already hated Key Priestlord Klovus, but what he's brought upon us in the name of his war . . ." She growled deep in her throat. "Hear us, save us!"

"We know the risk you are taking out there." Cemi put heartfelt emotion into her words, as Iluris had taught her to do. "But we also know this cannot go on much longer. If the people are restless, impatient with the key priest-lord and the Hethrren, maybe we can use that to our advantage." She looked at Captani Vos. "Our supporters continue to grow. We must plan the best time to emerge. When is the movement strong enough for us to reveal to the people that Iluris still lives? Maybe they will accept me as their temporary leader until such time as the empra awakens."

The other six hawk guards gave a full-throated agreement, but Vos was concerned. "Klovus would eliminate you, maybe even summon the godling to do it."

Analera also expressed her doubts. "Or the Hethrren would kill all of you. Magda would bash in your skull with that club of hers. How could you stop it?"

Vos rose to his feet, instinctively angry. "I would stop it! I'd do anything to protect Cemi."

"Magda would just kill you first." The old woman sniffed. "But do not give up hope. I am certain that parts of the Isharan army would rally around you, if you presented yourself and your case properly."

"That is what we have to decide," Cemi said. "Or else we just sit here for another day. And another."

Leaving the basket of food scraps, Analera slipped away, hoping to return to the upper levels unseen. Moments after she vanished down the tunnel, though, Cemi heard the old woman's anxious outcry. "You should not be here—" Her words were cut off by the sound of a hand striking flesh.

Suddenly, the new godling surged back into place, a shimmering presence that oozed out of the stone walls to create a mist of stone, hiding the entrance. As the entity covered the doorway, Cemi peered through the camouflage.

Far down the corridor, Analera sat against the wall, touching fingers to a bloodied lip. A muscular woman with a wolf pelt over her shoulders loomed over the cringing servant. "I go where I wish, and I wish to see what lies beneath the palace."

"Forgive me, Magda." Analera got to her feet. "But there's nothing down here but dusty storage vaults."

"I like dusty storage vaults." Magda raised a threatening fist again, and the servant scuttled away with a furtive glance toward the hiding chamber.

Behind the godling's stone illusion, the hawk guards rested hands on their weapons, ready to fight. The masking wall grew more substantial, forming a stone curtain. Cemi could barely see through, even when she pressed her face against it. She knew it looked completely solid from the other side.

The Hethrren leader stalked along, looking from side to side. She occasionally struck the walls with her club, as if she liked the sound of hard wood cracking against hard stone. As she approached the hidden vault, Cemi held her breath.

Analera ran back to the barbarian leader. "This way, Magda. I know these tunnels. Tell me what you're looking for."

"I'm looking for an excuse to kill you."

"I-I will try not to give you an excuse. I can be useful. I served Emprir Daka and Empra Iluris. I lived my life in this palace, and I can show you all the fine chambers, the treasure rooms, even the gold vaults. Come with me!"

Magda paused, only a few steps away from the hidden chamber. "Why would you do that?"

"To keep you and the Hethrren happy." The old servant's voice trembled. "And if you are happy, then you won't damage my beloved palace."

"A good enough reason." Magda pressed forward nevertheless.

The godling squirmed and solidified further. Cemi could feel the presence connected to her, and her vision penetrated between imaginary particles of stone. This deity must have been created by the people's deep faith in Empra Iluris, but if the empra was unconscious and the people also prayed to Klovus and his Serepol godling, how much longer would they strengthen Iluris? How would the new godling remain strong?

Cemi's faith remained intact, though.

Scowling, Magda strode past their hiding place, looking at the torches on the walls. Analera tagged along, trying to distract the barbarian leader, but Magda paused as if she detected something. Her brow furrowed, and she sniffed the air. "I smell fish. I smell sweaty bodies."

Analera said, "I have not bathed yet this week. And you . . . you have a certain musk of exertion."

"I smell like a woman who is not afraid to work or fight." Magda faced the illusory wall, standing only a few feet from Cemi on the other side of the camouflage.

Cemi couldn't breathe, and all of the hawk guards froze, making no jingle of armor or scrape of metal.

"Something isn't right." The Hethrren leader squinted. "There should be a room here."

"But it is solid stone, as you can see," Analera said.

Magda pressed the flat of her hand against the camouflage wall. The godling tensed, pushed back, but the woman pressed harder. The field rippled, and the big woman's expression brightened. "This stone is not real! Is it magic? What are you hiding in here?"

The godling turned into a kind of slurry, as if dissolving, and Magda pushed her way through, poking her head into the chamber. Cemi skittered back. The hawk guards raised their weapons and closed ranks to protect Iluris.

They knew the Hethrren did not worship the godlings. Cemi had no idea what the barbarians actually believed, but this partially formed godling, this invisible protector, did not stand against Magda.

As if pushing her body through a rushing current, the woman thrust herself into the vault. Captani Vos placed Cemi behind him and stood with his sword drawn, vowing to die to protect her. But she didn't want him to die. The hawk guards stood together, strong enough to kill even a fierce barbarian warrior, but Magda made no threatening move. She just looked at all of them crouched there, her face filled with curiosity. Then she let out a loud guffaw.

The godling sprang away from the doorway like a snapped thread. It coiled and curled like a presence of vapors along the stone, still there, still ready, but watching. Why didn't the entity just kill her in the same way it had smashed the assassins who tried to kill Empra Iluris?

Magda was most interested in the pale woman stretched out on the pallet. "Oh ho! Is that the missing empra? Klovus told me she was injured. He thinks she is worthless." She snorted. "And yet he is afraid of her. Why would he be afraid of . . . that?" She grimaced at the catatonic body.

Vos said defiantly, "The empra will awaken and lead Ishara again."

Magda was unimpressed. "Keep hiding here, little chipmunks. What do I care about you? Your empra is weak and powerless." She laughed again. "But the fact of her disappearance drives Klovus mad with fear. I like it when he is afraid, and I like to know you are hiding here."

The hawk guards could have swarmed Magda, but they held their defensive positions. No longer interested in them, the barbarian woman lurched back into the tunnels, where she grabbed Analera's scrawny arm. "Show me what else is down here. You mentioned treasure vaults."

They strode off. Cemi and Vos looked at each other in disbelief, trying to understand what had just happened.

84

WHILE Lord Bahlen's construction work took on a more frantic pace in the ancient ruins, Shadri convinced Thon to join her so they could uncover and solve wreth mysteries.

Broken stone had been excavated from the collapsed structures and used to shore up the defensive wall near the main gates, though peripheral sections showed intermittent gaps. Intact buildings had been cleared and reinforced, then converted to military headquarters, storehouses, and shelters for refugees who might rush there for protection.

Many of Bahlen's people had fought at Lake Bakal, and they knew what they were up against. His soldiers, carpenters, and stonemasons redoubled their efforts to shore up the city's defenses, sure that ruthless frostwreth armies might attack any day. But Mayor Cleff and many of his volunteer soldiers from Yanton had returned to their identities as farmers, carpenters, and woodcutters. The mayor had dispatched cartloads of supplies for the work crews, and some villagers even took up residence in the long-empty city.

Leaving Elliel with the laborers at the crumbling eastern wall, Shadri and Thon went to the intriguing collapsed crater. At one time the sinkhole might have been a dipping well in the center of a plaza, but a void had appeared beneath, as if something ate away at the source. The ground around the well had slumped down, but there was much more beneath—she could tell.

This time, they brought along a rope taken from one of the construction crews. Standing on the edge of the sloping crater, Shadri peered down at the intriguing hole at the bottom, which led deeper underground. She glanced at Thon. "When I showed this to you before, you said that there might be a magical wellspring in that hole, a source of power for the wreths."

Thon touched his lower lip. "Yes, but I wonder how I would know that information. I agree that something interesting must be down there."

Shadri reached into the foldpocket of her long skirts and withdrew her treasures. "I've never been very good with a flint and steel, but in my pack I had a candle and three sulfur matches." She held them up. "Down there in the dark, I can light my way and explore."

The buckled flagstones were overgrown with weeds, and clinging vines crawled up from the mysterious pit. Around the edge of the crater, the ornamental trees were stunted, but the roots ran deep. Shadri tugged on a trunk to make sure the tree was firmly anchored. "I want to know what's in there." She tied the rope around the tree. "I'm climbing down. You can come with me." She yanked the knot. "Do you think there's magic here? Maybe you can use the source to defeat the frostwreths?"

"I want answers, as you do, scholar girl. I can sense the power and the history here." His sapphire eyes glittered. His lips formed a thin smile. "Maybe the magic is strong enough to restore my own memories, or at least offer a clue to my past."

"If you really turn out to be Kur, then you could solve our problems."

He sighed. "If gods could solve problems so easily, there would be no problems." Thon looked at his hands, brushed his fingers through his dark hair. "Do you truly think I may be a god?"

She added with wry humor, "If you were merely a wreth shoemaker, no one would have erased your memory and sealed you beneath Mount Vada."

She braced her feet on the slanted flagstones and tugged on the rope. The long coil snaked downward and dropped into the black hole at the bottom of the crater. Shadri felt suddenly uncertain. "Do you think it's dangerous down there?"

"I think it is unknown."

"I like to explore the unknown." Holding the rope, she eased herself down, placing her feet on the uncertain flagstones, backing one step, then another. "Are you going to follow me?"

Thon looked toward the distant wall of the city and the main gates. Something had caught his interest, as if he heard something.

Just then battle horns sounded in the east, outside the city wall, accompanied by raucous shouts.

"Someone is coming," Thon said. "I sense danger . . . but it is not the frostwreths."

ഇൗ

After the victory at Lake Bakal, Elliel was prepared to face the frostwreths again, but she did not expect an attack to come along the road from Osterra.

Working at the main eastern gate of the restored wall, Elliel and her crew stepped aside as a surge of frantic people came down the road from Yanton begging for sanctuary. As the sun set, families guided mule carts, men rode old plow horses, mothers herded their children along the road. "An army is coming!"

Lord Bahlen rode up on his white horse to meet the first lines of refugees. "What do you mean an army? Which army?"

"They bear the rising sun of Osterra. And Commonwealth banners."

Brushing herself off, Elliel stepped up to a harried-looking mother. "King Kollanan requested Commonwealth troops to help us against the frostwreths. These must be the soldiers he asked for!" She allowed herself a relieved smile, though she couldn't believe it. "Why are you frightened?"

"They are not allies! They're burning the fields! They've killed dozens already, and they keep marching. They set fire to Yanton!"

Mixed among the groups of fleeing people, Mayor Cleff came forward, more harried than usual and his grin was gone. "I tried to get the townspeople out, but the army rode in so fast! They just started throwing torches. They even cut down some of my people with their swords."

The news created an uproar. Workers at the wall dropped their tools. A man on a high scaffold pointed urgently at smoke rising in the east. "That could be my farm! My fields!"

The refugees flowed through the open gates. The mayor urged them ahead of him, pushing them as fast as they could go. "We need shelter here. That was what we planned, my lord. They are destroying the entire village!"

Appalled, Bahlen stared at the rushing refugees. "Why would an army from Osterra burn our villages? What is the konag thinking?"

Cleff looked up at him, his mouth open. "I did not discuss politics or diplomacy, my lord! I just got my people away."

Elliel felt a heavy lump in her chest, remembering Kollanan's defiant letter. She knew that the capricious Konag Mandan was under Utho's influence. Utho could twist things to force an issue—as he had done when erasing her memory and sending her out as a tattooed pariah, just so that he could keep hiding his secrets with Lord Cade.

As the refugees rushed into the walled ancient city, Bahlen shouted for the work crews to take up arms. They raced back to their campsites to gather armor, swords, shields, many of which were still stained or battered from Lake Bakal. Others scrounged weapons of their own or used construction tools and staffs.

Approaching battle horns sounded as the invading army marched forward, and even more villagers hurried into the wreth ruins. Mayor Cleff and the work crews guided them to shelter. Fires blossomed in the nearby fields and homesteads. Bahlen rallied his army to form ranks outside the reconstructed

wall, but the ruins had vulnerabilities where the wall had not yet been repaired.

Before long, a haughty rider galloped down the road wearing a blue cape
and jerkin embroidered with the rising sun of Osterra. He nearly trampled
some of the refugees on the road. Sweaty and arrogant, the man halted a
fair distance from the city walls and shouted out into the gathering twilight,
"We come from Convera under orders from Konag Mandan. Because your
King Kollanan has defied a lawful decree, the konag has commanded that
the town of Yanton be eradicated as punishment. You may surrender, or you
may die. The army of Lord Cade is on its way." The rider wheeled his horse
about and galloped back down the road to rejoin his ranks.

When she heard Cade's name, Elliel's heart turned to ice. That man's vile
actions had set in motion a cascade of events that nearly destroyed her. But
Elliel had survived. She was a Brava again.

Bahlen frantically dispatched a rider to gallop back to Fellstaff and inform
King Kollanan. Then, as the fighters scrambled to take up defensive positions on the city walls, Elliel clamped the golden cuff of her ramer around
her wrist.

85

WHEN darkness set in over the Utauk heart camp, Penda found it impossible to get comfortable with her persistent cramps. Seeing the signs, Shella din Orr issued instructions to prepare for the impending birth. Thick layers of blankets were spread on the ground with stacked pillows for support. Hale doted beside her, tucking a blanket around her as if she were an invalid. Penda found his ministrations both endearing and annoyingly frequent.

"I'm not helpless, Father." She propped herself up so she could watch the bustling firelit camp. "You always talk about how Utauk women ride their horses until the last moment, then dismount, have their babies, wrap them up, and ride onward."

Hale snorted. "*Cra,* maybe that is true for some Utauk women, but you are my daughter and you are special."

"Yes, I am." She wrapped both hands around her belly and winced as her abdominal muscles squeezed. The contractions were persistent, stronger, and more regular. She could no longer dismiss them as false alarms. The baby would indeed come soon. Maybe tomorrow . . . maybe even tonight.

He dithered over her. "I remember when your mother gave birth to you. It was one of the most terrifying and wonderful nights of my life."

"I will keep that in mind," Penda said through clenched teeth. She had carried this baby for months, felt it growing, at first a bright spark that caused turbulence in her mood, making her prone to weeping and unbound joy. Now she let out a hiss and hunched forward. "*Cra,* this hurts!"

Adan had been with her throughout the journey, supporting her, adoring her and the child that was to come. But in the last two months, with so many traumatic things happening in the three kingdoms, the baby had become more of a burden for Penda to carry. Simply walking across the room or riding a horse was a challenge. She was anxious to be a *mother* instead of a pregnant woman.

Three days ago she had dispatched Xar with a message tied to his leg, and by now even the distractible ska should have flown back to Bannriya Castle. Her husband would be on his way, if he could.

"Ride swiftly, my Starfall! Ride swiftly."

The heart camp had stopped in a sheltered valley in the northern hills of Suderra. No known roads led here, only the blue-poppy paths used by Utauks. Shella claimed this was one of her favorite places, a spot where she had camped for many years in a row, and they would stay for several days. In no hurry to move, the old woman was glad to receive traveling Utauks who came to the same place.

The heart camp was not a large convocation of families as the recent gatherings had been, but it was still a place of joy with many tents and wagons, where close family members reunited with distant relatives. Penda enjoyed the music and fellowship; Hale enjoyed the food.

As the labor spasms faded, for now, she drew a circle around her heart, then placed her palm against her chest, concentrating, trying to locate Xar through the heart link. She could sense her green ska coming closer, guiding her husband here to the heart camp. She smiled as she leaned back against her pillows and looked up at the dark, open sky.

Suddenly the camp skas set up a shrieking clamor and took wing, hissing, clicking. Some had just wandered back home from their panicked flight a week earlier, and they remained jittery. Annoyed Utauk owners called after the reptile birds, while others stood at the edge of the large bonfire and looked upward.

Their shouts were filled with alarm as they pointed up at the sky.

Against the deepening twilight, Penda spotted a black shape cruising overhead, an enormous reptilian form with huge angular wings like sails made of stretched skin. Her heart stuttered in her chest. The Utauks ran about the camp snatching burning brands from the bonfire, yelling as if they could scare the monster away.

The dragon eclipsed the moon as it cruised above the treetops, pounding its wings, arching its sinuous neck. Penda had seen such a monster before, out in the desert with the sandwreths. This one circled directly above the Utauk camp, and with all their wagons, horses, and bonfires, they could not possibly hide.

The dragon swooped in with a roar that chilled Penda to the bone. It skimmed low, and the wind smelled of evil, rotting flesh, and a miasma of pure anger. Penda's stomach roiled not with fear, but with revulsion. The dragon was beyond powerful, beyond hateful, not merely some predatory reptile of enormous size. It sent out shuddering waves that resonated throughout the camp with the dark emotions that Kur had extracted from himself. This was poison, evil incarnate.

Utauks snatched hunting bows and arrows, tent poles, spears, heirloom swords. Standing together, they fired their arrows and hurled their spears in an attempt to save the camp. Many projectiles struck, and a few pierced soft spots in the reptilian hide, while others ricocheted off the hard scales. Even young Utauk boys flung rocks with their slings.

One stone punched a hole through the stretched leather, and the dragon flinched, then backflapped its wings as it crashed onto the outskirts of the camp near a paddock of horses. The frantic animals broke their hobbles and tried to flee, but the dragon crunched down on a stallion, snapping it in half before gulping it down.

Shella's bearded nephews ducked into the main tent and emerged holding the corners of a rectangular rug, which they used to carry the old woman. Scuttling as fast as they could, they bolted toward the shelter of the trees.

Utauk men ran out to throw torches and firebrands at the dragon. The monster snapped at the bright flames as if they were no more than bothersome sparks in the air. With a thrash of its barbed tail, the dragon flattened several family tents.

Hale grabbed his daughter, tugging her by the arm as they lurched to the edge of the forest. "I need to get you to safety!"

"We should all fight together."

"Not you," he said in a commanding voice that she had not heard since she was a little girl. "We cannot fight that thing."

The monster's rampage overturned carts, shredded tents, and destroyed crates of supplies. With a taloned foot it stomped on a wagon, bursting wooden barrels of ale as if they were grapes popped between fingers. It tore several Utauks apart. One had tried to attack with a wooden tent pole, and another had scrambled to flee with his young daughter. The little girl got away, but the father did not.

Penda held on to her father's arm as they ran. "Our only hope is to scatter into the hills. If we all flee in different directions, the dragon may lose interest."

"*Cra*, we will lose so many!" Hale said.

Two Utauk teens gathered something ethereal like knotted spiderwebs, unraveling a weighted bird net as they ran forward and separated. They threw the net at the dragon, catching its serrated wing, tangling it in the strands. The end of the net caught on the hooked claws, which made the monster lurch and tumble toward one of the large campfires. With brute strength the monster tore the net to shreds and snorted down at the fire.

Just then, one of Shella din Orr's nephews—Emil—dashed to the campfire and tossed a small wooden cask into the flames. As the cask fell into the fire, glittering powder spilled out, and a burst of colorful spangles and shooting sparks erupted in the dragon's face. It roared, lurching into the air. Its bellow was loud enough to knock Emil flat onto his back. He rolled away and dashed for shelter.

From a distance, sudden war cries broke through the night, a sound even louder than the dragon, high-pitched and musical, overpowering the screams of victims and the clamor of the beast. Penda spotted shapes thundering into the valley from the north, plunging down from the hills. She didn't believe what she was seeing. "Those are augas!"

Golden sandwreth warriors rode their two-legged reptiles with Quo at the lead. The wreth noble raised his spear, howling a challenge, just as he had done when killing the dragon out in the desert.

By quick count, Penda saw more than a dozen in the party, including a bald mage who unleashed magic in a whirlwind that snapped branches and tore leaves. The snarling force slammed into the dragon as it swooped in for another attack on the camp. It tumbled in the sky, then turned toward its new enemies.

Quo howled another challenge, riding in as hard as his auga could carry him. "A dragon! You have found us a dragon."

The wreth warriors closed in, and the Utauks continued to fight.

86

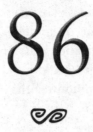

THE Hethrren showed no signs of leaving, even though the warships were ready to take them away.

In an imperious huff, Key Priestlord Klovus demanded to see Magda, but she saw through his bluster and exposed his fear as if flaying away tender skin. "With so much food and rest, we are growing stronger so we can be better warriors," Magda said. "I would be ready more swiftly if my lover stopped avoiding me."

He cringed, but dug deep into his heart. "If that is what it takes to make you board the ships and do as you promised."

Magda waved her beefy hand. "All in good time. Are your ships prepared to face ocean storms? Are your captains competent?"

"The ships are ready, and it is time to depart for war! You have nothing to fear."

She cuffed him on the side of his head. "I did not say I was afraid! But I am not convinced that the Commonwealth is a better place than this city." She indicated the entire palace she had appropriated as her own. "I think we will just take Serepol instead."

Barely escaping, Klovus stormed away from the empra's palace, unable to contain his anger anymore. He realized what he should have admitted before. The Hethrren did not intend to leave. Ever. He could no longer coddle or even tolerate the barbarians, and he had to bring his greatest strength to bear. He could not control the Hethrren, would not be able to make them abide by their own agreement. He had been a fool to trust Magda's promise, even if it would have given Ishara a complete victory. Now, instead, he had to save his land from these vermin. In the end, the people would see him as a hero. If he succeeded.

He felt the dark storm brewing in his heart and mind, lightning bolts of fury that were mere echoes of the godling's frustrations . . . which in turn reflected the feelings of the people. Everyone in Serepol was frightened, disgusted, and confused, and soon enough, their ire would turn against their key priestlord if he did not do something. They would blame him for bringing these repugnant barbarians to their capital city. It was up to Klovus to protect his followers, to purge the Hethrren from Serepol.

He knew the unruly warriors would never willingly board the warships and sail off to conquer the Commonwealth. They would stay here and grind down the people until nothing remained.

Hear us, save us!

Klovus had heard the echoing chant all his life, prayers to the godlings and the priestlords. Now, those words had a different meaning. *Hear us, save us.* He heard the people, and he knew of one way to save them.

He made his way to the Magnifica temple.

The structure had doubled in size since Klovus had started the work again. Previously, even when relegated to its vaults beneath the incomplete temple, the Serepol godling had been strong, and the people had fed it with constant prayers and sacrifices. Now, as the Magnifica grew, the godling's power increased exponentially. Though many people still prayed for the missing empra, whom no one had seen in some time, in this time of crisis they would turn their devotions where Key Priestlord Klovus directed them.

As he swept through the streets toward the temple plaza, intent on his mission, he instructed his ur-priests to summon the faithful. It was time. The barbarians were dispersed throughout the city, occupying buildings and taverns, sleeping outdoors because that was what they preferred. His followers obeyed the key priestlord's orders and tried not to provoke them.

Klovus reached the plaza, where three tiers of the stepped pyramid rose high, adorned with innumerable sculptures, manifestations of Ishara's godlings, symbols of hope and protection. Although each district had a different primary godling and countless local deities, the Serepol entity was the summation of them all, and the people channeled their powers there.

Klovus could feel the roiling strength of the power contained within his temple. Though the thing did not understand the specific details or facts, it felt his emotions and would do as he wished. And what he *wished* was for the godling to purge the invaders from Serepol.

Throngs came into the Magnifica square, some bold, some furtive. Many of the people had eyes shadowed with the fear that this gathering might become a massacre, that the Hethrren might ride in with their swords and clubs and slay them all. Others, though, placed their faith in the key priestlord, and thus in the godling. Hundreds came, and he knew the crowd would continue to swell.

Klovus needed to act swiftly, since word would surely get back to Magda. The Hethrren leader would not know what he intended, but she was no fool. She would try to stop him.

"Now is the time for your sacrifices!" he bellowed to the crowd. "We need your prayers, your strength, and your blood. Give to the godling, the defender of Serepol."

"But Serepol is about to fall!" someone shouted.

"Not if I can stop it." Klovus was afraid the worshippers would shift into an angry mob and turn against *him*. "The Hethrren lied to us! They promised to be our allies against the godless, but now they prey upon us instead." He raised a fist in the air. "This must stop!"

The crowd cheered. His ur-priests and dozens of minor priestlords spread out along the temple foundation, taking positions at the altar stations to receive sacrifices. Empty urns waited, and the priestlords readied their knives.

"Hear us, save us! The godling must be strong to root out this evil among us."

The Magnifica temple vibrated and shuddered. Particles of stone dust crumbled between the blocks. The entity within seemed ready to explode. Klovus placed a hand against his heart, concentrating. "Not yet, not yet!"

The crowd's faith and anger added a surge of power to the godling. As they pressed forward, some of them slashed their arms or palms, bleeding on the ground instead of into sacrificial urns. Their frenzy imbued the godling with even more uncontrollable strength.

Giddy from the outpouring, Klovus stood on the stone steps. People pushed closer with such vehemence that the key priestlord feared that he might be trampled in their zeal. He moved several steps higher on the huge structure.

But this was what he wanted.

Nearby, he noticed four workers in plain clothes, drab shirts and trousers. One man looked at him with a knowing expression, a shocking intensity. "Zaha," Klovus said in a quiet voice.

One of the nondescript men nodded. "We four will protect you if the crowd becomes dangerous."

"The *Hethrren* are dangerous," Klovus growled, more confident with his elite assassins nearby.

Inside the temple, the godling surged like a forest fire that had reached a pile of bone-dry deadfall. Klovus would have to release it soon. But not yet . . .

From where he stood on the raised foundation, he cast his gaze across the crowd. More people swelled their numbers, and their shouts resonated with waves of impervious belief. "Hear us, save us! Hear us, save us!"

Panic stirred at the edge of the plaza, and shouts turned to screams. He saw thirty or forty Hethrren charging in on their horses. The beasts trampled some believers who did not dodge swiftly enough, and broken bodies lay strewn about as the barbarians plunged into the crowd. Some people tried to stand against them, but the wild horses kicked out with their hooves. The Hethrren drew their weapons and began attacking the crowd.

Klovus felt an explosion of alarm, a lust for revenge, and he could not contain his anger. That, in turn, was reinforced and magnified by the godling, which absorbed and reflected the overriding emotions of the crowd.

He clutched his chain of office, closed his eyes, and shot his thoughts toward the godling that brooded deep inside the temple. The entity was also the heart of Serepol, the soul of these people, and it needed to come forth and fight for them. Klovus performed his mental workings and muttered the magic to release the angry deity from its realm behind the spelldoor and shadowglass.

A storm erupted through the scaffolding and bricks on the pyramid's incomplete third tier. The godling roared upward in a maelstrom of smoke and dust, unbridled anger and fear. It was a living hurricane made of claws and lightning, tendrils like vipers, fists like battering rams. The force knocked aside enormous stone blocks as it broke free.

The shock wave bowled Klovus from his perch, but Zaha caught him. Like an avalanche roaring down a mountain slope, the Serepol godling poured out of the temple and slammed through the crowd.

People screamed and howled, some in awe, others in pain as the godling plowed through anything in its way. Klovus could feel the entity swelling in the air and inside him.

The Hethrren riders raised their fists, and Klovus watched their expressions turn to terror.

The godling extended smoky tendrils, snatching barbarians into the air and battering them together before discarding the broken bodies. It stomped on the wild horses and flung more Hethrren high into the air. Some were smashed against building walls.

The worshippers in the temple square scattered in terror, though many were transfixed by the thing they had helped to summon.

Knowing its orders, the godling made short work of the first ranks of Hethrren. Klovus had summoned the entity for the purpose of purging the barbarians from Serepol, but it was a creature of violence and uncontrolled destruction. It did not have finesse, nor did it make fine distinctions.

The godling exploded away from the Magnifica, slammed into the buildings around the temple square, and flattened them, knocking down walls and crushing roofs in order to find and destroy the Hethrren.

It roiled along lashing out with lightning, hammering with bludgeons of smoke and steam. Klovus reached out through his link, trying to call it back. But the godling had brooded on its power for too long, and now it rampaged like a child in a fevered tantrum. Out of control.

87

~∾

I N Fellstaff Castle, King Kollanan met with his military advisors. Before the wreths returned, Norterra had been at peace for centuries, and each person tried to remember military strategy after a lifetime of calm. A handful of veterans from the Isharan war three decades ago had settled here, and now they offered their knowledge and experience.

Koll's initial strike at Lake Bakal had rallied his soldiers, and the second attack had seasoned them, but the death of well-liked Lord Cerus and so many fighters had driven home the reality of the coming battles. Through new conscription, the Fellstaff army had increased by more than a thousand soldiers, but after what they had seen of the wreths—both races—the king suspected that every human being would have to learn to fight.

Kollanan's great war hammer now lay on the council table in front of him, ready at hand. Queen Tafira sat beside him, and he reached out to take her hand rather than grasping the war hammer. Lasis stood behind him, always ready.

But Rondo infuriated him. The captain stood in the council room freshly shaven, his Commonwealth colors mended and laundered, his leather armor clean, his sword sheathed at his side. He looked as if he were about to attend a military parade. Instead, he spoke defiance. "I refuse, King Kollanan. Many weeks ago, Konag Conndur ordered us to escort you home to Fellstaff, and my men and I have done so. We remained long beyond the time required, and we even participated in your adventure up at Lake Bakal. Now we must present ourselves to our konag. The Commonwealth needs us."

Koll struggled to maintain his patience. "I need you here. You saw for yourselves how powerful the frostwreths are, and I have requested reinforcements from Convera."

Rondo flushed. "The Isharans have caused pain and destruction as well. You may choose to defy the lawful ruler of the three kingdoms, but my men and I will not be part of your rebellion." He nearly spat the words. "We are not traitors."

Around the table, the king's military commanders and vassal lords growled. One man rose to his feet, but Kollanan lifted a hand. Beside him, Tafira spoke in a calm, firm voice. "We are fighting to save the world, Captain, which is surely more important than a dispute across the sea."

Rondo rounded on her. "You have no right to speak on this matter. You are a foreigner and a spy!"

"Enough!" Kollanan snatched up his hammer and stood. "Captain Rondo, I have tolerated your insolence long enough. You are in my kingdom, and you shall follow my commands, or I will throw you and your men into manacles."

Rondo's face turned the color of hot coals at the base of a fire. Behind the king, Lasis said, "It would be my honor to restrain him, Sire."

The captain's hand strayed to the hilt of his sword. "Three of my men died in your folly against the frostwreths. If we are going to fight on a battlefield, we will fight for our true konag."

Before Koll could respond, running footsteps came down the corridor, and a flushed young man with sweat-plastered hair burst headlong into the chamber. He was so exhausted that he could barely keep his balance. He wore the colors of Bahlen's newly recruited army. "An attack!" The young man shook sweat from his hair, gulped hard, then wheezed out, "An army approaching my lord Bahlen's wreth city. Many soldiers!" The messenger grabbed the goblet of water in front of a surprised Lord Teo and gulped it down. "I rode so hard I nearly killed the horse!"

"What sort of army?" Tafira asked. "Is it the wreths?"

Captain Rondo remained standing before them, a statue composed of fury. He clearly resented this interruption and was not finished with his demands, but Kollanan concentrated on the frantic messenger.

The young man finally found his words. "An army came from the west, soldiers burning our towns and fields as they marched. Not wreths! They bear Commonwealth colors."

Alcock made a baffled sound. "Why would Commonwealth soldiers burn our villages?"

"By the orders of Konag Mandan. They attacked Yanton! The refugees took sanctuary in the wreth city."

A chill went down Koll's back. Mandan of the Colors was fragile and petulant, but he couldn't believe the young man would be so drunk with power that he would turn on his own people. He was Conndur's son!

"This is not possible," snorted one of his generals. "The Commonwealth would not attack Norterra."

"That's what they're doing," gasped the messenger after drinking more water. "Lord Bahlen sent me to call for reinforcements. Our defenses are not yet complete at the wreth city. We beg your help, Sire."

Kollanan rested his war hammer on his shoulder. "You shall have it. Lasis, with me! We will gather troops immediately and ride out." He knew that at a gallop, they could reach Bahlen's city while the battle still raged. Under normal circumstances, it would take half a day to move such a large fighting force, but Koll didn't waste a minute. He shouted around the room. "We move out with every fighter! Call in the patrols around Fellstaff. They are mounted and ready. There's no time to lose."

As the advisors and military commanders rapidly discussed which companies and squads they could call together, Rondo stood without moving. "My men will never raise our blades against the Commonwealth."

Furious, Kollanan wanted to raise his hammer and bash in the arrogant captain's skull, but he stopped himself. He had no time for that. "I no longer trust you or your men, Captain." He shouted out into the corridor, summoning five of the castle guards. "You are confined to the barracks, all of you, while the rest of my soldiers go defend my town. I will deal with you when I return."

Rondo looked cold and furious as armed guards surrounded him, waiting. Koll did not let his glare falter. "I will have you bound if necessary, Captain." The man turned his back on the king and strode out of the chamber. The king called after the guards. "See that they all are held and guarded. I want no trouble from them."

The agitated lords stood around the table, ready to rush off to fight for Yanton. Kollanan used his passion to sweep his wife into his arms, crushed her to him, and gave her a long, hard kiss. He stroked the side of her face, her hair. "I will be back after saving my people, beloved."

"I know you will."

With his loyal Brava at his side, the king ran out of the room as the urgency continued to build around him. He could raise a few hundred soldiers for an immediate response, and many more would come in a second wave within hours.

Kollanan the Hammer headed off to war, but it was not the war he had prepared for.

88

SHADRI lowered herself toward the mysterious pit, where unanswered questions drew her like a flame draws a moth. From above came the sound of enemy soldiers riding in at the main gate, a clash of swords, neighing horses, battle cries. Alarmed, she called up, "Elliel is there! Shouldn't we go help her?"

Thon stood where the rope was anchored to the tree. "I am confident in Elliel's abilities, but you, scholar girl—even with your skills and great knowledge—are not a warrior."

"I never said I was." She scolded herself under her breath. "Of all the things I've learned, why did I not teach myself swordplay? Too late now, I suppose."

At the main gates, where Bahlen's workers had been rebuilding, the roar of violence seemed to reach a crescendo. But would other groups of marauders spread out in search of another way in? The nearby city walls had crumbling gaps where attackers could break in . . . and Shadri and Thon were alone here.

Within minutes, Thon said, "Marauders have discovered a breach in the wall not far from here. They have horses and swords and torches."

From the rim of the sinkhole, Thon flashed a glance down at Shadri. "I am the only one to stand against them now." He looked around at the crumbling buildings, the strange sculptures, the soaring wreth arches, then nodded toward the pit at bottom of the crater. "Hide yourself. Leave the rest to me."

In a rush of worry, Shadri asked, "Can you handle them?" She lowered herself toward the gaping hole, her feet slipping on the slope.

"I have my own powers," Thon assured her. "They haven't seen me yet, but I want you safe."

"And I want *all* of us safe—" Shadri gasped as her heel caught on a loose flagstone that broke away, pattered down the incline, and plunged without sound into the black opening. Her heart raced and she wondered if this was a good idea after all. "I sure hope there's something down in that hole."

Thon cocked his ears. "You will find something, if only shadows and mysteries." He held a hand up for quiet, and then he dashed away.

Shadri sighed. "Shadows and mysteries it is." She couldn't understand why this conflict was even happening, and she worried about Elliel at the gates. Who was attacking? She swallowed hard and focused on her descent.

She reached the edge of the dark hole, where stones had broken off around the rim; others were loose, resembling teeth in an open mouth. Bracing herself at the edge as best she could, she wiped her hands dry on her shirt.

This is where I wanted to go, she reminded herself. Grasping the rope again, she lowered herself into the cold, whispering emptiness. Her feet dangled, and she kicked out, striving for some kind of foothold. Blackness seemed to snatch at her feet, but her toe touched something solid. She rested her weight and gathered her courage.

Questions called her from below, and Thon wanted her where the marauders couldn't see her. She drew in a deep breath. She was afraid for her friends, but she wasn't afraid of the dark and she wasn't afraid of mysteries, was she? No, this was where she wanted to be. Shadri descended into the blackness.

☙

Lord Cade's punitive army had arrived at Yanton, an unremarkable town, and after pillaging and setting the buildings on fire, had followed the refugees to a much more impressive target, the partially restored wreth city. While the central ranks confronted the workers and soldiers that Bahlen rallied into position at the main gate, Cade sent outriders around the perimeter to find any weaknesses in the defensive walls.

When she swore her service as a Brava, Elliel had never imagined she would have to fight Commonwealth forces. Horsemen rode in, followed by ranks of armed foot soldiers. They weren't supposed to be enemies!

She fixated upon the banners of Lord Cade, to whom she had first given her loyalty. From serving him, she knew about his illicit Isharan workforce, but her Brava heritage left her more inclined to hate Isharans than feel sympathy for them. She had grudgingly accepted Cade's work camps, without thinking much about them.

Now, however, she knew how monstrous Cade truly was. Elliel touched the rune of forgetting on her cheek. Why did she hate *Isharans*? They were far away, and their crime against Valaera was centuries in the past, but Cade had ravished *her*, disgraced her, betrayed her. She had never hated anyone so much in her life. She had reason for her own personal vengewar.

As the punitive troops charged forward, waving their swords and goading their horses into a full gallop, Elliel pressed her ramer hard around her wrist and barely felt the bite of the golden fangs that ignited her magic. Flames engulfed her clenched fist and burned in her blood.

Nearby, Lord Bahlen held his sword high, bracing himself. "Why would Konag Mandan order this?"

Elliel pushed her way to the front of the defenders as they howled a resounding reply to the invaders. Utho must be behind this scheme, for purposes of his own. The thought made her anger grow even stronger.

Bahlen's soldiers formed a solid defensive line along the repaired walls, ready to block the onslaught with spears and swords. Elliel felt sick as she watched Cade's forces split up, while the frontal charge slammed into the main gates.

The cavalry lines crashed with a thunderclap of swords, screams, and moans. Horses pawed the air. Cade's foot soldiers shoved forward, running at full speed as they found reserves of energy after their long march. Elliel's ramer burned brighter than all the torches at the wall.

As they fought, though, she sensed a hesitation in Bahlen's fighters. They were determined to defend themselves and protect the Yanton refugees who had taken shelter inside the city, but they had expected to fight inhuman wreths, not citizens of the Commonwealth . . . citizens who followed orders issued by Konag Mandan.

Elliel felt a knot in her stomach, too. Cade was the man who had steered them here, who had whipped them into a murderous rage. Anger reverberated inside her mind and radiated outward, as if it had taken on a life of its own. Surely everyone in the city could feel that dark force simmering here in the ruins. Elliel wondered if the wreth blood in her veins would help her now. With her finemail cape and blazing ramer, she felt invincible.

Among the charging soldiers, she saw a matching bright flare of fire from a ramer in among Cade's forces. Her heart froze as the sick suspicion shot through her. Was it Utho himself? No, Utho would ride at the front, and this Brava was several lines back. The second ramer slashed back and forth like a beacon.

After abusing and banishing Elliel, had Cade tricked some other Brava into bonded service? Knowing the lord's flaws and crimes, how could any Brava balance honor with a vow of loyalty to that man? Was it possible he didn't know what had happened?

The second ramer struck down two horses in Bahlen's cavalry advance. Norterran soldiers tumbled to the ground. She noted the fighting tactics and questioned whether the man was actually trying to kill the people or simply take them out of the fight.

Making up her mind to stop the opposing Brava, Elliel pushed her way through the fighting. Cade's soldiers raced toward her, some of them wild with bloodlust, others wise enough to show fear as they faced her. One tall warrior swung a two-handed sword in a blow that would have cleaved her in half, had she not blocked the blade with her ramer and slashed hard. The boiling fury seemed to be a living but unnatural thing within her, something she couldn't control, and the fiery blade melted her opponent's broadsword in half. Backing away, the man dropped the smoking, dripping red end. Elliel kicked him hard with her boot and knocked him backward without killing him.

Two other fighters raised swords against her, coming from two sides at once, and she also melted their swords. When a third man charged with a battle ax, she had no choice but to lop off his hand. He stared at the smoking stump and collapsed in a dead faint.

As she pushed forward, her incandescent ramer posed an obvious threat. Cade's soldiers backed away, their forward momentum broken by Bahlen's concentrated defense, and the front lines spread out.

Elliel kept fighting, striking at the weapons wielded against her, blinding one soldier, driving two others into each other. A volley of arrows streaked toward her, but her living anger seemed to enhance her reflexes. Her slashing ramer became a thick shield of fire that cut the smoking shafts in half. One arrow just missed her but pierced her finemail cape and hung there. She snapped it off and discarded the ends, feeling her anger intensify further. Elliel had never felt like this. The power seemed to be growing from the heart of the old city.

She meant to find and defeat the rival Brava, whoever it was, but as she worked her way toward the bright ramer, she saw something familiar nearby, a shield, a sword. But she could only see the man's sneer, emphasized by a thin and perfectly barbered line of beard along the jaw of a face that filled her with loathing.

Cade.

He saw her coming. "Elliel, I thought it might be you! King Kollanan couldn't send his other Brava?" Cade chuckled sarcastically. "You caused a crisis that could have rocked the three kingdoms, and now you fight against the Commonwealth itself." He grimaced. "See, you are exactly the traitor I made you out to be."

The wild, animated anger became a raging sun within her. Her ramer brightened, extended. This vile man had drugged her, forced himself upon her when she could not fight him off. Not satisfied merely to rape her, though, Cade had to humiliate her, strip her of her livelihood and all dignity.

Watching her expression change and the fluid rage take possession of her, Cade faltered. He raised his sword and backed away, but Elliel's threat continued to swell. Even though she wasn't herself, she was in perfect control.

"I remember, Cade. I remember everything."

She threw herself upon him.

☙

Once he saw Shadri descend into the darkness beneath the sinkhole, Thon went to face the marauding company that had slipped through the gap in the wall. He counted forty of them, leering and hooting as if this were a game rather than a military action.

By knowing Elliel, loving her, and understanding who she was as a Brava, Thon comprehended her core of honor. It was strange, but admirable. He carried a similar trait within himself, though it was far more ancient, more primal. He felt no loyalty to either faction of the wreths—who were still enigmas to him—but to something independent, neutral, and nurturing.

Now these brigands rode in search of refugees or stragglers. They would cause havoc inside the city, strike the defenders from behind. Thon was just one person, but he was enough to stop them.

The riders hurled their torches into the dead shrubbery or the open windows of ancient structures. "Come out!" one of the marauders mocked. "Come out and meet the konag's justice!"

"This is not justice," Thon said in a low voice. They had not spotted him yet, but he did not try to hide. His dark hair, pale skin, and gray garments gave him a ghostly appearance as he moved among the ruins. He could feel a lingering energy in the ancient sculptures, the dead fountains, the magical turrets that had once blasted celebratory flames into the air.

Thon paused. How had he remembered that detail? Or were the memories imprinted on the stone carvings and now leaked out for any susceptible person to receive? Around him, the city resonated with echoes. A great deal of fighting and killing had been done here long ago, and the ruins remembered.

At the main gate, the clash of battle grew louder. Thrumming through the air, borne on the cold night breezes, he sensed an awakening anger amplified by the wreth ruins. A long time ago this place had been under siege, and became a casualty of the ancient wars; now it was just a ghostly shell filled with legends and pain. Thon felt that pain, and he used it.

"I am here!" he shouted to the brigands, his voice amplified by the weight of history and legend around him.

The riders wheeled their horses about and charged toward him, seeing only one person standing there, one enemy they could easily defeat.

Deep within, Thon felt a change, something cracking . . . something awakened by the anger exuded by Elliel, by all the defenders of the city, and by the ruins themselves. That dark energy inside him formed a shadowy flame fed by anger and ugliness.

As Thon stepped forward to meet the oncoming soldiers, his movements were faster and smoother, as if he were *slithering*. His mind filled with shards of shadow, and his eyes widened to take in more darkness, more flickers of fire. When he opened his mouth, he sensed fangs. When he lunged forward, he grew stronger, larger. Within him, all he could feel were scales, claws, and exploding anger.

The darkness became an obsidian flame that drank all light and reflected back sharp edges and fear. Thon drew upon the anger in the air. He didn't know what was happening, nor could he control it, but he felt himself becoming invincible. He let out a roar.

89

THE godling rampaged through the Magnifica square.

The destruction would have seemed glorious if the ravening entity had harmed only its real enemies, but this was a disaster, creating a wide swath of collateral damage. Wielding massive arms of smoke and solidified vengeance, the godling rooted out Hethrren and ripped down the walls of buildings where they ran to hide. It blasted out timbers, extended roiling tentacles into windows, and tore apart any barbarian it found.

But in doing so, the thing left structures in flames with roofs collapsing and brick towers crumbling. The frenzied entity ricocheted around the temple plaza, energized by all the worshippers. Hethrren lay mangled and dead within moments, their horses crushed. And the godling surged on.

Though Klovus felt transformed by the power and struggled to exert control, the godling slipped through his mental grasp. Nothing could stop the pent-up emotions the people had created with their sacrifices and prayers. Back in Tamburdin, he had scorned Priestlord Neré for not being able to control her godling, and this one was far more powerful, far more enraged.

As people fled screaming from the plaza, Klovus saw four nondescript worshippers standing in front of him. They did not flinch. "You once trained us to fight a godling, Key Priestlord," Zaha said. "We will try to rein it in now."

"Go!" Klovus knew he might be sending them to their deaths, but it seemed his best chance to slow the godling.

On the perimeter of the temple square, the godling smashed the sacrificial stands in a storm of unchecked faith and primal desires. A food vendor's cart erupted into splinters. A wine seller's casks were thrown like pebbles into the air and exploded in a gush of red liquid.

The Black Eels fought their way to the rampaging entity and were joined by three more nondescript assassins who emerged from the panicked crowd. Everyone else ran away from the tempest.

When Zaha and his companions had once battled the Serepol godling during training in the underground vaults, several of them had died, and others had been injured. Klovus had been able to control the godling and pull it back to the spelldoor after the test.

But now it was loose. Klovus doubted anything could hold such a monster in check—the monster he had created, nurtured, and then unleashed. In search of more Hethrren, the godling continued to smash structures.

The terrified worshippers had scattered into alleys and streets, and now that the crowd had thinned, Klovus could run after the entity and try to bring it under control. His gold chain jingled against his chest and he panted with both fear and exertion. He fought to concentrate and use his link to pull back the deity, but the thing did not obey.

Klovus had ascended through the priesthood ranks because of his affinity for the godlings—and this godling was *his*. But now he fought and strained until his head was about to burst. Every time he thought he had a grasp, whenever he began to reel the godling back toward the temple, it slipped away.

The churning storm surged along a main boulevard that led all the way down to the harbor. Cobblestones flew up, scattering in all directions. The façades of buildings on either side of the boulevard were left charred with a black smudge of heat like a child's finger painting.

The exuberant entity was a firestorm, and that energy fed back into Klovus. Part of him relished this wanton, long-awaited destruction. He ran after the godling, still trying to restrain it. He felt like a boy chasing a runaway puppy.

The Black Eels raced after it. One assassin leaped into the air and dove into the indistinct mass of energy. Caught up like a dry leaf in a whirlwind, he continued to fight, swinging, punching, attempting to damage an intangible target.

Three more Black Eels bounded in to surround and attack the godling. One man was lifted up and hurled against a wall. Such a blow would have reduced any normal person to a smear of blood and broken bones, but the Black Eel temporarily hardened his skin into a shell of stone. The building's stuccoed wall cracked, leaving a divot from the impact. The assassin slumped to the ground, stunned, but he got up and ran after the godling again.

Klovus cried out, beseeching the deity. "Come back to me!"

Black Eels threw themselves into the formless whirlwind, trying to find some vulnerable point. Two more assassins were swept up in the cyclone of emotions, thrown high into the air. Their attacks seemed ineffective, yet the godling was distracted. It lifted hammer tentacles and crushed one man in a mammoth blow that even his stone skin could not withstand. More assassins were swatted away like annoying gnats, tossed onto rooftops, or flung down side streets.

Klovus stood in the middle of the boulevard and strained, pulling with his heart and his mind. "Stop! You are hurting your worshippers." The godling did not communicate in words or rational thoughts, only energy and emotion, reflecting what had been poured into it.

The streets emptied as people ducked into buildings for shelter, but the godling damaged walls, ripped down bricks, shattered stucco. Displaced roof tiles fell like grains of sand.

At last, Klovus established a tenuous hold and managed to tamp down the fury—until a group of angry Hethrren riders galloped in with raised clubs and swords. Recognizing the hated barbarians, the entity snapped the fragile restraints Klovus had in place, and surged forward again.

The barbarians yowled, challenging one another to bravery or foolhardiness. The godling elongated itself, swirled a cloud arm around a building, and smashed a wall down upon several victims, crushing them. Then it roiled forward and pounded the other Hethrren into broken meat.

The godling ripped along the main boulevard and tore open the doors and windows of a crowded tavern. Like a cruel child killing flies, it extricated several Hethrren inside and tore off their heads. In doing so, the entity also destroyed the tavern and left Isharan bodies behind. The surviving Black Eels kept running after it, attacking, distracting, trying to slow it.

Klovus pursued the godling through Serepol, dizzy and disoriented. The thing's destruction already far exceeded any damage the Hethrren had done. And he himself had caused this—he, Key Priestlord Klovus!

As the godling flowed toward the harbor, probing into buildings to extricate victims, Klovus sobbed from his efforts to control it. Ahead, he saw the crowded docks and the warships he had commissioned to transport the Hethrren to the unsuspecting Commonwealth. If the godling continued to rush forward, it could sink all those vessels, leaving Serepol Harbor a swamp of shattered masts and cracked hulls.

Klovus felt his heart lurch with despair, and he staggered to a halt. Another strong and angry presence emerged, different from the Serepol godling, but also familiar. An entity that he knew well.

Ur-Priest Xion emerged from the harbor temple at the waterfront, raising his hands. The wooden posts and tall carved doors cracked, then burst open as the temple's front wall exploded outward. Xion summoned his godling and came out to face its foe.

శ

Near Serepol Harbor, Mak Dur and his Utauk crew remained prisoners. Ever since Priestlord Klovus had impounded the *Glissand*, the Utauks had been held under guard, but at least this run-down waterfront inn was superior to a dungeon.

The Carp's Whiskers had fallen on hard times due to bad management and worse food. Near bankruptcy, the owner did not complain when the key priestlord commandeered the place, using Isharan guards to oust the two paying customers (who were actually weeks in arears on their rent), and declared that the captives must remain under house arrest.

The *Glissand*'s crew were forced to share beds—which were more spacious than the bunks or hammocks on their ship. The innkeeper fed them, glad to receive a stipend from the empra's treasury. The Hethrren had occupied inns and taverns along the harbor, but because the Carp's Whiskers had such a bad reputation, even the barbarians left the place alone. The Isharan guards stationed in front of the inn were bored and inattentive.

Still, despite the adequate conditions, Mak Dur and his crew were angry at being prevented from sailing home. Over and over, he drew a circle around his heart. "The beginning is the end is the beginning." Somehow, he needed to warn other Utauks to stay away, but he couldn't do anything unless he escaped from Serepol.

Then a miracle happened.

As the godling rampaged down to the harbor, the streets became a fiery cataclysm. Mak Dur and his sailors peered through the inn's open windows as the whirlwind of energy and faith smashed warehouses and shops, hunted down Hethrren, and roared toward the docks.

The guards assigned to watch them looked at one another in dismay, and without speaking a word, ran off to join the great battle.

Reaching a decision, Mak Dur pulled all of his sailors together. "No one is watching us! The *Glissand* is unguarded. *Cra*, this is our chance to take the ship back. We'll cut the ropes and sail away, and no one will be able to catch us."

"Those Isharan warships could pursue us, Voyagier," warned a crewman named Sarrum. "There must be at least thirty ships ready to set sail!"

"Not while that thing is rampaging," said Heith, the navigator. "Look at it!"

Mak Dur shook his head. "*Cra*, do you think any of those scows could sail faster than my beautiful *Glissand*? Do you think their captains are better than I am?" He rushed his men into the inn's main room. Outside, the shouts and roars grew louder, the unleashed deity smashing buildings even closer to the Carp's Whiskers.

The innkeeper ran into the room, looking harried. He was balding and prone to easy perspiration. He stepped behind the long wooden bar. "But you have orders to stay here! The key priestlord will be upset. You are prisoners."

Mak Dur flashed him a sardonic frown. "Do we need to kill you so we can get away?"

The innkeeper backed toward the bar. "No, no, that won't be necessary."

"*Cra*, we should at least subdue you."

With a chorus of shouts, the Utauk sailors all agreed. Grinning, Sarrum said, "I'm sure I can find a rope somewhere."

The innkeeper waved his hands. "Truly, that won't be necessary! Hear us, save us! Let's say I was out back tending the compost heap, and that I didn't even notice you escaping. I will blame it on those guards who fled, leaving the inn unprotected. They shouldn't have left dangerous criminals without supervision."

Impatient, Mak Dur gestured to his sailors. "It's best if we make this look legitimate. Just to be sure."

The stout innkeeper tried to waddle away, but Heith and Sarrum seized him, tied a rag around his mouth, then trussed him. "Now your explanations will be much more believable once they find you." The innkeeper grunted and struggled, but the *Glissand*'s crew ran out into the streets, rushing toward their precious ship tied up at the docks.

In front of the harbor temple, the wild godling rose up to clash with a second roaring entity. The two collided with tremendous fury.

90

WHEN Kollanan galloped off with part of the city guard and his standing army, some of whom were still lashing on their armor, he left Queen Tafira in charge of the city. Lasis joined the king, as a bonded Brava should, while Tafira remained behind the castle walls with her guard staff protected against any attack.

She could not guess how long they would be gone, how many fighters they might lose. Tafira sent castle guards up to the high turrets to keep watch for frostwreths, redoubled lookouts on the wall towers. Fellstaff Castle was secure, but she tucked two throwing knives at her waist nevertheless.

She wore embroidered slippers and a fur-lined robe that brought to mind the styles of the village where she had grown up, where Kollanan had rescued her from her own people—and his. That was so long ago, back when people had believed their only real enemies were other humans. The idea of resurrected wreths or an awakening dragon would have sounded ludicrous.

Tafira feared their worst enemy might still be human hatred. Konag Mandan's decree had proved that much. How could he have ordered an attack on an unsuspecting Norterran town? Captain Rondo's insolent attitude remained unchanged despite his having faced the frostwreths himself, and although he and his men had finally been confined, she did not feel a sense of relief. Tafira had seen hatred in the captain's eyes, while her husband likely noticed only a dispute. Koll did not grasp the prejudice Tafira had dealt with all her life, and she could read signs that were invisible to him.

Kollanan should have sent them back to Convera a month ago, but her husband had a huge heart and bravery to rival any man's. She loved him with all her being, and she would not have changed a moment of her life with him. For three decades she had tried to fit in among the people even as she retained part of her Isharan identity. All along she believed the Norterran subjects had accepted her. They loved their queen because they loved their king so much.

But Tafira was not blind to the occasional sidelong glances, the quickly covered expressions of discomfort when she walked in Fellstaff. She had never thought such uneasiness would become an issue—until now.

෴

Struggling to maintain his dignity, Captain Rondo marched alongside the Norterran guards. He had been kept in a holding room while Kollanan and his soldiers armed themselves, mounted up, and rode off for Lord Bahlen's besieged city. Now Rondo and his remaining sixteen men had been rounded up and were being taken to the barracks, where they would await judgment after the traitorous king returned. The captain kept his gaze forward, his blue cape over his shoulders. They had all been disarmed, without resistance.

Rondo's surviving soldiers fell in beside him, the ones left after the foolhardy and disorganized attack on the frostwreth fortress. Three good men had died on that battlefield. Now the others looked at one another, uneasy and angry. Rondo felt as if he were being torn in all directions.

The six Fellstaff guards were suspicious, their swords drawn as they marched Rondo and his men back to the sturdy barracks. "We'll hold you there until King Kollanan decides what to do." The man's voice had a sneering accusatory undertone. "Ancestors' blood, aren't we under attack from enough sides?"

A second guard said, "I'd rather be fighting with the king to help defend Yanton, but instead we have to babysit hooligans!" The remaining Norterran soldiers murmured in agreement.

Rondo still didn't respond, but he had been with his men long enough that he felt their mutual outrage, like spilled lamp oil just waiting for a spark. King Kollanan had prevented them from returning home for far too long, making excuses. Kollanan seemed uninterested in avenging his murdered brother, which made Rondo lose all respect for him. The wreths were powerful and mysterious, but they had made no move, beyond building a fortress on a distant and isolated lake. Meanwhile, the Isharans had declared overt war!

Rondo glanced to his side, where Sergeant Headan's face was ruddy with anger, his jaw clenched. They had served together for many years and knew each other's nuances. He saw that the man was ready to spring, and in a flash of decision he gave a slight nod.

It was as if lightning had cracked down from the clouds. Headan reached beneath his cloak to his back, snatched a knife hidden behind his thick belt, spun, and drove it into the throat of the escort guard next to him.

At the same moment, Rondo reacted like a released spring. He raised his

boot and kicked hard into the chest of the guard next to him. The blow sent the soldier reeling.

Like a stinging scorpion, Headan yanked his knife back out, lunged for the guard's sword even as the dying man reached up to his gushing neck, and ripped the blade free. "Captain!" In a swift motion, he tossed the sword to Rondo, who caught it and struck down the guard he had kicked.

"Men, defend yourselves!" Rondo yelled, and his well-trained soldiers sprang into action, even though they were unarmed.

Making quick use of his knife again, Headan fell upon a second guard.

Rondo disarmed the guard he had killed and handed the extra sword to one of his own men as he charged at a third Norterran guard. The Commonwealth soldiers outnumbered their armed opponents, and they threw themselves recklessly upon the guards, two and three at a time.

"For Konag Mandan!"

"We will not be held prisoner by a traitorous king."

Kollanan's great mistake had been in believing that Rondo and his men would respect his authority and supposed nobility.

The castle guards were well armed and well practiced, but Rondo's men were desperate. Two of his own men died—five casualties now—but they made short work of their minders.

Realizing that the clamor of the battle was much too loud in the night, Rondo held up his bloody sword. "To the stables! Quickly!" Like a band of brigands, they rushed across the courtyard. "We will head northeast, stay off the roads. We have to get over the mountains, out of Norterra, and report to Konag Mandan."

"He'll be pleased with the information we can give him," said Headan.

"I wish we could bring more than that," Rondo said under his breath as they burst into the stables. "Saddle up! Grab cloaks, blankets. We ride."

He heard a shout in the courtyard and looked through the stable's open gates. And saw exactly what he needed.

~~~

Lanterns were lit in the streets, and torches burned outside the castle, but Tafira continued to feel uneasy, always wary of danger from the frostwreths. Restless, she cinched her robe's waistband tight and stepped out into the night. She immediately sensed something terribly wrong. She heard running men, urgent but hushed shouts. She smelled blood.

In the shadowy expanse of the courtyard, she saw bodies sprawled on the ground. She ran ahead, bending over to see murdered soldiers wearing Norterran colors—the castle guards who had watched Rondo and his soldiers!

She crouched over one man with a gash across his chest and heard him gurgling his last breaths. She sprang to her feet and shouted, "Guards!"

On the other side of the courtyard, the stable doors were open. Men moved inside, grabbing tack, saddling mounts. Horses whinnied. Putting her hands on the hilts of her two throwing daggers, Tafira ran toward the furtive shapes. "Guards!"

Shouts responded from inside the castle. Guards would come soon, but she doubted it would be in time. Tafira ran to the stables. "Here! They are trying to get away!"

Leading horses and running, Captain Rondo and his men emerged to meet her with predatory expressions. Several of them had thrown on dark cloaks or stable blankets to hide their Commonwealth colors.

Facing them, Tafira drew upon all her experience as queen. She doubted they would follow her command, but maybe some of the men would hesitate. "You are defying the king's order. Stand down!"

Two of the men touched the hilts of their swords. Rondo said, "Kollanan is not my king, and I will not fight against my own people."

"We *are* your own people!" she snapped. She stepped forward, putting the full weight of command into her bearing. "Norterra is part of the Commonwealth, and I am issuing the *queen's* command."

"You are not my queen either," Rondo retorted. "You are a foreigner, and your commands mean even less than Kollanan's." He looked hungry. "Take her as a hostage. The konag can use her as leverage to make Norterra obey him."

Tafira drew both throwing knives and stood ready to defend herself. "Guards!" She heard the jingle of armor, running footsteps as her guards emerged from the castle, but they were on the other side of the courtyard.

"Take her. Tie her up and sling her over my saddle," Rondo said. "We'll ride hard tonight."

The Commonwealth soldiers spread out to close in around her. Kollanan always told Tafira to do what was necessary, to be prepared for an attack. She had trained, and she was deadly.

As the men sprang toward her, Tafira threw her knives, planting one up to the hilt in the first man's throat and stabbing another in the chest. The two fell onto the straw of the stable floor, but her actions only enraged the others. And she had no more knives.

They swarmed forward. Tafira tried to run, shouting again for her guards, but three men seized her. She thrashed like a wild animal, fighting, punching. She clawed Headan's face, hoping to gouge out his eye, but only left red streaks down his cheek. She screamed as they lashed her arms and ankles, and tossed her like a rolled rug on the front of Rondo's saddle.

Leaving their dead behind, two in the stable and two in the courtyard, the men galloped pell-mell into the streets of Fellstaff.

Tafira squirmed and saw a handful of castle workers and guards responding to the commotion as Rondo's soldiers stampeded past. Pokle, with wide eyes and a pale face, bleated out an alarm. "The queen! They are taking the queen!"

But most of the castle guards were away with Kollanan to help rescue Lord Bahlen. Only a few armed soldiers ran after Tafira, attempting to stop the abductors.

Rondo growled close to Tafira's ear, "Konag Mandan will know what to do with an Isharan captive."

Tafira tried to roll off the saddle, but he cuffed her so hard that her ears rang, and her vision faded to black.

91

⚰

K ING Adan gripped the reins as the bay mare trotted onward, finding
the way even at night. Though the group was exhausted, they took few
breaks, and Adan had slept only a few hours in the two days since riding out
from Bannriya Castle. Hom sagged forward, asleep in his saddle, though his
brother Seenan remained alert, taking the lead while Captain Elcior rode
beside the king.

Overhead, Xar darted forward then swooped back, urging them to hurry.
They knew from Penda's note that the Utauk camp was near the northern
border of Suderra, and Adan knew they must be close. His heart beat faster.
Soon he would be with his wife, and they would hold their newborn child.
He hoped he would be in time for the birth.

The horses snorted, and he heard shouts ahead, an unexpected clamor of
battle followed by a terrifying roar. Adan squeezed with his legs, urging the
mare to greater speed. "Penda!" Already tired, the horse tried to shy away
from the ominous sounds ahead.

Captain Elcior drew his sword and pushed his mount forward, joining
Seenan at the lead. "We should have brought a larger military escort, Sire!"

Hunched over the saddle, Adan spoke through clenched teeth. "Right
now I want speed, not numbers!"

Under the light of a gibbous moon they topped a forested line of hills
above a sheltered valley where they saw campfires and people swarming in
panic.

And a dragon.

Xar trilled and shrieked, swooped past Adan, then streaked forward.

Hom yelped, "Sire, the monster will kill us."

"Ride!" Adan shouted. He was glad to have the protection of his Banner
guards, but he would have ridden forward even if he were alone. Penda was
down there!

The dark dragon flew above the camp, pounding huge wings. Adan could see its angular silhouette, the reptilian neck, the arrow-shaped head. His pan-icked mare tried to bolt, but he knew he needed to get down among the Utauks who were fighting the monster. The previous dragon hunt out in the Furnace had shown him that swords could do little against a monster like that, but this time their weapons were inlaid with shadowglass, thanks to Queen Voo. He hoped that would make them more deadly.

As the dragon attacked the camp, Utauks either scattered for shelter or tried to defend their belongings and their people. They grabbed flaming brands from bonfires and fought using the makeshift torches. Utauks were not battle-hardened, ruthless warriors, but they were resourceful and deter-mined.

The dragon tore up several tents, and two men in bright clothing bolted forward, cracking long bullwhips. The braided strands snapped and slashed against the reptilian hide. One whip curled around and snagged the dragon's clawed foot, but the beast pounded upward and tore the whip free, wrench-ing the man's arm out of its socket. He dropped and rolled, cradling his limp arm as he bolted for the shadows of the trees. As the dragon turned to snap at him, the man's companion snapped his own bullwhip, cracking it on the beast's snout. The dragon roared, chomped at the whip, and the Utauk man dove under a sturdy wagon.

Elcior and Seenan drew their reinforced military bows, which were more powerful than Utauk hunting bows. And their arrows were tipped with shadowglass.

Adan pulled ahead of his companions, shouting, "Penda! Where are you?" His horse shied and stamped, seeing the dragon and smelling the rep-tile musk. Unable to control the mare, Adan swung down from the saddle, landed on his feet. He raised his sword. "Penda!"

Xar flew up to him, clicking and whistling, and led him toward Penda.

Out of the forested hills to his left, Adan heard rough snorts and loud shouts that were different from the Utauk sounds. He turned, ready to face another enemy, and to his astonishment he saw a group of augas racing toward the dragon as it circled around to attack the camp.

The monster let out a hiss like steam from a covered kettle. Wreth warriors—sandwreths!—charged in to challenge the dragon. They hurled spears into the sky, piercing its armored chest. In pain, the beast spun in the air, worked its wings, and lashed its barbed tail.

Adan kept following Xar, desperate to find his wife. He could not com-prehend why wreths were here. Two of the golden warriors drove their augas toward the monster as it slammed into an Utauk wagon before turning to its new opponents. The dragon snapped one rider from his auga and crunched down. It spat out the pieces of the body, bowled the auga aside, and raked the second warrior with a clawed foot before it sprang into the air again.

The rest of the sandwreths were not intimidated. One let out a foolhardy battle cry, and Adan recognized the wreth as Quo, Queen Voo's brother.

Xar circled in front of Adan's face, snapping at him. The ska's faceted eyes blazed bright. He followed the reptile bird to scattered blankets and cushions beside a collapsed tent marked with the crimson and black colors of the Orr tribe. He called out Penda's name again.

"My Starfall!" Her response made his heart leap. Penda and her father were moving into the trees. She tried to run, hunched over and hobbling. "My water broke. The spasms . . . I can't move."

Hale Orr helped her along. "*Cra,* dragons eat newborn babies, you know."

"Dragons eat anything they can catch," Penda said.

Adan reached them and spun around, holding his sword up to drive away anything that threatened her, whether it be dragon or wreth. "To the trees! We can take shelter there."

Once they were in the thick of the forest beyond the camp, Penda collapsed against a thick oak. She slid down and wrapped her arms around her belly. "Our baby chose a very inconvenient time to arrive, Starfall." She winced, and then smiled. "But your timing is perfect."

Xar fluttered in and landed on a branch just above her head. Adan stroked her dark hair.

In the middle of the camp, the two Banner guards, still on horseback, shot more shadowglass-tipped arrows at the dragon. The sandwreths rode their augas around Elcior and Seenan, as if amused by their efforts.

The dragon ripped up the large tent that belonged to old Shella din Orr, but no one was inside. Transfixed and terrified, young Hom ducked into a low supply tent, and the dragon tore the fabric away, exposing the boy. Hom darted for shelter, and the monster lunged after him as he crouched down, trying to hide under a stray blanket.

Seenan galloped in. "Leave my brother alone!" He launched an arrow that plunged deep into the glowing eye. The dragon reared back, lashing out with huge claws, but Seenan dodged away.

Now even more enraged, the beast attacked anything that moved, tearing at the wreth opponents as if the humans were mere distractions. As it swept past, one mounted warrior raised a spear, but the tail crushed both auga and sandwreth. On his own mount, Quo snarled at the massacre. Half of his war party had been killed already.

Leaning back against her large oak, Penda groaned and clutched her knees. Adan wanted to help Captain Elcior and the Utauks, even the wreth warriors, but Penda clasped his arm. He knelt beside her. "I'm here. I'm here!"

A sandwreth mage stalked toward the one-eyed dragon, extending her arms straight out at her sides. She summoned dust and fire and hurled it into the creature's open mouth, which made the dragon hiss and choke. The mage struck again with a skirling whirlwind that hit the creature's left wing. Two of the thin stabilizing bones snapped, and when the dragon lurched into the air, part of the wing flopped. The monster crashed to the ground again, falling on top of the standing mage and a nearby sandwreth warrior, crushing them both.

The injured dragon thrashed as it struggled to get its feet under it. Quo drove his auga in, screaming, but he sounded less reckless and cocky now.

The dragon spun and slammed Quo off the auga. He struck the ground with a sharp snap of breaking bones. Two wreth warriors ran to defend him, but the dragon tore them apart. Leaving the bodies on the ground, the monster heaved itself into the air again, beating its huge wings above the camp, though it flew erratically, with one eye blinded and one wing damaged. Even so, it clearly intended to attack again.

Suddenly, with a shrieking, buzzing sound, countless small shapes flew in across the dark sky. Hundreds of wild skas along with bonded Utauk pets flurried around the dragon, harassing it as it rose higher into the air.

Under the shelter of the oak, Xar flapped his wings as if he wanted to join his fellow skas, but Penda held him. "Stay! You must stay with me." The green ska made a strangled sound, turned his faceted eyes toward Penda as if she had betrayed him, but she would not let go.

The countless reptile birds were like sparrows harrying a large crow, driving it away. Their clamor was tremendous, drowning out even the tumult in the camp.

"The dragon's going away!" Adan said.

Xar continued trying to break free, but Penda held on, desperate not to lose him.

The wounded dragon flew erratically into the night, and the skas swarmed it, pecking, attacking. Soon they were all only silhouettes against the starlight. As Adan stared at the shapes, it seemed as if the skas drew closer and closer, like bees circling a hive, until they were *absorbed* into the giant reptile, but he couldn't be sure what he saw in the darkness and distance.

Then the dragon was gone, flying far from the Utauk camp.

Adan had just a moment of relief before Penda let out a sharp cry of pain, and he knew it was time for the baby.

92

ॡ

THE harbor godling protected the waterfront, the ships and sailors, the fish markets, the docks, and all of the harbor businesses. Klovus had once served the harbor godling as he rose through the ranks of the priesthood, and he had borrowed this godling when he sailed off to destroy the fishing town of Mirrabay.

Now, when Ur-Priest Xion summoned the harbor godling, Klovus felt a surge of hope. Perhaps the other entity would be strong enough to block the wild chaos of the Serepol godling.

Or perhaps not.

The harbor was in turmoil. Aboard the warships tied up to the docks, sailors and soldiers were unable to escape unless they dove overboard. Along the waterfront, people ran in all directions as the Serepol godling lurched toward the markets and boathouses. Finding three more barbarians who tried to flee, it snatched them up with a fluid tentacle arm and hurled their broken bodies into the swirling force of the harbor godling that rose up to meet it.

The two deities roiled and surged. Enhanced by the sacrifices that had just been poured into it, the Magnifica godling loomed over its rival. Ur-Priest Xion stood close as debris flew all about him, but he was just a tiny form. The winds roared and lightning bursts struck as the godlings faced each other.

Xion tried to direct his deity to wrestle the rampaging godling into submission. Klovus ran toward him with outstretched arms, trying to control his own entity. The two forces slammed into each other with a thunderclap, sending a shock wave through the air.

The key priestlord clawed outward with his thoughts. "Come back, damn you!"

But the godling would not listen.

ॡ

Escaping, the crew of the *Glissand* ran into the streets while the fighting godlings destroyed part of the waterfront.

Most people had fled, although some crouched in doorways or watched the titanic struggle from high windows. No one tried to stop the running Utauks, though. At the long docks, crews stood on the decks of the ready warships, shading their eyes. At any moment, the embattled godlings could crash into the water and capsize countless vessels in the harbor.

"Faster!" Mak Dur hissed, and the Utauks raced out along the far pier where the *Glissand* was tied up. Sailors aboard adjacent vessels shouted at them, but they were warnings, not curses. Mak Dur ignored them. His crew rushed aboard the ship, the first sailors already pulling up ropes even before their comrades scrambled onto the deck.

After untying the ropes from the docks, the sailors used poles to push the *Glissand* away, and when it drifted free, six of the men unshipped the long maneuvering oars and began to guide the graceful vessel away from the docks and toward the open harbor. Two men climbed the mast, releasing the sails from the yardarms.

"We'd better catch a breeze fast, Voyagier!"

The two godlings tore at each other with smoke, wind, lightning. Mak Dur looked at them in awe, then turned back to the business of escaping. This would be their only chance.

❧

Like opposing black clouds, the godlings tore at each other, grappling for dominance. Skittering arcs of electricity and flashes of primitive flame surged out, and Klovus experienced each blow as if his own body had been struck. He felt both the harbor godling and his own deity, as if he himself were being torn apart.

The godlings flowed back and forth, exploding, surging. Together, they slammed into a boathouse and upended the fishing boats stored inside. Klovus cringed and ducked as shards of wood like sharpened stakes flew toward him.

Ur-Priest Xion screamed, wept, held up his hands. The harbor godling continued to fight, but the Serepol godling was stronger. Even as Klovus tried to take hold of his entity, it ripped away one of its rival's thundercloud tendrils. When the incorporeal piece broke off from the main body, the fragment dissipated, diminishing the harbor godling.

Embattled, the smaller godling stretched itself, and the central mass focused into hundreds of screaming, angry faces with open mouths that tore at the Magnifica godling, which responded with even more manifested figures, symbols of primitive anger—wolves, bears, dragons.

The harbor godling transformed into a motley collection of sharks, huge squid tentacles, enormous whales, but the Serepol godling continued to grow stronger, feeding on the fear and damage it had caused.

Klovus could feel both godlings within him, struggling . . . and he sensed the exact point at which the harbor deity knew it was defeated. The Serepol godling engulfed its opponent, swarmed around it, pressing in, tearing, devouring. Ur-Priest Xion fought with every shred of energy he possessed, but Klovus could see the despair growing on his long face.

The Magnifica godling crushed and absorbed the last remnants of the other entity, taking the essence into itself. Klovus felt the second godling die, while the stronger one became wilder than ever.

In front of the harbor temple, Ur-Priest Xion collapsed onto the street, motionless, as his very soul was drained out of him.

*

The Utauk sailors moved faster than naval crews normally would. The men rowed until they thought their hearts and muscles would burst, and in a matter of minutes the *Glissand* pulled away from the last docks and set sail.

As they cleared the other ships, Mak Dur heard Isharan crews shouting at them as they realized the Utauk ship was escaping. He squeezed his fist and looked up at the circle painted on the billowing mainsail. Now more than ever he needed Utauk luck to work in his favor.

Even though several Isharan warships set up an alarm about the fleeing ship, the embattled godlings had thrown the city guard into complete chaos. One of the entities defeated and absorbed the other, and now the victor rose as tall as an ominous thunderhead.

The navigator worked the rudder; the sailors pulled the ropes. Every person knew every task. Mak Dur was the voyagier, but right now he had little to do but hope. He felt a breeze on his face, enough to stretch the sails, and he began to weep.

One Isharan warship set sail and started moving out after them, but by now the *Glissand* had reached the mouth of the harbor, leaving behind the burning wreckage on the waterfront. Unless the pursuing vessel had a priest-lord aboard who could summon favorable winds—which he very much doubted—his ship would gain an insurmountable lead out on the open sea.

"That's all right." He drew a circle over his chest. "No one can catch the *Glissand.*"

They sailed beyond the harbor, leaving the devastation of Serepol behind them.

93

THE pit beneath the wreth city whispered of terrors and the impossible weight of age, but Shadri was not afraid. Standing in the darkness, she looked around with wide eyes, seeing only black, but her imagination filled in details. Her ears were attuned to any rustle or draft that moved through the subterranean chambers.

From outside, she heard faint battle cries, the sounds of bloodthirsty combat. "Thon, are you still up there?" Her shout echoed, sounding as loud as an explosion, and she cringed at the noise. She didn't dare call out again. What if one of the marauders found the rope and cut it, leaving her stranded down here?

Shadri braced herself, found solid footing on crumbling blocks beneath the collapsed ceiling. The original wreths must have built underground tunnels, perhaps an entire warren of storage chambers and secret places.

She looked up through the opening at the deceptively peaceful starfield. She heard horse hooves, the jingle of armor, boastful threats in deep voices. At first she feared for Thon, then she allowed herself a small smile, remembering what he could do. Rather, she feared for the attacking soldiers.

Now that she was beneath the intriguing sinkhole, she needed to explore her surroundings. She ducked her head and extended a hand to feel her way along. She didn't know the size or extent of the underground vaults, but she sensed power here, sleeping beneath the ruins. Long ago, this city had been filled with thousands of wreths, working their magic, hurling their anger and prejudice. They had created powerful armies and inconceivable weapons.

Shadri ran her palms along the cool stone, feeling lines and curves of spiral designs in ascending messages. The blackness was like a living thing around her.

When she had gone far enough that the marauders would not see her light shining up from below, Shadri fumbled in her pocket, found the candle and the sulfur matches she had taken from her pack. She struck a match against the stone wall, and a small flame hissed out, startling the shadows. She touched the flame to the wick, and her candle caught, flickered, then grew strong. The orange pool of candlelight did not extend far into the deep, deep darkness, but she could see her way.

The tunnels were huge and winding, with side passages that curved off, plunging even deeper beneath the city, while others opened under the main wreth buildings. She walked cautiously, making sure she could remember her way back.

The stone walls were so smooth they glistened like metal, as if they had been polished by a release of extreme energy. As she moved forward with whispering footsteps, she felt a simmering presence, an energy like the glow of a dying campfire. But it was not light and warmth like the coals in a hearth; rather, this was dark and cold, throbbing.

The main passage turned, bent, snaked. Shadri explored cautiously, making as little sound as possible. Following a curve, she held her candle in front of her and came upon a monster.

Startled, she drew back. The flickering candle flame illuminated a ferocious visage, the angular form, the sharp spines and scales, the hinge of the jaw, the long teeth. It was a dragon . . . yet more than a dragon.

She froze, but the thing didn't move, and as its black surface drank the orange light, she realized it was a large carving of a hunched dragon, a hulking reptilian creature chiseled out of solid shadowglass. Instead of the familiar dragon wings and long lizardlike body, though, this dragon had a twisted torso, extra arms—human or wreth arms, as if meant to represent some kind of amalgam of a dragon and wreth. Or Kur, perhaps? Along with Ossus? The god and the dragon together as one?

Studying the terrifying sculpture buried beneath the wreth city—much as the world dragon dwelled beneath the Dragonspine Mountains—she thought about the evil and hatred extracted from Kur and manifested in the form of a giant dragon. Such potent evil and destruction could take many forms, not just the shape of a reptilian monster.

Daring herself, she touched the sculpture's smooth shadowglass surface. Had the dragon's intrinsic evil somehow manipulated the wreths, making the two races try to annihilate each other instead of carrying out their sacred mission? Had the dragon's insidious darkness leaked out and emerged as smaller dragons? Could this current war—the Commonwealth versus Ishara—be yet another manifestation of the great dragon's corruption? If the dragon at the heart of the world was the one thing that must be destroyed above all else, surely it was the evil of Ossus that drove great nations to fight.

Shadri began to wonder if Ossus himself was just a reflection of what was fundamentally wrong with the hearts and souls of wreths. And humans.

How was the human race supposed to fight against the flaws of a god?

The dragon sculpture suddenly turned intensely cold beneath her fingers, and frost crackled on its surface. She jerked her hand away, looking uneasily back down the passage. She was surrounded by the weight of ghosts from so many generations of wreths who had lived and died here.

Her heartbeat seemed to echo in the oppressive shadows. A cold, dark force seemed to be emanating from this symbol, this shadowglass figure, and it was growing stronger.

Far away she could hear a clamor of the marauders shouting, horses whinnying . . . and another sound that chilled her to the marrow. A roar erupted. Something predatory and reptilian.

Then she heard the marauders scream.

❧

When Elliel looked at Lord Cade's face bathed in the glow of her ramer, she felt disgust and shame. Her instinct was to cringe away from what he had done to her, but she drove those thoughts back. The ramer sizzled and crackled around her wrist, flames rising in a glowing blade.

Even as his soldiers crashed against Lord Bahlen's defenders, Cade had the gall to leer at her. "You are weak, Elliel. Any Brava with honor would have taken her own life after reading Utho's note describing your crimes."

"It was a lie," she said.

His laugh was loud even with the clamor around them. "A lie? Who decides that? Maybe I remember something different. I remember you with your legs spread."

She threw herself upon him, and Cade in his arrogance lifted his sword against the ramer, as if he could take a Brava by surprise, as if she would be distracted by her uncontrolled rage. He was nimble enough, but Elliel lunged closer. Her anger had become a living thing, inexplicable.

Cade howled for his Brava. "Gant!" He slashed with his sword again.

Elliel remembered how this man had poisoned her, wrestled her to the bed, and grinned in her face when he was on top of her. Elliel had detached her mind, unable to move her body. How she had hated him for that! She felt the tattoo on her face burn, remembered the abomination of a story that had made her believe she had slaughtered innocent children. All of it to cover up Cade's dishonor and Utho's complicity.

Fury boiled up within her, as if resonating among the wreth ruins, as if tapping into their energy. The burning emotion seemed to have a life of its own, an external fuel that made her anger even stronger. Something in this city was awakening, too.

Cade blocked her ramer with his sword, but she pressed harder, met his blade with her crackling edge. Her blood fire intensified, and the steel of his sword trembled, then melted. Her ramer blade cut through the metal, leaving only a stump of a blade.

Cade screamed and staggered back. The hilt was searing hot, but he flailed the broken weapon at her. Elliel struck again and cut off his hand at the wrist, leaving only a smoking stump. He howled, "Gant!"

The ugly Brava thundered up to loom in front of Elliel. She saw his black armor, finemail cape, and burning ramer.

"Kill her, Gant!" Cade shrieked.

She looked at the other Brava, noted his lumpy nose, pockmarked cheeks, and stony gray gaze. He was a powerful opponent, but she would fight him if necessary. "You are bonded to a coward and a criminal," she said, her voice remarkably calm.

Cade moaned and pulled his smoking wrist up against his chest. He began to sob.

Like a controlled thunderstorm, Gant faced her. "I know." Astonishingly, he lowered his ramer and turned away. "I am a Brava with Brava honor. This man does not deserve my service."

Cade screamed, but Gant stalked away through the battlefield without engaging any other opponents.

Elliel thrust her searing ramer through Cade's belly, holding him there. His outcry was loud enough to resonate across the battlefield. She could have lopped off his head, but Elliel didn't want to be swift and merciful. Instead, she drew the flaming blade upward, spilling his guts like steaming sausages, until she cut his black heart in half.

As her tormentor died, Elliel experienced a storm of emotions like fresh, purifying rain. She felt stunned, giddy, separate from the world.

And in the background, echoing through the ancient ruins, she heard a strange reptilian roar, the booming cry of a legend come to life.

◈◈

Though terrified, Shadri had to know what was happening up above. The monstrous roar had rattled the support pillars even down in the catacombs, and seemed to have frightened away all the ghosts and memories imprinted here.

Holding her candle, she crept back to the dangling rope and the starlit opening overhead. In the faint orange light, she could see the stepping-stones of blocks that had tumbled down into the sinkhole. She climbed, working her way up to the mouth of the pit.

As she reached the opening, Shadri heard something moving above, large and powerful. Any sensible person would simply hide in the shadows and hope the thing didn't notice her, but then she would never have answers, and she was not afraid of answers.

She held on to the rope for balance and raised her head above the lip of the pit. From the bottom of the sinkhole, she heard the distant battle, saw fires. Much closer, the shadow of a huge beast slithered and stalked across the dark metropolis. A barbed tail lashed out with a flash of scales, a body as big as a wall.

Screams rolled out from brigands who had bellowed their bravado only moments before. Next she heard growls and ripping sounds, saw bodies flung into the air.

Another roar resounded through the darkness, and Shadri caught the flash of a slitted reptilian eye. Biting back a scream, she ducked, feeling the deepest terror she had experienced in her life.

Shadri no longer wanted answers; she just wanted to survive the night.

my mother. I had the court jewelers reset them for this very occasion. I will wear it."

"Of course you will, my konag," Utho said, and no one challenged him.

The young man beamed as servants hung the heavy stones around his neck. Mandan's gaze grew distant as he stroked them. "Aquamarines . . . my mother's favorite stone. The color of blue poppy milk, mixed with tears."

Utho hardened himself, impatient for the ostentatious and lengthy ceremony to be over. "Come, Mandan, we must go to the remembrance shrine. We don't want to be late." Only he could speak so familiarly to the konag.

Mandan tugged at his sleeves and stepped over to the looking glass. "This is my wedding, and it will begin when I'm ready."

"But you don't want to make your beloved Lira wait. Imagine how nervous she is."

"Nervous? Anxious, perhaps. Or eager! She's about to become the queen of the Commonwealth."

The servants opened the door and scurried down the hall to clear the way as the konag toiled stiffly along. His fine garments were designed for appearances rather than mobility.

Convera City was filled with banners and pennants. Minstrels on every corner sang new songs for the royal couple. Ale and wine already flowed freely. Bakers had made a special knotted bread glazed with honey, which symbolized the love of the happy couple and the unbreakable bond of their marriage. Thousands of the pastries were distributed to the crowds around the main remembrance shrine.

In the crowd, women twirled and flashed blue and yellow ribbons knotted together, like the soon-to-be-bound lives of Mandan and his bride. Ribbon sellers worked their way through the crowd, snipping off lengths and exchanging them for a few coppers.

Utho had made certain the most important people comprised the front lines of spectators, nobles and merchants in colorful finery, the ones who had been first to swear loyalty to the new konag, to offer soldiers for the war against Ishara, to provide ships for the growing navy.

After the gloom and horror of Conndur's murder, the city was overjoyed with this bright celebration. Utho understood that the people needed such a festival, but he kept his face expressionless, since it was not appropriate for a Brava to smile. His gaze remained distant because his mind continued to turn the wheels of war. So much had to be planned.

By now, Cade's powerful army should have reached Norterra and laid waste to the town targeted by Mandan's casually thrown dagger. Utho would

94

∾

"I⊤ is a glorious day, Utho," Mandan said for the fourth time that morning. The young konag's eyes sparkled, and his smile looked sincere, but Utho recognized that it was part of a pose, like one of his portrait subjects sitting for a painting.

"A magnificent day indeed, my konag," Utho agreed, because he was expected to.

In normal times, Utho would have helped him dress, but this was Mandan's wedding day and such elaborate finery required a larger staff. His robes were heavy, lush, and frilled, Osterran blue trimmed with gold to signify the rising sun in a clear sky. He was not just a prince getting married, as his father had hoped for so long; Mandan of the Colors was konag of the entire Commonwealth. His marriage to Lira would be cause for great celebration, a symbol of unity, although Utho knew that unity was not what the three kingdoms were demonstrating at the moment.

The Brava regarded his own clean, black uniform in the looking glass. His ramer cuff was polished, but he did not intend to ignite the weapon at the wedding, despite Mandan's cajoling. In a chastising tone, Utho had said, "A ramer is not a parlor trick. It is a device of war. I will have enough occasion to use it when we clash with the Isharans."

Despite his disappointment, Mandan knew not to argue with him. Servants helped him don his ruffled shirt, jerkin, and blue cape lined with spotted fur. A woman fumbled with the fastenings, while a young man used a felt brush to remove any lint. Presenting him with a heavy necklace of aquamarines and gold, one servant regarded it critically. "Perhaps we should find something smaller, Sire? Is this a bit too much?"

Mandan was miffed. "I am the konag. What could possibly be too much?"

"We would not want you to outshine your beautiful bride, my konag."

His expression darkened with displeasure. "These stones belonged to rather have joined the assault himself, galloping forward to strike down the rebels who had defied the konag's decree.

Mandan brightened. "Look Utho, she's already here!"

A group of beautiful ladies stood in elaborate gowns, their hair coiffed high and ornate with braids. Lira was tall and thin, a vision of beauty with long tresses of red hair that hung loose, just like his mother's. "She is the loveliest bride in the history of the three kingdoms," Mandan declared, then said in a louder voice, "In the history of the world! Even the ancient wreths could not have rivaled beautiful Lady Lira."

Hampered by his garments, he trudged up the stone steps between the two regal stone lions, until he reached the entry platform, where the young woman waited for him.

As Konag Mandan took his place beside his bride-to-be, he looked like the victor of an entire continent. Lira giggled, obviously so far out of her depth she was ready to swoon. She greeted Mandan with a formal curtsy, and he gave her a bow. "I would rather sweep you into my arms with a passionate kiss, my lady. But there will be time for that later, just the two of us."

Blushing, she looked away as her mood changed. "I wish my father were here. This is my wedding day."

Mandan grew serious. "My father is not here either. We are much the same. And my mother is gone, as is yours. . . . Another thing we have in common. Are we not the perfect couple?"

Lira was troubled, but she forced a smile, then turned her shining expression to the gathered crowd.

The chief legacier stood in her robes, proud of her station. Vicolia was far less somber than when she had spoken of the death and legacy of Conndur the Brave. She raised her hands and addressed the crowd in a deep, husky voice. "People of Convera, you are here to celebrate a joining of two beautiful people, a unification of our hearts and minds. These two legacies will be bound together, forever written side by side in the book of eternity."

Utho heard wistful sighs out in the audience, saw their smiles and their bright eyes as they imagined the perfect romance. Having watched Mandan for years, though, Utho had seen little romance in the young man's heart. At least the konag made all the proper gestures, and maybe he'd even convinced himself.

Standing here, Utho paused to think about his own lost wife and daughters. But ever since the day the Isharans killed them, Utho had allowed no love in his heart.

The chief legacier droned on, and the people repeated the phrases she called out. All the citizens of Convera, and by extension the entire Commonwealth, were partners in this marriage. When Vicolia finished her pronouncement, a stonemason approached the sheet of white marble on which had been carved the names Konag Mandan of the Colors and Queen Lira of the Commonwealth. As the hushed audience watched, the mason used hammer and chisel to engrave a binding line on the stone's surface, joining the two names together.

Vicolia raised her hands. "Your legacies are linked in stone, in legend, and in our hearts."

Mandan took Lira's hand and lifted both their arms high. The crowd cheered. Satisfied, the chief legacier pressed her palms together. "It is a glorious day."

Utho was relieved the wedding was over, but his mind was preoccupied with thoughts of Lord Cade's victory. He finally allowed himself a thin smile. "It is a glorious day."

95

WHEN Glik awoke again, she felt disoriented. She also felt a strong pull in her heart, like a lifeline. She closed her eyes, held on to the feeling of strength, comfort, companionship. *Inside the circle. Outside the circle.*

Blinking up at the darkness and the stars, she smelled a sour odor in the air, the lingering stench of death from the distant past. Deep in her mind, she heard the whispered remnants of screams from all those who had perished here on this ancient battlefield.

She roused herself on the hard ground in the camp, felt the pain in her arm from a cut . . . blood! Then she remembered Mage Ivun slashing her with his shadowglass knife, pouring her blood into the basin so he could take her visions. Glik felt those images pound back into her mind, the dragon eye in the bottomless pit of obsidian, and the other huge but formless entity that felt even more terrifying, even more strange.

Ivun must have tossed her here, letting her revive from her trance on her own. She touched the cut on her arm, which had been bound up in rags now soaked with sticky red. She struggled into a sitting position, careful not to draw any attention until she understood what was happening. Was this the same night, or the next?

Visions had surrounded her, pulled her into a deep sleep where she continued to dream the alien experiences. She couldn't escape the images; worse, she didn't understand them. With her good hand, Glik drew a circle around her heart and pulled strength from repeating her words.

Wreth guards patrolled the encampment astride snorting augas. Several captives had died during the escape attempt, and the rest now hunched over meager fires, clinging to the thin comfort of ragged blankets. Others just lay on the hard ground pretending to sleep, counting the hours until they would be forced to excavate the black glass again. Cheth sat cross-legged at a small fire not far away, staring intensely into the coals.

Amid the turmoil and dread that filled her heart, Glik felt an unexpected strength as well. She pressed her good hand against her breastbone and closed her eyes as she inhaled. Now she knew what she felt. The heart link! It was Ari!

She peered into the clear, starry night. Because the Plain of Black Glass was a dead place, there were no night sounds of hunting birds or wild animals, not even insect songs. The only sounds were the augas and the wreth guards.

A shadow streaked overhead, accompanied by the quick flap of feathered wings. In a low whisper, Glik said, "Ari, you're here! *Cra*, I've missed you."

The reptile bird flew closer, but made no sound, not even her familiar clicks and burbles. The ska dropped into the shadows around Glik and fluttered her blue wings. The surge of warmth inside the girl's heart felt like melted honey. She reached out to let Ari land on her good arm, and she stroked the pale blue feathers and sapphire scales. Ari laid her head in Glik's cupped palm, and a low humming came from her throat.

Glik felt the ribbon collar around the ska's small neck. "What have you seen, Ari? What message did you bring me?" She rubbed her thumb on the mothertear.

Activated, the diamond spilled a glowing image into the air, and Glik forced herself not to gasp. Penda! She looked beautiful with her long dark hair and large brown eyes, but her face was drawn with concern. It had been so long since she'd seen her adopted sister.

"Glik, my dear sister, we know where you are. We know about the treachery of the sandwreths. Please don't give up hope! Adan Starfall and I will come for you. We are trying to find a way."

Another face drifted into the image—Hale Orr. "And the Utauks will help."

"We will come for you," Penda repeated and drew a circle around her heart.

Glik reached out longingly, and her fingers passed through the projection. When the message ended, her heart swelled even more. "The beginning is not the end," she said.

Ari made a low ratcheting sound, and Glik looked up to see a large dark shape. Cheth had crept up silently and also heard Queen Penda's message. "So they know about the camp. But will that help us?"

"She is the queen," Glik said. "Penda will help in any way she can."

Cheth clenched a fist and looked out beyond the fringes of the camp. "Then we have to be willing to fight, too."

Suddenly the ska reeled back, letting out an alarmed click. Cheth spun and dropped into a fighting stance. Three wreth warriors strode up, seeing the blue ska. One pulled out a spiraled spear, while the others grabbed their bows. "A little dragon! A spy."

Ari flapped her wings, and Glik snapped her arm up to fling the reptile bird into the air. Whistling, the ska soared up and away, but the wreth warriors nocked arrows and drew back their bows.

Glik screamed in alarm, and her cry startled the wreths. Their arrows flew astray. Ari dodged and swooped in the air, pounding her small wings to gain altitude. The third warrior hurled his spear, which grazed the ska's tail feathers.

"Leave her alone!" Glik could feel the ska's terror through her heart link. She threw herself onto the nearest guard, but he knocked her aside. The thrown spear clattered among the rocks on the far side of the camp.

The wreths shot another set of arrows. "Kill it!"

Ari squawked, tumbled in the air, then flew off again. She streaked down low and drove herself upward in an arc, gaining height.

Glik cheered when Ari flew far enough away that the wreth arrows could never reach her.

The warriors glared at her. "Vermin," one grumbled. "Little dragons." They stalked away.

Glik's heart kept pounding, and she drew a circle again and again, trying to calm herself.

Troubled, Cheth bent down to snatch something from the rocky ground. She returned to Glik, extending a long pale feather that the wreth spear had knocked loose. "Keep this, and Ari will always be with you."

Glik held the feather against her heart before tucking it into her loose tunic, where the wreths wouldn't find it. "Ari is always with me."

96

GALLOPING hard, King Kollanan led his rescue troops to the ancient city under siege. In the distance the orange glow from Yanton rose up from where the homes had been torched.

"Ride," Kollanan shouted as the walled ruins loomed in front of them. The din of fighting grew louder ahead. "Ride! We have to save them."

The Norterran riders circled to where Cade's troops had massed at the main gates. Koll let out a loud roar of challenge, and his soldiers added their voices, building the sound into a thunderous threat. "Ancestors' blood, they will know we are coming, and they will be afraid."

As Storm galloped forward, Koll reached down to snatch his war hammer from where it was tied to the saddle. He swung the weapon high.

Without slowing the horse, Lasis clamped his ramer in place and drew blood to ignite the fiery sword. He raised his blazing hand like a beacon to guide the Norterran army. It was still a pitched battle outside the gates when the reinforcements arrived. Two other ramers shone on the dark battlefield. One must belong to Elliel, but the other?

The charge struck Cade's standing army from their unprotected flank. The Commonwealth troops turned to defend against the unexpected assault, but the Norterran riders drove in and scattered the core of Cade's foot soldiers. The invaders waved the open-hand banner as if it would protect them, but Kollanan considered himself a Norterran, first and foremost—especially now that the konag had turned against them. He felt a deep ache in his heart as he swung his hammer into the helmet of one large, angry soldier who blundered in front of Storm. They should not have been enemies!

Shouts resonated among the invading forces, wails of despair, cries of disbelief. It took a moment for Koll to understand their words as the news spread. "Lord Cade is dead. Cade has been slain!"

Kollanan would rather have executed the treacherous man himself. His charging army drove a wedge through the punitive forces. Some of Cade's cavalry soldiers pulled their horses together and tried to make a stand, but the king careened into them and swung his hammer, crushing the chest of an opponent. "Stand down!" he yelled. "Your lord is dead!"

Soon enough, Kollanan's reinforcements overwhelmed the invaders, and Cade's army broke ranks and scattered, especially after they learned that their commander had been killed. Norterran riders drove the enemy forces apart in a wild rout. Seeing their defeat, many of the ranks dropped their swords and surrendered. Kollanan's riders pursued scattered contingents into the countryside. Even if some stragglers got away, it would be a long while before anyone could make it back to Osterra.

As the fighters milled about, Kollanan rode toward the two blazing ra-mers, drawn to the Bravas. Before he could reach them, though, the fiery swords extinguished themselves, one by one.

∾

The screams above finally stopped, but Shadri remained underground. The catacombs beneath the sinkhole had once seemed sinister and terrifying, but now they kept her safe. She blew out her candle and closed her eyes—a pointless gesture in the darkness—and pressed against the wall as she lis-tened to the large *thing* prowling about. She might have to retreat deeper into the tunnels, even though she didn't know where she was going. At the moment she was too fearful to move.

The monster outside seemed intent on killing the brigands, for which she was glad. Their screams had all stopped.

Before long, the silence stretched into a cavernous lack of sound, though she could hear the distant noises of continuing battle. She hoped Elliel was safe, and she wondered what had happened to Thon. . . . What if he had been killed, too?

After a long moment, the dangling rope twitched, jerked, then began to withdraw. With a yelp, Shadri snatched the end, and the rope went taut in her hand. She heard a patter of pebbles, footsteps descending the steep slope, and a familiar voice called, "Are you down there, scholar girl?"

Shadri shouted with great exuberance, "I'm here! There's a . . . monster out there. I think it's a dragon."

"I am safe," Thon said, and she realized that he hadn't answered her com-ment. "The battle is nearly over."

She found a sturdy foothold, pulled on the rope, and climbed out of the hole.

Thon was partway down the crater to meet her, steadying himself with the rope. "I believe we won."

Shadri spotted blood running down the opposite side of the sinkhole, leaking from mangled bodies in leather armor. She saw blue Commonwealth tunics saturated with deep red.

Thon didn't seem to see them as he reached down for her. "Let me pull you up."

&

Elliel's wrist throbbed from the bite of the golden cuff, and her hand burned with a fire that did not consume. She faced the other Brava who stood over the body of Cade. Even though the vile nobleman was dead, Elliel wanted to kick his corpse and keep kicking him for what he had done to her. But she was a Brava, and Bravas had honor.

Gant held his blazing ramer as if he didn't remember what to do with it.

Elliel made no move. "Are you going to fight me now? Are you aware of what your bonded lord did to me?"

The other man nodded. "Yes, I know. He destroyed your reputation. He drugged and assaulted you, and his jealous wife tried to murder you for what he himself did." His pockmarked face was ruddy as he looked at her. "Is there more?"

Elliel was surprised. "Probably, but you have the gist of it. In the name of justice, the name of honor, Cade needed to pay for his crimes."

Gant assessed the smoking wound. "And so he has." He extinguished his flame and let his arms hang limp, leaving himself vulnerable should Elliel choose to attack him. After a moment's hesitation, she extinguished her own ramer.

Lasis rode up, holding his fiery sword high. He looked down at the body of Lord Cade, then searched for explanations in the faces of the other two Bravas.

Gant continued, as if he were talking to himself. "Lord Cade was my bonded lord, and I did as he commanded . . . but I regretted my decision." He looked at his hand, which had recently been engulfed in bright fire. "Now my bond is broken."

Elliel felt sick, knowing it wasn't over. "Utho is worse. He did far more damage than this petty man did." She glanced at the battlefield around them, all the unnecessary deaths. "And he continues to do so."

"I know Utho well enough," Gant said. "I traveled with him to Fulcor Island, and he could not abide the fact that Conndur suggested an alliance with the Isharans."

Elliel felt unsettled. "Every Brava knows about Valaera, what Isharans did to us. That crime has never been punished, or even addressed."

"True, but the konag considered the wreths and Ossus to be a greater threat. I heard him speak to the empra during their parley session, heard him offer a truce. It seemed to me the empra was willing to consider the idea, but Utho did not want to hear it." Gant paused as if something had just occurred to him. "In fact, Utho was furious . . . and he was the last person to see the konag before he was murdered."

Before long, King Kollanan approached them on horseback. His face and beard were spattered with blood, and his war hammer dripped with gore. He rode through the unsettled enemy soldiers without striking out at them.

Lasis spoke to Gant. "Conndur was right. The wreths are our true enemy, and they are more powerful than all the armies of Ishara combined. Frostwreths have swarmed down from the north, and sandwreths have secretly taken human prisoners as slaves. After their own war—if any humans survive—they mean to wake the dragon and bring about the end of the world."

Listening, Kollanan halted Storm in front of Gant. "Will you fight with us? We could always use another Brava."

Gant took a step closer and gave a formal bow. "Kollanan the Hammer, king of Norterra, I believe Konag Mandan issued malicious orders in sending Cade's army against you. I know that the Isharans are not our friends, but by the wreth blood that flows in my own veins, I understand legends and legacies." He looked around the battlefield, which was lit by scattered fires and the light of the gibbous moon. "And I know where I must fight." He turned his back on Cade's corpse. "Will you accept my bonded service?"

Kollanan looked at the body on the ground, then faced the Brava man. "I accept your service. Come and join us in the real fight for the fate of the world."

97

RONDO'S men removed Tafira's gag after hours of hard riding, when it would do her no good to scream. The treacherous escort soldiers had been trained in the Osterran cavalry, and they knew how to ride through unmarked forests and live off the land. Because they were fleeing with the queen as hostage, they remained out of view on their way across the north.

"I can't decide whether we should dump her at Konag Mandan's feet trussed like an animal, or if we should let her surrender herself," Rondo said.

Chuckling, the men debated the matter while they set up an isolated camp in the pine forests. Though she seethed inside, Tafira held her silence as she sat with her arms bound, her ankles lashed together. She shifted her body to lean against a large rock.

Two of her abductors piled dead wood in the clearing and lit a campfire. The night was cold, much more frigid than Tafira expected, and she guessed that the frostwreths were working their insidious magic to spread the tendrils of winter.

"Nothing to say, my lovely queen?" Sergeant Headan prodded, a sneer dripping from every word.

"Not to any of you."

"Then we didn't even need the gag," Rondo said. Sitting on a fallen log across from her, the captain used the whetstone from his pack to sharpen his sword in a clumsy threat. "Even after all your years living here, I can still hear your accent."

Tafira's gaze was ready to strike sparks for another fire. She remembered the castle guards running out into the courtyard, sounding the alarm as they saw the Commonwealth men ride off with her. "You know my king will find you. He will crush your skull with his hammer."

Rondo laughed. "Hasn't he already committed enough crimes against the Commonwealth?"

The escort soldiers rummaged through their packs and took out pre-served food they had found in the saddlebags. Headan squatted in front of Tafira, munching on dried meat and sweet biscuits. Chewing loudly, he mused, "She's already forfeit, Captain. Even though she's a foreigner, she still has a certain beauty about her. Older than I'd like, but . . ." He sniffed. "I've never had an Isharan woman. Have you?"

Rondo shook his head, and the sergeant pressed his idea: "We can all take turns, maybe a few tonight, a few tomorrow. It's a long ride back home. By the time we reach Convera, we'd each have an Isharan woman—and a queen, at that! You can't make us pass that up, Captain."

Rondo stroked the side of his face. "Nothing says we have to deliver her in perfect condition. Konag Mandan wouldn't care."

Tafira knew these men were full of empty bluster, but she could see a dif-ference in their eyes. They were angry at what they had been through, in-censed because King Kollanan had not sent them home weeks ago. Under normal circumstances, she knew these soldiers wouldn't have the nerve to harm her, but these were not normal circumstances. Nothing had been nor-mal since the day the wreths swept over Lake Bakal.

"She is a beautiful woman," Rondo admitted. He rose from the fallen log and inspected her like a customer evaluating the wares of an unreliable mer-chant.

Tafira spat at him, and he flinched aside, scowling. She said, "If you dam-age me, I will be worthless as a hostage. If any harm comes to me, my be-loved Kollanan will declare his own vengewar on you, and all of Osterra will pay the price."

Rondo covered his alarm. "Ho! Listen to such boldness from a woman tied up on the ground and far from home!"

"Such boldness comes from the rightful queen of Norterra." She twisted against the ropes around her wrists. The men had been lax, tying her with sloppy knots, and she could probably work herself free in time. "Give me a knife and let me play with you. I am good with a knife. Ask your two men who are dead on the stable floor."

Rondo reddened and struck her hard across the face. "You make me think that a little bit of rape might be a fitting punishment for the murder of Com-monwealth soldiers."

"Why don't you let us throw knives and practice, Captain?" said another soldier. "I'm fairly good at it. Ancestors' blood, I even killed a rabbit once."

"Accidents happen," Tafira said in a mocking tone.

Rondo grabbed her by the arm and hauled her to her feet. "Practice is a good idea." She stumbled as Rondo and one of his men pulled her to a thick silver pine. "Get more ropes from the packs."

She twisted her arms. The bindings were loose and slick from the poor knots and her own perspiration, but she couldn't slip free.

Rondo pressed her against the trunk. A soldier offered another coil of rope to wrap around her waist and the tree. He looped the rope around her several times, lashing her to the tree, even binding her legs so she couldn't kick.

Rondo stepped back and drew his dagger. "Just how good are you, men? I don't want any mistakes." He sniffed. "A cut or two would be fine, but pray you don't kill her."

Tafira strained against the ropes.

"Don't worry, they will try *not* to hit you." Rondo stepped back and threw his knife first. The blade struck the tree just above her head, chipping off a chunk of bark. She flinched.

The brash young rabbit killer threw his knife next, and it skewered the tree to her left. He whistled at his prowess, but Tafira held her tongue. She thought he had been aiming somewhere else entirely.

The men took turns, egging each other on. Tafira steeled herself and hated them. A careless knife did cut her arm, and blood ran down the tree, mixing with hardened globs of pitch. One miscalculated throw could plunge through her throat or heart, and they were far from any village where they might find a doctor. Tafira would have been safer if they had raped her.

The men's laughter was so loud they didn't hear their horses snort and stamp, straining against their hobbles on the outskirts of the camp. Tafira looked across the campfire and felt a deep flow of fear worse than these raucous men had inspired.

Captain Rondo turned, knife in hand. "What's that?"

Pale figures emerged from the trees, strange warriors with ivory hair, corpse-pale skin, and eyes the color of dull steel. They rode shaggy white creatures larger than bears, and they were armed with swords made of ice and quicksilver. Their armor was a metallic blue.

"Wreths!" Tafira hissed.

The campfire had attracted the ominous warriors. Emerging from the forest, they exuded the power of magic and superior strength.

Rondo's men scrambled in alarm. One ran to snatch his throwing knife from the pine trunk beside her.

The captain stepped forward to meet the strangers. "We are soldiers of the

Commonwealth. We serve Konag Mandan." He squared his shoulders, as if those words might strike fear into the frostwreths.

The lead warrior sniffed. "We do not care." His wolf-steed growled, sounding like a cauldron about to boil over.

The escort soldiers stood tense and amazed, not knowing how to respond. Tafira could not move, lashed to the silver pine.

"We have no quarrel with you," said Rondo.

The wreths let out a resonant laughter that sounded like breaking ice. "We will make one."

With unhurried, even casual movements, the frostwreths advanced. The first spear skewered Rondo through the chest. The point was so sharp that it glided all the way through his breastbone and sprouted out his spine. The captain clasped the spiraled shaft, then collapsed backward.

The Commonwealth soldiers ran forward to fight. They barely had time to let out a battle cry before the wreths were upon them. The pale warriors hacked and stabbed methodically, like farmers harvesting a garden.

Tied to the tree, Tafira could only watch in horror tinged with satisfaction. Her abductors died—decapitated, impaled, chopped to pieces. The wreths unleashed the wolf-steeds, and the white beasts fell upon the hobbled horses, tearing the animals apart. The fighting came so close that Tafira was splattered with blood.

Though the battle-seasoned Commonwealth soldiers outnumbered the frostwreths two to one, the fighting was over in short order. Tafira had not made a sound. All of her captors lay dead in bloody disarray.

The lead wreth had barely exerted himself, although his long hair was tangled from the effort. "This is what Queen Onn commanded us to do."

"It is a success, Irri," said one of the blood-streaked warriors.

"It is a beginning." He produced a large snowball, which he held in the palm of one hand. As he concentrated, it glowed and became smooth and clear, a sphere of ice. The warrior—Irri—held the transparent ball and turned in a full circle, collecting images of the slaughtered soldiers. Still holding up the globe, he approached Tafira, bound to her tree. She remained perfectly still, like a rabbit staring down a viper.

"And you are another one." Irri regarded her with cold intensity. Tafira didn't know whether to thank the wreths for killing her captors. It was not the sort of revenge she had hoped for.

"I am the queen of Norterra," she said. "They were my enemies."

The wreth man continued to stare at her with eyes the dull gray of winter clouds. "Human squabbles do not concern us. You all belong to us."

A tangible chill rippled from the warrior's body. The white wolf-steeds continued to feed loudly on the dead horses. Tafira imagined the wreths would take her prisoner, bring her to the frozen palace.

The thought that she might see her grandson Birch gave her a glint of hope, but she hated these wreths as much as Kollanan did. They had marched down from the north and killed Jhaqi and her family, destroyed the village.

"Queen Onn told us to kill any human we found," another wreth reminded Irri. "As an example."

Still holding up his ice sphere, the lead warrior nodded. "She did. There is no mercy."

Without taunting, without threat, he drew an ice knife with his other hand and made a quick move. The edge was so sharp that Tafira barely felt the cut as he slashed across her throat.

if it might explode from the pressure. "But you also hurt Serepol! You caused too much damage. You need to control yourself."

He sucked in a deep breath. His throat and lungs burned. "I am your key priestlord." He kept his arms outstretched, his fingers splayed, and now he drew them into fists. "I am your master!"

Like a browbeaten child, the godling shuddered. For all its swooping magnificence, Klovus could feel that its essence was much more diffuse after such an enormous expenditure of energy. Even though it had destroyed and consumed its rival, it had begun to fade substantially. When he had used the deity to lift enormous stone blocks for the construction, the people had offered their full faith, fed it with their awe. But now the terrified worshippers had fled, withdrawing their support, and the godling was cast adrift from its temple, its source.

Some of the crowd watched the priestlord from peripheral buildings. They feared his strength as much as they feared the godling. "Hear us, save us." It started as a low chant, then others raised the prayer higher. "Hear us, save us!"

Klovus realized that they were chanting for his benefit, giving *him* strength to control the godling. "I need you to obey," he said to the thing. "There will be other battles, other enemies. The Hethrren have been hurt. You did your task, for now. You need to rest."

Like a deflating bladder, the godling shuddered, became less of a behemoth. Klovus used all of his power, all of his faith to wrestle it into submission. "Follow me!"

He strode off, and the godling moved like a ball of storm clouds behind him. The Hethrren visages roiling inside the entity's body had disappeared, but more faces appeared now, bubbling up—the face of Klovus, all of them. His heart filled with warmth, dedication, even love at this message from the godling.

The people withdrew as Klovus led the deity back down the ruined streets. He moved at a brisk pace, even though he was exhausted from all the running and shouting, and from his mental grappling with the godling. He saw several nondescript men following him along the side streets, blending with the crowd. Black Eels. Their clothes were torn, some were bloody; two of them had visibly broken arms, but they showed no pain. He was glad that some of them had survived.

He was also shaken to see the dead bodies that littered the streets. Wailing people bent over fallen family or friends; stunned merchants stared at the ruins of their businesses; fathers dug through collapsed walls and shouted

98

RAISING his hands, Key Priestlord Klovus begged his godling. The monstrous entity roiled like a terrible storm at the edge of the ruined waterfront. After consuming the harbor godling, it struggled to contain its form and incorporate new powers, which gave Klovus an opening.

The connection that he always had with the godlings reeled out, and he tried to capture, or at least calm, the gigantic deity. He had once experienced the same affinity for the harbor godling, and now he felt its loss deep in his heart.

Around him, a swath of Serepol had been ravaged, the buildings smashed and toppled. Fires crackled in the ruins, and bodies lay strewn about, some of them Hethrren, some of them local residents.

But Klovus stared only at the monstrous godling. "Please stop!" he said, and his words finally penetrated the thing's consciousness. He stretched his arms higher. "You must stop! This is our city. *Your* city, your people." He began to sob. "You hurt the followers who put their faith in you."

The godling lashed out with a pillar of smoke and fire, then clenched itself and withdrew. So many worshippers had placed their hopes and prayers into this entity, but now that belief was replaced with terror. On the godling's uncertain surface, heads and faces rose like bubbles in a boiling pot, many of them the shaggy heads of barbarians wearing demonic expressions, one face after another. The godling was trying to communicate something.

"Yes, the Hethrren," Klovus said, relieved that the entity had halted its rampage. "The Hethrren are our enemies. I told you to kill them."

Lightning flashed in the godling's heart, and additional cloudy arms stretched out. The enormous force swelled at the waterfront. The fish market was in ruins. The harbor temple had been damaged, its façade scorched and blasted.

"Yes, you killed many Hethrren," Klovus said. "That was what I wanted you to do." He felt the struggling force within him, and his heart pounded as the names of lost family members. Others just stood staring and broken. Many of the victims were barbarians, smashed and torn with obvious malice, but they did not outnumber the dead of ordinary Serepol citizens.

Klovus prodded the godling as he hurried toward the Magnifica. As soon as they approached the temple square, the entity expanded in the air and picked up speed, as if anxious to be home. It flowed formless, an inferno of dust and smoke, and became more substantial as it rose to the upper platform of the half-constructed temple. It towered like a snarling guard dog but chained, able to threaten but no longer attack.

Klovus stood below, looking up. "Go! Return behind your spelldoor. Gather your strength until I call upon you again. The people will make sacrifices to reward you for what you have done." He pushed aside his doubts and fears because he knew the thing could sense them. The godling pulled itself back into the temple like smoke retreating into a chimney.

Klovus climbed the thick stone steps to the first level, saw the shattered sculptures that were meant to represent other godlings across Ishara. He raised his hands and pushed with his mind one last time. "Back to your place."

The godling obeyed. As soon as it was gone, the key priestlord felt the last vestiges of strength drain from him, and he collapsed onto the temple steps. He placed his head in his hands, blind to everything else around him. Right now he didn't want to see the damage, did not want to count the dead.

He feared the people would pray to the empra again with redoubled fervor.

Klovus didn't know how long he rested there, drained and incalculably weak, but he looked up when he heard a gruff voice. Several battered Hethrren approached him, their hair knotted and tangled, their furs mangled. One man bled from his cheek down into his unruly beard.

And Magda. The ugly woman stood before him unharmed. She was massive, intimidating, as ominous as the godling in her own way. He could see traces of fear and respect behind her expression. She loomed over him, and Klovus tried not to cringe. He was vulnerable now. She could simply kill him.

"I thought you were weak and soft, lover. But you have a power that I did not realize before." Her grin revealed her sharpened tooth. "I have reconsidered my opinion of you. You are a poor lover, but you may yet be useful." She embraced him with a beefy arm, nearly crushing his shoulders. "Together, we can overwhelm the Commonwealth."

99

THE dragon had flown off, injured and defeated, but the damage it did lingered across the Utauk camp. A thunderous silence filled the night as the world settled into the numb aftermath. Adan heard the snap of fires and the moans of the wounded, smelled blood, smoke, and dirt.

Beside him under the oak, Penda hissed with her increasing labor pains. "I'm glad you are here, my Starfall." She reached out to hold him, then winced. "But I do want this to be over!"

Xar, calm now that the huge dragon had disappeared, fluttered to a lower branch above Penda. He bobbed his head and looked down at her as if ready to comment on the birth.

"It is not a quick process," said Hale. "*Cra,* a baby doesn't just pop out!" He flashed his gold tooth, but he was too worried for it to be a smile. "I have seen it before."

Adan stroked his wife's dark hair, then looked around the camp, distraught. "I am not a midwife, and I am not trained in this. I don't want to leave anything to chance." He rose and turned to Hale. "Stay here with her. I'll find some of the Utauk women. They've been through many birthings."

Hale agreed. "Even Shella din Orr will do, if you can't find anyone else."

"Hurry back," Penda said.

Adan did not want to leave her side, but he needed help with the birth. Carrying his drawn shadowglass sword, he sprinted out of the trees into the shambles of torn tents and overturned wagons.

Adan came upon a crushed auga, its large mouth open, black tongue lolling to the side. Another injured beast twitched its head back and forth, but its spine was broken, its slitted eyes were glazed with agony. He stood over the creature, seeing its pain, and remembered when brutal Quo had commanded one of the augas to batter itself to death against the gates of Bannriya. Feeling no hatred toward the two-legged mount, Adan thrust his sword beneath its chin and up into its brain. The auga gurgled and slumped in death, as if in relief.

Then he found the wreth corpses. Several of the golden-skinned warriors lay with broken spears and shattered swords. The bodies were mangled and red. Other wreths lay wounded and moaning. The entire attacking party had been defeated, their weapons and magic insufficient against the dragon.

As he hurried through the camp, looking for someone to tend to Penda, Adan stared at the fallen warriors. The sandwreths had been arrogant and seemingly invincible, but this massacre put the lie to their confidence. If that dragon had been merely a fragment of Ossus, then what was the huge dragon himself like? How large and powerful were the sins and dark thoughts of a god? He gazed down at the dead mage, sprawled with her arms and legs twisted at the wrong angles. "What folly!"

A pair of bearded Utauk men came up to him. "King Adan, we are glad you survived. Thank you for your assistance."

He recognized Shella's two nephews. "And your grandmother?"

"She lives. We will set up a temporary lean-to for her," Emil said.

"She says she has been through worse," Burdon added. "*Cra,* I don't want to know about it."

Adan pushed aside other worries. "I need a midwife. Penda is about to give birth. She shouldn't do it alone." He looked back over his shoulder. "I need to be there."

The nephews consulted with each other. "We will find someone. Don't worry."

They split apart and began working their way through the camp, shouting. As the one point of urgency faded a little, Adan looked around, hoping to find his young squire or the two Banner guards. "Hom!" he called. "Captain Elcior!"

Adan heard a muttered curse of pain, and a wreth noble clawed his way out of a collapsed Utauk tent. Adan recognized Quo with his gold and ivory hair, jewels and bangles. Severely injured, Queen Voo's brother struggled to get to his feet. He winced in pain, groaned, and fell back to the ground, pressing his hand against a deep gash across his torso. Adan stepped closer to the gravely wounded sandwreth.

Seeing him, Quo let out a sharp laugh. "Ah, Adan Starfall! You have joined us in another dragon hunt." He coughed, spat out a bubble of blood that formed between his lips. "This one was not quite so enjoyable." His side had been torn open, his ribs shattered. For any human it would have been a mortal wound, but the wreth held on, using his magic to keep himself alive.

Unlike the dying auga he had dispatched, this wretched man evoked no sympathy from Adan. "How did you know to come here? Were you hunting the dragon?"

"That was merely a fortunate coincidence." Quo coughed in an attempt to laugh, and more blood came out of his mouth. Annoyed, he wiped it away with his other hand. "My sister sent us to track down Penda Orr. You thought you could hide her from us, but Voo wants her." He tried to prop himself up. "Is the baby born yet?"

Adan glowered. "You cannot have my wife or child."

"It is not for you to decide." The wreth's eyes narrowed. "It is unwise to stand in the way of what my sister wants."

Adan felt a deep chill. Penda and her father had hidden among the Utauk tribes, but Quo and his wreth party had found her somehow, tracked her to this isolated heart camp. No doubt Queen Voo would keep hunting. With a sick hollow in his heart, Adan realized he could not keep his wife safe from the sandwreths. He also remembered the most recent mothertear images from Glik's ska: Quo was himself involved with the vile work camp and the enslaved humans.

The sandwreths pretended to be allies, but Adan knew they were just as evil as their rivals to the north. Worse, they were coming after Penda and the baby, and Adan could not abide that.

Struggling to push himself upright, Quo spoke in an annoyed voice. "Help me, human. I can tend to my own wounds. If there is a place for me to concentrate and enter a brief spellsleep, I will be healed."

Adan stared down at him, worked his jaw.

The wreth's topaz eyes bored into him with imperious command. "As soon as I am well, I will escort your wife and child to Voo. You cannot stop it." He tried to chuckle.

When Adan refused to respond, he saw the noble's expression change to uncertainty, then fear. Adan held his shadowglass-inlaid sword, the weapon Queen Voo had helped him to create. She claimed that the substance would help human weapons fight the frostwreths.

And sandwreths, too.

"You will not have Penda, or my baby. I *can* stop you." He leaned down and whispered, "I know about the labor camps you hide in the desert. The human prisoners you have taken." As the wreth's eyes widened in surprise,

Adan straightened. "Someday, legends might say that you died fighting a dragon . . . or maybe no one will remember you at all."

He thrust the point of his sword into Quo's chest, feeling the sharp steel and the thrumming shadowglass.

The wreth man struggled, raised his hands, but Adan shoved the blade all the way through his twisted heart, pinning him to the ground. Quo convulsed, grappled, and then died.

Adan could not allow himself to regret his actions. "Humans are not your slaves or your servants. We don't belong to anyone but ourselves."

Two horses approached, and Adan saw Seenan and Captain Elcior, with Hom stumbling behind them. The squire looked distraught, his clothes streaked with blood and dirt. All three had witnessed what their king just did.

Looking at them, then scanning the wreckage of the camp, Adan reached a snap decision. "Most of Quo's party were killed by the dragon. Find any other sandwreths who are wounded." He inhaled deeply. "You know what to do."

The two Banner guards looked at each other with hardened expressions, but Hom didn't understand. "Shouldn't we help them?"

"No. They cannot be allowed to leave. They came to take Queen Penda and our child!"

Captain Elcior raised his own sword. The dark shadowglass glinted in the starlight. "We will find any that still live. No sandwreth will survive this night."

Shella's nephews came running up to Adan. "We sent two midwives to Penda, and they say all is well. She will be fine." Their gazes went to the body of Quo, and then to Adan and his bloody sword.

The king straightened. "We can leave no wreths alive tonight. No witnesses. Quo and his party did not come here to fight the dragon—they came to steal Queen Penda."

"Wreths are not to be trusted," Emil agreed, scratching his thick beard. "Not sandwreths, not frostwreths. Mother Orr says that over and over." The two men reached a decision. "They were never here. We will dispose of them, remove all trace."

Adan thanked the two men, then ran back to help his wife.

100

WITH Lord Cade's scattered army on the run, the Norterran defenders galloped after them and rounded up prisoners. Although most of the soldiers surrendered, a few escaped, and Kollanan grimly accepted the fact that eventually word would get back to Convera.

For the time being, the king remained at Bahlen's wreth city, glad that the defenses had held against the main assault. The Yanton villagers emerged from the shelters, terrified but alive. They had so many questions that their king could not answer, devastated to know that soldiers under the Commonwealth banner had tried to kill them. Koll sent a contingent of his reinforcements to ride to the damaged town, leading the people in an urgent effort to see what they could salvage. It would take a long time to put out the fires.

While the survivors tended the wounded and counted the dead, Koll took counsel with his Bravas. Together, they grappled with the idea that Konag Mandan had now declared himself their enemy. Koll regretted every single soldier he had killed this night, but there had been no way around it.

Elliel said, "We requested help from him, and this is how he responds!"

Lasis shook his head. "I am not familiar with the deep politics of the three kingdoms, Sire, but I cannot fathom why the konag—*our konag!*—would send an army against us."

"Even as a prince, Mandan was weak and petulant. He lived under his mother's wing," Koll said, looking down at his bloody war hammer. "After she died, he was never right again."

Elliel looked pale, exhausted from fighting, from her confrontation with Cade, and from what she had realized. Her voice was dark and low. "This was Utho's doing, Sire. Mandan is just a puppet."

Bahlen approached. "What did my town do to deserve this? Why did the konag choose Yanton? Why would he order those soldiers to burn homesteads and harm so many innocent people? We were supposed to be protecting against *wreths!*"

"He was sending a message." Kollanan ground his teeth together. "And I will send one back to him." He looked at the bodies strewn on the battlefield, then turned back to the three Bravas. "You made the right decision, Gant. I believe in Brava honor. I beg you to hold to it."

The rough-featured man clipped the ramer band to his belt and rested his hand on the hilt of his sword. "For centuries, my race held on to hatred against the Isharans, always planning for a vengewar. The anticipation of revenge became its own reward. Yes, the Isharans hurt us long ago . . . but many generations before that, the wreths took advantage of our ancestors. We are half-breeds *because* they ravished our mothers, bred with our fathers. No Brava child was conceived out of love, but of assault."

Elliel said, "We owe the wreths nothing. Even Utho knows that."

Kollanan felt the heavy responsibility of leadership. As king, he had rallied his counties, his vassal lords, enlisting anyone willing to be trained as soldiers. Many loyal veterans had settled in Norterra after the end of the last Isharan war, and he had called them all to arms. It had been easy to convince them to fight against the evil wreths.

But now he had to fight a war on two fronts, two separate enemies—one of them entirely unnecessary. Looking at the dead from both sides on the battlefield, Kollanan considered how these Osterran soldiers had marched across the land for the sole purpose of attacking a harmless village. Why would Mandan pursue this useless conflict, when all energy should have been directed against the wreths? Why did he refuse to see the danger?

Would he now have to split his Norterran army and send troops to the border with Osterra? He needed all of his fighters to defend against a frost-wreth retaliation, but he could not ignore this unprovoked attack from Konag Mandan. He doubted anything good would come of this.

How he wished Tafira were here to counsel and comfort him. She was always his wisest sounding board. He hoped she had kept Fellstaff safe. The city was in good hands.

He scanned the bodies, saw dead soldiers bearing the mountain symbol of Norterra, while others displayed the open hand of the Commonwealth. Bahlen looked disgusted. "When we gather the dead, I want to separate my fighters from . . . those men. Shall we burn the traitors? Bury them in unmarked graves."

Koll felt the heat of anger in his face. "Ancestors' blood, I will not continue the mistake, the stupidity! These soldiers followed orders, but they were evil orders."

"And Cade was an evil man," Elliel said.

Koll nodded. "Mandan may have broken the Commonwealth charter, but I will not. I still believe in the three kingdoms. Treat their fallen with respect. Each soldier likely carries a journal or some sort of identification. Our legaciers will write down the name of every person who died here—on either side—and try to preserve their legacies." The thought made him glance up. "Where is Shadri? Didn't the scholar girl come with you? And Thon. Where is he?"

"They were exploring the northern part of the city." A look of deep concern crossed Elliel's face. "I will go find them." She snatched the reins of the nearest mount and galloped off.

☙

Elliel rode into the ruins, recalling that her friends had gone to investigate the mysterious sinkhole. She shouted their names, and let out a bright gasp of relief to find them both alive.

Thon waved at her. "Elliel, my love! Is the enemy defeated? Did you take care of them?"

"I had help." As she approached, the horse snorted, oddly reluctant to approach Thon, but she pushed forward. She looked past him, seeing the blood that covered his silver chestpiece and leggings, all the mangled bodies scattered around the abandoned plaza. "Cade's soldiers broke through? You fought them?"

"Only a few dozen, but I . . ." He shrugged and looked away with his deep blue eyes. "I do not remember exactly what happened."

Shadri was quieter than usual, obviously troubled. She wiped at her face, but could not smear away her confused expression.

When Elliel swung down from her restless horse and Thon wrapped his arms around her, she smelled an unusual musk about him, something dry and utterly unfamiliar, unlike perspiration or blood or dust.

He seemed in a daze. "I felt anger emanating from these ruins, and I also discovered an unexpected power inside me." He pulled away from her, as if her touch made him uncomfortable. "I felt real strength, and I felt *you*, Elliel." He offered her an uncertain smile. "I sensed your rage—and it made me stronger."

The Brava woman stared at the gleefully splashed blood, the mangled victims. "Those are not sword wounds. What happened?"

"There was a monster," Shadri blurted out. "It was dark in my hiding place, and I found the sculpture of a dragon carved out of shadowglass, and it gave off a kind of . . . angry power. It resonated everywhere. I caught a

glimpse of scales and teeth, claws." She glanced back at the torn bodies, nauseated. "I wish I knew what it was, but I'm afraid to know."

Thon withdrew, looking uncertain. "Something came out of me . . . I
think. I did not see." He spread his fingers, clenched them into fists, and
opened them again.

"The thing was huge," Shadri said. "All dark, with blazing eyes."

"A dragon?" Elliel was prepared to laugh, but she saw that Shadri was entirely serious.

"Or something like a dragon. It was huge and shifting." Shadri looked at
Thon, and he glanced away, as if in shame.

Elliel couldn't understand what the scholar girl was saying. Thon kept
looking helplessly at his hands.

Shadri finally said, "We don't know what Thon is, do we? He was buried
beneath the mountains, and we even thought that he was like the legends of
Kur himself. Gone to hide." She swallowed hard.

Thon seemed to be wrestling with his own thoughts. "I do not remember."

Shadri looked at Elliel. "Thon doesn't know anything about his origin. He
was sealed away from the wreth wars. You found him inside Mount Vada.
What if he was somehow . . . contaminated by the dragon?"

Elliel dreaded what the scholar girl was about to say.

Shadri often spouted questions, facts, or any random idea that occurred
to her. Now, though, her words were ponderous, as if she was afraid to voice
her thoughts. "Another explanation fits, though, doesn't it? We know what
else is buried beneath the Dragonspine Mountains, something powerful."
She blinked. Thon regarded her without arguing, not trying to stop her. He
seemed resigned to the possibility.

Shadri said, "What if Thon himself is Ossus?"

101

KORU'S frostwreth warriors had defeated the stunted dragon, but the effort required all of their magic and weapons. Weeks ago, her war party had set off from the frozen north, confident and determined, ready to face Ossus, their destiny. And a small, crippled dragon had nearly destroyed them. Koru had failed. All of her warriors and mages had failed.

One more warrior died on the second day of their trek home. He coughed blood during the entire ride, spitting scarlet down the white fur of his mount. All their wreth magic and innate healing powers had been insufficient against his injuries, and finally he slid off onto the frozen ground and died.

Koru called a halt. The rest of the war party piled rocks and ice around the body, then Mage Elon called up a searing blue fire that reduced the body to white ash. Their mood was subdued, but Koru did not let it linger. They moved on.

How were the wreths supposed to destroy the great Ossus, as Kur commanded, if the two races squandered their strength fighting one another? Queen Onn did not grasp the magnitude of the challenge. As the battered survivors rode their limping oonuks back north, Koru felt anger. "My mother is a fool," she said aloud.

One of her warriors touched the crusted wound in his side and muttered sourly. Koru couldn't tell if he agreed with her or felt obligated to defend the queen's honor.

"We have seen real dragons now," Koru continued, "yet my mother considers them a problem to be dealt with in the future while she obsesses about the sandwreths. Are they our real enemy?" She growled deep in her throat and tossed her long hair. "Even if sandwreths and frostwreths join forces, will we be strong enough to kill Ossus?"

The wolf-steeds trudged along on bloodied paws. When they reached the snows again, the animals moved with an added burst of energy, but it faded quickly. Now they seemed exhausted and in pain.

They rode for days, traveling north, to where the frigid air felt bracing, refreshing. The scour of ice crystals numbed her cheeks. When Koru at last saw the ice towers in the distance, she realized that the gigantic palace was just another symbol of Queen Onn's arrogance.

She dug her fingers into her oonuk's thick pelt. The beast panted heavily, as if its lungs had been seared. Koru needed to have words with her mother.

֍

Birch sat beside the throne again, hiding his real plans. Onn ignored him as always, but insisted that he remain nearby. She would glance at the boy, reassure herself that he was there, that he adored her, and then pay him no further mind.

Birch had become skilled at hiding his emotions, maintaining a docile mask. In hidden places within the palace, he looked at his reflection in polished ice to remind himself of who he was. He would run his fingers through his ragged brown hair, remembering how his mother had hummed nonsense songs as she clipped his locks. Now his hair was long and shaggy, and Birch didn't like it. He knew his mother would not cut his hair, not ever again.

In the mirror he would observe how the anger and sadness showed in his expressions, and he practiced smoothing his cheeks, keeping his mouth in a straight line, so that nothing showed in his eyes. He did not want Onn to guess that he hated her with all his being.

Birch sat silent and well behaved on the throne dais. He was cold because the air was cold, the floor was cold, the walls were cold. There was no escaping it here in the palace. He had his blanket, and he still had the carved wooden pig that his grandfather had made for him, which he kept well hidden, like a talisman. He was amazed that Onn had not taken the keepsake from him.

The drones had served food earlier and retreated, leaving him alone with the queen as she mused. He had listened to Onn discuss strategy and make war plans. Her lover Irri had gone off to hunt a few token humans in Norterra, but she planned a more complete strike against those who had offended her. Frostwreth armies would wreck Fellstaff, turn the castle to rubble, tear down the walls around the city. She seemed unaware that Birch was listening.

He could never forget how she had blithely massacred so many innocent drones, his friends, as she vented her rage when she'd learned of the Lake Bakal attack. The drones took care of him, considered him special. He had started teaching them, and many now possessed hidden weapons, although the drones didn't know what to do with them—or were unwilling to try. Birch remembered playing pretend battles with his brother and their friends in the village, and he remembered listening to his grandfather tell stories of the Isharan war.

Irri marched pompously into the throne room. He had pulled back his hair and tied it behind his shoulders. He lifted his chin and announced, "I have good news to report, my queen." His bare arms and armor bore dark specks of dried blood.

Onn rose from her throne, noting the red smears. "You do not bother to bathe before presenting yourself to your queen?"

"I thought you might find the smell of human blood enticing, that it might drive you to greater lust."

She laughed. "That is all you think about, Irri!"

Stealthily, Birch retreated to the back of the dais, taking shelter. He managed to slip behind the frozen throne.

Intent on the queen, Irri paid the boy no attention. "I missed you."

Onn sniffed. "Tell me about your victory, and then I will decide how much I missed you."

He squared his shoulders and delivered his report. "You dispatched me to ride south, find human victims, and punish them."

"As a start. We will do much more, but I was impatient." Her voice had a flirtatious lilt. "Show me what you accomplished."

Irri produced an ice sphere, a transparent globe that gleamed and flickered, full of images. Holding it in his palm, he projected the images in the air. "We found a party of their soldiers camped in the forest and killed them all." Turning the sphere, he displayed slain humans in blue Commonwealth jerkins now soaked in blood. "We believe they were some of the soldiers who attacked our fortress at Lake Bakal."

"Good," Queen Onn said. "You are making me more glad to see you."

Irri rotated the ice sphere and showed another image—a woman tied to a tree, a bound hostage. "This one was with them. She said she was their queen."

Birch leaned forward, eyes wide as he recognized his grandmother Tafira. He didn't know why she was bound with ropes, why the soldiers had taken her. In the image, Irri used a frozen blade to slash his grandmother's throat. She bled out quickly and died without a word.

In shock and horror, the boy jerked back, his shoulders striking the ice wall. He clamped his lips together, trying to keep his teeth from chattering.

Irri dissolved the images and pocketed the ice sphere. Onn clasped her hands together. "You have pleased me with this, and I expect you to please me further—after you bathe."

Covering his grin, the warrior bowed and departed.

Birch was sickened and silent, despite the roaring anger inside his head. He squeezed the carved pig in his pocket until his hand ached. He could not let the frostwreths keep hurting him and the people he loved! They had killed so many already, and he needed to do something.

He thought of his grandfather Kollanan, his war stories, his legacy. He remembered his doting grandmother, how she let the boys help in the castle kitchens, peeling and chopping turmeric roots until their fingers were yellow. He thought of fishing with Tomko at the end of the dock on Lake Bakal.

Birch was just a boy, but he would be a warrior someday. King Kollanan had promised that. He was brave, and he knew it. He had proved as much just by surviving.

No other human could get so close to the frostwreth queen. No other human would have such a chance.

Onn stood facing away from him, paying no attention to her human pet. She obviously relished the murderous images Irri had just shown her.

Birch felt the secret knife he hid in his waistband. As he fingered the rough hilt, though, he realized that the blade was just too small—sharp, but short and stubby. It would never kill a powerful frostwreth queen. He needed something deadlier.

Birch didn't think. He reached up, silent as glass, and removed the broken spear from the wall. The weapon was heavy, and the shaft felt cold in his hands, but the long point was sharp, still stained with the blood of Ossus. It was a good weapon.

Birch took two steps forward, leveling the long spear at Queen Onn's back.

His footsteps must have made a whisper on the frozen dais, since she turned at the last moment, arching her eyebrows in amusement. Her large, cold eyes stared at him. "Child, what are you . . ."

Birch shoved the spear into Onn's side. The sharp blade plunged through her filmy gown, cut between her ribs. She let out a grunt and a gasp, but the boy didn't make a sound. He pushed harder, ramming the spear deeper with all the force of his small body.

Queen Onn choked, looked at him in disbelief, and grabbed the spear shaft as if helping him guide it inside her. Her blood blossomed out. With a quiet growl, Birch shoved even harder, and the spear sprouted from her back.

Onn tried to scream, but she had no breath. Blood bubbled from her mouth instead of words, and her knees went weak. The queen collapsed in front of her throne, nearly dragging him down. The spear shaft was the only thing that held her up. "Boy . . ." she gasped. Her face went slack with astonishment.

Birch heard footsteps outside the throne room just before another wreth strode in. Though he knew he was caught, he refused to let go of the spear. He twisted the spiraled shaft in Onn's body, making sure the wreth queen was dead. He didn't care what happened to him now. This was his legacy. Though he was just a child, Birch knew someone would tell his story, would remember him as the one who had killed the leader of the frostwreths.

Covered with Onn's blood, he turned and saw an armored female noble, pale and beautiful. Queen Onn's daughter.

Koru stared at the tableau. Her mother collapsed the rest of the way to the floor like melting ice, and Birch released his hold on the broken spear shaft.

In disbelief, Koru strode to the dais, and Birch faced her without moving from the corpse. They stared at each other. Queen Onn ceased making the sounds of dying, and the room filled with tense silence.

He heard more wreths approaching outside in the corridor, moving with heavy boots and thick armor. Koru's eyes flashed at him. With a sudden motion, she pushed the boy aside just as the other wreths entered the chamber—Irri, along with several battered wreths who had accompanied Koru's war party.

Onn's daughter defiantly grasped the spear shaft that impaled the queen's body. She turned to face the newcomers, who stared at her in shock. Birch backed away.

"I killed my mother, because it is necessary." With a wrench Koru twisted and ripped the spear out of the body. The frostwreth queen slumped in a puddle of her own blood, and Koru held up the spear, which was now stained with the blood of her mother as well as a dragon.

Into the shocked silence, Koru said, "Queen Onn was a poor leader. She would have brought our race to ruin."

She gave a quick glance at Birch, who remained silent, trying to become invisible again. Koru turned her back on the boy, but she didn't seem to be ignoring him. He thought she was somehow protecting him.

"I am now the queen of the frostwreths," Koru said, "and together we will fight the dragon."

102

⁓

AFTER escaping from Serepol Harbor, the *Glissand* caught favorable winds and headed west, back toward the safety of the old world. The navigator set a course far north to catch another current, avoiding Fulcor Island by a wide margin.

During the first day, lookouts spotted distant red-and-white-striped Isharan sails in pursuit, but the warships were slower and poorly guided. The nimble *Glissand* could dart like a silvery fish, while the Isharans used brute force, with little finesse. Before long, the pursuers were too far behind to be a threat.

As the breezes blew his dark hair, Mak Dur sketched a quick circle on his chest with one finger and admired the similar circle painted on the sail. They were almost home.

The voyagier and his crew celebrated their freedom by eating provisions they found aboard, knowing that they would reach the coast of Osterra within a few days. The sailors became raucous, reckless, giddy with relief. Standing on deck beside Mak Dur, Heith asked, "Do you think those godlings will wreck Serepol? I've never seen such destruction."

"I could not care less if those monsters tore the city apart. The priestlords were fools to unleash them. *Cra,* maybe it will teach them a lesson." He grimaced. "I do not intend to trade with Ishara ever again."

"I vote we just sail up and down the coast of Osterra," said Sarrum, looking at his fellow crew members. "Plenty of towns, ports, and customers there."

"A voyagier does not go against the wishes of his crew," said Mak Dur. "I will enjoy being home and safe. Inside the circle again. Utauks were not meant for war."

A thunderstorm rolled in that evening, drenching the decks and filling the water barrels. The sailors came out to stand in the heavy rain, washing themselves and feeling refreshed.

Two days later they spotted the hazy gray-green coast, and the Utauk crew cheered. Ahead, ships sailed around the Rivermouth harbor like bees swirling near a hive. Raising Utauk pennants, the sailors pulled on the rigging, and the *Glissand* arrowed toward where the Joined River spilled into the sea.

Mak Dur stood at the prow, feeling more relieved than victorious. He chastised himself for risking another trade run, despite knowing the tensions with Ishara. He had hoped one last voyage would result in a large profit, but instead he had lost his ship, cargo, even the valuable shadowglass. His crew had faced an ordeal none of them would ever forget. Now that the danger was over, however, their ordeal seemed more like an adventure. He considered the stories he would tell in Utauk camps from now on.

As the *Glissand* approached the harbor, two Commonwealth warships sailed out toward them, their sails marked with the rising sun of Osterra. They were loaded with soldiers, and they reminded Mak Dur of prowling guard dogs. The crew mumbled uneasily, but the voyagier pointed up toward the clear circle on their sail. "They know we're Utauks. *Cra,* we are neutral and no threat."

As the burly vessels closed in, though, he felt less confident. He spoke in a low voice to Heith. "Keep sailing toward the harbor. We have nothing to hide and an important story to tell. The konag himself will want to hear our report."

One warship pulled alongside the *Glissand,* and the grim soldiers shouted across to them. "You have entered Commonwealth waters. What is your business here?"

"We are Utauks!" Mak Dur called back. "We escaped from Ishara and are back to trade information."

The large ship came so close that their hulls briefly ground together. Without asking permission, the Commonwealth soldiers threw ropes and boarding hooks, and the Utauks were indignant as a dozen men in leather armor bounded over. Mak Dur blustered, "I did not grant permission for you to come aboard! Why are you . . ."

"We will escort your ship into Rivermouth Harbor. Konag Mandan has commandeered all viable sailing vessels for his navy."

"His navy? This is a trading ship, not a war vessel."

"It can become a war vessel," said the lieutenant in charge.

Now that the *Glissand* had been occupied and secured, the soldiers detached the boarding hooks, and the two ships drifted apart again. Twelve soldiers took up threatening positions on the deck, intimidating the unarmed Utauks. The lieutenant raised his voice. "I command you to sail to the

Rivermouth docks, where your ship will be inspected and your crew will be interrogated."

"There's no need for this!" Mak Dur said. "We were going there anyway."

"Good. Cooperation makes things easier."

The Commonwealth soldiers stood with drawn swords, offering to do none of the ship's work, but Mak Dur's crew knew what to do. With strong breezes, the *Glissand* made good time toward the harbor. As they approached the crowded docks, he saw countless ships, many more than the usual bustle of fishing boats, trading vessels, and patrol ships. Every ship in the harbor, even smaller fishing scows, bore Commonwealth colors. Mak Dur's heart felt like lead.

"We escaped from Serepol for this?" Heith whispered.

The lieutenant said, "After the murder of his father, Konag Mandan is preparing for war with Ishara. His navy will be larger than Konag Cronin's legendary fleet from the previous conflict, and your ship will be part of it. Your crew should be proud."

Mak Dur muttered, "The beginning is the end is the beginning."

The officer frowned at him. "No need for that Utauk nonsense. We will teach you war songs of the Commonwealth."

The *Glissand*'s crew grumbled. The navigator wove a path among the other vessels in the harbor, and a pilot boat guided them to an open dock. As soon as the ship was tied up, more soldiers swarmed aboard, remarking on the sturdiness of the Utauk ship.

"She seems a fast enough craft," said one military officer, who ignored Mak Dur and the Utauks. "After we add armor to the hull and a battering ram at the prow, she'll be ready to go to war."

Mak Dur was offended. "You cannot just take my ship! The *Glissand* is an Utauk vessel."

The soldier frowned at him. "We are not taking your vessel—we are conscripting it, along with you and your crew. We will provision you and train you to fight in the Commonwealth navy."

More soldiers clambered aboard and took over his beautiful ship.

103

KING Kollanan stayed at Bahlen's wreth city to help the survivors recover. Legaciers collected the stories of every person they could find, and the dead were burned in respectful funeral pyres. He also sent Lasis and Gant along with teams of his soldiers to nearby Yanton to work in the damaged farms and homesteads.

As he met with his Bravas, vassal lords, and battle commanders, he was sick at heart. They discussed what had happened and, more important, how Norterra should respond. Koll felt exhausted and sad. He had no desire to engage in a civil war with Osterra, but his outrage grew by the hour. Even before leaving the ruins, he wrote and dispatched a rider on a fast horse with an urgent letter to King Adan in Bannriya, informing him of the disastrous news—and warning him of what Mandan might do to Suderra as well.

Wanting to get back to Fellstaff, he gathered part of his hasty rescue army and rode off, accompanied by Elliel and Thon. He was confident Tafira had held the city together, as she always did, but the frostwreths might choose any moment to launch their full military strike against the city.

Kollanan followed the main road back to Fellstaff at a weary pace, but when he arrived at the city walls he found the people in an uproar. A haggard guard just inside the gate waved his arms, calling to the king. "The queen has been abducted, Sire!"

As the man blurted a few details, Koll spurred Storm at a gallop up to the castle. With Elliel and Thon beside him, he charged into the courtyard, shouting for the staff until his voice was hoarse. Pokle scurried out, pale and wide-eyed, his hair mussed.

"What happened here?" Koll demanded. "Tell me! Now! Where is the queen?"

The young man ran forward, waving his hands. "King Kollanan, it was those terrible Commonwealth soldiers! They stole horses from the stables, and the queen tried to stop them. She threw her knives, killed two of them, but they . . . they took her!" He sniffled. "They just left the bodies there. Didn't even take their own comrades."

Koll felt rage building in him. "If Tafira had more knives, she would have killed more of them. Where did they go? How long have they been gone?"

Another guard rushed into the courtyard. "They rode out in the middle of the night. Just after you took the soldiers to help Lord Bahlen."

"Riders went after them, tried to catch them," Pokle said. "They haven't returned." Other guards and castle staff swarmed into the courtyard, shouting over one another, but Kollanan got the gist. Rondo and his men had fled the city and they would have stayed away from the primary roads. Queen Tafira was their hostage.

One of the castle guards was distraught. "We sent out four search teams, Sire. They will find them."

"You should have dispatched the rest of the army!" Koll's urgency raged through him. Tafira! They might be halfway to Convera by now.

The guard's mouth dropped open with alarm. "But Fellstaff was defenseless! You had already taken all of the soldiers who could ride. With the frostwreths out there, we couldn't—"

Koll pulled out his war hammer as he wheeled Storm around. He had cleaned off the gore, and wrapped leather around the weapon's handle. "I will find her. Tell me which direction they went." He had no time to rest.

A handful of castle guards emerged from the barracks. "Search parties are scouring the countryside. They will hunt them down. We sent the best trackers we had left."

Another man said in a trembling voice, "There is nothing more you can do right now, Sire."

"There is always something I can do." Koll ground his teeth together. "They wouldn't dare hurt her." But then he remembered what Mandan had already done. He wanted to scream. After defeating Cade's troops, he had hoped to come home to triumph and further strategy planning. Now he felt an urgent need to leave again. "I should have known not to trust that vile Rondo." His heart was ready to break. "In truth, I never trusted him, but I did not believe him capable of such treachery." He growled. "Nor Mandan."

"I think . . . I think it was a surprise, Sire," Pokle said. "Rondo's men were just trying to ride off, and the queen must've got in the way. They kidnapped her."

"They will no doubt ransom her, take her to the konag," Elliel said.

Koll snapped, "Ancestors' blood! She's lived in Norterra for three decades as my queen, and she has ruled by my side. But she is Isharan. Mandan will use that. He will make her a scapegoat."

"*Utho* will use it," Elliel said. "We have to find her before they reach Convera."

Koll slid out of the saddle and handed Storm's reins to a stable boy. "I need a fresh horse so I can ride out again soon." He strode into the castle, calling another search party together. Wanting to vent his anger, but finding no appropriate target, he swung his war hammer in the air.

Yes, the wreths intended to destroy the human race, but why would his own *allies* strike Norterra? Why would the rightful konag declare war against one of the three kingdoms? Mandan was tearing the Commonwealth apart.

Before long, the head of a search party galloped in on an exhausted horse. Distraught and bedraggled, he shouted out his news as he stumbled off his mount. He yelled into the courtyard, "We tracked down Rondo and his men, Sire!" The man looked as if he had been weeping on the ride. "And we found the queen."

Kollanan's rumpled shirt flapped loose around him as he ran into the courtyard. He grabbed the man's arm, bellowing for the stables to hurry with the new horse. "Take me there." Elliel and Thon joined him, ready to rush off.

"It's too late," the man gasped, his voice breaking. "Too late!"

Koll threw him up against the wall. "We'll get you a fresh horse, too. Climb in the saddle and ride! Was your party able to engage Captain Rondo? Why didn't you bring the queen back with you?"

"Too late, Sire. Much too late." The scout began sobbing. Stable boys brought out hastily saddled horses, and Elliel and Thon mounted. The scout seemed in a daze as he climbed into the saddle on a fresh horse.

A growing horror left Koll speechless.

Elliel and Thon galloped alongside as they raced out into the hills, led by the weary messenger. Elliel shouted over the pounding hoofbeats, "Tell me—what happened?"

"All dead!"

"Rondo's soldiers are slain? Who killed them?" Koll demanded. "And the queen?"

"All, Sire. All dead." The man hunched over his horse and rode faster, as if he could outrun his news. Koll refused to hear.

He saw only a red haze as he urged the new mount to as much speed as the animal could handle. He didn't want to accept what he had heard. He kept thinking of his beautiful wife with her exotic wisdom, how she had always been loyal to him. "Ah, Tafira . . ." He was still in a daze of denial, his throat dry, his body aching from combat and days in the saddle. He blocked all thoughts from his mind.

Wrung out, gray skinned with grief and dread, the messenger slowed in a forest clearing where other horses were tied to trees nearby. "This is the place, Sire."

Elliel and Thon joined Kollanan as he slid from his saddle and stood on unsteady legs. Now that he was here, he felt slow, wary. Despite his disbelief, he knew what he would find, and he hated each step.

The scout began weeping again. Four Norterran soldiers stood guard around the site. Kollanan smelled blood in the air.

In the clearing, he found dead soldiers strewn about—Captain Rondo and his escort party. All had been butchered.

"Who killed them?" Elliel said. "I've never seen such a massacre."

With the gait of a dancer, Thon moved among the bodies, inspecting them. Elliel drew her sword, while her other hand strayed to her ramer, but the threat was long gone.

"We found them like this," said one of the scouts.

Koll's words were strangled by a sob that fought to escape. He saw the large tree at the edge of the camp, the figure tied to the trunk with ropes.

Someone had slashed her throat.

He walked forward on weak legs. Each footstep was like a boulder falling. He stood before Tafira, who hung limp but tied in place with a rope. Her head lolled forward, her chin down, her eyes closed. Blood from her neck had soaked her fur-lined robe, and her lush dark hair was loose and tangled.

Kollanan wept. He wrapped his arms around her body in a last embrace and buried his face in her hair. "They killed you, beloved. Ah, they killed you!" He held her for a long, long time while the others remained silent, giving him his space.

He thought of all the times he had held Tafira over the course of thirty years. "They did this." He finally pulled himself away from her, thinking only of Cade's punitive army, the assault on Bahlen's city, Mandan's appalling orders. "They did this," he said again. "*They did this.*"

He had fought the frostwreths. He had faced Isharans in the old war, and he knew what they done to Conndur on Fulcor Island. But as he looked at his murdered wife, he decided the real monsters were his own people. "They did this!"

Thon crouched in front of the slaughtered Commonwealth soldiers. "But who did *this*?"

A scout said, "They were all dead when we found the camp. Even their horses were torn apart."

Wary, Elliel turned in a slow circle, watching for some terrible force that might emerge from the dark silver pines that surrounded them.

Thon touched the gashes in the dead soldiers, cuts in their armor. He bent closer, narrowing his deep sapphire eyes, and sniffed the air. He went over to crouch beside Captain Rondo, who had a mortal wound in his chest where a spear point had plunged through his heart. Thon snapped back to his feet in a liquid motion. "These wounds are from wreths. A wreth hunting party murdered everyone here." He nodded toward Tafira. "Including the queen."

Kollanan cut the ropes and slid his wife's body to the ground as gently as possible. He felt dead inside while at the same time his mind blazed and shouted in denial. "Or Captain Rondo murdered her first, and then wreths killed the entire party. Why else would she have been tied like that?"

Thon shrugged. "There is no way to be certain."

"Even if the frostwreths killed her, she was only here because of *them*." Koll glared at the dead escort soldiers. Tears ran down his cheeks and into his beard. He felt hollow, but he would find the steel inside that emptiness, the hammer. The king of Norterra had enemies all around.

"They did this," he said one more time, meaning anyone and everyone who dared to stand against him.

104

⚘

Utho had a secret that ran as deep as rot within his bones, and Onzu knew it.

All Bravas were connected by a common thread, a bond of blood, and only under extreme circumstances could they be extricated from that community. His son Onder had been one of those purged of his memory, cast out from all Bravas. As had Elliel because of the unspeakable crime she had supposedly committed.

Unless Utho had lied. Unless he had concocted a scheme that ruined the warrior woman's life and legacy for "the good of the Commonwealth."

Onzu feared that perhaps the legendary Brava, advisor to the konag himself, might have tainted their united half-breed community with his dishonorable actions. The training master had to know. His own loyalty was in question, and his actions would be—*must* be—predicated on the truth.

As deep night fell across the training village like a smothering shroud, all the young wards had bedded down to rest for an early morning of combat exercises, and Onzu walked along the darkened paths between dwellings. He carried a lantern, although he could have walked every inch of the village wearing a blindfold.

The visitors' hut remained untouched since Utho had spent the night. The Brava man had left early that morning after a cold and uncomfortable conversation with his veteran trainer. Onzu had convinced him to ride into the mountains and look for the truth of the stirring dragon. He had hoped the other Brava would reach an epiphany, but alas, Utho had not returned. From the reports of Tytan and Jennae, it seemed the vengewar was still Utho's obsession, to the exclusion of all else. That was when Onzu had determined they were on fundamentally separate paths.

A disagreement was one thing. A lie—for whatever purpose or justification—was another. The contents of King Kollanan's alarming letter disturbed him deeply. Onzu needed to know what Utho had done with Elliel, whether that deception warranted cutting ties with him completely.

He opened the door of the hut, shone the lantern on a sleeping pallet. No one had touched the pillow or the thin woolen blanket since Utho had left. The bed was neat, blanket straightened. Onzu entered, shining the pool of yellow-orange light and looking for any telltale remnants that Utho might have left behind.

Though no one else was awake, the old trainer crept like a thief as he approached the pallet and studied the bedding, the stuffed pillow, the blanket. He narrowed his gaze and leaned forward.

There, a steel-gray hair, a single strand caught on the woven fabric.

With nimble fingers that had killed many men, Onzu plucked the hair and brought it close to his eye. Yes, this would be enough, but the rest of the magic would require more than lantern light. It needed pure fire, fire fueled by blood.

Outside, listening to the muted sounds of forest creatures and the conspiratorial whisper of breezes through the pine boughs, Onzu sat on a stripped log that served as a bench beside the carving of the ancient Brava leader. He placed the single gray strand on the smooth wood where he himself would often sit in contemplation.

Onzu set the lantern on the ground and removed the ramer cuff. As a training master, he rarely used the magical weapon. It was not a toy, and he did not show off for the young men and women who learned their fighting skills here. A ramer was meant only as a last resort, a weapon for the most dire battles.

This was a different kind of battle.

Now he clamped the cuff tight, and the pain of the golden fangs was like a sharp sigh of relief. Dark blood ran down his forearm, and he *pushed* with his magic, calling forth the flames that burst around the metal band, then engulfed his hand.

Bright fire, innocent flames.

Each Brava carried his past and his truth within him. They were half-breeds, wreth magic intertwined with human honor and decency. Every fiber of a Brava's being reflected the choices he made and the deeds he did. Given a master with a strong enough command of his own innate magic, those echoes of deeds could be peeled away and revealed like the rings in the trunk of a tree.

For decades, Onzu had carefully shaved his head, keeping his scalp clean. If he let his hair grow back, the strands would be pure and white. Although he had made bad choices in his past, Onzu had no regrets, no shadows that lingered behind his heart.

Utho had left this gray strand behind.

He raised his flaming hand and pinched Utho's hair between two fingers. Inside the thin strand, Onzu could recall the memories and see what resided within the man he had considered to be his greatest student.

As the strand touched the purifying fire, a tiny puff of smoke curled up, then expanded into a panoply of images. Concentrating hard, Onzu pulled and guided the images. With dismay, he saw Utho fighting a horrendous godling in a seaside village. Mirrabay. Another Brava paladin fought beside him, a young man—Onder! And Onder fled in terror, leaving Utho alone to face the wild, destructive deity. Just as the story said. . . .

The old Brava master swallowed. It was the truth he had feared, and his eyes were blurred as he saw the next set of images of Utho and other Bravas gathered in a dark remembrance shrine, including Jennae. Together, they marked Onder with the rune of forgetting on his face, then turned him loose with no memories, only shame. . . .

Though heartbroken to see the confirmation of his son's cowardice, Onzu had a different purpose. He wanted to see what Utho remembered of *Elliel*, whether or not she was guilty of the vicious massacre of which she had been convicted. Was Utho's account true, or should Onzu believe the letter that King Kollanan had sent to Convera?

The ramer fire blazed brighter, and the strand of hair gave up its secrets.

Before long, the training master saw the truth—Elliel lying on the edge of death, stabbed by Lord Cade's viciously jealous wife . . . after Cade himself had raped Elliel. Utho and Cade had crafted a false story in order to maintain the dark political stability of the Isharan prisoner camps.

Poor Elliel had paid the price. Utho had made the Brava woman believe she'd committed a monstrous, despicable crime.

The hair continued to burn, continued to bring forth images, but Onzu was so angry he could barely see them. The sheen of tears in his eyes formed a film of rage. The ramer's heat strengthened him.

Sitting on the log, he saw out of the corner of his eye that several young trainees had emerged from their homes. Now they watched wide-eyed as their master called up images from his blood.

But Utho's dark memories were not done yet. As the hair strand burned down to the root, the deepest, blackest visions appeared, a bottomless cavern of secrets that the man had never wanted anyone to know.

Images flickered in the smoke and fire, revealing Konag Conndur in stone-walled private chambers . . . on Fulcor Island. Onzu knew where it was and what was happening, because as he saw and inhaled the smoke of memories, they became his own.

Utho came to the old konag secretly in the night and bolted the door with a terrible purpose. Locking himself inside with Conndur, his friend, his konag. Konag Conndur had invited Empra Iluris to the isolated island garrison, wanting to forge peace between the two continents because he, Conndur, believed the wreths were a far greater threat to the human race than the old feud with Ishara.

But Utho was blinded by his own purpose. He saw the world and the future only through a red rage of hatred for Isharans, the need for the venge-war and what he thought was the good of the Commonwealth.

In revealed memories, Onzu watched as Utho methodically and savagely murdered Konag Conndur.

Utho.

Mutilating him, spraying the blood everywhere.

Utho.

Blaming it on the Isharans in order to provoke a war.

Utho! Utho! *Utho!*

The hair was gone, but the damned memories remained. The ramer fire continued to burn bright in his hand, and Onzu surged to his feet. The stinging blur over his eyes vanished.

He saw his young trainees staring at him. They had seen, too.

He extinguished the ramer fire, shaking and drained, but also energized. This was not finished.

Master Onzu knew what he had to do.

105

◜◝

MANDAN of the Colors was painting again, and that disturbed Utho. After the young konag learned of Cade's disgraceful defeat in Norterra, his reaction seemed displaced and worrisome. "I am the one who writes the legacy of my Commonwealth! As konag, I make the history that anyone will remember." He looked at his canvas and gave a defiant nod.

Utho spoke in a guarded tone. "That does not alter what happened, Sire."

Mandan sniffed. "I will change it in my painting, and then I count on you to make it true." He dabbed the brush into his pigments, swirling the colors together. "You are my bonded Brava."

His new project was too large for a simple easel in his quarters. Instead, he had erected a large canvas in the open throne room. When army commanders, court advisors, vassal lords, and ministers of state came to deliver their reports or request funds from the treasury, Mandan was there painting.

Previously, he had at least pretended to make decisions and issue important commands, after consulting with Utho. Now, the konag had abdicated that responsibility and only made offhanded comments. Nevertheless, his mind was fixated on the battle at the old wreth ruins. He painted the bloody spectacle of what he envisioned *should* have happened there. It had very little bearing on what had actually occurred, as Utho now knew.

Defeated stragglers had trickled in from Norterra, weary members of Cade's army, who could tell only small parts of the story. They had fled when the battle turned, having seen King Kollanan's arrival with unexpected reinforcements. Finally, when two line commanders reached Convera, they described the complete rout, how Bahlen's people had put up a remarkable resistance in the fortified wreth ruins and how the Fellstaff forces had turned the tides of battle and scattered Cade's army.

Mandan was sickened by the failure, outraged at the king of Norterra. He railed against the fool Cade for being such a disappointment. Unable to control himself, he struck his new wife. Lira bawled with grief over the death of her father, and Mandan slapped her across the face again. When she shrank away sobbing, he slapped her a third time, and when she collapsed on the floor, he kicked her. He would have continued to do so, but Utho pulled him away. Lira curled into a ball, wailing.

"Your father failed me," Mandan yelled at her. "He had a vital task, and now my uncle thinks Norterra can ignore the konag's commands."

Lira whimpered, not hearing his words.

The wheels continued to turn in Utho's mind. This loss was far more disastrous than a mere personal affront to Mandan. Cade's standing army was one of the most powerful military forces in the Commonwealth, and Utho needed it for his vengewar. Now all those soldiers were either killed or defeated, the survivors dispersed across Norterra.

"What of Lord Cade's Brava?" Utho demanded of the returning soldiers. "Why did Gant not protect his bonded lord?"

The first soldiers did not know the answer, but by the second day, a wounded cavalry soldier reported that he had seen Cade killed by a Brava woman, and Utho knew that it must be Elliel. A chill went down his spine.

"Cade's own Brava let it happen," said the rider, shaking his head. "Gant just stood there and watched while Elliel cut down his lord. I think he threw in his lot with King Kollanan afterward."

Utho could not believe what he heard, but too many things were incomprehensible right now. He squeezed his fist as if he could ignite deadly flames even without his ramer. "We need every fighter for our war against Ishara, every Brava! Our navy is growing. Our soldiers are being trained. Our smithies are manufacturing thousands of swords."

A mass of frenetic energy, Mandan snapped, "We cannot let this defiance stand. Our gathered armies must march on Norterra!" His gaze suddenly shifted. "And what of my brother Adan? Which side will he take? We need to secure Suderra as well, before it's too late!" His pinched face grew stormy. "Is Adan in league with Kollanan against me?"

Utho lashed out at him. "If the Commonwealth is engaged in a civil war, then our enemies will thrive and plot against us. We must fight now, set sail and attack Ishara while they are leaderless! An Utauk trading ship just returned from there and reported that their godlings are on a rampage. Serepol is nearly destroyed and Empra Iluris has vanished. Now is our chance, during this turmoil!"

Curled in a corner of the throne room, her back pressed against the cold stone wall, Lira continued weeping.

☙

Over the next several days, Utho made cold, rational plans for his war, while the young konag withdrew into his paints and colors. He sketched figures on the enormous canvas, using charcoal sticks to draw the combatants in a broad scene of chaos and carnage. This was how Mandan envisioned the events in his mind, even though he himself had never been to war except for the naval skirmish on Fulcor Island.

"There, the battle in Norterra." Mandan stepped back to admire his painting. "This is how the legacy will be written."

His depicted battle scene was filled with blood, bodies hacked to pieces, dead soldiers strewn about the ground, their faces twisted in agony. Every fallen soldier in the painting bore the colors of Norterra. In his version of the event, not a single brave Commonwealth fighter had fallen. More disturbingly, the central figure in the artwork was a rearing stallion ridden by a victorious warrior, whose upraised sword dripped the blood of vanquished enemies. Mandan.

The konag had painted himself in the middle of the fight, a proud and powerful commander leading his troops to crush the upstart traitors in Norterra. Now, Mandan's satisfaction rolled off of him in waves.

Deeply troubled, Utho stared at the painting and came to a reluctant decision. So long as the konag was under his control, he could manage the plans for the vengewar. "I am your bonded Brava, my konag, and that will be your legacy—as you command. We can display this mural proudly in the throne room. We should call your vassal lords to come see it."

"They will admire my work," Mandan said. "And we will make them tell the story when they return to their holdings." He dipped his brush onto the palette, swirled the rich crimson, and painted more red around the fallen bodies on the imaginary battlefield. "It inspired me."

Utho made sure the young man kept his priorities, though. "We must bring the Commonwealth back together, unite all three kingdoms against the Isharan animals. Together, we can conquer the new world."

"We deal with King Kollanan." Mandan sounded like a petulant child insisting on his dessert. "My uncle first!"

Utho's head throbbed, and his heart ached. He didn't wish to engage in outright war in the three kingdoms because that would cost so many Osterran and Norterran fighters—and he needed the whole army against Ishara. He could see that Mandan would not be swayed, so he suggested an alternative. "In order to unify the Commonwealth, we have to remove Kollanan. And quite probably your brother Adan as well. All three kingdoms must be ruled by leaders who are loyal to the konag."

Sitting on a stone bench against the far wall, as if she avoided the throne dais and the empty chair reserved for the queen, Lira sat dull eyed, a wisp of herself. She had changed so much since Mandan had first met the lovely but fragile girl in Cade's holding house. And the young man already seemed tired of his bride after only a week.

Lira sat on the stone bench, her skin as pale as milk, her long red hair limp and tangled, as if she hadn't brushed it in several days. She didn't weep any more, but simply stared. Her shoulders slumped as if the spark had been snuffed out of her.

She raised a goblet to her lips and drank. Utho knew she was consuming the milk of the blue poppy, more and more each day. So like Lady Maire . . .

"I ride for Rivermouth this afternoon, my konag," Utho announced. "I need to inspect the ships. New Bravas are coming in to join our army, and they will throw their swords and ramers to our cause."

Mandan spoke up, quoting: "A vengewar is not a quick thing, but it is necessary."

Utho was pleased that the young konag remembered. "Exactly, Sire. Soon enough, the real battles will begin."

Mandan of the Colors went back to his painting.

Hale propped the stump of his left wrist on his hip. "Penda did the important parts."

She sighed. "I just want to hold my baby and rest."

The midwives brought more pillows to make her comfortable, then spread blankets over her. The baby instinctively sucked at her breast. Penda tucked the fabric around the delicate head with its fuzz of dark hair. Within moments they were both fast asleep.

Hale Orr turned to look at the Utauk camp. "I had hoped this night would bring only joy, but we must face what just happened. Let us go find our dead, Starfall."

Most of the fires had been put out, and the Utauks gathered their scattered possessions. At first they were reluctant to build another bonfire, afraid the flames might bring back the dragon, but Shella din Orr told her people to remember who they were, and their community formed a wall against fear. From the wreckage, they created a bright, cheerful blaze.

Four Utauks had been killed during the dragon attack, one man crushed inside his tent, two snapped up in the monster's jaws, and another died from a deep gash that bled out. The Utauks carried their dead with reverence to the side of the camp. They gathered stones and laid out a large, perfect circle. Soon, they would have a traditional funeral, singing songs around a pyre.

Adan regarded the dead sandwreths with both anger and disgust. Quo's body was pale, his face drawn, his topaz eyes open but dull.

Seenan and Captain Elcior rode up, issuing their grim report. "All of the injured wreths are dead, as you commanded, Sire. The shadowglass weapons easily dispatched them." Elcior's horse snorted and pawed at the ground.

Adan nodded. "What about the augas?"

"The dragon killed most of the beasts and the others scattered and ran off."

Seenan spoke up, sounding shaken. "Do you want us to chase them down? They are loose in the forest."

The augas seemed to be stupid beasts, and without the wreths to command them, Adan doubted they would cause problems. "Let them run loose. Queen Voo will not be able to tell what happened."

"We also found something else," Captain Elcior said. "A strange creature, not human and not wreth."

Adan frowned as they led him over to a dead auga. Lashed to its saddle was a small creature, gray skinned and poorly formed, like a sketch of a person. "It was dead before tonight, Sire," Seenan said. "Long dead."

106

♋

WHEN King Adan held his newborn daughter, his heart felt as if it would burst with love. Utauk midwives had tended Penda through the birth, smiling and conferring with one another, while she squeezed his hand until he thought she would crush his bones. She sweated and cried out with the effort.

Afterward, the midwives called it a safe and easy birth, but Adan saw nothing easy about it at all. They had wrapped the baby girl in a colorful blanket someone had retrieved from Shella's damaged tent. Penda slumped back on the grass beneath the oak, exhausted yet with a glow of magic about her. And it was magic, Adan thought—the magic of giving new life.

Xar dipped and dove around, performing aerial tricks, looping and trilling as if proud of himself or enthralled with the baby.

Penda reached out and touched the rough bark of the sturdy tree and let her eyes fall closed, as if drawing energy from the forest. "I want to name her Oak," she said. "Our daughter will be sturdy and majestic, and strong when we need her to be."

"Oak . . ." With the child in his arms, he gazed into the sweet, tiny face, and she responded with a twisted and puckered expression. "Yes, Oak is a fine name." The baby girl let out a high-pitched cry that sounded exuberant and joyous after the violence of the night.

"She is inside our circle, my Starfall." Penda's voice sounded like music to him. "The beginning is the end is the beginning."

The king held his daughter tight. "The beginning . . ." Penda reached out her arms, and Adan handed the baby to her mother.

Hale Orr strutted about beaming, showing off his front gold tooth. "A perfect child. *Cra,* absolutely perfect!" He bent close to Penda. "I remember when you were that small, dear heart. And now you have done it yourself."

"I also had something to do with it," Adan said.

"We think the wreths might have been taking it back south," said Elcior. "Though I don't know why."

"King Kollanan told me the frostwreths had new slaves, drones . . ." Adan studied the creature. "Queen Voo wanted to see one."

"Well, she's not going to get this one!" Seenan said.

"No, she won't." Adan's expression hardened as he turned to his Banner guards, then back to his father-in-law. "The sandwreths must never know. We cannot leave any sign of their fallen warriors. Come with me."

They returned to Quo's body, where Hale Orr continued to regard it with a queasy expression. Adan explained what he wanted, and his father-in-law agreed, "*Cra,* we will take care of it." Hale looked down at the sprawled wreth corpse. "Utauks are good at hiding things."

Emil and Burdon listened as Hale issued instructions. Once the Utauks took care of their own dead, they would burn the wreth bodies and pound any blackened bones into powder. They would keep none of the trinkets or weapons, leave no sign that the people had ever seen the wreth war party.

"Not a trace," Adan said. "As far as anyone is concerned, Quo and his companions were never here. They must have encountered some mishap as they wandered my kingdom."

"And why were they wandering the kingdom in the first place?" Hale wanted to know. "Why were they here, this far from the desert?"

"They came searching for Penda," he said. "And our child."

"*Cra,* and they found her!" Hale scowled at Quo's body again. "I thought we would be safe in the heart camp."

Adan knew that Queen Voo was so arrogant she would never believe any humans could possibly kill her brother and his sandwreths. It would never occur to her that Adan or the Utauks might have the courage to do so. The secret would be safe.

His heart ached. Was the end of the world truly at hand? If so, what was his best course of survival? What could he do for his people?

He thought of the images within Ari's mothertear of the desert camp and the enslaved human workers. Although dragons could wreak havoc, Adan knew the sandwreths were the real enemies.

He walked to Shella din Orr's new tent. The Utauks had raised support logs and stretched the fabric to create a makeshift shelter. The old woman sat on her rumpled rug with the threads of the bloodlines she represented. She picked at the tapestry. "The legacy of humankind is unraveling, King Adan Starfall."

For a moment, the ominous reality suppressed even his joy over his new

daughter. "The only way we can win is if we all fight together, all of humanity. Alas, I doubt that will happen." He thought of his brother's impetuous
decree, the konag's outrageous demand for the armies of Suderra to sail off
and fight across the sea. Even though the Isharans had killed his uncle Conndur, how could Adan throw all his forces against Ishara when the wreths
were at his own doorstep? He, Adan Starfall, was the king of Suderra, and
he was bound by the terms of the Commonwealth charter. He wanted to be
loyal to Mandan, but how could he do that and save his own kingdom?

The old crone sat impossibly cross-legged, her knobby knees barely covered by her skirts, her legs like bent sticks. She nodded and sent him away,
apparently realizing that Adan needed to go back to his wife.

He trudged across the camp and found Penda still dozing with their
daughter. He sat beside them and made himself comfortable, resting against
his wife and child. If the wreths wanted to bring about the end of the world,
then Adan would do anything necessary to save his family and protect his
kingdom.

Penda stirred, and the baby woke. Without rousing his wife, he took the
child in his arms and planned to save the world for her.

107

STILL hidden in the chamber beneath the empra's palace, Cemi reeled to hear about the disaster in Serepol. Analera said, "Key Priestlord Klovus is a fool! His workers constructed the Magnifica temple even though Empra Iluris forbade it, and now the godling has grown much too powerful. And he unleashed it!"

"The great godling is our protector," said Captani Vos.

The old servant scoffed. "The people strengthened and enraged the godling until it became greater than anything we've ever seen. The idiot priestlord sent it to attack the Hethrren, and so the thing ripped apart buildings and homes, killed hundreds of innocents on its rampage. The godling didn't know what it was doing." Her raspy voice dripped with anger. "Oh yes, a great many Hethrren were killed, but so were many poor citizens. And it consumed the harbor godling! Ripped it to shreds and defeated it!" She moaned. "Hear us, save us! We haven't even put out all the fires in the city yet."

Cemi's words were a low growl. "Now they will listen if we come back." She felt the strange new godling swelling and swirling nearby, anxious to move forward. It was its own deity anchored to Iluris, even to Cemi herself. "The people need an empra."

"Ishara needs a leader now more than ever," Vos said.

Cemi knelt beside the pale woman, who was obviously wasting away. She did not want to admit that her beloved mentor was effectively dead, even though her heart kept beating. The wounds had healed, but her mind remained gone. "Do you think the army is ready? Do we have enough loyalists there? Supporters among the people?"

"The citizens of Serepol are outraged at what Klovus did," Analera said. "They know he is responsible, but they are still too stunned to grasp what it means."

"They must stop building the Magnifica if the godling is already too powerful for the key priestlord to control," Vos said.

"Klovus will not let them stop, even though he knows what he did." Disgusted, the old servant gathered the basket of food she had brought. "I continue to serve you, and you know I am loyal to the empra. I have already given most of my life to her, and I would give it all if necessary." Analera walked to the door and turned back to them. "But you had better decide what to do—and soon. Give them an alternative."

Cemi did not need the warning. She looked up at Vos, and the handsome captani stared back at her, worried for her, for the empra, and for all of Ishara.

After Analera departed, the formless new godling flowed out of the stone walls and became more tangible, shimmering as it camouflaged the opening. Cemi should have felt safe under its protection, but instead she felt trapped. "Iluris, are you ever coming back to us?"

During their agonizingly quiet days here, she had often held conversations with the silent woman. Vos also talked to his adoptive mother, even though she didn't respond. Every one of the hawk guards here had confessed to the sleeping empra; they had told her their stories, beseeched her to come back—all to no avail.

"It will have to be you, Cemi," Vos said, then spoke louder as all the hawk guards listened. "Empra Cemi. We need to make our move."

The hawk guards gathered close. "Empra Cemi," they repeated. "That is what our mother would have wanted."

"We will make it happen," Cemi said, trying to sound strong.

Vos placed a hand on her shoulder and pulled the young woman against him in an embrace.

Then something changed. Cemi looked down and saw a flicker in Iluris. The old woman's breathing shifted, and the girl sensed a crackle, a strengthening of the godling that sheltered them in this grim and unlikely sanctuary.

On the pallet, Empra Iluris let out a sigh and her eyes fluttered open.

ACKNOWLEDGMENTS

Writing a big, complicated series with so many characters and story lines is something like one of my characters leading a large army across the landscape. I keep a lot of it in my head, but I also rely on help from many other people. I'd like to thank my editor, Beth Meacham; my agent, John Silbersack; my wife (and first reader and line editor), Rebecca Moesta; as well as Diane Jones, Lauren Moore, Brian Herbert, and all my readers.

GLOSSARY

ADAN—king of Suderra, husband of Penda, son of Conndur the Brave. Also called Adan Starfall.

ALCOCK—one of Kollanan's vassal lords in Norterra.

ALMEDA—wife of Lord Cade, who attacked and nearly killed Elliel.

ANALERA—old servant of Empra Iluris.

AORON—sandwreth mage.

ARI—blue ska, heart-linked to Glik.

AUGA—reptilian mount ridden by sandwreths.

AXUS—sandwreth mage.

BAHLEN—one of Kollanan's vassal lords in Norterra. His holding has extensive wreth ruins.

BANNER GUARD—city guard force in Bannriya.

BANNRIYA—capital of Suderra, first city founded by humans after the wreth wars.

BHOSUS—Utauk prospector found dead on the Plain of Black Glass.

BIRCH—Kollanan's grandson, taken from the frostwreth destruction of Lake Bakal and kept by Queen Onn as a pet.

BLACK EELS—elite Isharan assassins, capable of magic and shape-shifting.

BLUEWATER RIVER—one of the two main rivers in the Commonwealth.

BOLAM—older brother of Conndur and Kollanan, destined to be konag but died of a fever during the Isharan war.

BRAVA—mixed-blood race of wreths and humans, sworn defenders of the Commonwealth.

BURDON DIN ORR—one of Shella din Orr's grandnephews.

CADE—one of Mandan's vassal lords in Osterra. He keeps Isharan prisoners in his holding, forcing them to harvest saltpearls. Elliel served him as Brava, and he raped her.

CAPTANI—highest rank in the hawk guard.

CEMI—young street girl chosen by Empra Iluris as her heir apparent.

CERUS—one of Kollanan's vassal lords in Norterra.

CHETH—Brava woman, prisoner in sandwreth labor camp.

CLEFF—mayor of Yanton.

COMMONWEALTH—the three kingdoms of Osterra, Suderra, and Norterra, ruled overall by the konag, enemy of Ishara.

CONNDUR—former konag of the Commonwealth and king of Osterra, father of Adan and Mandan, murdered on Fulcor Island by Utho, but blamed on the Isharans. Also called Conndur the Brave.

CONVERA—capital city of Osterra and the Commonwealth.

CRICKYETH RIVER—one of the two main rivers in the Commonwealth.

CRONIN—former konag, father of Conndur and Kollanan.

DAKA, EMPRIR—emprir of Ishara, father of Iluris, fell to his death from a high tower window.

DAR—ancient frostwreth warrior who attacked and injured Ossus.

DONNAN RAH—Utauk courier and spy.

DONO—ur-priest in Serepol.

DRAGONSPINE MOUNTAINS—rugged mountain range that separates Osterra from Norterra and Suderra. The dragon Ossus is purported to live deep beneath the peaks.

DRONE—bluntly formed servant creatures created by the frostwreths.

ELCIOR, CAPTAIN—head of the Banner guards in Bannriya.

ELFAS—Suderran military advisor.

ELLIEL—Brava, bonded to King Kollanan, originally stripped of her memories by Utho and left to believe she had committed a great crime.

ELON—frostwreth mage.

EMIL DIN ORR—one of Shella din Orr's grandnephews.

EMPRA—female ruler of Ishara.

EMPRIR—male ruler of Ishara.

ENNETH—child of Onn, brother to Koru, killed long ago in battle.

ERICAL—priestlord of Prirari.

FELLSTAFF—main city in Norterra.

FINEMAIL—tough, flexible metal armor worn by Bravas.

FRENIK—old manservant of Empra Iluris.

FROSTWRETHS—northern faction of the wreth race, currently ruled by Queen Onn.

FULCOR ISLAND—strategic island between the Commonwealth and Ishara, long contested. The site of a disastrous peace conference, where Konag Conndur was killed and Empra Iluris left severely injured.

GANT—Brava, bonded to Lord Cade.

GLIK—orphan girl among the Utauks, explorer, Penda's adopted sister.

GLISSAND—Utauk trading ship.

GODLING—entity created from faith and magic by the Isharans.

GORAN—one of Mandan's vassal lords in Osterra.

GRAO—child of Onn, brother to Koru, killed long ago in battle.

GURA—frostwreth mage, died in his spellsleep chamber.

HALE ORR—father of Penda, Utauk tribe leader, grandson of Shella din Orr.

HAWK GUARD—elite personal guards of Empra Iluris, adopted by her as surrogate children.

HEADAN—sergeant in the Commonwealth army, part of Captain Rondo's group of escort soldiers.

HEITH—Utauk navigator on the *Glissand*.

HETHRREN—barbarian clans from beyond the boundary of Tamburdin.

HOM—squire to King Adan.

IBER—one of Kollanan's vassal lords in Norterra.

ILURIS—empra of Ishara, in a coma after a severe head injury during the battle on Fulcor Island.

INOD—sandwreth mage.

IRRI—frostwreth warrior, Queen Onn's lover.

ISHARA—continent ruled by Empra Iluris, enemy of the Commonwealth.

IVUN—sandwreth mage, leader of the human prisoner camp.

JHAQI—daughter of Kollanan and Tafira, mother of the boys Birch and Tomko, killed by frostwreths at Lake Bakal.

KLEA—Brava assigned as new watchman of Fulcor Island.

KLOVUS—key priestlord of Ishara.

KOLLANAN—king of Norterra, brother of Conndur the Brave. Also called Kollanan the Hammer.

KONAG—the high king, leader of the entire Commonwealth.

KORU—daughter of Queen Onn.

KRESCA—early queen of the Commonwealth, credited with bringing the three kingdoms together.

KUR—the god of the wreths and creator of the world, who vanished and left them with the mission to destroy the dragon Ossus.

LAKE BAKAL—mountain lake and village, destroyed by frostwreths to create a site for their own fortress.

LASIS—Brava, bonded to King Kollanan.

LEGACIER—historian and scholar.

LENON—Suderran military commander.

LERAN—frostwreth warrior.

LERO—bully on the streets of Prirari.

LIRA—daughter of Cade and Almeda.

MAGDA—leader of the Hethrren barbarians.

MAGNIFICA—grandest temple in Serepol.

MAIRE—mother of Mandan and Adan, took her own life with milk of the blue poppy.

MAK DUR—voyagier of the Utauk trading ship *Glissand*.

MANDAN—new konag of the Commonwealth, son of Conndur, brother of Adan. Also called Mandan of the Colors.

MAREKA—wife of Utho of the Reef, murdered in an Isharan raid.

MELIK—Utauk caravan leader.

MIRRABAY—Commonwealth seaside town attacked by Priestlord Klovus and a godling.

MOR—frostwreth mage.

MOTHERTEAR—diamond used in ska collars to collect images.

NAURA—legacier from the Convera remembrance shrine.

NERÉ—priestlord in Tamburdin District.

NEREV—chamberlain to Empra Iluris.

NORTERRA—northernmost of the three kingdoms, ruled by King Kollanan.

OLAN—legendary leader of the doomed Brava colony at Valaera.

ONN—queen of the frostwreths, mother of Koru.

ONZU—Brava training master.

OONUKS—frostwreth wolf-steeds, synthesized from horses and wolves.

ORI—Glik's former ska, lost in a storm.

OSSUS—the legendary dragon beneath the mountains who personifies all the evil and flaws of the god Kur.

OSTERRA—easternmost of the three kingdoms, ruled by the konag.

PENDA—wife of King Adan, queen of Suderra, daughter of Hale Orr.

PIRO—boy from Lake Bakal, killed along with Tomko.

PLAIN OF BLACK GLASS—ruins of ancient wreth battlefield, source of shadowglass.

POKLE—young man rescued from Lake Bakal village, does menial labor in Fellstaff Castle.

PRIESTLORD—leader of Isharan religion, able to commune with godlings.

PRIRARI—Isharan district, original home of Cemi.

QUO—sandwreth noble, brother of Queen Voo.

RAAN—ancient wreth, lover of Kur, ancestor of the sandwreths, poisoned her pregnant sister Suth out of jealousy.

RAMER—Brava weapon, a golden cuff that draws blood from the wrist and ignites into a fiery blade.

RAO—ancient frostwreth warrior who attacked and injured Ossus.

REMEMBRANCE SHRINE—archive of life histories.

RIVERMOUTH—main Commonwealth port, where the Joined River flows into the sea.

ROKK—frostwreth warrior, lover of Onn, killed at Lake Bakal.

RONDO—captain in the Commonwealth army, part of a contingent sent to escort King Kollanan back to Norterra.

SALTPEARLS—precious items harvested from the sea by Isharan slaves in Lord Cade's holding.

SANDWRETHS—southern faction of the wreth race, currently ruled by Queen Voo.

SARRUM—Utauk crewman aboard the *Glissand*.

SEENAN—young Banner guard, brother of the squire Hom.

SEREPOL—capital city of Ishara.

SHADOWGLASS—obsidianlike substance found melted on ancient wreth battlefields, possesses strange magical properties.

SHADRI—scholar girl now serving at Fellstaff Castle.

SHELLA DIN ORR—matriarch of the Utauk tribes.

SKA—a reptile bird, often kept as a pet and heart-linked to Utauks.

STORM—King Kollanan's warhorse.

SUDERRA—southernmost of the three kingdoms, ruled by King Adan.

SUTH—ancient wreth, lover of Kur, ancestor of the frostwreths, sister of Raan.

TAFIRA—queen of Norterra, Isharan wife of King Kollanan.

TAMBURDIN—Isharan district farthest from Serepol, frequently raided by Hethrren.

TEO—one of Kollanan's vassal lords in Norterra.

THOOMA—legacier of the Fellstaff remembrance shrine.

ULLA—sandwreth mage.

URGAR—Suderran military advisor.

UROK—Brava, bonded to Lord Bahlen in Norterra.

UTAUKS—independent tribes that travel and trade throughout the Commonwealth and also occasionally Ishara.

UTHO—Brava, bonded to Konag Mandan, instigator of vengewar against Isharans, also called Utho of the Reef.

VADA—largest mountain in the Dragonspine range, which recently exploded and devastated a vast area.

VALAERA—original Brava colony wiped out by Isharans and their godling.

VENGEWAR—Bravas' long-foretold war of vengeance against Isharans.

VICOLIA—chief legacier of the Convera remembrance shrine.

VITOR—one of Kollanan's vassal lords in Norterra.

VOO—queen of the sandwreths, sister of Quo.

VOS—captani of the hawk guards protecting Empra Iluris.

VOYAGIER—title of an Utauk merchant captain.

WRETHS—ancient race that created humans as servants and soldiers. Warring factions of frostwreths and sandwreths drove themselves to near extinction.

XAR—green ska, pet of Penda.

XION—priestlord of harbor temple in Serepol.

YANTON—village near Lord Bahlen's wreth ruins.

ZAHA—head of Black Eel assassins.